Paula McLain was born in Fresno, California in 1965. After being abandoned by both parents, she and her two sisters became wards of the California court system, moving in and out of various foster homes for the next fourteen years. When she aged out of the system, she supported herself by working as a nurse's aide in a convalescent hospital, a pizza delivery girl, an auto-plant worker, and a cocktail waitress, before discovering she could (and very much wanted to) write. She receivd her MFA in poetry from the University of Michigan in 1996. Now a *New York Times* bestselling author, Paula's works have appeared in magazines and newspapers worldwide. She lives in Ohio with her family.

You can discover more about the author at paulamclain.com.

# LOVE AND RUIN

In 1937, courageous and independent Martha Gellhorn travels to Madrid to report on the atrocities of the Spanish Civil War, and finds herself drawn to the stories of ordinary people caught in devastating conflict. She also finds herself unexpectedly — and uncontrollably — falling in love with Ernest Hemingway, a man already on his way to becoming a legend. In the shadow of the impending Second World War, and set against the tumultuous backdrops of Madrid, Finland, China and especially Cuba, where Ernest and Martha make their home, their relationship and professional careers ignite. But when Hemingway publishes the biggest literary success of his career, they are no longer equals, and Martha must make a choice: surrender to his suffocating demands, or risk losing him by forging her way as her own woman and writer.

Books by Paula McLain
Published by Ulverscroft:

THE PARIS WIFE

PAULA McLAIN

◆

# LOVE AND RUIN

*Complete and Unabridged*

# CHARNWOOD
*Leicester*

First published in Great Britain in 2018 by
Fleet
an imprint of Little, Brown Book Group
London

First Charnwood Edition
published 2019
by arrangement with
Little, Brown Book Group
An Hachette UK Company
London

A catalogue record for this book is available
from the British Library.

ISBN 978–1–4448–4058–2

Published by
F. A. Thorpe (Publishing)
Anstey, Leicestershire

Set by Words & Graphics Ltd.
Anstey, Leicestershire
Printed and bound in Great Britain by
T. J. International Ltd., Padstow, Cornwall

This book is printed on acid-free paper

For Julie Barer

There is nothing else than now. There is neither yesterday, certainly, nor is there any tomorrow. How old must you be before you know that?

— ERNEST HEMINGWAY,
*For Whom the Bell Tolls*

# Prologue

Near dawn on July 13, 1936, as three assassins scaled a high garden wall in Tenerife hoping to catch the band of armed guards unaware, I was asleep in a tiny room in Stuttgart, waiting for my life to begin.

The killers were professionals. They moved without sound, slinking up hidden ropes, never looking at one another or thinking of anything but the next moment's action. On cat's feet, they fell from the wall to the ground, passing invisibly through the shadows and creeping softly toward their target.

It was like a symphony unfolding. Their plan was to take the guards one by one by slitting their throats. Then they would force the door beyond the veranda and climb the marble steps to the little girl's room. María del Carmen, she was called, ten years old and sweetly sleeping until a rope would gag her quickly and pillows would crush over her small face. Then to the master bedroom, where they would dispatch the last few guards. Everything would be done without firing a single shot. The general and his beautiful wife wouldn't need to stir even a little in their bed beyond the door, their bodies still as a painting by Velázquez, until death came.

All of this had been set in motion, but then one of the guards turned suddenly and machine-gun fire cut the night. The assassins scattered, barely escaping with their lives. The general woke at the sound of gunfire, but after hearing from his men what had happened, he only stumbled back to bed. Attempts on his life were not rare and particularly not just then, when he was on the cusp of the thing he'd waited for, as a tiger waits, just out of sight.

Five days later, the planned uprising in Morocco began. The general broadcast a message urging all military officers to join the insurgence and overthrow the Spanish government. Then he sent his wife and daughter into hiding in France, and was taken through the streets of Tenerife, where already the shooting had begun, to a waiting de Havilland Dragon Rapide. He wore civilian clothes and dark glasses and, by way of further disguise, had shaved off his familiar mustache.

It was nothing after all this for the trim little plane to take flight, ferrying its passenger to North Africa, where he would prepare the army that would soon overtake mainland Spain. On the way, he donned his uniform, crisp khaki with a red-and-gold belted sash. And just like that, he became General Francisco Franco, newly escaped from exile. Ready to start a war the whole world would be forced to finish.

★　★　★

And what was I doing then, at twenty-seven, when Franco made his play for Spain? Standing in a deepening shadow, as everyone was, whether they realized it or not.

German troops had recently marched into the Rhineland, and the Nuremberg Laws were being enforced, banning Jews from marrying or bearing children with 'pure' Reich citizens, restricting them from public schools and certain businesses, and essentially branding them, along with Afro-Germans and Gypsies, enemies of the *Volksgemeinschaft*, so the Nazis could protect their Aryan blood in a race-based state. It was all so shocking and so absolutely wrong. And yet you could almost pretend it wasn't happening by going on with your life and thinking it had nothing to do with you.

I had lived in Paris on and off for years, trying to be a writer and also falling in love a lot, without being terribly successful at either. I was dying to write a character as glittering and sharp as Lady Brett from *The Sun Also Rises*, but since I couldn't, I would settle for trying to be her. I wore long skirts with knit sweaters and sat in cafés smoking too much and crinkling my eyes and saying, 'Hello, darling,' to near strangers. I ordered cocktails that were far too strong for me, and laughed at things that were desperate, and threw myself hard at experience, by which I mean married men. But the worst of it was walking home alone afterward under a smeary purple sky feeling not at all like Lady Brett but sad and lonely and thoroughly confused about what to do and who to be.

Something was missing in my life — in me — and I thought writing could fill it or fix it, or cure me of myself. It was only a notion I had, but I'd been following it faithfully, from St.

Louis to New York, New York to Paris, Paris to Cannes, to Capri, and now to Stuttgart, where I meant to do research. I'd recently begun a novel about a young French couple that would do bold and important things in the name of political pacifism — go on strike with coal miners and endure the metal truncheons of the gendarmes, all in the name of social justice.

The story felt brave and serious to me when I was hunched over my notebooks in the Weltkriegsbibliothek, but there was a moment every day when I stepped out of the library and was confronted with the actual world. How naïve and hopeless the idea of pacifism seemed when the streets were full of brownshirts.

One day I was at the cinema when two Reich soldiers came through and dragged a young Jewish woman out of her seat in front of me and into the street by the back of her neck like a dog. The lights came down and the film reel began to spin, but I couldn't be still in my chair and be entertained, not now. Walking back to my pension, I startled several times as I caught my reflection in a shopwindow. I looked Aryan enough, with my blond waves and light blue eyes and strong straight nose. I'd inherited my features from my parents, after all, who had easily passed as Protestant in anti-Semitic St. Louis. But there was Jewish blood in my family on both sides.

From Stuttgart, I moved on to Munich, where things grew even darker and more ominous. I read about Franco's coup in Nazi newspapers, which recounted everything in a boasting,

4

sneering way. The rapidly falling Republican regime was described as a pack of 'Red Swine Dogs,' while Franco glowed, a prince of the Spanish people. Never mind that the government he and his henchmen were overthrowing was the product of the first democratic election in sixty years. Never mind that innocent people were being butchered so that a few could claim power and total dominion.

By the time I was back in Paris, Franco had declared martial law and vowed to 'unite' Spain again at any cost, even if it meant slaughtering half the population. Most of Spain's military had joined the Nationalists, while untrained civilians struggled to defend cities and villages. Pamplona, Ávila, Saragossa, Teruel, Segovia, and the whole of Navarre fell like dominoes before a month had passed. Anyone who spoke against the coup was a target. In the old Moorish city of Badajoz, the Nationalists marched almost two thousand into the Plaza de Toros — militiamen and peasant farmers, women and children — and opened fire with machine guns, leaving the bodies where they fell, and then pushing on to Toledo, where they would do the same.

Worse still were the terrible alliances being formed. Nazi Germany sent state-of-the-art Luftwaffe bomber planes and three thousand troops to Spain in exchange for mineral resources, raw copper and iron ore that would soon help Hitler with his own deadly goals. Submarines were sent and more bombers, hundreds of shiploads of supplies and skilled officers to train Franco's men and sharpen their ability to kill and torture.

Mussolini came to Franco's aid as well, 'loaning' him eighty thousand troops and forming the third deadly prong of the Fascist triangle. And just like that, after years of sinister plotting, and almost overnight, Europe was a different place, and a more threatening one. It seemed anything could happen.

Stalin in the Soviet Union had his own agenda, but for the moment there was much to be gained by aiding Republican Spain. He waited to be joined by the major democracies in the West with arms to sell, but France's government was bitterly divided, and Britain seemed more concerned with the salacious happenings between King Edward VIII and Wallis Simpson. In the States, Roosevelt was busy trying to manage the crippling effects of the Depression and also in the throes of his reelection campaign. And after all, there was much for America to debate in regard to Spain's pleas for help. There were troubling rumors of arms being given to anarchists and labor-union militias if they would join the Republic's cause — a difficult stance to support when there was already so much fear at home about communism.

Roosevelt decided on a blanket arms embargo, vowing to keep America out of foreign wars as long as possible. But for some of us who watched the shadows deepen all through that fall of 1936, there was no such thing as a foreign war. Nationalist forces spread through innocent villages, killing tens of thousands as they went.

As they shelled the capital of Madrid, surrounding it on three sides, we felt responsible. The Republic of Spain had tried for democracy only to be slashed down and tortured. Why was it not our concern?

Slowly, slowly, and then all at once, thousands of people began to come forward as volunteers. International Brigades were formed out of troops from France and America, Canada, Australia, Mexico. Most of the men weren't trained soldiers. Most, in fact, had never held a gun, and yet they grabbed what weapons they could — revolvers their fathers had left them, hunting guns, pistols, gas masks from the hardware store — and boarded trains, ships, cargo planes.

It was a beautiful crusade, and though I wasn't immediately sure how I would find a role for myself, later I thought only this: It may be the luckiest and purest thing of all to see time sharpen to a single point. To feel the world rise up and shake you hard, insisting that you rise, too, somehow. Some way. That you come awake and stretch, painfully. That you change, completely and irrevocably — with whatever means are at your disposal — into the person you were always meant to be.

For me the war in Spain will always shine with the light of hard-won transformation. It was like falling in love. Or looking up into the sky to see a burning arrow, which screamed to be followed. It was that simple and complicated all at once. And if more would be set in motion than I could possibly predict or even imagine, I was still ready to say yes. And if I would soon lose my heart

7

forever, never to retrieve it, lose absolutely everything — I was ready for that, too. My life seemed to be demanding it. It was calling me forward. There wasn't any choice to be made, in the end. I would have to go to it, with my eyes wide open, and my hands open, too, willing to pay the price.

# *Part 1*

## RACING SHADOWS

### JANUARY 1936-MARCH 1937

# 1

For better or worse I was born a traveler, wanting to go everywhere and see everything. My clearest memory, at five or six, was the morning I wrote not crookedly or hurriedly but with care: *Dear Mother, how pretty you are. You are lovely to me. Goodbye. Martha.* I found a thumbtack and fixed my letter to the newel post at the top of the stairs, and walked out the front door taking nothing with me and not making a sound. Trotting down the block with purpose — for I had thought this out long before — I stole onto the cart of the man who delivered our ice, hoping to end up far from St. Louis, and in the world.

All that long summer day I was completely hidden and also exhilarated. Being stowed away was part of that, and how I'd gone off alone, in secret. But even more convincing was the strangeness of what I saw through the cracks of the carriage — factories and neighborhoods and whole rambling expanses of my own city that I'd never seen or guessed at. I was happy and even forgot that I was hungry until dusk, when I caught a glimpse of Forest Hills Park and realized we'd traveled only in a wide, known circle.

That first solo journey had disappointed me, but it set my course anyway. I was a traveler, and that was that. By age twenty-six I had seen most of Europe, swum naked in three oceans, and met diplomats and Bolsheviks. College couldn't hold my interest, so I'd abandoned it, earning my own way. It seemed imperative not only to be on the move, and feeling things, but also to be my own person, and to live my own life, and not anyone else's.

But in January of 1936, my mother called me home to St. Louis with a cable saying my father was ill. I went by train, nervously shredding the cable in my coat pocket as I went. For as long as I could remember, my mother had been careful never to let anyone see her worry. But tension and anxiety had come through even in her telegram's few dashed-off words, and I didn't know how I would find her, or my father, and if I was up to facing him, ill and frail. To facing things as they were.

My mother, Edna, was always the North Star in my sky, and also kinder than anyone living. She was warm and intelligent and good all through, and though she'd devoted her life to tirelessly championing women's rights and was ready, always, to be on the right side of things and people and causes, somehow the campaigns and marches and community speeches never got in the way of her being a mother, or a wife. Every evening she would stop whatever she was doing the moment she heard my father's key in the lock. Then she'd hurry to the bottom of the stairs just as he sailed through the door, planted his gray felt hat on the wooden stand, and kissed her.

This evening ritual was a tender thing between

them and their oldest habit. But it also seemed to be an inked-in promise of the future. Of utter reliability going forward as far as it was possible to see. Of all the kisses to come. I remember feeling, as a child, that it took no effort at all for my mother to be at the door every evening. Time obviously colluded to arrange it — slowing so she could stop everything to be exactly there whenever the door swung open every day. But of course I was mistaken. It took tremendous effort and will, too. And choice, and determination. Other things tumbled so she could be at the stairs. They did, though I had never seen or heard them as they fell.

My father, George Gellhorn, was a celebrated and esteemed obstetrician, with a busy practice and teaching positions at two hospitals, and a glowing, impeccable way of being in the world. He was that pillar father, straight out of a George Eliot novel, managing his family with smooth care, precise as the inner workings of a Swiss timepiece, and his patients, too. And everything.

In his study, there were thousands of books in alphabetical order with their spines perfectly aligned. And he had read all of them. I thought he knew everything there was to know when I was a girl, and everything about me, too. Maybe that's why I was forever trying to please him and win his approval, so I could finally be the daughter I saw flickering with promise and possibility in his eyes. It was perhaps the greatest difficulty of my life, coming to terms with the truth. Of course that daughter didn't exist. She never could.

★ ★ ★

From St. Louis Union Station, I hired a car to take me to McPherson Avenue, where I stood in front of the wide, polished door and let myself fantasize for one long moment about running rather than facing the music. The last time I'd been home, my father and I had fought so terribly I couldn't remember his words without flinching. And now he was gravely ill, possibly dying.

The door swung open, and my mother was there, looking at me as if I'd lost my senses. 'Marty! Come in. You'll catch your death.'

As she pulled me inside and into her arms, her smell alone undid me. Lavender water and face powder, and good linen. Every moment of my life was hers to hold, the fortnightly dances and Saturday breakfasts, her humming along to running water, or reciting bits of practice speeches she was always working out in her head. Picnic lunches, just us two, at Creve Coeur, near the burbling falls, where I prayed that she would never die. And evenings on our front porch, books tented in our laps as the light faded, and white moths stuck to the screen door.

It was like floodgates opening, being there on the same stretch of the crimson Persian carpet where I had lost countless games of marbles with my brothers. All the distances I had traveled, trying to be myself, didn't matter here, where nothing ever changed. Not the mahogany furniture or the art or the books in their placement on the shelves. Not the eggshell sheen

14

on the walls, or the quality of light coming through the stained-glass window on the landing. This was the light of childhood. I was all the ages I had ever been.

'How is he?' I asked when I was able to compose myself.

'We'll know more tomorrow.' Her face was tight and drawn, hard to look at, or to look away from. She was still a beautiful woman and always would be. But I could see her cares etched around her cornflower-blue eyes and along her jawline, and the sleepless nights, too. Silvered strands of her hair had fallen loose from the low knot she always wore, and her navy shirtwaist was creased under her strand of pearls.

I didn't want to ask if the doctors had mentioned cancer, and couldn't somehow. The word had been on my mind all the way out from Connecticut, but I simply held it, leaded and razor-edged, as I trailed her quietly to where he was resting. Down the long hall, past the secretary and round mirror, the heavy chandelier, each known thing was sturdy and anchoring, exactly where it should be. At an angle under the stairs, the grand piano sat with sheets of one of Chopin's nocturnes open on the scrolled music stand, though no one had played it in many years, not since my youngest brother had gone off to medical school in Virginia.

'Is Alfred coming?' I asked.

'At the end of the week if he can get away. He's just started a new round of courses.'

I waited for her to mention George and Walter, my older two brothers. They were both in

15

the East and married with young children. If they were coming as well, then it really was as awful as I feared. But she only kept walking.

Upstairs, my brothers' childhood bedrooms had long since been converted to guest rooms, while mine on the third floor under the eaves had been preserved with all the care of a time capsule. I looked forward to escaping there later, but now there was this, my father as thin as I had ever seen him, his complexion nearly gray against yellow linens. He was propped on a pillow, with his eyes closed. But he wasn't sleeping.

The cable had said that he was suffering terribly with his stomach and that his doctors would operate. Later I would know more, how he'd kept secrets from us for years, fighting to hide his symptoms, his pain, from everyone, even my mother, because he guessed he was dying. During his months and months of silence, things had grown dire.

'Marty's here,' my mother's voice called out now.

His eyes opened and his lips tightened over a smile. 'Martha.'

I felt very small, suddenly, and that there were two of me, the girl I was and the one he wished he could put in her place. Both loved him but had never been able to say it. Because anger was there, too, side by side with the loving feelings, the wish to hurt him, the wish to pull him close forever.

My mother urged me forward, into the chair that had been pulled up alongside the bed, and

16

then went over to the window seat and opened a newspaper. His hand, when I took it, was thin and riddled with veins, but warm. When was the last time I had held my father's hand?

'I'm going to be perfectly fine,' he said before I could speak. 'I have the very best surgeons in St. Louis.'

'I thought you were the best surgeon in St. Louis.'

The joke was stiff, but he smiled for me before being caught up by a spasm. It took hold, changing his face so that I had to look away, anywhere. When the pain cleared, and he lay there, breathing heavily, taking some water, he said, 'I've been reading your book. It's wonderful.'

There it was on his nightstand. The plain paper manuscript of my latest effort, *The Trouble I've Seen*. I had sent it just before Christmas as a gift, though it hadn't been an easy decision. He hadn't been able to finish my first book, a novel, and told me so, calling it vulgar. I had worked on it for two years while in Europe, then found a publisher on my own and even gotten a small advance. But you would have thought I'd made a deal on the black market from the way he laid out the terms of his disappointment in a long, impassioned letter. My characters were immoral and frivolous. He didn't know why I had bothered when there were so many worthwhile things to write about. *What Mad Pursuit* followed three college girls who were desperate to find themselves, who travel everywhere and take men to bed and contract

17

syphilis, and otherwise stumble along, developing a dingy film of loneliness. Obviously he'd seen my own failings in the pages, though I'd only meant to show him how clever my dialogue was, and how gaspingly well I'd described the sea.

I read his biting letter over and over, fuming and wanting to spit all sorts of terrible things back. But behind my anger was a bottomless kind of hurt. At some point, I crumpled the pages and threw them in the bin, but that didn't solve anything. Every last word was still with me, way down in one corner of my seething heart, where they ticked and smoked as if they might detonate at any moment.

This latest book was utterly different, a collection of stories about people struck hard by the Depression, and I had taken it on meaning to do social good.

'You really liked it?' I asked him now, unable to keep the plaintive tone out of my voice.

'A lot of it is sad, of course. And I imagine it might be more difficult to get a contract for this one after the reviews you received for the last.' He said it with no malice whatsoever, as if he were talking about eggs, or rain. 'But maybe it doesn't work that way.'

'It does, actually, but I won't give up. I couldn't bear working so hard for nothing.'

'Of course you won't give up.' My mother rose to stand at the foot of the bed. 'We Gellhorns aren't quitters. And for the record, I think it's marvelous, too. You've made those characters come alive. I felt them as terribly true.'

'Thank you,' I heard myself say as I wrestled an array of competing emotions. I wanted my parents to be proud of me and to take me seriously. I also wanted to be well past caring, complete and needing only my own validation. That was the bar I always tried for, anyway.

'We have to be at the hospital at six sharp,' my mother reminded, and then offered a hand. I took it, suddenly as tired as I had ever felt. 'Let's leave your father to rest.'

# 2

The next morning before dawn, my mother and I got my father downstairs and packed into the car, tucking blankets around his legs as if weather were the problem, and not whatever it was that ate away at him from deep inside. It was beginning to snow.

At Barnes Hospital, they admitted him and then whisked him off through swinging wooden doors while the two of us waited in the cafeteria, drinking terrible coffee, and then moved to a bland visitors' sitting room. Outside, the storm picked up, dropping a soundless sheet of white. It seemed the only way to keep time, watching the drifts pile higher and higher on the windowsills and on the tops of the cars five floors below us in the parking lot, looking more and more like mounded sugar.

'He's going to be fine,' we kept telling each other at intervals.

'He is.'

It was a talisman we were braiding back and forth, repeating the words without variation until they were links in a chain of hope, or faith, or whatever lies between.

And then late in the day, one of the surgeons walked toward us carrying his cloth cap in his hands, and I thought I would rather step out of my own skin than hear what he had to say. I could barely stand to watch his mouth move. But then the surprise came. The news was good.

It was cancer, after all, but the tumor had come out easily and whole, and didn't appear to have spread anywhere else. They would keep my father at the hospital until he was stronger, but there was every reason to be hopeful.

'Oh, thank God,' my mother cried, and we held each other. I felt her shake as we both laughed through tears, and my heart lightened all at once. A magician's dove set free.

\* \* \*

On the way home, later, after we'd seen him and felt even more assured that all truly would be well, we drove miles out of our way to stop at the German bakery at Soulard Market for poppy-seed cakes. In our kitchen, my mother warmed milk in a saucepan, and it felt like Christmas had come again, only with a better gift. The milk went into a heavy mug, and I savored its heat in my hands as she asked how I'd been. Now, on the other side of so much worry and strain, we could finally talk naturally.

I told her all about the borrowed house in New Hartford, Connecticut, where I'd been holed up writing of late. How I loved my little room with its desk that faced a long meadow, and how it felt like an incredible treasure to have months of time, and nowhere else to be, and nothing pressing to think of.

I hadn't noticed her expression shifting while I talked.

'You should come home,' she said after some

21

silence. 'It's not polite to impose on friends for so long.'

'Oh, Fields doesn't care.' W. F. Fields was my current benefactor. I didn't yet think of him as a friend; we hadn't known each other long. 'It's not like that. He's never there anyway, since he works in the city.'

'What about his wife?'

'He's a bachelor, Mother, and his house is enormous. He hardly knows I'm there.'

The moment the words left my mouth, I realized my error. Of course she would be far more troubled by no wife in the picture than the possible impingement on Fields's generosity. And though she didn't say these next words, I heard them anyway, reading the tension in her shoulders: *What will people say?*

'It's really all right,' I tried to explain. This wasn't the stuff of tawdry melodrama. Fields had never been my beau or even a conquest. He was a stuffy UN type with an encyclopedic knowledge of China. I'd met him at a party in Washington, and we'd gotten to discussing my writing, and this new work, a collection of long stories based on some of the people I'd met when I was traveling the States as a narrative reporter for FERA, the Federal Emergency Relief Administration. I hadn't been able to forget those people — that's all I had said, and that it would be nice to have a place to dive in completely, the way Fitzgerald and Hemingway had had Paris.

'Well, it's hardly Paris,' he'd replied, and then extended the offer of his weekend house upstate.

I saw no reason not to accept. And that was really all there was to it. Later, he made a pass at me when he came to use the house for a snowy getaway, but it had been after three very severe martinis, in his defense, and I had fought him off easily enough. We'd been able to laugh at the whole thing later.

I knew my mother couldn't hear any of this and feel reassured. So I simply said, 'I really can take care of myself,' and then changed the subject to the articles I'd lately been pitching to magazines. For the past several years, I'd made a stab at serious journalism, but apparently didn't have the right background. Or maybe it was the way I looked. When I could arrange a meeting at all, editors eyed me up and down, taking in my long legs, my good clothes, my hair, and pegged me as more socialite than Junior Leaguer. The only work I was able to find was penning beauty tips for women with time on their hands: youth treatments, suntanning techniques, the latest hairstyles. Twenty dollars for a thousand words. The writing felt mindless and constricting, and required only the smallest sliver of my intelligence or point of view. It chinked away at me. But what alternative was there?

My mother listened without comment as the milk in both our mugs went cold. I knew she wanted more for me, and for me to want more for myself. As a girl I'd written poetry every day, dreaming of literary glory. Now there was bubble bath and cuticle cream, and I was barely scraping by.

'I'd like to have you here,' she said when the evening had grown still, and it was time for bed. 'That's selfish of me, I know.'

'You've never been selfish a day in your life.'

'We've put some money by. If you want to work on something that's, well . . . ' Her words trailed as her meaning wavered, but only for a moment. 'We'd like to help. Come home. Write here.'

'Oh.'

She hadn't surprised me, exactly. The last months had been difficult and exhausting for her, and of course she would worry far less about me if I were just upstairs. I felt her watching me as I thought how to answer her.

'It's a lovely offer,' I finally said. 'Let me think about it, if that's all right?' Then I kissed her, and placed our mugs in the sink, and headed up the stairs quietly, the thick carpet swallowing my steps, while inside, I felt a pinching sensation and small flickerings of panic.

★ ★ ★

If my parents had had their way, I would never have left college except to win the Nobel Prize in Literature, or for a marriage as long and stable as theirs. But I'd gone to Albany for a newspaper job, instead, where no one had ever written deathless prose or poetry, covering wedding announcements and women's society luncheons, and trying to live on four dollars a week in a tiny room that smelled of sauerkraut. When that wore me out, I revolted. I took my two suitcases and my typewriter and seventy-five dollars, and sailed to Paris.

I'd tried for journalism jobs there, too, all well over my head, I was quickly informed. So I became a junior shampoo girl instead, writing when I could, and sleeping very little, and buying fistfuls of violets rather than breakfast whenever I was feeling down.

Meanwhile, my parents worried, first silently, and then openly. My father began to lob letter after anxious letter at me, meaning to bring me home, no doubt, or to settle me down in some other way. But they only made me want to live faster, and cast a wider net.

That's how I met Bertrand de Jouvenel, a smooth, good-looking, and very married left-wing French journalist. It all happened so quickly I didn't have time to weigh my own questions. He'd once been the storied and much-sought-after lover of Colette. She was his stepmother, and had seduced him when he was only fifteen. All of that should have sent me running in the opposite direction, but I felt only intrigued, and then dazzled by his hunger for me, and the desperation we felt trying to be together when it was impossible. His wife, Marcelle, wouldn't grant a divorce.

We were involved for nearly five years. Occasionally I would catch a glimpse of what I was doing and bolt away from him, my knapsack stuffed with the tattered draft of my first novel, meaning to finally get serious. But he quickly raced after me, again and again, and the same old chaos resumed.

I spun in circles. I cried an ocean. I spun some more.

★ ★ ★

To be fair, it wasn't just my parents who disapproved of Bertrand. Every friend who had ever cared about me worried aloud for my happiness. He wasn't free to love me. Marcelle's hand wouldn't be forced, no matter how he promised he could change her mind. That I stayed even so gave off the general impression that I was extorting myself like a low-rent geisha. I'd become a cautionary tale.

When Bertrand and I finally broke free from each other, I went home to lick my wounds, but quickly realized my mistake.

'What are you up to with your life, Marty?' my father railed. '*Experience* shouldn't be a dirty word, but it seems to be with you.'

'Don't be unfair, Daddy. I'm going to get back to my book now. I want to write. You know that. It's all I've ever really wanted.'

'So write,' he'd said bloodlessly. We were in his study, and I couldn't help feeling as though I were one of his patients waiting for the worst sort of pronouncement. I sat in front of his heavy, orderly desk, while behind his straight shoulders medical dictionaries and texts and the other books he'd read and loved all his life sat lined up on their shelves like a custom-made firing squad. 'Write, and do it now instead of capitalizing on your nice figure and your pretty hair. Stop being so charming.'

The sting of his words made me dizzy. My ears rang. 'If I am charming it's your fault and Mother's.'

'You're just afraid to be lonely.'

I stared at him, feeling hurt and angry but most of all sad. Sad that I couldn't dare tell him he might be right. At that very moment, there was already another suitor waiting in the wings, though I hadn't confessed it to anyone. And he was married, too.

'You need to learn to live with yourself, not others,' he went on. 'That's the difficult part. When you learn to accept your own nature, it will start to feel peaceful, not frantic. Maybe then you'll stop throwing yourself at such terrible choices.'

'I don't have any problem with how I'm behaving,' I told him, though that wasn't true. I actually couldn't seem to help myself. 'I'm not asking for advice.'

'No, you're not. I'm aware of that.' He turned away, looking out the window. It was autumn, and the sycamores on our street were tawny and unspoiled, as only nature seemed to manage. They glowed. When he gazed back at me, he said, 'You're collecting people because you need their opinion about you. It's not pretty to watch.'

'Don't watch, then,' I had said, and then left before I could scream everything I felt. That I hated his blinding scrutiny. That I loved him so much my guts felt twisted with it. That I was lost and afraid. That I was trying with all I had, though that never, ever seemed to be enough.

# 3

The next day and all that week, my mother and I went to the hospital to see how much better Father was doing. His eyes weren't hooded anymore, and the surgery had unburdened him, lifting away dread and secrecy as well as pain.

Now that the tide had turned, I felt lighter, too. He would heal and strengthen, returning to his own patients. He would live. But I was also aware of a small inner voice whispering that our battle over my character would continue as before. It wasn't that I wanted him to die. That thought would have been beyond imagining. But I had wanted something to be simpler between us, finally.

Instead, my mother found it necessary to tell him about Fields and the house in Connecticut. Even from his hospital bed, he began to pressure me to return home, brandishing words like *inappropriate* and *selfish* and *childish*. He meant to hold up a mirror, not a hammer. But I felt only blows.

I finally made it clear to him — and Mother, too — that I was going back east to do what I had been doing no matter what they thought; that I didn't see at all how I was hurting anyone. He'd gripped the sides of the hospital bed, then, and pulled himself taller and straighter. I saw the effort that took and felt weak with it.

'Marty, there are two kinds of women,' he

28

said. 'And for now, at least. Well, for now you are the other kind.'

I don't remember what I said in return, only that I couldn't imagine ever forgiving him. Pierced and small, my head full of wasps, I raced home to pack my things and found the next train east.

Once on board, I headed straight for the club car. It was filled with businessmen, exactly the type I knew my father would warn me against. Even my being there, ordering a martini and slipping off my coat, he would say, would mean I was asking to be picked up.

I ordered a whiskey and soda as St. Louis dropped away, and it wasn't long at all before a man in a Brooks Brothers shirt and knit tie came and sat across from me.

'Can I buy you a drink?'

'I have a drink, thanks.'

'Let me get that one, then. Or you can have one for each hand.'

'Sounds messy.'

He smiled. 'We can fetch you a towel. Where are you headed?'

'New York.'

'City girl, eh?'

'Trying to be.' I didn't want to say more or explain myself, not to him.

He had a pinkish, compressed-looking face, though his shirt was handsome. His shoes were cordovan with a high sheen, and he wore a thick, burnished wedding band, not that it mattered. I wanted nothing at all from him, only the distraction of this single moment.

When the steward brought my second drink, it wobbled on the narrow table and threatened to spill until I drank it, quickly, on the heels of the first. He was in bonds, he said. I don't remember what else we talked about, except that he bred greyhounds. Later, somewhere in the middle of Pennsylvania, he compared me to one of those slender, flighty dogs and then tried to kiss me.

I had gone out to the lavatory and he had followed, as if I'd given a sign. I hadn't, but his nearness was all right for the moment, for how it pushed other things away. As his shoulders held me to the shuddering wall of the passageway, I closed my eyes, tasting the insides of his mouth, green olives and pure alcohol. But then he began to move heavily, his breath loud. His stomach pressed into mine as he grabbed for my waist, then my breasts.

'Say, what's this all about?' he asked when I stopped him.

'I just like kissing.'

'You're a funny girl.' He looked puzzled and a little annoyed. 'Why are you here with me anyway?'

*I'm not with you,* I thought to myself, feeling the liquor I'd drunk surge through me like smoke. 'No reason. I'm happy, that's all.'

'You don't seem happy. In fact, you look about as sad as anyone I've ever seen. That's why I noticed you.'

A porter came through, carefully keeping his eyes straight ahead, trying to be invisible. I stepped back, feeling hot and seen through anyway. I thought of my father. 'Do you think there are two kinds of girls?' I asked the man when the porter had moved on.

'I don't know. The world's a big place. Seems to me there are probably more than two kinds of everything.' He eyed me curiously for a moment. 'Say, what are you playing at?'

'Just shut up,' I told him.

'What?'

'You can kiss me again, but please, *please* shut up.'

★   ★   ★

The next morning, I crept out of my Pullman berth and looked both ways as furtively as some kind of spy. I didn't know where the bonds man was and didn't want to know. It was challenging enough to slink all the way to the other end of the train with only myself to answer to. I roiled with small flashbacks, clever things I'd said for effect, where his hands had gone on my body, and mine on his. Keats would help, I hoped, and buried myself in my book all that day, my head swimming a lot at first, and then less and less as my nerves settled and my memory grew a thicker skin.

On the train pushed, and when we finally arrived at Penn Station, I stepped out into the cold afternoon air that was cleaner and colder than anything in St. Louis, because it allowed for more. None of these marvelous people knew or expected anything of me. I could be whomever I chose. I could burn my candle at both ends if I wanted, or right from the center, or I could

31

throw the damned thing away.

I had arranged to stay with an old girlfriend for a week or two before returning to Connecticut. She lived on Grove Street, in a little walk-up in the West Village, and had hidden a key for me in her philodendron. I'd forgotten completely that I'd given my mother the address. Forgotten everything by then but the way my cheeks stung, chapped, and how good it was to be moving on my own steam. But just through the front door, on my girlfriend's rickety yard-sale table, another cable lay waiting for me.

While I'd been in the middle of Pennsylvania in a stranger's arms, my father's heart had failed. He had died in his sleep.

OH, MARTY. I'M SORRY YOU DIDN'T HAVE A CHANCE TO SAY GOODBYE. PLEASE COME HOME.

# 4

Over the next twelve months I think I aged twelve years. I lived like a maiden aunt at the top of the stairs, seeing no one but my family, and guessing about the world only when it trickled through in newspapers. The hermit's life might have been good for writing if I'd felt less awful about my father's final words to me, and less stricken by the reality of his death. I'd been wrong, I now knew, to think his going might solve anything for me, and even more wrong to have wished for it, for even a single second.

I wanted him back in a howling way. I needed to make things right, to forgive and be forgiven, which amounted to the same impossible thing. I needed time to prove to him that my character was only a little bent and raw at its edges, and that I could yet make him proud of me. But clocks don't turn backward. I was having a hard time believing they turned forward, either. At least from where I stood.

My brother Alfred had taken time off from school and come to live at home, too, for a time. We ate all our meals together in the kitchen and listened to the radio after dinner in our bed slippers. By day I was trying to write something new, but primarily I gnawed on pencils and stared out the window, and waited to see what my mother might need.

She was being brave, as brave as anyone ever

could be, but my father had been her North Star just as firmly as she'd always been mine. One day, I went to post a letter and found her standing still at the bottom of the stairs. It was nearly the dinner hour and the light was blue. It tipped sideways, throwing shadows on the door as she stood there, and when it came to me why, my heart cracked for her. She was listening for his key in the lock. Waiting for her kiss.

I went to her and took her in my arms. She was still as air, thin enough to blow away.

'I don't know what to do,' she said against my shoulder. 'I keep wondering who I should be now.'

'Can I help?'

'You've already done so much. I know you'd rather be off somewhere being gay and free.'

'I'm happy to stay.'

It was partially the truth. I would have given anything to make something easier for her, but being home was also like living in a mausoleum, or behind glass. I couldn't breathe except shallowly most days, and then there was her face, full of a misery that unstitched me. For thirty-five years she'd been a wife. Who could stand that kind of emptiness and reversal? Who could avoid it, except to love no one and live alone?

★ ★ ★

After a while, I began to write again, and also to hunt for someone to publish *The Trouble I've Seen*. I sent the book to multiple publishing

34

houses, and then bit my nails down to nothing as the rejections began to trickle in, my hopes dissolving like teaspoons of sugar in water. Finally, I decided I had to do something else or chew off my own paws, and began to look for journalism jobs out east. I wallpapered Manhattan with energetic letters and my résumé, such as it was. After a deluge of no-thank-yous, *Time* magazine agreed to let me do a trial story for them. I was determined to win them over, and killed myself, working twelve hours a day for a full week. The piece was personal as well as newsy and gripping, I thought. It was about a trip to Mississippi that Bertrand and I had once taken from New York in a rented car, and how we'd come terrifyingly close to witnessing a lynching.

The writing overtook me. I poured everything into the piece, but when I'd finished and sent it on and then spent a week pacing, desperate to have this job and no other, the *Time* editor sent his regrets by mail in a single discouraging paragraph. The tone was wrong for them, somehow too serious and also not serious enough. He hoped I would try again at some point, when I had more experience behind me.

'I don't understand,' I complained to my mother. 'Too serious *and* not? How is that even possible?'

'Maybe he just means you have more to learn. That's not a bad thing.'

'I could have learned *there*. I don't see why not.'

'Maybe if you set your sights a bit lower, you

can work your way up and try them again,' she offered.

'Who has time? I want to be in the middle of something wonderful already. I can work hard. I don't mind that.'

She looked at me gently, seeming to weigh her words carefully, and then said, 'Beginnings are important, too, darling. You should be patient with life.'

'That might be easier if something were actually going well. Who knows where I'll find work now, and my novel's at a complete standstill.' I meant the new book I'd recently begun, about the pacifist French couple and their noble adventures. I was doing the work, dutifully writing my scenes and working through the dialogue, though mostly it seemed as if the story had nothing to do with me, but had only followed me home one day, like a stray. 'My characters feel like strangers, and I don't know how to get closer,' I went on. 'Maybe if I could be in France now, or walk the famous battlefields of the Great War, or only sit and think, looking at the Seine.'

'Why shouldn't you, then?'

'Don't be silly. I'll go another time.' I meant to reassure her, but I saw immediately that she was upset. She felt she was standing in my way.

'You can't give up your plans for me, or your freedom. That wouldn't be fair to either of us.'

'I'm not staying here because I feel sorry for you. This isn't about duty.'

'Let's call it love, then. But love can grow heavy, too. You need to live your own life.'

'I know,' I said, and I did. But as I hugged her hard, feeling her goodness pass through me like a transfusion, I realized I had no idea which direction to face looking for that life.

★   ★   ★

Winter turned slowly to spring that year. I winced from room to room, smoking too much and staying up late, and sleeping some days until one or two. And then I heard from an editor at William Morrow who was offering to take a chance on *The Trouble I've Seen*. The advance he held out was shockingly small. He also made it clear both by letter and by phone that he didn't believe the book would sell well, if at all. All of this was hard to hear, but at least the book would see daylight. I accepted, gratefully, hoping to prove the editor wrong, and also wishing to God I could share my news with my father.

I felt terribly small now when I remembered how angry I'd been with him, how I'd spat and seethed under his scrutiny. Maybe he'd been too hard on me, or maybe he'd only meant to help shape me, or challenge me to rise while there was still time. All I knew was that, where all the rage and rebellion had been, I felt only a yawning emptiness. Somehow, my mother's words — 'I keep wondering who I should be now' — had attached themselves to me, too. I didn't know what came next or how to find it.

Finally I told my mother I was thinking of considering Europe again.

'I was hoping you'd change your mind,' she

37

said. 'Think of it as a work cure. Go and throw yourself into this book.' She may as well have said, *Please figure out who you are. And hurry.*

★ ★ ★

I sailed that June of 1936, heading first for England and then France, both of which had shrunk and faded since I'd last been in Europe, not two years before. Unemployment was rampant and tensions high. In Paris, labor strikes were shutting down the city, so I moved on to Germany to begin my research in earnest. That's how I came to stand outside the Weltkriegsbibliothek, watching Nazi soldiers march and posture, trying to terrify, while most of the city cowered, as if under a terrible spell.

Hitler's influence had been swelling gradually, but at a distance from my life. Now I saw all sorts of things in a new relief. Conflict and tumult bubbled. An alarming number of Europe's countries — Greece and Portugal, Hungary and Lithuania and Poland — were under military rule, or in the thrall of dictatorships. Spain was the only place that was even trying to push back. A newly elected democratic government was trying to break essential ground. But then Franco struck.

It wasn't a surprise at all, I remember thinking, as I read about the coup in Nazi newspapers. The signs had been looming, tiptoeing blackly forward. But that didn't make it all any less horrifying. I went back to Paris, wanting to bury my head and focus on my book, but that was like racing a shadow. The strikes were still on, and half the restaurants were closed. There were riots in the Parc des Princes as French Communists tried to assert themselves and the Fascists pushed back. All of France seemed vulnerable to me now. Frighteningly close to the maw of a dragon.

I ran home, arriving just after the release of *The Trouble I've Seen*. Somehow, the book was not only selling but also receiving wide and glowing reviews. I had expected nothing, and could scarcely believe it. The *Boston Evening Transcript* called my writing 'fearless.' The *New York Herald Tribune* ran a full-length feature review with my picture, and described the book in rapturous terms from start to finish. Lewis Gannett, in his syndicated books column, said my writing burned with 'stinging poetry,' and predicted mine would be one of his favorite reads of the year.

I wanted to pinch myself. After the failure of my first novel, it felt wonderful and gratifying to be taken seriously as a writer — like long-prayed-for sunshine breaking through storm clouds. I was happy, and I felt vindicated. And yet there was something missing. I read the notices over and over, wondering why they weren't quite enough. And then turned to the newspapers again. The *St. Louis Post-Dispatch* ran the latest story, along with the *Times* and the *Chicago Tribune*. More and more papers seemed to be sending correspondents over because daily coverage was only growing, and Spain was on everyone's mind.

'How can this really be happening?' I asked Alfred and my mother, waving the latest story like a terrible flag. After a sixty-eight-day siege at the Alcázar, Franco's rebels had broken through the fourteenth-century fortress and taken control of Toledo, slaughtering hundreds of hostages as well as Republican soldiers. Elsewhere in Spain, there were daily executions and firing squads as Nationalist forces gained momentum.

'It's too awful,' Mother said. 'And who knows what Roosevelt's thinking.'

'He's thinking how to get reelected,' Alfred said. 'You can bet he won't send anything, not even water pistols.'

'I hope you're wrong,' I said. 'What if it's like the Balkan Wars? That's what everyone seems to be predicting. War could come for all of us soon, and no one's doing a thing to intervene.'

Anxieties only built through the fall as the death toll mounted, reported by all the major papers. The Nationalists had moved on to Valencia, and then Madrid in early November, attacking from the north and southwest, while hundreds of thousands of Republican refugees streamed into the city from the east. Daily shelling started, and German bombers began targeting the center square.

'I will destroy Madrid,' Franco declared to the whole world, but then the first International Brigades of volunteers arrived in the city, marching up the Gran Vía while crowds of Madrileños cheered. Maybe the brigades could turn Madrid and stop Franco here. Maybe Franco would have another crushing victory. All we could do was watch and wait to see what would happen next.

# 5

That December the anniversary of my father's death loomed, and Christmas, too. Mother took the box of fragile balsam ornaments down from the attic, but then couldn't bear to unwrap them. The glowing Nativity in Forest Hills Park seemed to belong to other, happier people, as did the skaters in pairs on the frozen river, and every other symbol of the season. We enlisted Alfred to choose a place on the map, anyplace at all as long as the sun shone there. Then placing a pillow on the best chair next to the stove where he had liked to read Robert Browning, we let Daddy's ghost have the house, and ran away. Ran away as only widows and orphans can.

Miami was where we meant to stay. By lunchtime on our second day, though, we had already tired of the shuffleboard tournaments and charades. Every third dish on the hotel's luncheon menu came with Mornay sauce.

'It isn't very wild here, is it?' Mother frowned at an arrow-straight, well-oiled stand of picture postcards. 'We only have a week after all.'

I felt it, too — that we hadn't gone far enough yet, or fast enough. Hadn't fully escaped.

'We can do better,' Alfred chimed in, and before an hour had passed, we'd collected our things from our still-tidy rooms, settled our account, and were dragging our luggage through the center of the town toward the bus station, all three of us happy — finally — with a sense of adventure.

Out of the city, Florida's orange-juice-colored sun fattened, and the heat grew wonderfully heavy. A single tired road stretched south through swamp and marsh flats, like an enormous python digesting the slow line of cars and wagons one by one. The twisted mangrove and saw-grass marshes released a salty, earthy *living* smell, while roadside signs offered pan-ready turtles and bonefish, and ominous biblical quotes.

Nearly every turn and crook of the place was different and mysterious and as far away from home as I could imagine, and I could imagine a lot.

Three hours later, after much bumping and jostling, we were delivered to the southernmost tip of the whole country. Key Languid. Key Desultory. Key *Wonderful* West.

The entire town would have fit in an unwashed teacup, and was hotter than anything and falling apart. The dusty streets were overrun with chickens, ready to riot over breadcrumbs or pebbles, it didn't seem to matter which. We found a hotel on Petronia Street and walked to Mallory Square for ice cream and an unobstructed view of the sea. Neither disappointed. On our way back toward the center of town on Whitehead Street, we passed the fattest, most senatorial tree I'd ever seen. I wanted to marry it, or maybe just sit forever in its circle of shade, but Mother had other ideas. Her pretty hair was sticking to the back of her neck, and liquor was called for. She dragged us farther on, to a low, whitewashed stucco watering hole on a little side street off of Duval.

It was the middle of the afternoon, and inside, the bar was dark as a cave, nearly empty. There were sawdust shavings and peanut shells in not-entirely-fresh drifts on the floor and a bar that jutted out of the wall, held in place by a hulking, mountain-sized barman. His name was Skinner, he told us, and we were welcome in his Conch bar because he could see we were lost and had no idea what we were in for.

Mother smiled. 'We're not lost.'

'If we are,' I corrected, 'we mean to be.'

Skinner laughed, and then set about making us daiquiris with a mound of chipped ice and fresh lime, while a grizzled-looking fellow at the other end of the bar looked us up and down. I was wearing my black cotton sundress and a pair of strapped low heels, an outfit that set off my hair and my calves, and generally speaking didn't fail to make an impression on the opposite sex. But he didn't seem more than politely interested in me, and anyway, I stopped thinking about myself the moment I recognized him.

He wore a ragged T-shirt and shorts that seemed to have come from the bottom of a fish barrel — both of which weren't doing him any favors. But it *was* him. His dark, nearly black hair fell over one side of a pair of round steel-wire spectacles. He caught me watching him, and our eyes met for a split second before he passed his hand through his mustache absentmindedly and went back to a stack of

44

letters he was reading.

I didn't say a word to Alfred or Mother, just let myself look at him for a moment, as a tourist looks at a map. His legs were brown and muscled as a prizefighter's. His arms were brown, too, and his chest was broad, and everything about him suggested physical strength and health and a kind of animal grace. The whole picture made an impression, but I wasn't going to trot over there and confess that I had his photo in my handbag, marking the page of my mystery novel. I'd clipped it from *Time* magazine, and also the long article alongside it, that he'd written about bullfighting. I didn't want to stammer out how meaningful his writing was to me, or abase myself by claiming I was a writer, too.

While still at Bryn Mawr, I had pinned my favorite quote from *A Farewell to Arms* above the desk in my dormitory room: 'Nothing ever happens to the brave.'

It was meant to be a daily reminder as I worked on my own writing, and a challenge, too, though I secretly hoped that everything happened to the brave. That life came hot and bright and loud if you flung yourself fully in its direction.

In the dark close bar, I tried to galvanize myself to approach him somehow. He was my hero, and not twenty feet away. *Nothing ever happens to the brave*, I thought, pinching myself and waiting for something clever to come to me, but nothing seemed good enough.

I swallowed hard and a little breathlessly and turned away to face my family again, and my daiquiri. The drink was tart and strong, with floating bits of ice. Overhead, the blades of the fan clipped round like a slow-breathing animal. Beyond the open door two seagulls harassed each other, wrestling over a black mussel shell. And Mr. Hemingway continued to ignore us, reading his mail until Skinner, chipping more ice for a second round, asked where we were from.

'St. Louis,' Mother said proudly.

That did it. He stood up from his end of the bar and came over. 'Two of my wives went to school in St. Louis,' he said to Mother in a neighborly way. 'I've always liked that town.'

*Two of my wives?* The way he'd phrased it, you'd think he'd had a dozen — not that I would have dared risk pointing it out.

'It suits us most of the time,' Mother said. 'Though down here you have better rum. The sunshine isn't bad, either.'

When he smiled at her, his brown eyes shone warmly and a dimple stretched along his left cheek.

'I was born in the Middle West,' he told her. 'Near Chicago. It always looks better to me from a distance — the country as well as the people.'

Alfred had been quiet, but suddenly stood and shook hands, and we traded names all around. I was proud of him and Mother for not startling or seeming overimpressed at the introduction. The whole country knew who Hemingway was, and most of the rest of the world, too. But here in his town, it was obvious that he liked to be taken for a regular Joe. The T-shirt alone proved that.

'Let me show you around while you're here,'

46

he said to us all while looking pointedly at Mother. She was still a very handsome woman. She kept herself up, as they say, and had lovely silvering hair, open blue eyes, a perfect mouth, and absolutely no vanity. Except for our recent loss at home, I'd always thought she was the most contented and well-adjusted person I'd ever known. Luck came to her often, as it did now. And it was almost as if a roulette wheel had been set spinning the moment we got on the bus or even before, the black marble spit out precisely here with a winning, effortless, inevitable click.

*A private tour of Key West by Ernest Hemingway?* Of course. Sure thing. Don't mind if we do.

★   ★   ★

In Hemingway's black Ford coupe, we made a stitching loop around the outside of the island, beginning at the southernmost point, where there was a barrel painted red and white like a barber's pole. There were two anemic-looking beaches, but Ernest assured us the swimming was good.

'This doesn't seem at all a literary place,' Mother said to him from the passenger seat. Her hat was off, and on her lap. She trailed one hand out the open window. 'How did you manage to end up here?'

'The long way, I guess.' He grinned. 'Paris to Piggott, Arkansas, to Kansas City. Montana after that, and then Spain, then back to Paris.

47

Wyoming, Chicago, New York, and Piggott again. And Africa was in there, too, actually. I don't think we spent a month in one place the first two years we were married.'

'Goodness. How did your wife manage?'

'Beautifully, actually. Managing is what she does best, I think. She runs absolutely everything and is a fine mother, too. We have two boys.'

'How wonderful,' Mother said, 'to see so much of the world.'

'Yes. But you need a quiet place as well to come and let the dust settle. You can't really work on the run like that. You can, but the work will show the strain. And all the footprints, too.'

At the last, I felt he was talking to me directly. It was just the thing I'd been worrying about. That I was trying too hard in my new novel, and the effort was everywhere in my pages, translated into stiffness, or sometimes desperation, but there.

'I'm not sure I'd get anything done, what with all the sunshine and the daiquiris,' I said, trying to joke, when in fact he'd rattled me.

'If you force yourself into the yoke before dawn, you can do whatever you like after.' His eyes cut sideways at me in the mirror, and my pulse quickened. It was something to have his attention, even briefly. Like a bright light passing my way before moving on. But there was also a feeling that he really saw me, and understood how my mind worked. It didn't make any sense, as we'd just met — but he was a brilliant painter of people in his work, and I believed that he probably did see all kinds of things, perhaps without even trying.

Later, just as the sun was beginning to drop behind the palmetto trees, he drove us up to a small cemetery and parked, leading us on foot through a creaking wrought-iron gate on Angela Street. Jacaranda blossoms flared high above the grave markers. We wove through them, slowly, toward a central copper statue, where Alfred stopped and squinted to read the memorial placard.

'Hey, there are sailors here from the USS *Maine*.' He sounded pleased.

'It sank in Havana Harbor,' Hemingway said. 'Cuba's just over there.' He gestured to the south over his shoulder. 'Ninety nautical miles and half a world.'

'I think I read something about the conquistadors at the hotel,' Mother said.

'That's right. 'Cayo Hueso' means 'Bone Reef' in Spanish. The whole island was a mound of skeletons when Ponce de León turned up.'

'What did they do with all of them to make the place livable again?' I asked.

'Is it livable?' He was smiling. 'I think they're all out in the shoals somewhere. Every once in a while I drag a thighbone for a mile thinking it's a marlin.'

'Not really?' Alfred said.

'Not really.' Then, with a wink, 'A thighbone weighs nothing.'

49

# 6

The next afternoon, Hemingway invited us to Whitehead Street to meet his family. His wife, Pauline, was small and dark and handsome more than pretty, with short, boyish hair and a slender figure, and very intelligent eyes. She made us a pitcher of lemonade and rye whiskey we drank in the back garden, right where the swimming pool was going to go soon. It would be the first on the island, Ernest told us, and the workers would have to dig through solid coral first. He seemed to like that it wouldn't come easy.

The boys, Patrick and Gregory, had been playing badminton when we arrived, and came over when the game was finished to say hello. They sat nearby, cross-legged and on the ground, natural as anything, their faces pink with exertion. *This famous man is their father*, I thought, looking between them and Ernest, who sprawled in a chair. But they had beautiful manners and didn't seem spoiled in the least.

The house and grounds were well kept up, with banana and date trees and frangipani adding lushness to the large dollop of paradise. Ernest's writing studio was a separate building that had been converted from a small garage, and was attached to the main house by a rope bridge. Nothing could have been more romantic or better situated. In fact, everything I turned my eyes to seemed perfectly designed to hand-deliver happiness, right down to his funny, pleasant wife, his boys, easy in their bodies. The shade as it fell. He had quite a life, I thought, but of course he would.

Before we left, Ernest went to fetch something and came back with a copy of my latest book for me to sign. I shot a look at Mother, wondering if she'd mentioned it while I was out of earshot. But no, Ernest quickly told me. He and Pauline had both read it a few months before, and thought it very fine. He'd known immediately who I was in the bar, in fact, but hadn't wanted to embarrass me.

*Embarrass* was hardly the word. I was overwhelmed. Ernest Hemingway had read my work and liked it. Had recognized my name. Had thought well enough of the book to want my signature inside. Flushing, I thanked them both and then sat awkwardly with the volume in my lap, not knowing what to write that would adequately describe my feelings. The whole situation felt like a fantasy, surpassing my wildest imaginings.

Then, just when I thought I couldn't be more flattered, Ernest offered to let me read pages of his new novel, which was about fishing and Bimini, and 'rich people,' and getting ruined a little, he said.

I couldn't quite believe he meant it, or that any such thing could happen outside of dreaming. But he went and got the pages and handed them to me, seeming shy, suddenly.

It was almost finished, he explained, but now he was going to have to set it aside for a while.

51

He was headed to Madrid soon to report on the conflict for the North American Newspaper Alliance.

'Oh, let's not talk about it now,' Pauline said. Her eyes did something complicated and she smoothed the lap of her simple white dress.

'Poor old Mama,' he said affectionately. 'I wouldn't go if I could help it. You know that.' He looked at her tenderly for a moment longer, and then turned back. 'I try not to be political. Politics ruins writers. But Franco is a bully and a murderer, and the Fascists seem determined to wipe out the Spanish working class. I don't know if there is a middle ground now. Not for anyone who's paying attention.'

'It could be the war that never ends,' Mother said. 'I know that sounds dramatic.'

'I only wish it were,' he said.

'Well, I'm glad you're going,' I told Ernest. 'It's hard to leave your family, I know, but Spain needs writers like you.'

'Spain needs all sorts of writers. There promises to be plenty of bloodshed,' he added darkly.

'Do you think any journalist could get over?' I didn't think before I asked the question, and now felt my mother's gaze swinging around pointedly, and Alfred's, too.

'Could be.'

'I'm not working for any magazine now.'

'You're not really serious, Marty,' my mother said.

'I might be. I've wanted to do *something*.'

'It's so dangerous, though.'

'I can promise to watch out for her,' Ernest said. 'If she finds a way to get there.'

'That's kind of you to offer,' Mother said, though it was easy to see she was unsettled by the idea. I was, too, and yet I'd said it.

★   ★   ★

After the visit was over, we walked quietly through the yard, passing good wishes back and forth and promises to keep in touch. It had been a wonderful evening, and an important one, I thought. I wanted to hold the moment still as long as possible, but finally there was nothing to do but say good night one last time.

We passed through the gate and turned onto Whitehead Street, in the direction of our hotel.

'Please don't do anything rash,' my mother said.

'I'm only considering it, that's all. I'm not going to bolt for the nearest ocean liner.'

'I liked him,' Alfred said. 'He's hardly what I expected, though. More like us than you'd think. Like anyone. Who would have thought?'

Who indeed? But as he and Mother talked about how kind Ernest had been to us, and funny, too, and how beautiful his house was, and how charming his wife, I found I was only half listening. In my mind, I'd already turned toward Spain, and was wondering hard about what it would take to actually get there, and what it would cost me in all sorts of ways.

Was this all a dream? A beautiful illusion? Or was it a sign, finally, of what I was meant to be doing, and Hemingway, the signpost.

'Marty,' my mother called, and then again, louder, 'Marty!' I'd walked right past the hotel. I probably could have walked all night, thinking.

# 7

January in St. Louis had never been easy to bear, but with Key West behind me, the weather now seemed to draw a very particular target on my soul. Wet snow fell and then freezing rain until the streets and walks were slick and black and treacherous. The sky drooped heavily, pushing chimney smoke down until it thickened the air, clinging to the houses and lampposts. I thought I might scream, and then Hemingway rang.

When Mother called me to the line and I heard his voice, I was surprised, and also a little breathless. 'How did you find my exchange?'

'"Gellhorn" isn't that common a name.'

'Well. I'm flattered.'

He was silent for a moment, and I wondered if I'd embarrassed him somehow. But then he immediately began to talk excitedly of Spain. The Republic needed ambulances now most of all and he knew something about that from the Great War and it was all he could think about. He and some literary friends were getting together in New York soon to talk of how to raise money for them. 'Maybe you should come,' he threw out.

'To New York?'

'Sure. Unless you weren't serious about Spain.'

'I am. I just don't know how. I'd need papers, credentials.'

'Maybe you just need good friends. There

might be a way I could help fix it.'

I fell quiet, feeling amazed, and then I told him that would be wonderful. It was hard to take in just what was happening. My mind whirred at his interest in me, how unlikely it was, how promising. After a moment, I said, 'I've been reading your novel. And feeling sick with jealousy, too, especially to read your dialogue.'

'Well, all I really do is listen.'

'If that's all it is, anyone could do it. You have all sorts of secrets. Don't think you're fooling me for a minute.'

'Maybe, but this book still needs something. I know that much. Maybe the kind of miracle ending that wraps everything up and spits you out whole. I don't quite see it yet, though.'

'You will.'

'Already she's so sure.'

The affection felt heady. 'About this I am.'

'Just come to New York,' he said suddenly. 'You'll sort everything and then I'll buy you a steak and you'll show me a story or two.'

'I want to. I'm determined to finish this book first, though. I might need one of those miracle endings, too. I can't quite see it yet.'

'But you will,' he said.

'Goodbye, Ernesto. I'm awfully glad we're becoming friends.'

'Goodbye, daughter,' he said gently, and then rang off while I was left holding the receiver, wondering if I could trust this strange turn my life was taking.

★ ★ ★

56

All that month and into February Ernest called every few days, his energy high, wanting to talk of Spain. He said he was thinking of himself as an anti-war correspondent, but that it felt imperative to go. He hadn't really done journalism in years, and it was the damnedest thing, but he was looking forward to it. To not being so safe and cared for as he was now. It had been a long time since he was cold, or had lived simply. Close to the bone. 'Being too comfortable can ruin a writer as much as anything,' he explained. 'And no one ever saying no to anything you want. It's dangerous.'

'I know what you mean,' I told him. 'After my father died last year, and I moved here to be with Mother, I knew it was the right thing to do. But I feel too swaddled, and too fed. Like a seal in a zoo exhibit.' I paused and said, 'I must sound ungrateful to you.'

'Not at all. You make sense to me.' Then, 'I'm sorry about your father. Mine shot himself.'

'How awful for you.' I had read that in a newspaper, but it was something again to hear him say it and know it was him, the man and the writer and not the celebrity we were talking about.

'More awful for him, I guess, but it never feels that way. I was twenty-nine. My son was born that summer and nearly killed his mother. Then winter had my father blowing himself to smithereens, and no one saw it coming, except maybe me. I wasn't surprised, just torn in two. It was the damnedest year of my life, I guess, or one of them.'

'I'm hoping it gets easier at some point,' I told him. 'I still feel awful about the things we said. The things we didn't say. Do you think it's possible to make peace with the past?'

'Hell. You can try, I guess. But I'm not sure anyone gets forgiven. Not even then.'

We fell silent for a time, the line between us stretching with the weight of what we'd shared. It was baffling to me, how comfortable I was beginning to feel with him, speaking so freely to a near stranger. And of course he wasn't just any stranger, was he?

I had recently sent him a short story I'd written while still in Germany the summer before, called 'Exile.' It was about a German man who decides he can't take the Nazis for another moment and moves to the States, only to realize that life is still terribly difficult, and that he doesn't fit there either, or maybe anywhere. Ernest said he had liked it tremendously, and the next thing I knew he'd sent it to his editor, Max Perkins, who wanted to publish it in *Scribner's Magazine* if I'd agree to a few cuts and changes. Soon, Perkins and I were exchanging letters about the story, and just like that, I'd slipped into a life that seemed to belong to someone else.

'*Scribner's*,' I said to my mother. 'And they're paying me, too. Ernest is really becoming a champion for me. I can hardly believe it.'

'Well, I hate to say it, but you are a beautiful young woman. Are you quite sure he doesn't have other motives?'

'It's not like that, Mother. We talk of real

things, important things. And there's never a time when he doesn't mention Pauline and the boys. He's very loyal to them.'

'As he should be. Be careful. That's all I mean to say.'

'You don't think I could actually have designs on him, do you?' I interjected. 'He's my idol, Mother. A marvelous glowing idol, and a rare sort of person. I only want to be near him awhile and soak up his light. I don't know how you can blame me for that.'

'No one's blaming anyone. I'm on your side, don't forget.'

'How could I ever? You've always been on my side, always. Even when I wasn't.' I went to her, and gripped both her hands lightly, and met her blue eyes with my own. 'It really will be okay. I know what I'm doing.' Then I went upstairs, wrapped myself in a quilt, and stood at the window for a long time, thinking of New York.

★　★　★

As much as I wanted to get my way to Spain sorted out, and to see Ernest before he sailed, I was determined to finish my book first. I locked myself in my little room for the next two weeks, and hammered out the last twenty pages all in one strenuous, nerve-shattering day. I pushed so hard I didn't even know what I'd created and was more than a little afraid to find out. The pages themselves were satisfying, though. I lined them up neatly, and bound them with fat rubber bands, and then held the manuscript in my

59

hands, weighing it silently before sliding it into a desk drawer. Someday I would feel strong enough to look at what I'd done, or hadn't, as the case may be.

I felt depleted and also anxious to be moving, as if I'd been sequestered for several dark years in Siberia without a single glimpse of the sun. Dragging a weathered canvas duffel out of the attic, I packed quickly, trusting that there would be time to prepare more fully once I arrived in New York.

'What does one need for a war, anyway?' I asked my mother.

'Courage, I suppose. But I'd throw a cake of soap in there, too. And warm socks.'

'You know I'm going to be perfectly all right, don't you?'

'Of course,' she lied, then kissed me and left me to my packing.

# 8

Before I had stepped off my train in Penn Station, I was counting pennies and frowning. I'd scanned the fare schedule for European sailings and would need one hundred sixty dollars for even a broom closet. Then there was the money I'd need for my time in Madrid, a number that went up or down depending on how long I stayed. For the moment that was utterly a mystery to me. Actually, everything was.

I went first to my girlfriend's house in Greenwich Village, stopping long enough only to throw my duffel in a corner and swipe on lipstick. Then I went to search out Ernest at the Barclay, where he told me he would either be or leave word as to where I could reach him. But he wasn't to be found. I must have puzzled the concierge, standing there like a wooden duck on the marble parquet, wondering what to do next. I had just sat down, spinning through my possible options, when the revolving doors whirled in from the street level, and there he was at the center of a large, loud group.

'Daughter,' he shouted, when he saw me, and then scooped me up in one large paw, moving me toward the bank of elevators without bothering to introduce me to his friends. The doors slid closed, and we all began to climb. Everyone simply went on talking over one another, the cold seeping from their overcoats,

61

while I stood and bit my lip to keep from saying anything stupid. I didn't know why I thought I'd find Ernest alone, that we'd go to a café and talk about writing and maybe go someplace for spaghetti and talk. Now all that felt incredibly foolish. He was at the center of a whirlwind. He *was* the whirlwind, making it go.

In his suite, I found a blue velvet chair and tried to stay out of the way while two different phones were picked up and orders for booze and caviar rattled off to room service. Ernest had thrown his overcoat onto a corner of the bed and now sat on it, loosening his tie. He smiled at me in a lopsided way, and our eyes met for the briefest moment before he turned, barking out, 'And three bottles of Taittinger. Make that four.' Facing me again, he said, 'You do like champagne, don't you?'

If that was a real question, there wasn't time for me to answer because a very smartly dressed woman flared over and began talking to him, standing close with her fists on the hips of her slim-cut skirt, blocking him from view. This was Lillian Hellman, I would soon learn. She and Ernest and the others in the room made up the newly formed Contemporary Historians, a corporation bent on funding a documentary film that would help Spain acquire ambulances and other kinds of support. The filmmaker was Dutch, apparently, and already over in Spain with his Norwegian cameraman. Other members of the Historians were John Dos Passos, Archie MacLeish, and Evan Shipman, all writers big enough to cast shadows. The room seemed full of them as I sat in my blue chair, wondering how I might break in.

Finally, Ernest saved me. He pulled me over and introduced me all around, saying, 'This lovely blond giraffe is my good friend Marty Gellhorn. She's coming to Spain, too.'

'Once I sort it out,' I explained to Evan Shipman while Ernest headed to answer the door. The liquor had arrived, an ocean of it as far as I could see. '*If* I sort it out.'

'What's standing in your way?' Evan cocked his head like a lion. He was a poet, but looked more like a film star to me. His hair was as perfect as his shirt, his oxfords, the crease running up his charcoal flannel trousers.

'This nonintervention pact against foreign involvement,' I said, squeezed against the doorjamb as Ernest came through with a crate of champagne on ice. 'You need real credentials and all the right paperwork, and I have nothing. At least for the moment.'

'Just go to a magazine and say you'll be a stringer for them.'

'You mean freelance?'

'Sure.' He rocked his drink back and forth, the ice clattering, and then downed the last of it in one go. 'You'll be a woman in a war zone. That's not typical in the least. Seems to me someone will at least give you a fair read if you send good work on.'

'It's worth a try,' I told him. 'At the moment I don't have any other ideas save stowing away or being baked into a cake.'

Dos Passos came over holding a massive bottle

63

of Taittinger that was streaming foam onto the floor. No one seemed to notice or care. He filled our glasses and gestured at Ernest, who now sat backward in a chair nearby, leaning on tented elbows and talking a mile a minute. 'So how do you know this character anyway?'

'Hem? We met in Key West. My family was on holiday and we fairly stumbled into him.'

'Huh. That stumbling typically goes the other way.' Dos's smile was leering, and obviously for effect. I didn't know what to make of him even before he said, 'I see he's got you already.'

'I beg your pardon?'

'Hem, you're calling him. He's probably got you using Hemingstein, too. It's all right. Everyone plays up to him, and nearly everyone manages to talk like him if they stick around for two minutes together.'

I stared at him, feeling pinned in place. 'I'm not trying to talk like anyone,' I began to say, but he only grinned and moved on, continuing to play barman. Suddenly I felt off-balance and over-warm. I grabbed my cigarettes and stepped out onto the balcony to get some air. It had rained earlier, a drenching mist that now left everything strung with cold little beads. I touched the wrought iron, collecting moisture on my fingertip, and let myself fume for a minute at Dos's words. It had been mean of him to expose me when we'd only just met, but he was right, wasn't he? It had taken no time at all for me to parrot Ernest, behaving like his sidekick, believing we were good friends, and that our alliance meant something. But all those writers on the other side of the heavy curtains, they were bona fide and terribly busy, too, swirling like the polished stars they actually were. What was I doing here?

'Thinking of jumping?' Ernest had stepped through the French doors and came to stand beside me.

'Maybe. I don't think I'd even feel it with all of this champagne.'

'It's good champagne, isn't it?'

'It is. The best. Thank you.' My words came out fast and clipped, as awkwardly as I felt. He was looking at me.

'Did you finish your book?'

'I did, God help me, but I haven't been able to face it. How's yours coming?'

'Finished, too. At least that's what I've told Perkins. But frankly this is taking all my time at the moment and then some. I haven't done journalism since twenty-three.'

He meant the year, I realized. Nineteen twenty-three, when I was fourteen, taller than all the boys at the dances, and terribly shy. It made me a little dizzy to think of the gap in our ages. He was thirty-seven, and had already done so much with his life, while I'd accomplished so little with mine. The thought came again: *What am I doing here?* 'How do you think it will be, getting back to it?' I asked him. 'They're very different kinds of writing, aren't they?'

'Like riding a bike?' His smile slid sideways. 'Honestly, I'm not sure the whole job isn't just a way to do something for Spain, and to see it again. I love that country. The people are as

65

lovely and decent as any you'd ever meet. And they don't deserve what's happening to them now. Hell, not even a dog deserves Franco.' He was watching my face again, and now said, 'You feeling all right?'

'Sure. Why not? I'm tired, that's all.'

'Well, get some rest. There'll be a lot to do over the next few days, and no one really sleeps here.' Something in his face softened. 'It's nice to see you, kid.' Then he folded his large frame back through the doors and I faced the city again, smeary and twinkling and indecipherable.

★   ★   ★

The next day I woke late to a couriered message from Ernest, saying that he had to run back to Key West the following morning, but that I should come to the '21' Club that night if I was free. He was sailing at the end of the week. So much to do before then and no time. He'd signed it *Ernestino*.

I sat back down on the bed I'd only recently crawled from and held the cable between two fingers, reading his words again. A soft, spongy feeling came up through my chest. I was disappointed. For weeks I had been thinking that if I simply pointed myself here at Ernest's feet, he would shine his light, and my next steps would be clear. But that had been silly, and girlish. He owed me nothing, and anyway, it was Monday now. He was sailing on Friday and had to race to Florida and back before then, with his own affairs to settle and a family to worry about, too.

The fact remained that even if he had meant to help, I was alone now, and over my head. Maybe I always had been, but the only cure, it seemed to me now, was to stop feeling sorry for myself, and kick for the surface hard. Time was passing, and my pennies were dwindling. Even if I meant to stay in New York, I had to find a job, but I would do more than that. Whatever it took, I would find passage to Spain, earning my own way, figuring it out as I went. I'd always been good at that, if I was honest with myself. It was other people who made things tricky, even if they were incandescent ones, like Ernest.

Making two cups of strong builder's tea, I drank them searing hot and then bathed and dressed. I had one nice sweater from home — black cashmere, hardly what I'd need for Madrid — and wool slacks, and my Bryn Mawr coat, and it would all have to do. Stepping out onto Grove Street, I hurried for the subway. I had slept too late. It was almost the lunch hour already, and I had at least one elephant to shoot, possibly two.

A few years before, when I was still working and writing for the FERA and at a party in Washington, I had met an editor at *Collier's* magazine and we had stayed in touch occasionally. His name was Kyle Crichton, and he'd recently sent me an awfully nice note about liking *The Trouble I'd Seen*. I thought now might be an excellent time to remind him he thought I could write, though showing up in his office took some cheek. *Collier's* had a circulation of several million, and hadn't I just been turned down by *Time?*

Still, I plunged ahead, buying a bag of warm chestnuts for his receptionist, and then dragging Kyle away for a drink at the Stork Club. It was an incongruous place to bring up war and sacrifice, I realized too late. White coats wheeled and spun around us. The dining room tinkled with luxury and privilege, each table a who's who of the notable, the glamorous, and the altogether gilded. It was all very dazzling. It was beside the point.

'I'm not asking for an assignment,' I tried to explain to Kyle. He had already more than guessed I wanted something from him, and I felt myself teetering on an edge. This dance took every ounce of my courage. 'There are border guards, though, and I have to pass muster or they won't let me in the country at all, let alone near the action. I have to have credentials. Real ones.'

'You want me to hire you as a stringer.' His hands grazed the stem of his glass, his skewer of stuffed olives bobbing in the liquor, which had the sheen of lighter fluid.

'*Hire* is maybe too strong a word. I know I haven't proven myself as a journalist yet, but I mean to one day. Maybe you'll actually like what I write, and want to publish it.'

'Maybe.' His eyes gave nothing away.

'All that is its own question. For now, I only need a letter or something to say I'm with you. This is bureaucracy plain and simple. It's paperwork.'

68

'And then what?'

'I don't know, actually. I don't have any idea how this will go. But I can't sit on my hands when so much is happening, when so much is at stake.' As my words tumbled out, I thought of how I must sound to him. As if I had three heads, each more romantic and stuffed between the ears than the next. 'You think I'm a fool.'

'No, just idealistic. And very young. You're an interesting kid, Marty. If you were my daughter, I'd probably burn your passport and chain you to the cellar door. War isn't any place for a young woman, it seems to me. But you have a good heart.' He turned back to his drink, considering something privately, and then said, 'If you're really determined to go, I'm not sure it's up to me to stop you.'

I lunged at his free arm, relieved and elated. 'Oh, thank you, Kyle. You won't regret this.'

'I hope you're right.' His expression clouded over and I was puzzled for a moment until I realized he wasn't worried that I might embarrass his magazine or myself. But that I could die in Spain. The body count in each day's newspapers sometimes included Americans who'd been fighting in the Abraham Lincoln Brigade since January. It was only a matter of time before a correspondent was killed.

No one was safe. I knew that, and yet also had been trying to stand apart from it. The thought seemed to hang suspended between us now, a thread of fine-spun glass, while Kyle and I locked eyes for a moment, understanding each other perfectly. Then our waiter glided up with the bill in a discreet leather box, and I shook the foreboding feeling off, aiming to be breezy again. 'I'm going to be fine,' I told Kyle. 'You'll see. Now, what should this letter say?'

# 9

'*Collier's* has named me 'special correspondent,'' I said to Ernest and the other Historians
that evening at '21.' 'It works utterly, if *special*
means 'fraudulent.' But I don't care. Beggars
can't be choosers.'

'It doesn't matter what's in the damned letter,'
Ernest said. He sat across from me, his shoulders
square with the top of the banquette. They
seemed to balance his whole side of the room.
'You've found a magazine to claim you. That's
the main thing. What about the fare?'

'I stopped at *Vogue* a few hours ago and
abased myself. I said I'd take absolutely
anything, and they believed me. You're looking at
the new expert on the middle-aged woman and
her beauty problems.'

'What would you know about middle age?'

'It gets worse. There are all sorts of skin
treatments and I have to try them, and then
write about my results.' I puffed out my cheeks,
trying to make him laugh. 'But the truth is I'd do
the cancan through Central Park if that's what it
took.'

'Wouldn't that be amusing?' Lillian Hellman
said. She'd drawn on a deep-red lipstick, and the
lines were perfect and a little brutal against her
face powder. I realized she terrified me, how she
talked and walked and leaned and smoked, all
intensely and pointedly. Her remark had felt like

a cuff, too, though in fact she'd barely flicked her eyes at me before turning back to Ernest and more serious matters. 'Now about these ambulances?'

'Forget about the ambulances for a minute,' Dos Passos said. 'We have to talk about the film.'

This was the documentary they were funding, and apparently the shape of the film was still in question. The Historians couldn't agree on what mattered most. Dos Passos seemed bent on making the common people the focus, while Ernest was far more interested in the soldiers, the tactics, and other military elements.

'I don't see how anyone can make a war film without warfare.' Ernest's voice rose easily above the din of the bar, cutting through. 'Any battle means tanks and guns, men in trenches. It means death. Tragedy on the simplest and most absolute scale.'

'But what about the people in the villages?' Dos challenged. 'They deserve to be seen. They haven't asked for any of this, you know? Nothing's in their control.' He was sweating and repeatedly pushed back a skein of slick, dark hair that clung to his round forehead. 'I'm only saying their story matters, too. Besides, the world might very well show up more to defend mothers and farmers and children over soldiers.'

'Sure, they will. And why not?' Ernest snapped back. 'Let's save the blood for your filet mignon.'

Though I hadn't known either of them for very long, I felt myself agreeing with Ernest. Part of it was his conviction. When he really got going on something, his feelings came through in his voice. His face grew expressive, and his eyes snapped to life. I could also tell that he believed what he said. That he felt all these things deeply, and wasn't afraid who knew. It was hard not to be won over by him.

'Good grief,' Lillian piped in. 'Can we eat before we duke this out? You're not likely to agree anyway, even if everyone plays nice, and that's a long shot.' She readjusted her fox stole with purpose. It was a biting February night, but all practicality aside, the stole made her shoulders flare out commandingly. I would have to get one for Spain, I thought, making a mental note, and maybe for everyday life, too.

'Okay. Go on,' Dos said, ignoring her. 'Shove gore in everyone's faces, and see if they don't run for the hills.' His face was pink and vehement. 'I don't even think this is about the film at all. It's you. *You* want to go to war again. You're the one who needs to see the blood.'

Ernest glared at him. 'All right, Sigmund Freud. Is that how it is?' The bite of his joke was probably meant to deflect or diffuse things, but I caught how Ernest's pupils shrank and his hands tensed. Dos had hit a nerve.

'Boys!' Lillian cried, and everyone fell silent, as if she held a wooden ruler instead of a highball glass. Nervous laughter gradually filled in.

The bar was dark and close and the ceiling pressed down, seeming to collude with the shifting mood. I had been squeezed into the center of the banquette, and as the Historians made noises about heading to the dining room,

73

and then stood, downing the last of their cocktails, I waited to be released. Even with the current tension, they drifted in pairs toward the maître d', talking and conferring, planning — united and serious, and more than a little dazzling to watch.

I had recently heard a rumor that after *The Children's Hour*, MGM had put Lillian Hellman on retainer for twenty-five hundred a week, just in case something clever and deathless came to her in her sleep. It was almost impossible for me to imagine that kind of money, or the freedom she'd won. Until a few months ago, it had been my general understanding that if you were a writer, you pummeled your own soul until some words trickled out of the dry streambed, enough to fill a saucer or a teaspoon or an eyedropper. And then you wept a little, or gnashed your teeth, and somehow found the fortitude to get up the next day and do it again.

But these writers were like magazine covers. Like skyrockets, too. That I was here, even glancingly lit by the wake they cut, was still a little stupefying. Not that I didn't have ambition. Sometimes I thought I was entirely made of it. As I'd said to Kyle, I meant to show him and everyone else that I could be a proper journalist, a writer others admired and respected and remembered. I wanted my name to count but for the moment was still an apprentice, and particularly in this crowd, where heroes were milling about, ready to be clung to. It would take time for me to earn my way. To prove myself, and to rise.

'You're not a fraud, you know,' Ernest said, as if he'd read my mind. He'd sat back down to say it, reversing his steps. 'Your work is good.'

It meant everything to hear him say it, and I told him so. 'More and more, it's the only thing that really matters to me,' I went on. 'The only thing that never bores me, and never lets me down. You know what I mean.'

'It just so happens I do.' The wall behind him was mirrored and threw back half-a-dozen fractured likenesses. White shirt. Black mustache. Tight-fitting jacket. Squared jaw. Strangling tie. He didn't look like a hero at the moment; he looked like a man. Confident about some things and not at all about others. Like all the men I knew. Like all the people I knew. Like me.

'I'm not sure when I'll sail,' I said. 'It could be weeks from now. Make sure to leave a bread-crumb trail for me, all right?'

'I will.'

'I'm very fond of you, you know, Hemingstein.' To hell with Dos and how I sounded, I thought. I believed we were friends. I felt an understanding between us, a coming together of like minds, and I wanted to trust that feeling. 'I'm happy we're going to be in the same union.'

He took off his wire-rimmed glasses and looked at me. In the three months since we'd parted in Key West, all of our talk had happened over the phone or in hastily scrawled letters. All these things that could happen in his eyes, or with his moods, or what each of his smiles meant, were a mystery to me. New people were complicated, but they were also wonderful.

75

Everything was a code not yet solved.

'I'm fond of you too, daughter.' His eyes changed a little as he spoke, and he seemed about to say something else. But then Lillian ducked back around the corner, tugging on his arm and saying how famished she was. Before I knew it she had pulled him out of the dim bar and into the next room, out of sight.

# Part 2

# TO SPAIN WITH THE BOYS

## MARCH-MAY 1937

# 10

I didn't see Ernest again. He raced home and back, and then sailed for Paris on the ocean liner *Paris* (naturally) while I scrambled through slush-worn Manhattan, collar up, chin out, huffing and puffing to get my work done.

The last instruction from Ernest before we parted was that I should look for Sidney Franklin when I got to France if he and the others had already gone ahead. Franklin was a famous matador friend of Ernest's who was improbably from Brooklyn, and Jewish besides. The Torero of the Torah was the joke about him, but apparently his work with the cape was no joke at all. He was an absolute wonder in the ring, Ernest had told me, and of course I'd read the pages and pages of admiring stuff about him in *Death in the Afternoon*. Sidney had also lived in Madrid for a time and knew the lay of the land. If he could get all the right visas, Sidney would be Ernest's majordomo and factotum, his common-law wife — that was another frequent joke — since Pauline was needed at home with their two boys.

I knew it couldn't be at all easy to be attached to a person as big as Ernest. He wasn't just famous; he was unforgettable, with a pull that seemed to work on everyone powerfully and tidally, like the moon. But Pauline seemed to carry off her role gracefully, keeping the entire ship of Whitehead Street running smooth as glass. According to Ernest's stories, when friends rolled through at regular intervals from near and far, she was the one who ordered just the right oysters and tins of pâté and bottles of wine, entertaining everyone at her perfect table while he worked, tending his singular fire. And if that wasn't enough, Pauline read Ernest's work and encouraged him, while also keeping Patrick and Gregory behaving like princes instead of beasts. Even at five and eight, based on my brief visit they seemed to have a lot of her style in them and were awfully well behaved. If I ever had children, I imagined I would probably be impatient with them, distracted by my own moods in a way Pauline never seemed to be. Or maybe she hid it terribly well?

And now she would have to be proficient in another way — watching him launch off to a battlefront, with no guarantees that he'd return. To me, it seemed so much more difficult to be a wife, at such a time, than one of the boys. She would sit at home waiting for a telegram — happy or tragic. He had feet and wings and purpose. He was on the move, and that's where I wanted to be, too. And the sooner the better.

★ ★ ★

Paris was the meeting tree then. The place we all swung out from.

When I arrived in the middle of March, Ernest had indeed gone on ahead, and there was no sign of Sidney. The boulevards were windy and cold,

80

the cafés full of trench coats and cigarettes and wan light. I rooted around for several days, hoping to find other journalists to cross the border with. Frankly, I was afraid to go over alone, but it looked like I wasn't going to have another choice.

Swallowing my anxiety, I began to focus on wading through the necessary bureaucracy, trying to procure whatever stamps or papers were needed, but that was a shifting target, it seemed. Even two months before, crossing over to aid the Republic had been fairly easy. A daily train nicknamed the *Red Express* had sped volunteers south from Paris to the Spanish border, where buses took them the rest of the way. Now you only had two options, either to find a boat over, which might very well be torpedoed by patrolling Italian subs, or to steal over the Pyrenees in cloaking darkness, hoping not to get caught.

I studied maps and talked to as many people as I could about how to go about it. There was a train, apparently, that would take me to Bourg-Madame, only a few kilometers from the French border. There were no through trains. I would have to disembark and walk out of the village and over the countryside on back roads until I came to the Catalonian village of Puigcerdà, where I would catch another train if I wasn't turned back first, or something worse.

I left Paris alone on a soggy afternoon in late March, under a sky that was dense and wet and gray. Afternoon became evening, and I squinted as I tried to write impressions in my journal to

81

remember later. The window beside me frosted over, rattling the countryside into a kaleidoscope of black and white. This wasn't the France I knew, which had always been as much about swimming in the sea as about anything else, about languorous holiday sunshine and whole days spent drinking wine and staring up at clouds. No, this country seemed to be offering something dark and strange and new to me, in an entirely different language. If only I could learn to understand it.

Spring was still far away, and I felt that immediately when I disembarked after midnight. I wore trousers in warm gray flannel and a gray jacket meant to block the wind, which it didn't quite. In my duffel I had a comb and a change of clothes and also a dozen tins of peaches and potted meat. I could feel the cans through the canvas as I walked, pounding like small fists at the backs of my thighs, reminding me of my body again and again, that I was what I appeared to be, a tall blond woman walking alone in a frigid country, awfully far from St. Louis.

Bourg-Madame was probably charming by day, I thought as I walked. It clung to a hillside behind stone walls and was tucked into a string of such villages, all nestled high above the surrounding valley. But the village was boarded up tight as I passed through. I readjusted my duffel and blew on my hands, then turned east, away from the village down a steep, cobbled road, the moon above a wispy, glazed-looking crescent.

It wasn't exactly legal, what I was doing, and

for much of the time, I was too anxious to even whistle to keep myself company. I had only a little Spanish, and wasn't sure what I would even say if I was stopped, beyond proffering my passport and the hard-won *Collier's* letter. I was cold, too. The stones beneath my feet were slick with frost, and the air cut through my jacket. I hunched my shoulders, digging my free hand into my pocket, glad that it was only a few miles farther to find my next train, at Puigcerdà.

This part of the Spanish Pyrenees wasn't in Nationalist territory, not yet. The town had a slumbering feel as I approached, and of course the borderline itself was invisible. One moment I was in France, at peace, and the next in Spain, at war. And what it all meant for me — and all that would happen — was still ahead in the dark, entirely unknown.

*Ah, Marty,* I heard my father say, as if I were suddenly carrying him on my shoulder, just under my right ear. *You think you can just traipse off to war, do you? Have you thought this through?*

Had I? Did I really know what I was doing here? Perhaps not, but I was on my way.

★   ★   ★

Just before dawn, I boarded my second train, this one bound for Barcelona. It was unheated, knitted together out of icy little wooden cars that shuddered through the countryside. Each carriage could seat six, but I was shoehorned into one with half a dozen beautiful Spanish men in civilian clothes. They might have been students, they looked so young. All sorts of people had become soldiers overnight, drawn into battle because there was no other way, now, with Franco on the loose. Liberty was entirely contingent. Life was in the crosshairs. Of course they would fight.

They wore what clothes they had as a uniform, brown peasant cotton shirts and rope-soled shoes. One pulled a long, flat loaf of simple bread — almost black in color — from a carpetbag. Another carried sausages, dense with garlic and chilies, in his handkerchief, along with a wedge of flinty sheep's milk cheese. When they shared their meal with me, thrusting the offering into my lap without saying a word, I wanted to write a poem for them and say it out in Spanish. I would have to learn more Spanish immediately. I would have to learn all sorts of things. For the moment, I smiled gratefully, and ate.

For the rest of that day and into the night we rode together. I fell asleep at some point and woke in the very early morning, my head on the shoulder of the boy next to me. For a moment, before I was really awake, I felt like his sister. That he could be Alfred and we could be anywhere, headed to Key West, maybe, on a dusty but promising bus, looking forward to whatever lay just ahead. But of course this was another place. A more perilous one, too, though for the moment I saw only the beauty. Outside, as I yawned and stretched, dawn light streaked through falling snow, broad flat flakes that swung their way to the frozen ground, looking like

84

petals. The trees were glazed with ice. Everything seemed to be made of crystal.

A few hours later, we reached Barcelona. The whole city seemed to whirl, even from the train, a carnival of bodies and busyness. Spanish, English, French, American — everyone talking excitedly, their eyes bright, though they shouldered guns. One had a canteen bumping along under his waist on a knotted cord. Another had a wine cask instead, and boots strung around his neck, and a face out of Botticelli.

I said goodbye to my traveling companions at the station, hoping they understood what was in my eyes, since we shared no proper language. I could still feel them behind me as I walked off to find my next move, and I wanted to say a sacred prayer for them, though I had never really known how to pray. Would they live to find their way home to their sisters and mothers and sweethearts? Would I survive even a week in Spain when already my heart felt so wide open and so susceptible?

I took a room at the first hotel I came to. I was dying for a bath, but apparently the entire city was flush out of coal. So I fell face-first into the bed as if I had never seen one before. Clothes on, boots on, I slept the thick and cottony sleep of the displaced. I didn't remember dreaming or moving at all until cold sunshine pierced the shutters facing the square. I rose and stood blinking at an enormous silk banner that read WELCOME COMRADES FROM AFAR. Morning. Barcelona. I was actually here.

I needed coffee desperately, but there was only

minute coffee, dark crystals you poured boiling water over and tried to pretend it wasn't too bitter to drink. I took myself to the crowded little café off the lobby, but before I could down enough espresso to even think straight, I found everyone was talking about what had happened the night before. There had been a fierce attack in the wee hours, the air-raid sirens wailing as the city shook.

'I can't believe I slept through it,' I told the concierge, who spoke English well. 'I wouldn't have thought it was possible.'

'You are lucky to have such a skill.'

'Sleep isn't a *skill*.' I laughed at him.

'But of course, señorita. The innocent have it. They're born with it. Somehow you lose it as you age. Worry steals it away.'

I was about to explain to him that of course I *was* worried, but suddenly realized it didn't matter, because I had slept, right through everything. Skill or gift or accident, the result was the same, and I would take it.

# 11

I stayed in Barcelona another twenty-four hours, just long enough to see how alive the city was with revolution. Anarchist, Socialist, and Communist banners hung everywhere. The streets were strewn with what looked like confetti but was really thousands of colored propaganda leaflets and manifestos all swirled together brilliantly. Workers and servicemen had taken over the once-privately-owned villas and businesses and turned them into collectives. The ruling class had either surrendered their possessions for the greater good and stayed to fight, or fled to France. Everything belonged to everyone, and that was extraordinary to see. When I got into a taxi, the driver refused my pesetas. He was a servant of the people, he insisted, in Spanish I barely understood because it was Catalonian. Still, we smiled at each other. And it was wonderful.

The next day I packed my things quickly and found a munitions truck that would take me as far as Valencia. Apparently, skirting the coast to the south and then angling north again across La Mancha, toward Madrid, was the safest route for the moment — though that was always changing as the front changed. For two days, we bumped along with a large caravan of vehicles on a coastal road, with sloping, climbing hills, now and then coming to small villages that appeared all but deserted. In the distance I could see the Mediterranean, bright and hard and blue, sometimes flat looking as starched cloth, and sometimes whipped and angry.

North across the span of water, I knew, was the Côte d'Azur, that sun-drenched paradise where a decade before, newly sprung from Bryn Mawr, I'd swum and guzzled oysters and bicycled along sandy cypress-lined roads. That place had been beautiful beyond words, but also seemed like a confection now, compared with Spain. This was another kind of country altogether, rougher and simpler and purer, and so clearly worth fighting for I felt it as a clenching in my throat.

Like the recruits on the train before, when I was pointed at Barcelona, the men on the munitions truck had become like family to one another very quickly. They sang snatches of wistful Catalan songs that seemed to bring the sun out of hiding. The air warmed as we rode, and I realized that at least for the moment, at least in this place, spring was on its way. Not here yet, not quite, but a clear promise.

No one seemed to mind my being there, or my being a woman. They hardly noticed me, in fact. I could simply look at everything and absorb it, jostled by the great tires shuddering along the road, while sunlight palmed the top of my head, and lightly brushed the tips of my eyelashes. This was a country wracked by war and chaos, but already I knew that it wouldn't take much at all for me to love it.

★   ★   ★

At Valencia, I walked into the heart of the city, intent on finding a place to sleep and getting the lay of the land. I took a room at the Victoria in the central square, and the next morning went looking for the press bureau office, to see about arranging transport to Madrid — a train or truck, or some sort of caravan. But I didn't even make it two blocks from the hotel before a car pulled along-side me, a dinged and dusty coal-colored Citroën that looked like it had tunneled its way through a mountain or two.

A small, dark Spanish man leaned out the open window as the car rolled to a stop beside me. For a moment I thought something terrible might be happening, but then a voice called out from the backseat, and another man pushed his way forward, smiling at me as if he were a friend.

'You're American,' the man said as he angled out the back window. Ashy hair fell straight over his forehead. He had a large, rubbery nose, rather like a handsome yam. His eyes were deep set and sensitive looking under full brows. He looked familiar somehow.

'Martha Gellhorn.' I offered my hand.

'Gellhorn,' he said. 'Say, it's lucky we met. Sid Franklin.'

'Sidney! How'd you find me?'

'By not looking at all.' His smile tipped and widened. 'You've been all right? No trouble?'

'No. Everyone's been so kind. Your visa must have come through, then.'

He shook his head. 'Hem tried like hell, but it was nothing doing. This car isn't exactly sanctioned. I guess I'm not either.'

'Ernest found the car for you?'

He grinned. 'I sort of borrowed it.'

'I'm even more impressed, then.'

I couldn't help noticing how heavy the Citroën was on its wheels. I leaned in and saw the backseat was piled with flats of supplies — fruit and coffee and chocolate and canned tomatoes. Somehow Sidney had found prawns, too, in large tins, and marmalade, and fresh oranges in a bushel basket. Stuffed in around the boxes and suitcases and baskets were several large cured hams wrapped in cheesecloth.

'You're going to eat well, at least,' I told him.

'That's the idea . . . if we don't get blown off the road. Get in.'

I had them drive me to my hotel, where I ran and got my things and was out in minutes, feeling excited about this chance meeting, and ready to be in Madrid. Sidney's driver looked like something out of a painting, with a narrow and swarthy face, and heavy eyebrows under a brown cap. His name was Luis, and as we navigated our way out of Valencia, he told us in heavily accented English of the recent Loyalist victories at Guadalajara and Brihuega. Mussolini was aiding Franco, and had sent twelve thousand troops over, but our own troops had defeated them. Had crushed them, in fact.

'It's the biggest Italian defeat we have heard of,' Luis said proudly. 'You should have seen the fiestas that followed. My father is still drunk at home, and may be that way for a month. Viva España.'

'Viva España!' we echoed, beaming, and

90

passed out of the city and over the pale green Valencian plain, past healthy-looking orange and olive groves, and up into the dry, tan hills.

★   ★   ★

Madrid was several hundred miles northwest over the coastal range and across the great plateau, La Mancha, flat brown fields that went on and on, possibly forever, full of trees and goats and the kinds of windmills that Don Quixote had flung himself at. It was mountainous and broad, rolling in every direction, and there was a sense, as you drove, of how old it was, too, how full of history.

For more than a day we drove steadily, on tamped and dusty and curving roadways, past sentry posts and roadblocks that rattled me each time we saw one coming. My palms dampened as I offered my flimsy letter from *Collier's* with my passport, sure it wouldn't suffice this time, and that I'd be sent packing. Sidney had a document Ernest managed to have written up in Paris to look official, saying that he was a part of the war effort, and bona fide, and somehow it all worked, over and over. Somehow, improbably, we got through.

Since early November, Madrid had been an entrenched front line in this civil war. Franco's Nationalists had dug in to the west and north, while the Republican forces fought to push them back, reinforced by volunteer brigades. The city was under siege, and bombed at regular intervals. Any day, Madrid could fall — that was a real possibility — but for now you could still approach from the east and southeast, and that's what we did.

When we arrived, it was nighttime, and blacker in the dark than anyplace I had ever been. We drove in through the center of town, along the Gran Vía, which was ravaged from shell fire. The roads were deeply rutted and entirely dark, visible only in the beams of our dim headlamps. At several places the street was splintered and impassable. Gutted buildings yawned to either side, and my heart went cold at the core, suddenly, because I knew, at last, that this was really war. And there would be no escaping the reality of that again.

At a sentry point near a hulking arena, we were stopped and asked for a daily password Sidney knew — thank God — from a telegram Ernest had sent to Valencia.

'That's the Plaza de Toros,' Sidney told me while we waited for clearance, jutting his chin at the shadowy arena. 'I've been there many times.'

'But not like this,' I said.

'No, it's a different city. I didn't know what to expect, only that it seemed important to come.'

All I could do was nod, feeling very moved.

Back in motion we passed buildings smashed and ransacked, storefronts covered with plastic sheeting and also cardboard. We drove slowly to avoid the shell holes and because it was so dark. It was strange to be in a place that was so black and ravaged, as if the city were dead and this place were its ghost. I had never been fearful as a child, but if I had been, this would have been the stuff of my nightmares.

Finally we reached the Hotel Florida, on the Plaza del Callao. Much of the surrounding neighborhood had been brutalized, but the exterior of the hotel was still intact. It looked like an aging starlet, with a marble façade and black iron fretwork, all of it climbing into the black sky.

Inside, the lobby had a vaulted ceiling and broad curving staircase, but the tile and decor had seen better days. It was empty, too. There was only one man other than the porter, and he was stooped behind the reception desk, his face mottled with candlelight, poring over what looked like a stamp collection. He barely looked up from the pages to tell us that Señor Hemingway wasn't in his room. He'd gone to dinner at the Hotel Gran Vía, the designated mess hall for correspondents. We could find him there.

I followed Sidney up the street, keeping my eyes on my boots. The street was uneven, littered with rubble from recent explosions, I guessed. In the distance I heard a thundering sound that I knew was gunfire. I clutched my jacket nearer, feeling like I was floating a little apart from my body. Here I was at war, where anything could happen at any moment. Nothing could have felt stranger or sharper or more sobering.

Farther along the boulevard, past several sets of barricades and sentries armed with bayonets, we finally arrived at the Hotel Gran Vía and were directed down several dark flights of stairs to a snug, dim sub-basement. The whole place swam with smoke. Long planks were set up as makeshift tables and Ernest was at the end of one of these, surrounded by men in uniform. He wore his wire-rimmed glasses and a light blue shirt rolled-up at the sleeves. As we made our way over, he stood up, shook Sidney's hand, and then folded me in for a quick, breathless bear hug.

'Hello, daughter, you've made it.'

Suddenly I was aware of everything that had transpired to get me there. I felt cold and dusty. My knees and shoulders ached from being too long cramped in the small car. So much had happened, but somehow all I could say for the moment was 'Yes.'

There was a bustle of trying to squeeze us in at the table, finding chairs, calling over the waiter, and was there enough food? 'You'll have to hold your nose,' Ernest warned. 'This isn't the Ritz.'

On the table was some sort of fish served on a pyre of jaundiced-looking rice with oily bits of salami and hard chickpeas. I managed to shovel it down somehow between sips of my drink. The gin was surprisingly good.

'This is a war after all,' Ernest said when he saw my expression. 'If they spared the booze, everything would go to hell quick.'

'I brought all the supplies,' Sidney said. He'd pushed away his plate after a few bites. 'I can start cooking for you.'

'Sidney here makes eggs that would break your heart,' Ernest told me. 'He's also a terrific bloodhound. I knew he'd find you.'

Sidney and I locked eyes and grinned at each other at the hidden joke. 'Yes, he's clearly gifted. Thanks for sending him, and for worrying about me.'

I felt Ernest appraising me, his eyes fastened to my face with something like pride. *Daughter*, he'd called me again. He seemed to use it with other younger women, too. It felt affectionate and concerned more than proprietary, and didn't bother me at all. It was actually nice to hear him gathering me toward him. My days of solitary travel had felt smooth and even fated, but it was so much better to be among friends now. Vouched for and understood.

★ ★ ★

After dinner, the three of us walked back toward the Florida. The city was densely black and cold. I had my shoulders hunched for warmth, my back full of knots. In the distance, gunfire came again, a chattering stammer of sound.

'That's University City,' Ernest explained. 'That show goes on all night.'

'How far away is the fighting?' I asked him.

'A mile or more. I'll take you up tomorrow, and also to the Telefónica to get you your safe-conduct vouchers. It's the tallest building in Madrid, and built like an iron battleship. That's where the censorship office is. You'll file your stories there. They have lines to London and Paris. It's all pretty cozy, you'll see.'

*Cozy* didn't begin to describe anything I saw or could imagine, but I felt safer than I had all day, walking between Ernest and Sidney, whether that was actually true or not.

'You have your rooms sorted yet?' Ernest asked as we went inside the Florida.

I shook my head.

'Sidney's next to me. I have two rooms on the third floor toward the back. It's safer there, but harder to breathe. All the dust drifts that way and hangs there. I don't know why.'

We stood at the desk and waited for the concierge to see about me, and Sidney made noises about needing to arrange all the parcels and supplies. In one corner, the tired-looking porter leaned against a tired-looking wicker sofa, as if they each needed the other desperately. A potted palm listed in another corner, its leaves painted with white powder that was clearly ceiling plaster and not simple dust. Madrid had been under fire for five months. Nowhere, I guessed, was there simple dust.

By the time I had a key in my hand, I was nearly falling down from exhaustion.

The lift had recently been damaged by shelling, Ernest informed us, so I told the men good night and hoisted myself up four flights of steps, to the floor above Ernest and Sidney, then down a long carpeted hallway to my simple room. I had a bed and a bureau and a radiator and a small bathroom, the kind where you have to fold yourself up into a handkerchief to properly wash. Near my bureau, a single lamp threw murky gray shadows. I took one look at myself in the mirror, pronounced myself a spook, and went to bed without washing my face.

The blanket was woolen but too thin, and I had been cold for days. I drew it all the way up to my nose and lay listening to the muffled repeat of machine-gun fire. The front line was a mile away, Ernest had said? I tried to imagine what the trenches looked like from film reels I'd seen, but somehow could only picture the six beautiful Spaniards I'd met heading to Barcelona, lying huddled together on a broken earthen floor. And that wasn't a good direction at all for my thinking.

I curled my knees into my chest and wished I had something strong to drink. It was strange to be here, in a besieged city, where people were trying to kill one another and not get killed themselves. In the corner, the radiator clanked on, startling me, while in the distance, artillery fire came soft and stuttered. I felt too many things, and all at once, and wondered how I would ever sleep.

# 12

There were other, safer hotels in Madrid, I would soon learn, but most of the foreigners found their way to the Florida — American journalists and French photographers, German filmmakers and British aviators. There were prostitutes, too — curvy or thin, young or old, some with long braids down their back, some with blond streaks through jet black that made me think they'd watched too many American movies.

'The *whores de combat*,' Ernest told me the next day as we made our way through the lobby and out onto the Gran Vía, crossing the Plaza del Callao in cold sunshine. It was midmorning and I had slept for twelve hours. Only now was the fog beginning to lift. Meanwhile Ernest strode comfortably beside me, swinging his arms, skirting piles of rubble and broken glass. I didn't know how he was so at ease, unless this was the kind of world he felt most comfortable in. Unless disaster suited him perfectly.

Here and there, work crews were sweeping up the chaos and trundling it off in wheelbarrows. Other crews were laying fresh concrete to fill the holes. I looked up at a ruined apartment building as we passed, the whole structure sagging, windows exploded out. 'Where have all these people gone?'

'Elsewhere in the city, or in the parks like

gypsies. Some have fled, of course, but most refuse to leave.'

'That's beautiful, isn't it?'

'I think so. Though I don't like to imagine what can happen to them here. I try very hard not to, actually.'

A tram passed us, running right along the side of the boulevard, right past the barricades and ruined squares.

'You can take it all the way to the front. Isn't that the damnedest thing?'

I told him I'd never seen anything like it, though that was true of anything and everything in Madrid.

Soon we came to the Telefónica Building. It was thirteen stories high and white, or what passed for white in that blighted district, rising up bravely from the bones of decimated houses and cafés, all concrete and steel, more modern than anything nearby. We passed into a courtyard, where an armed guard took our credentials, then went down into the building, into the cellar where the censorship office was located. Inside, a wiry Spaniard greeted us.

'Arturo Barea, this is Marty Gellhorn. Be nice to her, will you? She's a friend of mine, and she's writing for *Collier's*.'

'She is too beautiful to be a journalist. And too beautiful to be with you,' he barked as he laughed.

I took his hand, which was warm. 'I don't know about all that.'

'Welcome to Madrid.'

Arturo's partner, Ilsa Kulcsar, came into the

99

room then, and Ernest took something from his jacket pocket, holding it out in his palm. It was an orange.

'He never forgets me, this one,' Ilsa said. She was Austrian and young and very pretty, with a thick accent and a warm smile that made me feel instantly at ease.

'This is where you'll post any dispatches,' Ernest explained. 'There are two lines, one to London and one to Paris. Censorship is strict here. These two will check every word you write, and they do the work of ten,' he went on. 'Their energy is astounding.'

Arturo shrugged good-naturedly. 'Who else will do it? The war does not stop because anyone is tired.' He sat down on top of one of the two desks in the room and lit an American cigarette, telling us that the price had now gone up to fifteen pesetas a pack on the black market. The week before it had been ten.

I reached into my satchel and gave him a pack of my own. The smile he gave me was everything.

'That's the fastest way to his heart, you know,' Ilsa said.

'That and beautiful hair,' Arturo said. 'Yours is gold like a cloud. Are you sure you're a writer?'

'Not at all sure, actually. If my hair is a cloud, I can assure you it's a filthy one. There's no shampoo in the hotel.'

'At least there's hot water,' Ilsa said. 'Think of that.'

We stayed for a while, talking about a message that had just come over the wire. A heavy concentration of Italian troops was currently north of Madrid and moving at a speed of twenty kilometers a day.

'That isn't what I would call good news,' Arturo said. 'But at least I have fine cigarettes.'

'I want to be just like Arturo when I grow up,' I told Ernest as we left.

He laughed. 'You want to be a bantamweight Spaniard? And deprive the world of those legs?'

'Stop teasing me. He seems to have such a good, rich heart, even in the midst of all this.'

'They all seem to have that, these people. It's something about being connected to each day as it comes. You should see all this during fiesta sometime. Spain knows how to be alive like no other country.'

'It's even more of a shame, then, that all this is happening.'

'I'm hoping the film can make some sort of difference.'

'With the ambulances, you mean?'

'More than that. If we do it right, then whoever watches back in the States will know how it really is here, and then they'll have to help. A whole world can shift that way. From telling the truth.'

'You sound like a writer,' I said gently.

'Oh, brother,' he said. 'Don't get me started.'

We had come back to the Gran Vía. On one side of the boulevard the great plane trees climbed, the branches still bare and almost sculptural, awaiting spring. Beneath the trees, a long stone wall stretched for many blocks, and was full of shell holes. Everyone seemed to be walking on that side of the street, though there was less obvious destruction on the other side. I stopped for a moment, thinking about this, about habits and what it meant to feel safe, even when you weren't. 'I wish you hadn't told him about *Collier's*,' I said. 'I haven't proven myself yet.'

'That's only semantics.'

'Do you really think so? I can't tell you what it means to have you in my corner.'

'You don't have to tell me. We're the same that way. Maybe in other ways, too, I'm thinking.'

I glanced at him to see if he was teasing me somehow, but he only walked on, swinging those arms, true as an arrow.

★   ★   ★

When we got back to the hotel, Sid had cooked up piles of breakfast — fried ham and slabs of dense bread browned in lard, and real coffee, not the instant crystals I had in my room. We fell to eating in happy silence, and then Ernest yawned and said he needed to try to do some writing or he'd fall asleep and waste the rest of the day.

I decided to explore a little on my own, taking the Baedeker with me because Ernest insisted I should. He also suggested I stick to the main thoroughfares.

'What should I do if there's shelling?'

'Duck into a doorway, preferably a stone one. You should be all right, though. Mostly they shell at night.'

'How will I know?' I asked.

'It's a high whistling scream that turns your insides into jelly.'

'You certainly know how to reassure a girl.'

'I can't imagine you'd have gotten this far if you were the needy type.'

'Maybe not.' I stood a little taller, pocketing the Baedeker, and then emptied my cup, thanking Sidney for the breakfast.

I stopped in my room and grabbed my windbreaker, and then went down through the lobby, which was nearly empty. At the open front door, a small well-dressed Spaniard stood with a newspaper tucked under his arm. He glanced at his watch and then looked out at the street again.

'I thought I heard sniper fire a few moments ago,' he said to me.

'Are you sure?'

'No. It could have been something else.' He looked at his watch again while I waited beside him. Anything was out there, beyond the door, a sniper, a high whistling shell, a grenade, a death. But the door was also only the slimmest idea of protection, and the lobby, too. No one was ever safe anywhere, not really. I stood a moment longer, thinking all this and wanting to be brave, or at least moving somewhere, pretending to be. The man wasn't going to budge anytime soon; that was clear. Finally I excused myself and wished him a good day. Then I stepped around him and out into the street.

# 13

There were plenty of first-rate correspondents in Madrid, and other writers who came through briefly, wanting to be part of what was going on. Some of them were famous already and some would be much later, and some never would be. They all had something to say, and I wanted to listen.

In the evenings, we would gather at the Hotel Gran Vía for some ghastly food and then retreat to Chicote's, the best of several cramped bars in that area of Madrid. Sometimes we went to Gaylord's instead, or Tom Delmer's room, which was one of the largest at the Florida. He wrote for the *Daily Express* and kept a cache of good whiskey and also chocolate in a little blue tin he must have brought from home. I wasn't sure I liked him. He had thick rounded shoulders and a high laugh that could sound like a hyena's. When he had too much to drink, his face went deep red, too. But I liked his chocolate and the Beethoven he often played on his phonograph.

Ginny Cowles wrote for Hearst, which was sympathetic to the Nationalist side, but no one faulted her for that. She was only doing her job. Just before Mussolini had invaded Abyssinia, she'd interviewed him and written smartly and objectively, which was a feat in itself. She often came to sit near me when we were in Delmer's room, the gold bangles on her wrist clinking musically as she passed her glass from hand to hand.

I felt closest to her and to Ernest, and to Herb Matthews, who wrote for the *Times*. He was tall and slender everywhere, and wore gray flannels and nice shirts that he kept fresh looking somehow when Ernest's always looked like he'd slept in his. Matthews was also intelligent and serious in a way that you felt every time he said anything. I liked him more all the time, and also felt lucky to know him, to be thrown together like this, even for a few weeks or months.

One night, Antoine de Saint-Exupéry came and drank with us. He'd flown into Spain in his own plane, which I couldn't even imagine as I watched him sitting sideways on Delmer's bed. He wore a peacock-blue dressing gown belted over silk pajamas and leather slippers that looked exotic enough to have come from Morocco or Dar es Salaam.

'What do you think of this country?' Saint-Ex asked Tom as he lit two cigarettes simultaneously, one for himself and one for Ginny.

'I think it's in the middle of the most enormous change of any country on earth.'

Saint-Ex nodded three times quickly while waving his match. 'They seem to be fighting for the truth.'

'And paying dearly,' Matthews added.

'Freedom has only ever been paid for with lives,' Tom said. 'It's always the same story. We just happen to have a front-row seat this time.'

'I'm not sure it's the same. Something feels

105

very new to me,' Ginny said.

'Think of the people who've come to fight and possibly die for Spain from all over the world,' Ernest added, leaning forward. 'Forty thousand volunteers, I heard, and it's not their freedom at stake, it's *all* freedom.'

'The courage is beautiful,' I said. 'But do you think these boys really know what they're doing?'

'Sacrificing themselves?' Matthews asked.

'We have to think they do,' Ernest said.

Tom passed a carton of cigarettes around. I'd been smoking too much already, but took another anyway. The smoking and the talking and the whiskey were all part of the fabric of the evening, the way time slid forward. I had never been a great drinker, but I was learning to hold my own in this crowd, mostly out of self-preservation. So when the bottle came around again, I took more of that, too.

'You seem quiet tonight,' Ernest said at one point, coming to sit next to me in the cretonne-covered chair Ginny had just vacated. 'What are you thinking about?'

'Just how happy I am to be here. That seems silly to say, I guess. But I've been wanting something to care about for a long time, something larger than myself. It makes me afraid to go home again.'

'You're not leaving soon, are you?'

'I don't want to leave at all. I told you I was being silly.'

'I think I understand what you mean. Everything is clearer here. I've been in a kind of fog for the last few years. This new novel I'm on

106

is fine, but it's not costing me enough. It's not doing anything new.'

'Is that why you came? To be jolted toward a different kind of book?'

'Maybe. Or maybe I'm just hoping to remember who I am and what brings me alive.'

It still surprised me that we could talk so openly this way, about substantial things. Ernest listened to me with his brown eyes half closed, as if he had all the time in the world, and didn't want to be anywhere else. It was a wonderful feeling, that what I said mattered. I thought that it would take very little for me to tell him anything, possibly everything.

'Sometimes I wish I weren't so young,' I told him.

'It's a fine thing to be young. When I was your age I was a father with one marriage behind me and all the awful feelings still inside me from hurting other people.'

I thought he must have meant his first wife, the marriage that had ended before Pauline, but didn't want to pry. 'Sometimes hurting others can't be helped,' I offered.

'That's what we tell ourselves, isn't it?' The slimmest shadow passed over his expression. 'See this scar here?' He pointed to a shiny, jagged shape above his right eye. 'I walked into a skylight in Paris when things were about as dark for me as they ever were.'

I only nodded, waiting for him to go on.

'I think Freud might say I wanted to hurt myself.'

'Did you?' It was a hard question to ask, but I

107

wanted to know if he was willing to share such a thing.

'I can't say for sure, but it makes sense, I guess. That I felt too rotten not to show it somehow. In a physical way, I mean. To break through to the hurting place.'

I wasn't sure how to answer him. It was terrible, the kind of pain he was talking about. I looked at the scar again, silvery white as a fish just below the surface, and then made an effort to be lighter. To be kind. 'I don't know much about Freud. Do you talk to him often?'

He squinted and smiled a little. 'Only when it can't be helped.'

★ ★ ★

It was past midnight when the party finally broke up that night. In my room, I washed my face, changed into cotton pajamas, and collapsed into bed. I was asleep in moments and don't expect I even moved until sometime in the middle of the night, when a squadron of Junker planes flew over the hotel.

The motors sounded like the end of the world. The room shook with a juddering I felt in my chest. I sat up fast, my head swimming with panic, and bolted from my bed. Then I froze. Did they have bombs, I wondered, and if so how many? Should I hide in the bathroom, or under my bed? Whatever the rules were, I hadn't learned them yet.

A quick hard knock came at my door. I nearly jumped out of my skin, but it was Ernest. He

108

had his trench coat over his pajamas, and his feet were bare. 'Are you okay?'

'I think so.' We stood there for a moment, listening. The sound of the motors seemed to hover, as if the planes weren't moving at all, though I knew that was impossible. 'What are they going to do?'

'Maybe nothing,' he said. 'Why don't we have a drink?'

'I've already had too much.'

'It might help anyway.' He crossed to my bureau where I kept a bottle and poured a few fingers for each of us into water glasses.

I went to the edge of my bed and took the glass he offered as he sat down beside me. But I only held it in my hand. The growling of the bombers was finally beginning to dim a little, but other sounds were starting up from University City, the *carong* of rifle fire in bouncing volleys, and then a series of short metallic bursts. The hand that wasn't holding my glass began to flutter in my lap. I tucked it under one leg.

'It's okay to be afraid,' he said. The curtains were open. Moonlight pushed in through the windows and made small pools along the wooden planks of the floor. But Ernest's face was mostly in shadow as he said, very quietly, 'Do you want me to stay?'

'Oh.' He'd caught me off guard. Somehow I hadn't let myself think this could happen, though he was very much a man, and I was a woman. I had kept him high above all that in my mind, where he was my hero and also my teacher, my friend. I tried to think of what else to say, but it was all too thin. 'I'll be fine. Thanks for worrying about me.'

'Maybe I'm worried about me is the thing.'

Even in the darkness, I had a hard time meeting his eyes. The sounds from the front went on, as alarming as ever, but there was also a strange stillness as he reached to draw his hand through my hair, pushing it to one side and exposing the base of my neck above the rumpled collar of my pajamas. In a moment, before I could begin to catch up, he was kissing me there, lightly as a moth might touch down, and with incredible tenderness.

'Ernest.' I pulled back. My heart was making a terrible racket. I had no idea what to say or do.

He leaned to kiss me again, and the pressure of his mouth on mine drowned out every other thought. I put my hands against his chest, fully meaning to push him away, but then gripped the cotton fabric instead, urging him closer. His tongue moved between my teeth and he breathed, warm and slow, an exhalation that seemed to go on and on.

'Ernest,' I said again. 'What are we doing?'

'I don't know. I don't care.'

Before I could respond, the building convulsed, and I was bounced to the floor hard. The hotel must have taken a direct mortar hit. Everything quaked, the ceiling raining plaster. Ernest helped me up, and then we both raced to the door and threw it open. Door after door spilled bodies into the hall. We all looked at one another, wondering where we should run or hide. At least three Spanish prostitutes appeared

110

and stood blinking as if disoriented. When Sidney Franklin came out, he was with a woman I'd never seen before. Her sweater was on backward, her hair rumpled with sleep. I knew I looked as guilty as she did in that moment. I felt Sid looking at me with a question in his eyes, but it was easy to avoid it in the chaos.

Suddenly, Saint-Ex appeared in his beautiful dressing gown, like some sort of mirage. The attack seemed to be over, and he offered coffee. Ernest and I followed a small group of friends and stragglers to his room. But as we all sat, talking, waiting for the coffee to boil and wondering aloud if the hotel would be a real target now, or if tonight's barrage was an accident, I felt exposed in more than one way. I didn't think I could bear it.

Standing awkwardly, I was careful not to glance at Ernest. 'I'm going back to bed. Good night, everyone.'

'Be safe,' Ginny said.

'Take this,' Saint-Ex said, and handed me a heavy pink grapefruit from a wooden crate, his private store.

I thanked him and moved out into the hall, carrying the grapefruit in front of me, as if it were some sort of offering or sacrifice to foreign gods. Plaster dust was strewn everywhere, like a speckling of fine snow. There were thick cracks along the wall on both sides, and a tipped-over table. And a broken lamp. Inside, I was in disarray, too. I wasn't sure what might have happened with Ernest if the hit hadn't come, but I had felt myself tumbling faster than I thought possible away from my own good sense and resolve. He was my friend, and that meant the world to me. *He* did, just as he was. And anyway, hadn't I learned my lesson with married men?

With a lingering unease, I went into my dark room and closed the door behind me, sliding shut the bolt.

# 14

The next morning I woke to a pale, still dawn, everything quiet as quiet could be. It was cold in my room, the radiator having turned to stone sometime in the night. I could smell good coffee wafting up the staircase from the third floor, and also the sharp fatty salt smell of ham and eggs frying on Sidney Franklin's magic hot plate. But as dizzyingly wonderful as the odors were, I didn't want to turn up at their place, not today.

I reached for the slacks I'd draped over the back of a chair and a linen shirt from the bureau and my wool jacket. Then I went downstairs thinking of the café across the street, even though that meant a day-old roll and bitter coffee crystals and perhaps an orange.

The week before, in the middle of a morning quiet as this one, three men had been at the window of the café when it exploded inward. Now there was thick brown paper and cardboard taped over the shell hole. Inside, the rubble had been cleared and the blood scrubbed; when I stepped near that place, I stopped for a moment, remembering for them. They'd had wives and children, probably, rituals and small pleasures, and a future that had been wrenched away. That's what you could never wash clean or get back.

I decided to take my breakfast with me, not stopping until I came to the Plaza Mayor, where

I sat at the base of one of the grand lampposts, and watched the pigeons settle and scatter and settle again in some rhythm only they understood. The shoeblacks were setting up their stations around the square, avoiding the places where there were new shell holes in the cobblestones. I studied them awhile and drank my coffee, feeling a headache squeeze at my temples and the base of my skull. I couldn't shake Ernest from my thoughts. The memory of his hands in my hair, the smell of his skin rising between us, prickled and unsettled me. Almost nothing had happened, and already it was too much. What would I say when we next spoke? What would he want from me? Did I want things from him, things I was ashamed to admit to myself?

There were no answers, not that I wanted to face. Pushing all these thoughts away with force, I stood and crossed the square. I'd arranged to meet Ginny Cowles at the Palace Hotel, which had been converted into a military hospital. The façade still looked like old Madrid, creamy and grand as a tiered wedding cake. Once inside the doors, though, I was immediately hit with the high sharp biting smell of ether, and beneath that, a murkier and more complex one of human illness and blood and suffering.

Ginny was waiting for me near the concierge desk in a slim black wool coat and good gold jewelry and the high heels she favored. In truth she looked dressed more for the Upper East Side than for any part of this besieged city, but I liked her, and I was grateful that she'd offered to

114

introduce me to the doctors and show me around so I might come back again on my own.

'That was some party last night,' she said as I walked up.

'Did you sleep at all?'

'Not really, but I never sleep much. There's always too much to think about.'

'I know what you mean,' I said. 'Even without the shelling.'

Beyond the foyer with its neat wicker furniture and nesting tables was the hotel's old reading room, which had been transformed into an operating theater. There were sheets pinned up to form partitions and more sheets draped everywhere to give the general impression of sterility. Ordinary dining tables were now surgical tables. Cut-glass chandeliers stood in for operating lamps, crystal bulbs replaced with harsh brilliant ones. Along the wall, all the books had vanished from the shelves, changed out for bandages and penicillin and contraband peroxide.

Ginny introduced me to one of the surgeons, explaining that I was an American writer, and that I wanted to know as much as possible about the conditions here. The surgeon was Catalonian, middle aged and reserved, with a sad mouth and very black delicately curved eyebrows.

'It is difficult to do my work here,' he said, 'but so much more difficult in the field. My colleagues at the front in Teruel, or Jarama, Brihuega, they have everything to deal with and also the weather. And no such luxuries as we have here.' He pointed above him at the bastardized chandelier which was suddenly — I could see it, too — a small miracle.

'What was your training?' I asked him through Ginny. 'From before?'

'Before . . . ? Before I was a foot doctor. Now I am all things and none of them quite enough.'

He led us to a recovery ward on the sixth floor, where blood-mottled stretchers lay stacked like cordwood in the halls. The rooms were full of the wounded, four or six cots squeezed into small but clean spaces. Sunlight spilled in through the tall sash windows, tumbling onto the floor and resting in the corners, but bringing very little warmth.

One of the men was a wiry bearded Russian pilot. His plane had been shot out of the sky and he'd burned with it before being rescued. *Rescued* wasn't quite the word, though, I thought, taking in his hands and arms and scalp, the flesh transformed to leathery knots and ridges that gave him so much pain he couldn't sleep without paralyzing doses of morphine. Looking at him made me want to weep — but you couldn't weep for all of them. Or could you?

Another man, a Canadian infantryman — Fisher was his name — had one leg up to the hip in plaster and was using his time to write letters home for everyone else in the ward. He was practicing penmanship with his left hand, since his right had been taken above the elbow. He had a round face and a thatch of coarse reddish hair that made him look tufted and also rather magnificent.

116

'You two should be movie stars,' he said to us, looking up from his letters. 'I'm not kidding.'

'Where were you wounded?' I asked.

'Right up the street . . . University City. Isn't that the damnedest thing?'

'Were you trained here, too?'

'Trained? That's not what anyone would call it. We were holed up for a week in a small farming village after I arrived, mostly freezing to death and eating burro meat. Ever try it?'

'No.'

'Well, make sure you don't. It's pure rubber and tastes like your granny's shoe.'

He smiled, twisting his lips at one corner, and then told us how one day a convoy from the International Brigades had rolled into the training base, scooped hundreds of men up, and taken them out onto the plains west of Madrid and taught them to fire Remington bolt-action rifles against the steep side of a quarry. 'I fired three times, or maybe five times. I'd never held a gun before. Then they said enough, we couldn't waste the ammunition, and back in the trucks we went.'

'And they sent you into battle that way?' I looked back and forth between his face and Ginny's and the Catalonian doctor's, but no one was incredulous or even surprised except me. 'Aren't you angry?'

'What good would that do? Besides, I volunteered. I knew I could get my head blown off over here. That was a very real possibility.'

'Why did you come?'

'Same as everyone else, I suppose. 'Cause I

was too furious and too excited to do anything else. I'd just gotten my diploma from McGill, but I couldn't think what good it was going to do me if the world went to hell. You know? It's Spain's turn now, that's what I was thinking, but anyone's turn next if we don't stop Franco.'

'I believe that, too. But it's hard to die for ideas, isn't it?'

'It's hard to die any way.' Color had risen to his face. The pen in his left hand twitched. 'At least our ideas are the right ones.'

★ ★ ★

Ginny and I toured several of the other rooms. In one, a boy with a massive caved-in sort of head wound was sketching another boy's portrait with careful, tender strokes. In another, a French soldier whose stomach had been blasted open, his entire abdomen wrapped in layers upon layers of gauze, showed us a branch of mimosa a pretty Hungarian nurse had brought him. He held one of the blooms, pink and feathered and silky. Stroking it with one thumb, he told us how there was a tree in Marseille that dropped flowers like this, sticky as honey as they decomposed on the road near his childhood home.

'Will you be going home soon?' I asked.

'I don't know.' He blinked several times, as if this might help him see the future. 'If I recover, I've promised to stay and fight. But I'm not sure I believe in wars anymore. They only make ghosts and they don't change anything.'

118

'I'm sorry,' I said, because I didn't know what else to say, and then praised the beauty of his mimosa, which was all I could praise just then. 'I hope you do make it home to your tree again, and to your family.'

A short while later, Ginny and I stood outside in the cold bright April sunshine. My thoughts were still whirling, but Ginny seemed detached and coolheaded, somehow, as if she'd seen all I had, but then set it down immediately, the way you would any thorny burden. I hadn't learned how to manage that, if I ever would. I wanted to ask how long it had taken her to grow such a thick skin, and if sad, impossible things still slipped through sometimes, and what she did then. But we weren't friends like that, at least not yet.

We said goodbye, and then she walked off at a clipped pace to some other appointment or to meet a secret source or contact, or to type up that day's story. Something important, that much was obvious.

I wanted to be of consequence in this war, too, but didn't yet see a clear path. I had come to write, but there were journalists literally everywhere, and everyone more experienced than I was. In one sense, it felt important merely to be here, to witness everything without turning away, and to write it all down. But then what? Would I really be bold enough to send an article to *Collier's* if I managed to finish one? How could I break out of this pack of writers covering the same battles and tragedies when I wasn't sure I had anything to add that hadn't been said many times before?

In my room later, I sat thinking as the light faded, a volume of Blake's *Songs of Innocence and Experience* in my lap, cold tea on the table nearby. At some point, my eyes fell closed. It must have been past midnight when I woke again. My room was bathed in total darkness, and there were tentative footsteps in the hall just outside my door. Then I heard a knock. A whispered voice came. 'Gellhorn. You up?'

I went rigid.

'Gellhorn, it's me. Open up. We should talk.'

I was afraid to make even the slightest sound, and closed my eyes, listening.

'Marty,' the voice hissed again.

After a few more agonizing moments, I heard Ernest's steps retreating. Only then did I dare to breathe. Rolling to the wall, I placed my hand on it flat, feeling the surging and siphoning of water moving through the pipes as through the arteries of a body.

Sometimes I thought I could almost reach into the different rooms this way, where the others slept curled on their sides or stared at the pages of a magazine, or drank alone in the dark. The hotel was a kind of honeycomb, in my mind, and we were all connected. That was one of the most surprising things about coming to Spain. That I was finding my sort of people, perhaps for the first time. That I belonged.

And then there was all the rest of it, too, how noble this revolution was, and how crucial, quite possibly one of the most important moments my generation would know. And I was here for it, incredibly enough. I couldn't let myself ruin this experience, not when I was so close to figuring everything out. What mattered to me, and what I wanted out of life, and who I really was, deep down.

Spain was a chance to find my voice as well as my compass. Tumbling into anyone's arms would be a grave mistake now, but being with Ernest would be riskier still. I couldn't lose this lovely bridge of friendship and understanding between us, not when it was so new. Not for sex alone. I also couldn't begin to imagine anything like an actual relationship with such a man. He was like a film star here. When he said anything, everyone leaned nearer. His scribbled-off dispatches, almost unintelligible if you didn't know what you were looking at, earned him five hundred dollars each. I had fifty dollars to my name and no idea if I had the talent to earn more.

I turned over onto my back again and looked up into the swirling dark of the ceiling. Ernest would have reached his room by now, and was sitting on the edge of his bed, perhaps, removing his shoes. Perhaps reaching for his flask, baffled, or merely tired, ready to be done with women and the trouble they caused.

I didn't want to cause trouble; I only knew what I knew. That Ernest could eclipse me, large as any sun, without even trying. That he was too famous, too far along in his own career, too sure of what he wanted. He was also too married, too dug into the life he'd built in Key West. Too driven, too dazzling.

Too Hemingway.

# 15

'We're going to have to run for it,' Ernest said. We had come to an exposed part of the street, twenty-five yards or so between the cover of ruined buildings in a neighborhood gutted by bombing. 'Snipers like this spot. Two or three people die here every day.'

I only nodded, a live fluttering at my throat, while he straightened his hunter's cap. His body pitched forward, bent at the waist so sharply I thought he might fall, but he didn't. When he reached the other side, he motioned for me to follow, just as he'd done, and though I wondered if I could even make my legs move, as wobbly as they were, I plunged forward.

As I came to the safety of the wall and crouched behind it, my pulse in my ears, I was euphoric. I could see he felt it, too — a sensation that was less like whistling past the graveyard than dancing furiously atop your own tombstone. Energy rippled between us. This was as close as we'd been since the night in my room, and that was here between us, hooked into the electricity and risk as we set off again.

We passed a six-story building that was open to the street, its façade ripped cleanly away. There was something almost vulgar in it, how you could look all the way through to the china cabinets and beds and wing chairs and bathtubs, the furniture of any life rattled apart and suspended. Some of the apartments seemed untouched except for the small matter of having no front wall — like some abandoned life-size dollhouse you could reach into and rearrange to suit yourself. Someone's home should be a haven, a fixed and unshakable thing — I thought — but this was more proof you couldn't count on anything but people, and only the right sort. The ones who could be like walls for you once you found them. This was my first war and I didn't know anything yet, but I knew that.

We were on the Paseo Rosales, once the most elegant address, Madrid's version of Park Avenue, now a ruin. Above us was the battered apartment building the Dutch filmmaker Joris Ivens was using to gather footage for his documentary about the war, which by now had a title, *The Spanish Earth*.

When we climbed the darkened staircase and came out again, we could see over all of the Casa de Campo and the front lines. That's why Ivens was so excited to have found this spot for shooting. You could see absolutely everything, clear across the broad sweep of the valley to the hills and the stark-looking pine trees, to where the infantry moved across the broken land. Here and there, you could even look right down into pieces of trench, where the men bent over their tommy guns like dust-colored toy soldiers.

Just shy of the balcony, Ivens and his cameraman had created a sort of viewing blind, propping the telephoto lens on a bier of old furniture and crates. The camera was wrapped in rags and ruined curtains, to camouflage it. Any glint of sun off the lens could draw a sniper and give our location away, Ernest explained as we moved toward the back of the apartment.

It was warmer there, out of the wind, though large chunks of the front wall and most of the windows had been blown out. I took off my coat and sat so I could lean against the wall between Ernest and Matthews. Herb handed me a jug of water and we looked out through exploded windows and watched the war, the feeling of safety and distance playing an odd game with my mind. A grenade blew a patch of ground into a cascade of earth and debris. Some of the men fell, bent over by the explosion, and they didn't get up. I kept watching, willing them to move, but they didn't.

As ill as the whole thing made me feel, I understood why it was going to be important to the film. You could see the entire shape of the battle from this distance without being swallowed by it. The shifting clouds of smoke and flashes of light. The sudden spoutings of dust as shrapnel rained along the ridge. The way the infantry moved forward by the inch and then pushed back, losing men, and taking men, until it seemed the same action. Maybe it was.

I reached for the notebook in my satchel, suddenly terrified that if I didn't write everything down that very second, I would lose it all. I felt my hand shake a little with the intensity and noticed Ernest had taken up his notebook as well and was scratching away at it, caught in the same wish to hold time still and make it behave. The world needed to see this, and that's why we had to see it first. Why we'd come.

★ ★ ★

'You need another,' Matthews said at Chicote's that night. The bar was so crowded we had to sit on top of each other or nearly.

'Tell me,' I asked him, 'why do you write about war instead of something else?'

'Someone has to. And I guess I believe we can change something. If we do it well enough.'

'If it's not already too late. I keep thinking that. That this is our one moment to fight for good in the world. It's now, *now*, and here. But what if the world stays asleep and won't see it no matter how loudly we shout?'

He shrugged. 'Then God help us all, I guess.'

I handed him my empty glass and he forged off through the wall of bodies. Half a second later, Ernest tumbled into his place and we were crushed together, elbow to elbow, knee to knee, laughter and serious talk to every side of us. I could barely breathe and he was part of it. He would want to talk now, when I only wanted to forget. Actually, I wanted to kiss him again, just once, very hard, and for a long time, because the taste of him had stayed with me, whether or not I could stand to admit it. One more kiss, and then I could begin forgetting.

'You're avoiding me,' he said.

'We were together all afternoon.'

'You know what I mean.'

'I guess I do.' There was nowhere to look away.

'I'm sorry. I haven't known what to say.'

'How about what you actually feel? That can be a fine place to start.'

'Who feels just one way?'

'I do,' he said. 'At least about some things. About you.'

'This isn't exactly the place, is it?'

But it was, ironically. The interesting thing about chaos is that it provides perfect privacy. Everyone we knew was there, which gave us a kind of seclusion we wouldn't have had anywhere else. We probably could have stripped naked and done a fan dance without drawing notice.

'You're afraid to let something happen between us. But it's already too late as far as I'm concerned. Maybe it was from the beginning. From the moment you walked into my damned bar.'

'Maybe. But we don't have to give in to that. I'd hate it if anything changed between us. You're too important to me.'

'That's something, I guess.'

'That's everything in my book. I can be an awfully good friend to you if you let me.'

'If I didn't know better, I'd think I was being ditched.' His tone changed to acid. 'It's been a while, but I think I remember the feeling.'

'Stop it. That's the last thing I want. Aren't you listening?'

'I'm listening.' His look was level, skewering. 'I've got plenty of friends.'

Before I could even think to answer him, Matthews was sliding through the fray to squeeze beside us. He held three big glasses of gin, all precariously full, and looked back and forth between us. 'Have I interrupted something?'

'Don't be silly,' I said, while my heart raced and rattled. 'But Christ, let's have that drink.'

# 16

It's late when Ernest crosses the darkly flowing Manzanares and skirts the southern corner of the Parque del Oeste, walking fast. It isn't at all safe here, particularly at night, when most of the shelling happens. Sometimes bombs fall, too, the great hulking Junkers or Heinkels passing over and sounding like death, turning his knees to butter.

Alongside the river, the park stretches out black as anything except for the cooking fires and barrels burning for warmth. Thousands of refugees are camped with their sheep and donkeys and children, each group huddled and separate around crackling red cinders. They've been there for months, since the siege began, and now can only wait by their small fires for the tide to turn. But will it?

Already the war has gone on months longer than anyone thought it would and shows no signs of stopping. Behind him smoke is still rising in columns from the front line at Garabitas Hill. The attack had lasted for only ten or fifteen minutes, but that had been long enough. In the trench, stray bullets had zipped over his head like May beetles, and when he had closed his eyes, trying to focus on the different voices of gunfire as a way of staying calm, he had thought of Marty instead, and knew then he was in a real jam, and that no one could help him out of it.

He hadn't planned to fall in love with her, but what did that matter now? The day she'd turned up in Key West, he'd only been reading his mail — that was the funny thing — and enjoying his daiquiri like any other afternoon. Then the door to the street had opened and sunlight had streamed in, and that was her.

Later, he would repeat a joke to friends about how she had legs that began at her shoulders, but the thing he'd actually noticed was her hair, which was the color of a wheat field, and her skin, which glowed as if some incandescent summer day had been stored in a jar for a century and then loosed all at once.

She was a beautiful girl, as beautiful as they came, but in his hometown bar, in the middle of his life, he felt protected and quite safe. He had a routine he'd built up very carefully and knew what it was, and what it meant. He had friends he could count on and others he couldn't, and he was learning to know the difference. And anyway, what really mattered was his work. There were books he had written and stories he liked a great deal, even if others didn't always see their value. After the Africa book, the critics had come at him hard, wanting to draw blood. But they couldn't get at the thing he'd built inside him or the stories and books that were waiting for him to be ready, the ones he hadn't touched yet.

He had every advantage; that was the feeling he had, and so he would drink a second daiquiri and read his mail and maybe the paper, and then go home to his wife and sons. Even shining as

129

she was, and not at all the typical thing, this beautiful girl was not a threat to him. When he talked to her he let himself notice everything, the length of her calves, and the way the black fabric of the dress fell against her skin, and how her eyes were somehow every color at once so that you had to look at them over and over to see how they changed.

Her mother was a beautiful woman, too. He liked her immediately. He liked them all, even the brother, and felt easy and natural talking with them. It was only after he'd gone that he realized he was still thinking of the girl. She followed him home, flaring softly in his memory, like notes of a symphony heard only once. She was still there when he closed the door behind him at Whitehead Street and stepped out of his shoes to feel the cool tile. Then Fife had appeared saying that they'd held dinner for him if he still wanted it. She was not a woman who missed much. She had cocked her head to the side like a raven and asked him where he'd been and why he was late, and he had known immediately that he needed to lie, and that this would not be the last lie he would tell his wife about this particular blond.

*   *   *

Now, at the edge of the park, he stops and turns to look behind him, the hill coarsely rounded and in shadow. Tomorrow he knows he'll hear the number of casualties on both sides, strict accounting being one of the things you do in a war to keep you from thinking about the actual people who have fallen. But it never works well, not for him, anyway. A drink is almost always the more effective cure. He'll go to Chicote's, then, and hopefully he'll see her there, too, and begin to feel better before he feels worse again.

All he can see for the moment is what's in front of him, only that, and she is part of it. It might be the war changing him, being at the knife-bright edge of things for the first time in many years. Whatever the reason, she's gotten through whatever defenses he's built up and now he doesn't want to stop thinking of her and trying to be closer to her, no matter what it ruins.

There was what you meant to do and what you had to do. There was who you thought you were, and who you became on a night like this, in Madrid, in the dark chaos of the street, following your feet where they needed to go.

# 17

After three weeks I felt I'd been in Madrid for years, and also that I never wanted to leave. I'd never experienced such intensity, ever. It was like living with my heart constantly in my throat. When the German batteries on Garabitas Hill began shelling the city steadily, life grew even sharper and more precious for everyone. In the daytime, the volleys came in short bursts — sixty or a hundred shells in ten minutes while we waited it out in doorways or in cafés or in the bathtubs of our hotels. Later, at the Hotel Gran Vía or at Chicote's or in Delmer's room, we would talk about the number of shells that had come, and how many people had been killed, and if there were any other battles that day, elsewhere, and what had happened then, and what might happen tomorrow. It felt comforting to go over everything again and again. It was a way of knitting ourselves together and feeling safer. It was a single language, and we all spoke it.

Very quickly I had learned to recognize the different sounds of gunfire, how to walk through fountains of exploded glass, and how to breathe when the air grew thick with lyddite smoke and dust. My Spanish improved and soon I could talk to the women who waited for hours in food lines, and the children who went to school in any building that would have them, walking past sprinkled trails of human blood to get there, and stopping sometimes to dig for souvenir shells to barter with one another, the way children in St. Louis did with marbles and baseball cards.

One evening I'd just come from the military hospital when I stopped at the square at Santo Domingo to listen to a flamenco player. Couples were strolling hand in hand, walking slowly through the soft air and talking as if the heavy shelling that morning had been only a dream.

At one corner of the square pigeons were trying to sleep while a group of children threw pebbles at them. The guitar player sat a little apart and hugged his instrument closely to his body while his other hand plucked bright notes. The song was beautiful. I sat to hear the rest, wondering about where courage comes from. Since the previous November, when Franco had locked his sights on destroying the capital, nearly every day had brought fire and death. But most Madrileños had still refused to leave. They would take the armed guards and the barricades and the blackouts as long as they could stay in their homes. They would take the shell holes and the buildings stove in by trench mortars, too, and the avenues cut off to block the movement of tanks. When their homes were gone, they would stay anyway, and walk after dinner if they damn well pleased, saying to themselves and to each other that it was better to die on their feet than on their knees. And wasn't it?

The guitarist had just reached the end of his song when there came a chuffing sound. I shrank without thinking, my shoulders clamping tight.

And then the shell. It spun and screamed its way into the square, exploding the cobbles on impact. And while everything in me tensed to run, my heart galloping ahead with panic, I crouched instead, counting seconds to myself until the whistling came once more, spiraling in louder and louder until it flashed on impact and the whole square rattled.

The children scattered, thrown like coins. The flamenco player collapsed onto his guitar and I finally bolted, hardly breathing, pushing my way into an already crowded doorway along the square. The lyddite smoke floated past, like lace made of poison. We counted and waited, but nothing happened.

'*Que Dios nos ayude*,' the woman in front of me whispered. *May God help us*. An empty market basket balanced in the crook of her arm. Her black-haired son gripped the edge of her dark shawl, carefully watching her face.

After five or ten seconds more of silence, she darted out into the square without glancing back. The boy scrambled after her, thin dark socks slipping into his rope-soled shoes, her shawl becoming the edge of a kite tail pulling him along. I could guess what she was thinking, that she needed to get the boy home to safety.

They had just reached the center of the square when the air shredded. The shell whined past and burst into countless fragments, like pieces of the sun. Faster than anyone could see, faster than thought, one pierced the boy's throat. He crumpled, his hand still in hers, while shells kept falling all around, one every few seconds. The woman bent over him. She screamed again and again for him to get up.

I had never seen death like this, right before my eyes, let alone the death of a child. Something in me cracked. My pulse was racing so violently I thought my heart might explode. But I went on living, while two men ran out to tenderly carry the boy's body to the edge of the square, and his mother stumbled after, walking in the trail of blood as she always would now, going forward, wailing and wailing and not stopping.

# 18

'You okay, Gellhorn?' Ernest asked that night. We were at Chicote's, but the greater part of me was still at the square.

I took the whiskey and water he put into my hands. 'I don't know. Is it always this way?'

'There aren't any rules for how to get through it, but it sometimes helps to remember that it's not you death has come for. Not you, and not anyone you love.'

That couldn't be right, I thought. Every death was equally horrible, and this had been an innocent boy. But I knew he had meant not to be callous, but to comfort me. There was something in his voice that did work to make me feel calmer, and more settled. And then there was simply being near him and the other people I'd come to count on. I had never been so grateful for friends.

We ordered more drinks and made room for stragglers. Tom Delmer had a five o'clock shadow. He and Matthews had just come back from the Tajuña Valley where they had interviewed some of the men from the Fifteenth Brigade who had survived the attack on Pingarrón Hill. Suicide Hill, it was called now, because four hundred Americans had gone over the top of the trench in one battle, and only one hundred and eight were still standing. If you could even call it that.

They had terrible stories. The mood was dark all the way around, but we stayed, knowing it was far worse to be in a bad place in your mind when you were alone. Sometime past midnight, we walked the few blocks back to the Florida. The city was black and cold, and we huddled together as a group, leaning against one another and lightly bumping shoulders, only separating when we came to the barrel-shaped lobby. Stringing our way up the curving staircase, we called good night to each other blurrily and repeatedly. In a few moments I was alone, the inky carpet in the long hallway swallowing my steps, a pleasant rubbery sensation there in my limbs and the muscles of my face, and in my mind, too. But I only thought I was alone.

I turned to place my key in the lock, and saw that Ernest stood a short distance down the hall in a pool of shadows, waiting for me to turn around.

'Hello,' I said quietly.

'Hello,' he said, and moved into the light.

Once inside my room, we didn't speak at all. I could smell the smoke and whiskey of Chicote's on his clothes. The heat of his body was a kind of pressure in the air, and his tongue against mine set off a series of small shock waves. His hands dropped to my waist, tugging my blouse free, and then sliding along my ribs and then higher. It was rash, what we were doing. We would both probably regret it, but I didn't want to think of that, or anything else for now. Not guilt, and not Pauline. Not how much time we had left in Spain, or what we would say or feel in the future.

Maybe the future didn't even exist. That was more than possible. War made its own rules, after all, and we could only guess at them.

He pulled me tightly to him and I heard my heartbeat roaring back at me from the wall of his body. And as I let myself tumble to the floor with him, what I felt more than anything was terribly lost. What I wanted more than anything — anything — was to be found.

★   ★   ★

Much later, we lay side by side in the dark. It was strange to be near his body this way when we'd spent so much time together never touching at all.

'What have we done?' I asked him.

'I don't know.'

In the dim room, without his glasses on, his face looked young and exposed. Even where there were deep lines around his eyes, I could see the boy he'd been. I liked him, that boy, and I also wanted to hurt him, suddenly. To bring up his wife, for instance, the real one who stoked the home fires in Key West, who had his name and also the grace of a warrior queen. She wasn't going to go away because he blinked once or twice at me in the dark.

'Maybe you should go.'

I felt him stiffen against me. 'I'd like to stay.'

I was quiet for several moments and then finally said, 'I'm tired,' because it was easier than saying any of the things I actually felt.

'Sleep, then. It was a hell of a thing you saw

today. I think you're very brave.'

'I don't feel brave. I don't know what to feel.'

'I'll be right here. Just try to put it all out of your mind if you can.'

'All right.' I rolled away from him, closing my eyes. Of course he was deeply part of 'it all.' But there was no sorting that out now. All I wanted was to be alone on a sea of unconsciousness, slipping away as the bed became a raft and my mind let go of itself.

'Good night, Marty,' I heard him say as I drifted, bobbing, in the dark.

# 19

A few days later the boys came to collect me and we set out across the valley for the Guadalajara hills, brown as bread in the distance. Not everyone could find transport out of Madrid, but Ernest could always get a car or even two, and drivers to take him where he needed to go, and as much petrol as he liked.

After the night we'd spent together, I had been doing my best to avoid him, but when he offered to bring me on this trip, I'd said yes immediately. His reputation meant that commanding officers and troops in the field were always happy to see him coming. I would get to witness some extraordinary things, I guessed, and hear the kind of stories I came for. Women were so rare at the front they might as well have been nonexistent. I wasn't going to miss this chance, not for the world.

As we went, tiny villages were strung along the road at intervals. They probably had been pearls once, these little towns. Now they sagged with defeat. Dirty, hungry-looking children perched on pyres of rubble to watch us pass. Their eyes were huge and slightly accusatory — not because we'd done anything wrong, but because we had the freedom to come and go this way, leaving only a spiraling arm of dust behind the car to show we'd been there at all.

At the top of a high pass, we let the car idle

and got out. The whole of the valley lay furled below, long stretches of olive groves and vineyards and the broken earth that meant a battlefield. In the distance, a blur of white stucco smoked. It was a farmhouse, burning. High above, in a sky flat as ironed cotton, a vulture spun one long slow circle that sent a tingling up the back of my neck.

We drove down into the valley and maneuvered the car to one side of the dusty road. From several miles off, we could hear the sounds of artillery coming, the layered stutter of machine-gun fire, the sharp graduated hammering of tommy guns. Walking across sharply broken ground, we came to a lip of earth, and this was the trench. In moments, we had dropped down into it.

It was wide enough for two to stand or kneel side by side, with a dry crackled earth bottom and earthen walls that climbed crudely and sharply. Here and there, the earthworks widened into a small square 'room,' if you could call it that. When we came to one, there was a simple table laid over with a map and a military phone. Several folded cots were stacked in one corner, making me think the men slept here, when they slept. There was also a small fire and coffee boiling. It smelled burned, and yet I wanted some badly, if only so I had something to do with my hands.

All the men we met — or they were boys, really, most of them — seemed to look at me with astonishment, as if a wedding cake had turned up, or a gazelle. Some of them were Spanish, some American, some Canadian, some

Mexican, it seemed. They had been on the line for forty-five days, one said, and expected an attack every day. Firing came at them all the time, of course, but a real attack would be something else.

We went down farther along the trench, where the ground became so hard and uneven it felt like trying to walk along an arid, stony riverbed. Many of the soldiers held rifles at the ready. Others stood beside theirs, or sometimes lay with their guns like sleeping dogs at their sides. Something I noticed was how many books there were, in back pockets, on carved-out earthen shelves, in straw, in the hands of the men. I saw a copy of *Candide* and also *Leaves of Grass*. When we came upon a young man who was reading *Walden*, I had to stop. He was tall and slender with a shock of blond hair that reminded me of just-shorn fields. The skin on his hands was pale and pink-white, the hands of a poet-philosopher.

'I love Thoreau,' I said. 'What's your favorite part?'

'All of it, I guess. He knows the names of so many flowers and trees. That's something. I'd rather think about that any day than what we have here.' His eyes were light blue with small black irises, like pinpoints, and they struck me as very beautiful and also unnerving.

'What's your favorite part?' he asked.

'Oh, all of it, too, I guess. He talks about the gift of being lost in the woods. I've always found that comforting, somehow. That maybe you have to be truly lost before you can find yourself again.'

He squinted one eye and looked at me sideways, seeming to gaze right through me. 'He does say that, doesn't he?' Then, 'I think you're going to be all right, you know. Don't worry too much.'

It was presumptuous, the way he was talking to me, and strangely intimate. And yet as exposed as I felt, there was also the consoling flicker of being seen — even for a moment, even by a perfect stranger. 'Good luck to you,' I told him.

'You too,' he said, and returned to his book.

When I caught up to Matthews a few moments later, I had the queerest feeling that I'd just seen a ghost.

'What was that about?' he asked.

'I don't even know. Just a boy, I guess. It's something being here, isn't it?'

'I'll say. It's important, though. We can't know what these kids are up against, really, but we can feel our way across the same bit of land and look in their eyes.'

'And see the books they're reading.'

'Sure. That's the main thing they say about journalism, you know,' he went on. 'Don't trust reportage. Don't let other people tell you what happened, not if you can help it. You have to take it all in with your own senses. To write what you see, and what you feel.'

That stood me still for a moment. 'What about being objective?'

'Don't try. There's no such thing.'

'I guess I'm glad to hear you say it. I've been thinking about the boy I saw die at Santo

Domingo. I want to write something, but I don't think I can without being emotional.'

'Just make a start. Begin anywhere.'

'It might be terrible.'

'It might be. That's not the worst thing.'

'No,' I agreed. And it wasn't. The worst thing — I already knew it — would be feeling too scared to try.

★  ★  ★

For four days, we drove between battalions and slept in encampments next to the soldiers' tents, eating as they did and sharing their fire. I knew that many of them were inexperienced — like Fisher, the Canadian infantryman I'd met in the hospital in Madrid, who'd never held a gun until he needed to use it with purpose. Some were smooth skinned as babies, their eyes long lashed and frightened, but devout. After talking with many of them and seeing how they lived, I realized they didn't have an endless supply of bravery, because no one ever did. When courage failed them, they would find a way to stand their ground anyway and fight on spirit alone. They had grit rather than bravery. That was why the Rebels were going to win this war, I thought. Why they had to.

After dark, the tents were thick with stories and red wine we passed in enamel cups. One night, when I grew restless, I slipped away to stand under the stars, smoking. The camp was notched into a hillside surrounded by tall spare pines. I stood in the quiet, taking in the fresh smell of pine resin and liking the feeling of being alone. Then the tent flap opened and Ernest was there beside me.

'Aren't you afraid out here?' he asked.

'It's beautiful.' I drew on my cigarette, the paper hissing as it flared.

There was no moon, and the hillside and the pines were shrouded in heavy blackness, as if curtains had been pulled down from some great height. From inside the tent, we heard laughter, but it seemed to have nothing to do with us.

'I meant what I said the other night. It's too late for me, with you. You might not want to hear any of this. Maybe I'm being a selfish bastard, but I feel more alive now than I have in years. Marty. Marty, look at me.'

'No.'

'Don't be a child, dammit. I'm in love with you.'

In seconds, he'd crossed the space between us and loomed beside me, blotting out the sky. His hands reached inside my field jacket and he kissed me in a crushing way. I couldn't breathe, and didn't care. The ground beneath me tipped sideways. The trees bent in and the whole night did, too, and whatever part of me could usually hold to reason was washed away. His fingertips felt hot along my back and shoulders and neck, and under my hair. Everywhere. I pushed at his clothes, wanting to get closer, to feel his skin, to have him.

'My God,' he said against my neck. 'We've lost so much time.'

'It doesn't matter.' I kissed him again, not

wanting to stop and also wishing futilely that this moment and everything between us could be finished already. The affair begun and ended, the damage done and the repairs under way, my battered heart on the mend. Because he would break my heart. I already knew that if nothing else.

And yet here we were, anyway, hurtling through the dark toward each other under a hundred million stars, and set to collide disastrously. Logic wouldn't save us and neither would the dwindling pile of days. We had all the time in the world to make a terrible mistake.

# 20

The Florida at night was a hive of shadows. I learned to read them all as I made my way to Ernest's room, my trench coat belted over my pajamas, determined that no one have any inkling that we'd become lovers. It was one thing to hurt ourselves, and another thing entirely to drag other people down with us. His wife couldn't ever know. My mother couldn't either, because I wouldn't survive the look on her face. *Again, Marty?*

No. It was hard enough to face myself.

Once inside his room, I didn't say anything, just dropped my coat where I stood at the door and found him in the dark. Our teeth jarred as we came together. He pulled me beneath him, his arms braced over me, a small drop of his blood or mine on my tongue. I felt dizzy and reckless and wondered if I might be falling in love with him, too. Or maybe this was just what it meant to be wholly awake. My nerves seemed to hover exposed around me like a raw kind of halo. I was being turned inside out, and whether it was the war or Spain or Ernest that was doing it, how did that matter? Maybe there wasn't any difference at all between them anyway.

★   ★   ★

Almost as soon as we returned from the field, I began to write, finally. I wasn't sure what would really come. Combing through my notebooks, I worked to flesh out moments and impressions — the sound of the shelling from my own bed at the Florida, the incongruity of the trams that ran up and down the Gran Vía, all the way to the front. The poisonous veils of smoke after an attack, and the lines for bread next to the lines for Charlie Chaplin's *Modern Times*. The perfume shops where the smell of cordite mingled with bottled gardenias, and the opera theater, which still sold tickets, and the beautiful young tenor who was a volunteer and often turned up for the matinee fresh from the trenches, with traces of blood on his shoes.

I wrote and wrote until I knew that the story I most needed to tell, and the one I was most afraid of, was about the boy and his kite tail of blood, my first long look at death. That day war had stopped being an idea and became personal. I could still see his hand clutching his mother's shawl. What had happened to her? How had she gone on with her life?

Thinking of either of them made me feel helpless, every cell in my body vibrating with an outrage bordering on despair. But despair didn't write well. Maybe there was no such thing as objectivity, as Matthews had said, but I didn't think I could tell the story at all unless I tightened my grip on my emotions somehow, and stripped my language down to the bone.

★ ★ ★

In 1934, when I was a young journalist newly in the field for the Federal Emergency Relief

Administration, coolheadedness had been my only lifeline. Like many of Roosevelt's New Deal programs, the FERA was young and untested. I was hired by Harry Hopkins, one of the president's senior advisers, with a handful of other writers to investigate the impact the Depression was having on real people. I would travel state to state, gathering firsthand observations of families on relief, and then send in my reports. Hopkins wanted stories and impressions, not statistics, and I was desperate to be useful.

I was only just back in the States after my disastrous affair with Bertrand, and feeling slightly hopeless. I'd managed to purge some of my despair about the relationship in my first novel, *What Mad Pursuit*, but after the initial rush of hope and undiluted maternal pride, when I held the first bound copy in my hands, thinking of how it would be shelved in libraries, my hopes had been dashed almost immediately. My father's bad opinion had stung more painfully than any of the reviews, even the ones calling my characters 'hectic' and the whole effort 'palpable juvenilia.'

I was completely unprepared for how awful it felt to be kicked this way. I wanted to skulk off under a rock somewhere and hide my head in shame. Instead, I took the FERA job, which felt like a great gift from the sky. I could forget my heartbreak, my wounded pride, and my crushed ambitions of being a celebrated novelist. I could forget myself entirely, in fact, and do something good for the country.

I was sent to North Carolina and then New England with thirty-five dollars a week and a bus voucher. More often I hitched rides with social workers to the saddest towns I'd ever seen. I would have told you I was prepared to be objective in my reports. But day after day, I saw families so wretched and beaten down by poverty they made me want to howl. In Lawrence, Massachusetts, I visited a woolen mill where skeletal girls hung over shuddering spinning frames for eight or ten hours without rest, their skin bleached looking and raw. They ate standing up. In the latrine I nearly walked into three young women trying to sleep on the icy concrete floor next to the toilet. One had a blue headscarf the color of faded cornflowers and such defeat in her eyes I had to grip the wall behind me.

I tried to visit five families a day on the road, the women and children often ashamed to leave their houses because their clothes were in rags and they had no shoes. One family of four slept in a single bed and they all had syphilis, even the infant daughter, who was so advanced in the disease she'd become paralyzed. They weren't seeking treatment because the mother insisted it was 'bad blood' and everyone knew that had no cure.

In another village, I sat in a sagging kitchen with oilcloth tacked to the walls to keep the wind out, because they'd run out of coal. A ten-year-old girl named Alice knelt on a pile of rags clutching a white duck to her chest. Her father had won it in a prize drawing where each chance was a penny.

'I thought we'd eat it,' he said, 'but you can see. It's all she has to play with.'

When he walked me outside later, I asked how he thought they'd manage to go on.

His shoulders made a flinching sort of shrug. 'If you'd told me even a year ago we could get by on what we have now, I would have called you a liar.'

'You're doing all you can. More, really.'

'I can't do anything.' He looked past me, past the rain-soaked street into the pitted sky. 'Sometimes I pray an angel will take us in our sleep. So far no one's listening.'

Back on the train that night, rattling toward Boston, I had to drink several shots of whiskey before I could begin my report. I'd been sent to look at darker things than I even knew existed, and still, they were mere drops in an ocean of human suffering. How could I write about Alice and her duck without sounding hysterical? About the girl with her headscarf, about syphilitic babies with no chance at all? Hysteria would help no one. If anything was ever going to change, Harry Hopkins and the FERA needed to see exactly what I saw, no more and no less. I had to be a camera, just as frank and unflinching as that, only one sentence at a time.

When I brought my reports to Hopkins in Washington, he arranged for me to meet Eleanor Roosevelt, who had once worked on social causes with my mother, and whom I'd always admired from a distance. I grew so intense as I laid out the scenes for her I'm surprised she didn't throw me out. But she only listened, really listened, and asked intelligent questions, her pen racing back and forth as she set down notes for herself. She wore a dark, unflattering dress, and her graying hair sprang up in wisps here and there. Middle age had been hard on her looks. She had no chin to speak of and her teeth protruded oddly, but I didn't think I'd ever seen anyone so beautiful. It was her dignity that shone through.

When I returned a few months later, I'd just been fired for encouraging a handful of mine workers in Idaho to rise up against a crooked relief contractor. They'd broken out all the windows at the FERA offices, and I was sent packing. But the Roosevelts thought I'd done the right thing, and offered to let me stay at the White House until I got my bearings.

I was given a simple room with a narrow chintz-covered bed and a rickety corner desk. Mrs. Roosevelt was so sensitive to the plight of the country that she would rather have broken the bones in her own hands than live in luxury while others suffered. The meals were plain, seasonless rib-sticking things. Wine was served rarely and by the thimbleful, and alcohol never — but the president would sometimes pull the more liberal and amusing guests into the cloakroom for one of his murderous martinis and a good joke. He found me charming and diverting, I think, like a minimally trained Pekingese, while Mrs. Roosevelt pressed me for news and the 'young person's view' of the country.

I liked her. Actually, I loved her — and almost immediately. I'd never met anyone with so much goodness and humility and tireless concern for others. Sometimes she let me help her answer her mail, which was absolutely bottomless and often heartbreaking. People asked her for help when they had no idea where else to turn — like a young man in Minnesota who had lost his arm in a hunting accident and could no longer help his brothers and sisters as before. They didn't have clothes fit enough to wear to school and desperately needed a horse. Could she find one?

I sat in a covered chair next to her simple cherrywood escritoire. She wore a shapeless blue dress and bent over the letter, her hands — they were lovely, strong hands, her most beautiful feature — pressing the page in thought.

'Will you send them a horse, then?'

'I'll try to find someone who can. We can always do better than nothing. It's a fine letter. Think of the time it took him to write it.'

I watched her for a few moments, filled with admiration, as I always was when I was anywhere near her. She had a kind of light, fueled by decency and wisdom and utterly inextinguishable. She made me want to be a better person.

'I've been thinking of turning some of my reports into character studies,' I told her. 'If I wrote stories or a novel, they might become real breathing people instead of figures and numbers on some graph no one will see. I want to help them. I want to try, anyway, and perhaps this is how.'

'You want to help them,' she repeated, looking

153

at me with those deep clear blue eyes that could be shy or filled with unchecked loneliness or steely and terrifying. I knew she never agreed with anyone unless she meant to.

'Yes, I do.'

'Then you will.'

★   ★   ★

I left the White House soon after that and went to Fields's house in Connecticut, a decision that would greatly rattle my family, as it turned out. But the golden chance to work without distraction was worth it. Over the next four months, while snow fell thickly, accumulated, then melted into spring, I wrote every day, feeling stoked by a conviction that was utterly new, at least in my writing life. It occurred to me that the reason *What Mad Pursuit* had failed utterly in the commercial realm was the same reason my father had despised it. My choice of subject. My characters were more than 'hectic,' I saw now. They were trite and narcissistic. Whom had that book helped? No one. This new idea, though, could be something else. It had nothing to do with ego or self-importance or with me, Gellhorn. I was only the burning bush.

I was still enormously proud of that second book, that it had sold well, and received nice notices, that Eleanor Roosevelt had written about it twice in her 'My Day' column, calling it fine and useful. The only regret I had at all was that my father hadn't lived to see me redeem myself. I still wanted to feel his pride and validation, I realized, though that was impossible. I suppose that was why my horizon line had newly shifted to include others — Matthews and Ginny Cowles and Tom Delmer, and Ernest. I wanted them to respect me as a writer, and I wanted to respect myself, more than anything.

I missed the driving sort of holiness I had felt in Connecticut when my characters were way down in my bones. Alice in her sad kitchen joined with all the other girls I met to become Ruby. And though I changed details and filled in things I couldn't have known, the thrust of the truth remained.

Did I still remember how to burn like that? Could I do it now, for the boy? For Madrid?

Yes, I thought I could.

# 21

I woke in Ernest's room at dawn, pushing the blankets back and turning away from him, beginning to dress, while he propped himself up on his elbow to watch me.

'You're off to work now, aren't you? Are you writing something new? I'd like to see it.'

'I'm a little afraid of it just now.'

'Oh?'

'I like it too much. It feels new, I guess. Like I've broken through something. I don't know.'

'Show me.'

'I could. But what if I'm wrong and it's terrible? What then?'

'You know, when you're young it can be important to hear other voices and test them against what you've done. I've told you about Stein, haven't I? She cut me to shreds, and Pound, too, but I needed it and then some.'

I bent over my shoes, feeling blood rush to my face. He was the last person in the world I wanted cutting me to shreds. I couldn't think of a writer I admired more. And then there was everything else about him. How he seemed to eat up every day's experience, even the terrifying stuff, when others turned into nervous cats. *Who is this person?* I found myself wondering more and more. *The one in the filthy brown trousers and a blue shirt full of holes? The one who prays to typewriter keys and also bourbon and also,*

156

*more than anything, the truth? Who steps over shell holes where the earth has been opened all the way down to the sewers? Who meets my eyes when the ceiling begins to shudder and tells me with no words at all that I'll be okay because he's with me? How does someone arrive at love with such a person?*

I didn't at all know, but that's what was happening to me. I was falling in love, and it was wonderful, and it was awful. I wanted to run like hell and never look back. I wanted to shut the lid down tight and stay in this room forever.

'Give me some time, all right?' I finally said, sitting up straight and meeting his eyes. 'I'll show you soon. I promise.'

'We don't have time, do we?'

'Not for Madrid, maybe.'

He fell quiet. I had another week or ten days left. He had a little more, but not much. We had been careful never to talk about it, but now it seemed we had no choice.

'Over here, nothing at home feels real,' he said after a while. 'I don't have a wife or three sons or a novel to write. I don't have house payments or people counting on me, or anything except each day's dispatch and trying not to get shot. And you.'

'But as soon as you're back in Key West, all of this will fade,' I finished for him, flatly, while inside I swayed, lurching off-center. 'That's what you mean. Everything will change places and Madrid will be the thing that's not real.'

'Something like that.'

I had expected this, and yet it still surprised

157

me. His words seemed to fit exactly into the thing I'd been fearing. That he would break my heart without having to lift a finger. That there was no way to actually have him. From the beginning I had known that he would go back to Pauline. But I'd also been telling myself that we'd somehow manage to build a bridge into lasting friendship. We were friends, weren't we? I couldn't believe we could simply vanish from each other's lives after all this, but he seemed to be suggesting as much. That we had been a fleeting thing, an interlude. Something inconsequential. And that soon I would mean nothing at all to him. It hurt in a dizzying way to feel him pulling away, and just when I'd begun to trust my feelings.

'You're a rare person,' I told him, trying to keep my voice even. 'I'm going to miss you.'

His look softened. 'We still have a few days.'

'I can't,' I said. I bent toward him until my forehead rested on his, and held still, breathing in the smell of his skin, the warmth of the cotton sheets, each detail of the room as it faded and became a ghost. Then I stood up, squaring my shoulders, and let myself out without looking back.

Walking to my room, I felt loneliness and fear come wisping down from wherever they had been waiting. They draped themselves over me, snug and familiar. Filling my pockets and all the spaces inside and out until I thought I might have to lean against the wall to stay upright. In moments, I'd been kicked out of love and was alone again.

*He was never yours*, a voice in my head said. But what did that matter? I had lost him just the same.

# Part 3

# HALFWAY HOME

## MAY 1937-FEBRUARY 1939

# 22

I should have gone back to St. Louis, I realized later, to see my mother and sleep in my old bedroom under the eaves in the house on McPherson Avenue until I'd cleared Madrid from my system like a fever. But I went to New York, where instead of bread lines and lorries filled with wounded dirty-faced men, there were chestnut blossoms and pink-tinged clouds and streams of yellow cabs. Instead of tanks in the streets or Junker planes roaring high above, polished cars glided toward cocktail parties. Shopwindows glittered with all sorts of things no one needed — evening wear, sapphire watches, cakes too elaborate to ever think of eating. It was all so beautiful. It was all so wrong.

New York meant I could help Joris Ivens, though. He was there to usher *The Spanish Earth* through its final stages, editing footage and cutting in the sound, which needed to be as visceral and arresting as the images were. This took some imagination. For weeks we met with a group of engineers in a padded studio on the Columbia University campus trying to reproduce artillery fire with an air hose and a football bladder, finger snaps and foot stampings, and fingernails dragged over a wire-mesh screen, not quitting until the result gave us chills.

'I think I can get us a viewing at the White House,' I told Ivens when the film was finally

163

done. 'Mrs. Roosevelt is keen to hear what we've been doing. You'll love her. Everyone does, though she can be awfully fierce, too.'

'If you can fix it we can meet in Washington in July or maybe August. I'll write to Ernest. He'll be over the moon.'

'I'll write, too,' I said, as if it were a simple thing. I had been thinking of him almost constantly, and then torturing myself about it. It was foolish to go on this way, missing what we'd had when it had probably been nothing at all. I also understood it was Spain as much as Ernest that had gotten under my skin, and the experience of the war. How important and real and raw every day was. How useful I felt, and understood. I had found a place at last where I actually fit, just as I was. The people around me seemed to be those I was meant to know and to care about. Now it was all over, and what was the cure for that?

I took to staying up late at night, smoking too much, and gazing into darkened windowpanes, thinking about Amelia Earhart. Everyone had been following her world flight, tracing her path with daily headlines and imagining what that kind of freedom must feel like. Then she'd vanished, her radio signals fading and spotty at first, then nonexistent. President Roosevelt had dispatched half the US Navy at an unheard-of expense to search for her, but so far it seemed the sky or the sea had simply opened up and swallowed her.

It made me feel shaky and horribly lonely — and brought Spain back more sharply.

Anything and anyone could disappear on you, and you could disappear, too, if you didn't have people around who really knew you. Who were there solidly, meeting you exactly where you stood when life grew stormy and terrifying. Who could find you when you were lost and couldn't find yourself, not even in the mirror.

★　★　★

We settled on July 8 for showing the film to the Roosevelts, and met up at Newark's Penn Station. I arrived first and waited under the vaulted blue-tiled ceiling, feeling excited and edgy in equal parts. When the boys arrived, first Ivens and then Ernest, I tried to cover my nervousness by joking about the food in the White House. We'd need contraband sandwiches — loads of them. Giddy, I pretended to tuck one into my shoe as we boarded our train, chattering a stream about how magnificent Mrs. Roosevelt was in all ways except menu planning. I couldn't stop cracking jokes because if I did, I knew I might burst into tears.

That night we dined on squab that chewed like a raincoat, milky, flavorless soup that was impossible to identify, and salad swamped by damp slices of pineapple. Ernest and I were never alone, and I was grateful for that. I wouldn't have known what to feel, what to say, what to want.

The film was a wonderful distraction. President and Mrs. Roosevelt seemed gratifyingly interested. They asked thoughtful, insightful questions about our experiences in Madrid, and so did Harry Hopkins, whom I hadn't seen in years. Each of them agreed the film was something truly useful and powerful to watch. If they had any advice, it was that the narration could be less restrained. One expected a strong anti-Fascist argument, and even propaganda, rather than artful subtlety. Since the film was finished, this more passionate stance could be delivered as a speech to any audience before a showing.

Ivens was delighted things had gone so well. We'd all been invited to stay the night, and while Ivens and Ernest stayed up late, working furiously on the speech, I knocked on Mrs. Roosevelt's door.

'I can't thank you enough,' I said, settling in one of her Spartan chairs. 'You and the president were awfully kind to my trench buddies.'

She looked at me for a moment, her gaze cutting through even before her words came. 'I hope you'll keep your head about you. Hemingway seems a complicated man.'

I thought about protesting or throwing up some lie, but she'd easily seen what I'd worked hard to hide, even from myself. 'He is. I don't have any fantasies where he's concerned, if that's what you're worried about. How could I? But when you're around someone like him, a fiery sort of person, a genius, really, and then you're not. Well, it leaves a hole, doesn't it?'

'Perhaps. But no other person can actually fill you up. You know that, don't you?' She looked at me piercingly for a moment, and then dropped her gaze. 'I must sound like your mother.'

'No. I'm always happy to have your opinion . . . you know that. You're very wise.'

'Not about everything.' There was a pot of petroleum jelly on her escritoire, which she dipped into, beginning to rub it into her hands. She was a deeply private person and would never have discussed her romantic life with me, but there were always rumors flitting around about the president and his women. His secretary, her secretary, foreign princesses, distant cousins by marriage. If even half of these affairs were true, I knew she must have suffered shame and loss, and a recovery that had changed her. What she and F.D. had now was so obviously a partnership, not a proper union. Not love.

'I don't pretend to know anything about marriage,' I tried to explain. It mattered to me that she saw me plainly and understood my intentions. 'Ernest isn't free. There's no cliff to fling myself from even if I wanted to. And I don't.'

'How could I possibly judge you? We each have to make our choices, and then find a way to live with them. And if we can't, well, then, that's when we know something has to change.'

I thanked her for her advice, wished her good night, and then sat up late in my room, pretending to read but really staring at shadows. She'd said that no one could fill anyone else up, and that sounded right — but maybe she herself still felt the emptiness of trying. Her heart had been badly damaged, whether or not she'd ever let anyone glimpse the truth. And when she'd talked about living with choices, I felt that she was sharing the smallest corner of something with me, a secret sorrow, a regret. She was a stronger woman than I was by a mile, the strongest woman I knew or could even imagine. She lived truly, and with dignity. And she slept alone.

★　★　★

The next morning Ernest and Ivens headed to Hollywood to show the film everywhere they could possibly drum up support, and I went to Connecticut to plot a novel about the war with a heroine who was a lot like me, only wiser with her heart. But before I could even properly dig in, an editor at *Collier's* reached me with news. They were going to publish the article I'd written in Madrid. Millions would read my piece, and see what I had seen.

That night I called my mother, crowing my elation and feeling with every cell in my body that I'd been saved.

'You're a real journalist, then,' she said.

'Yes. They've also promised to consider anything else if I wanted to go back under their moniker.'

'You want to go back.'

I heard the distress in her voice and rushed ahead. 'If you could only know what the people are like. How bravely they're fighting, and how everyone is working together. I'm not sure anything like this war has ever happened. I have to be there.'

'You'll go alone?' I hadn't told her about

168

Ernest outright, but his name had peppered every letter I'd sent from Spain, and she was no fool.

'I'm not sure.'

'Well, I trust that you'll know what's right for you.'

Her words echoed what Mrs. Roosevelt had told me. I wanted to believe both of them, but frankly I was already in over my head. Perhaps Ernest's marriage meant, as I'd said, that there was no cliff to fling myself from. But what did that matter when love itself was an ocean, and you could drown in even a teacup of it?

For the moment, I focused on what I did know. '*Collier's* is sending me credentials and my correspondent's badge, and everything. It's exciting, Mother. I know you're worried, but this is just what I've wanted. Please be happy for me?'

'Of course I will be. I am.'

As soon as I hung up with my mother, I wanted to call Ernest and tell him about *Collier's*. He'd believed in me from the beginning. Whatever else had happened between us, or not, he'd encouraged my work and seen potential in me as a journalist long before I had. I also wanted to tell him about going back to Madrid, of course, because as complicated as everything was now, the truth was that I couldn't even imagine being in Spain without him. I stood there for a long time, holding the receiver, listening to the hum going out in all directions to no one. Then I put it softly in its cradle, and went for a long walk instead, hoping to clear my head even a little.

*   *   *

Within twenty-four hours, almost as if Ernest had been reading my mind or could feel my dilemma in the air like a storm, a cable came. Hollywood had lit up for the film. Celebrities had thrown fistfuls of money after them wherever they went, and already they'd raised twenty thousand dollars. THAT'S 20 AMBULANCES UP AND ROLLING ON THE FRONT LINE IN FEW WEEKS' TIME, he wrote. JUST ARRANGED TO GO BACK 17 AUGUST FROM NY ON USS CHAMPLAIN. YOU'LL COME TOO ON DIFFERENT BOAT. SAY YES.

# 23

I met Ernest in Paris, at the Café de la Paix, one afternoon in late August. He'd found Matthews and brought him along, and we fell on each other in a crush, talking over each other and taking in each other's faces and smiling like crazy. We ordered two-dozen oysters for the table and enough red wine to choke an ox and stayed there, shoulder to shoulder, long past the time when the waiters and everyone else wanted us to leave.

This time, when we made for Spain, there was no caravanning or walking down cold dirt roads, but civilized transport, ever efficient. Once we reached the border at Andorra, we boarded a small plane loaded with supplies and bound for Valencia, first, and then to the Loyalist offensive at the Aragon front. The lion's share of Spain was in Franco's control now. Bilbao had fallen, and San Sebastian, and all the Basque territory to the west. There were still a few small victories for our side, costly ones. In recent fighting below Zaragoza, the Loyalists had managed to liberate the city of Belchite — what was left of it.

The smoke hadn't yet cleared when we arrived there. It clouded the ruins of the city with a haze that lent a dreamlike quality to what you were seeing. And what you were seeing was mostly terrible. The Loyalists had won this battle, and now the dead needed to be dug out of the rubble, often by hand. Men needed to take the bodies to a place and line them up, waiting for the trenches to be carved out, big enough to hold them. At one place the dead were piled eight feet high, with wretchedly stricken faces, dusty feet, and hands that stuck out at unnatural angles. And the smell, the smell was something I hoped I wouldn't remember later when I tried to write about this day. It made me feel sick and terrified and small — and glad I wasn't alone.

On the narrow streets, shelling had loosed the houses from their stone moorings. They listed and tipped toward one another. We walked through searing late-summer sunlight, through air that was thick and orange with dust. Bits of paper flew around us and we had to step over things — shutters ripped from windows, a crushed bicycle. Café chairs reduced to kindling. In the center of the road, I saw a heavy black sewing machine on its side, as if it had crawled out into the street to die.

Robert Merriman was still standing, somehow. Back home he'd been a history professor at Berkeley, but here he was chief of staff for the Fifteenth Brigade, and had led this final assault. Half-a-dozen times he'd taken grenade flak to his face and neck and hands, but seemed mostly to ignore his wounds, which looked jagged and brutal to me, like raw meat. In the hospital tent, he told us how he and his men had marched from Quinto and sometimes belly crawled to encircle Belchite with their bodies and a sheer force of will, moving toward the center of the city.

'It was house to house,' he told us, his clothing still blackened with soot and smoke and dust. 'House to house, bombing our way forward. We had to take the cathedral was all I could think.'

'You left some blood along the way,' Ernest said, his look full of a deep respect.

'Almost nothing. The boys did their best. They were wonderful.'

We could see that for ourselves, too. They had fought with everything they had and now were looking after their dead with an attention that was almost sacred. Down the hill along a narrow, shallow stream, some soldiers had stripped to the waist and were trying to rinse the blood and dirt from their faces and hands. They were American. I could hear Ohio and New Jersey and California in their voices, and while Ernest went on talking to Merriman, the two of them wrapped up in mutual admiration and memories of battles past, I walked down to the river where one young man stood a little apart.

It only took us a few moments to realize we were both from the same neighborhood in St. Louis, and that his mother had been a patient of my father's. When I asked him what he missed most about home, he didn't hesitate.

'Creve Coeur. Just before I sailed, my girl and I had a picnic there, right down by the lake. We sat there all day.'

'That's one of my best places, too. You know the waterfall? Under the weeping willow?'

'Yes.' His face seemed to register a hundred emotions at once. 'That was our spot.'

I had to smile, because I could see it, all of it,

173

on the best brightest day of the year, the sun like melted butter, my mother near me in tall grass, thousands of insects stirring the air. 'You'll go back.'

'Sure, I will.'

'You will,' I insisted. 'You'll go on a perfect spring day with egg-salad sandwiches and lemonade in a basket. Maybe you'll pick some lilies of the valley. That's what I'd do.'

'I should have asked her to marry me,' he said, and his eyes clouded over.

'You still can. Do it with those flowers. She's going to say yes.'

His lip trembled. 'That's a nice picture.'

'It's not just a picture,' I insisted, hoping with everything I had that I was right, and that he would get there in one piece, and claim his happy ending. 'It's the truth.'

When I walked back to the hospital tent a short while later, I felt a strange mingling of happiness and sadness, and remembered something my father had told me once, lifting a human skull that sat propped on one of the bookshelves in his medical office.

'These bones more than any other separate us,' he said, cradling the skull in his palms. 'We can never really know each other, never reach each other, though we try.'

I must have had doubts even then about his kernels of wisdom, but now it struck me clearly that I'd learned all sorts of things, things he didn't know. How we were all connected. How personal this life was, and how every time we grazed against one another even for a moment, we weren't the same afterward.

'Where did you go?' Ernest asked when I reached him.

'To St. Louis.'

He thought I was making a joke. 'All the way there, eh?'

'It's nearer than you think.'

# 24

In Madrid, we took our same rooms at the Florida and fell into our old routine as if we'd never been away. Ernest and I became lovers again without speaking a word. He never said Pauline's name, nor did I. Letters from her and his three sons littered his desk, and he never tried to hide them. They were there to remind me of the limit he'd set when he cabled, the one we never mentioned or looked at directly. YOU'LL COME TOO ON DIFFERENT BOAT. SAY YES.

I had said yes. And yes always came with a price.

★   ★   ★

Still, there was this, there was now. Bolting toward the Telefónica in the evening to post my dispatches, shells whizzing by my head, my eyes on my feet and the dusty road and nothing else. My editor at *Collier's* had cabled to tell me how good my work was, and that they were adding my name to the masthead. We celebrated at Chicote's and then at Gaylord's, with terrible sherry and then even-more-terrible gin. Later, whoever was still around headed to Ernest's room to eat something warming out of a can, oily sardines with their salted sea taste, potato soup, beans, corned beef. Coffee thinned with evaporated milk that clung to the side of the enamel cup. The tin opened with a penknife.

As it grew late, we talked about Hollywood, whatever gossip we could glean, or what we could invent. We almost never spoke about what had happened that day. Not the brigades, the offensive, the mud, the smoke. Not the battlefield where bodies were waxen with rain. Not the city reduced to rubble, or the house that had been there just the morning before, now a pile of bricks and splintered wood. Not the glass and rags and paper and plaster crushed to paste and white dust.

Just after midnight, we heard the shelling begin, like clockwork. Ernest rose from where he was sitting on his bed and opened the row of windows so they wouldn't break. I got up and went to the small gramophone Ernest kept in the corner and wound the crank and heard Chopin flare up. The first few bars of the Mazurka in C Major.

'I love this song,' Matthews said. He sat hugging his knees, looking very young and hopeful.

'It's not a war song,' Ernest said.

'Exactly,' Matthews replied.

'I want to hear it again,' I said.

'It's still playing,' Ernest said with a half smile.

'Yes, and when it's finished, I want it again.'

★   ★   ★

One night a group of us got to talking about what came next. I could scarcely stand to think

177

about leaving Madrid and what that meant, but Ernest seemed to be half packed already. His new novel, *To Have and Have Not*, was about to be released, and he was anticipating the sales figures and notices.

'The reviews have to be better this time,' he said.

He meant better than those for *Green Hills of Africa*, the long nonfiction account of his safari trip to Kenya, which had as many literary references in its pages as hunting stories. I'd read some of those notices, too, and still remembered how John Chamberlain had ridiculed the book in the *Times*, 'Thus Mr. Hemingway murders one whooping crane and the symbolism of *Moby-Dick* in the same motion.' I was already so loyal to Ernest's work then, I'd silently fumed for him, incensed.

'At least no one ignores your books,' Matthews said. 'That's what most writers face, isn't it?'

'Almost all of them, actually,' I agreed. 'You write, desperate to publish something so you can write something else. Then nothing sells and no one reads you, and you realize you're chasing yourself backward down a hole.'

'There's journalism for security now that you have *Collier's* on your side,' Ernest pointed out. 'It's always worked for me.'

'We're not in the same situation at all. Here I have the chance to write something meaningful, but back home I'll just be offered the 'woman's angle' again. You'll always have choices.' I heard the edge in my voice, but couldn't stop. 'You'll never write a book that isn't a bestseller, no matter what the notices say.'

'Haven't I earned that?' His eyes held a challenge, and suddenly I realized we were actually talking about the future, how his was as bright as it had ever been, and mine was full of uncertainty. *To Have and Have Not* was his title? Yes, that about said everything.

'What do you want to do?' Matthews asked me, wisely trying to change the subject.

'An agency wrote me about doing some lectures for Spain in the States. There's a whopping fee, and I'd be helping, too.'

'You're joking,' Ernest said.

'Why shouldn't I say yes?'

'No reason.' His voice had gone eerily flat. 'If you don't mind money-grubbing, there isn't any problem, is there?'

I blinked at him a moment, not quite believing the mood could turn so quickly. He was speaking to me as if we were adversaries, not friends. Certainly not lovers.

'Why pretend to be honorable at all?' he went on. 'A whore in wartime is still a whore, isn't she?'

Matthews shot me a look, but it was too late. Without thinking, I slapped him.

Ernest's eyes glittered as if he had succeeded at something or were daring me to do it again. Instead, I turned on my heel and raced out of the bar, not stopping until I was behind my own door. I didn't bother turning on the light, just poured myself a drink and worked at it shakily until I heard his knock at the door.

'Marty, open up. Let me in.'

I sat still as a stone on the edge of my bed. I wasn't going to him or even considering it after that little show. But then his voice came louder. He began to bang on the door, shouting my name, and I understood that in his current state he couldn't be bothered with tact or caution.

'Stop,' I hissed, swinging open the door, but he wasn't near finished. He began spitting insults at me. He told me he'd thought I was a real writer, but now it was clear that I was only after experience. I had probably been using him this whole while.

'I'm using *you*?' I swung for him again, unable to stop myself. He blocked my arm with his own and sent the lamp crashing across the floor. It exploded into dozens of shards while we stood looking at it and at each other, both of us frightened, I think, at how much we could stir in the other in no time at all.

'I think I should go,' he said.

I only stood there fuming, shock waves continuing to pulse in the room.

★   ★   ★

The next day I woke feeling like concrete had been poured over my shoulders and neck. I forced myself out of bed and out of the hotel, and spent the day touring Madrid with a small team of architects and stonemasons who were determining what was salvageable in the buildings that had been shelled. They examined foundations, measured the damage, and considered the risks.

I was doing the same, of course, still seething about things Ernest had said. How could I possibly be using him, unless he meant that I was a mercenary climber, a career girl. The thought made me feel numb and murderous simultaneously, and I had no one but myself to blame.

★   ★   ★

'We've got to end this now,' I said to Ernest when we were alone in his room after dinner.

'This is about last night. I'm sorry, Marty. I don't know what got into me.'

'It doesn't matter. I told myself I'd never be in this situation again.'

'Me too. It's funny how some people never learn. I wish my conscience wasn't so sharp, and that I had a terrible memory. I'd sleep a damned sight better.'

'I'm not built for forgetting,' I said. 'I never was.'

'What are you built for?'

'I'm doing my best to figure that out. And making a mess of it, too.'

He was quiet. So quiet I thought I could hear shadows tick in their corners. 'I wish I could marry you. I would, you know. I don't think there's another woman like you anywhere.' His voice was low, and then it fell away and the room was still again and I almost couldn't bear it. The truth was I had imagined the possibility many times. I had conjured a place for us off the map somewhere, an oasis where we would write and

181

talk of books, make love, and drink sherry and sleep in the sun. But that was a fantasy, and marriage as a thing whispered in the dark while he was married to someone else was even less than that. Less than a cloud. A dream. A mirage.

He belonged to Pauline, and I had never belonged to anybody.

'I should go,' I said.

'Please don't run out on me. I love you, and I know you love me, too.'

'I wish I didn't.' My throat felt tight with held-in tears. 'Love doesn't solve anything. It's not an answer. It's not some bright beacon showing us the way. It's not any of that.'

'No. No, it isn't. But what else do we have?'

He kissed me, and I couldn't breathe. *Nothing*, I wanted to shout at him, but that was already understood.

# 25

Sometimes the only antidote for pain is more of it. In our last few weeks in Madrid, we made love every day, sometimes twice a day, desperately, trying to push through each other to what couldn't be gotten at. His bed was an operating table, and this was heart surgery. It was awful. It was over too quickly.

'Tell me something,' I said quietly, not looking at him. The night was so still I could hear the blood tunneling through my body, the stopping and starting of each breath. Over our heads, the walls touched lightly as the corners of a picture frame. 'Tell me anything.'

He nodded his great square head against the crumpled pillowcase, and then lay quietly. Finally he said, 'Today I was thinking how wonderful it would be if we could wake up in Paris.' His voice seemed to fall to the back of his throat. The sheet was wound around part of his chest and twisted like a tourniquet. 'We should have years in an apartment in Saint-Germain with almost no space but wonderful light. But we'll never have Paris. Not the way we should.'

'We won't have Nice or St. Moritz either,' I said, catching on. This was a game of loss. We were giving the future away in bright fistfuls. 'All those champagne cocktails with slivers of pink fruit. Or Monaco. We definitely won't ever have Monaco.'

'Or Cuba. You should see Havana, the colors of the buildings, and the Morro and the Gulf Stream. I'd show you how to make a proper daiquiri with plenty of lime with no sugar and we'd stay up all night under the palms in a warm wind.'

I was quiet for a moment, only watching the high ceiling painted with cracks that day by day would stretch wider. Time would have its way with everything, because that's what had always happened and always would, out into infinity. But we were doing something else. We were wrenching ourselves free. Throwing love into the fire before the flames could rise and take it.

'We won't ever have a house together with two good armchairs side by side and loads of books,' he said.

'We won't have mornings of lazing in bed in our pajamas. We won't have anything regular happy people do. Not years to know everything about each other. Not children.'

He nodded soberly and then said, 'Sometimes it feels as if we've already lived out a lifetime together. Because we never will. I don't expect you to understand.'

But I did understand. It was how I felt about what was happening all around me. Spain was falling and we were falling with it. But the loss came with moments of incredible happiness, and the feeling of being seen and understood, of being found. There might be no future, no future at all, but time had sharpened into an unforgettable point. And that was a version of forever. That might be the only version of forever worth reaching for.

No matter what else happened going forward, Ernest and Madrid and this awful, marvelous war were tangled up together inside me, like the story of my own life.

I wouldn't keep them; I couldn't. But they were mine.

# 26

Teruel was colder than anywhere else he'd been in Spain, with snow blowing sideways, and a wind that shrieked like a wounded animal. From behind stacked boulders, frigid as steel to the touch, Ernest crouched with Matthews and Delmer and watched the Loyalist forces bear down. The first target was Muela, 'the Tooth,' a jagged and strange-looking hill outside the village, which was rigged with mines and tank traps and flanked heavily by the Nationalist troops, but hopefully not for long.

This was a surprise offensive from the Loyalist side that had been a long time coming. It wouldn't end quickly either, not in this storm. It was so cold that sometimes, as the assault went on punishingly, they had to duck into a railway car inside an abandoned tunnel for a nip of brandy and to feel their hands again. It was almost bearable there, away from the wind. There was a burlap sack of frozen oranges. To eat them, you had to hold the fruit over an open fire, feeling it going soft in your palm. Afterward, when they headed back to the ridge and their position, he could smell the citrus oil on his hands, and taste the singed sugar of the orange on his tongue, and it was almost better than the brandy, but not quite.

On the fourth day of the offensive, the Loyalists finally liberated Teruel, and he and

Matthews and Delmer had gotten to ride into the village in the convoy of tanks and trucks. Ernest had never seen surrender before and wasn't sure it looked much like victory at first. The people in the town came out of their houses slowly, looking confused and terrified, but when it dawned on them that they weren't going to be shot, they began to thump the soldiers on the back. An old woman brought out a ceramic pitcher full of tangy Rioja she'd made herself and poured it into any available cup, smiling a beautifully toothless smile.

★　★　★

After the surrender, Ernest went to Barcelona to have Christmas dinner with Marty. She was sailing home the next day, and he had no idea what to say to her. They'd said so much already, and nothing helped soften the fact that they were both headed away from each other, possibly forever. So he held her. He braided his hands under her hair, breathing her in. He said goodbye very softly against her neck. He said it five times, or six times, and still it took everything to let her go.

In Paris a week later, on his own way home, he found Fife waiting for him at the Hotel Elysees. It was blizzarding outside nearly as badly as it had been in Teruel, and Fife was on edge because she'd been there for days, sending cable after cable to Madrid, where she thought he was, and growing more and more distraught. As soon as he really looked into her eyes, he

187

knew why she'd come. Lots of people passing through Madrid on their way to New York had big mouths and narrow consciences. She'd no doubt heard rumors swirling. It didn't really matter who'd done the talking, because Fife knew, and now before him there was a battle needing to be played out, and his hand was being forced. In a way, the battle had already started without him, because she'd had the whole of her passage over to think of how she'd confront him and was so jangly now she reminded him of frayed wire.

Would he confess it? she wanted to know. If not, she was going to throw herself from the balcony.

Ernest was standing by the bed when Fife made her threat. He watched her open the French doors and then climb up onto the wrought-iron railing in her stockings. The snow fell thick and fast, and clung to her dark hair. Her eyes were wounded and wild and he felt pinned and wrecked simultaneously. He didn't think she would really jump, but who knew what anyone was capable of when you got down to it. Hadn't his own life proven that, if nothing else?

There was a long moment as Fife tottered there, not crying, not saying terrible things anymore, but simply waiting for his move. Either they faced off for a very few seconds, or it was years and years, but either way he found he could only plunge ahead with his lie. She'd gotten it all wrong, he swore. Someone had been telling awful tales, but the girl in question was only a friend, a trench buddy.

188

'A trench buddy?' Fife sneered. 'You don't think I know who we're talking about? She's too young for you. And anyway, I don't even think she's very talented.'

He remembered the night at Whitehead Street when they had all been in the garden together, talking over drinks. Whoever those people were, they had nothing to do with this moment. He stood fast and held his grip on the lie. And slowly, though her eyes had never softened, she'd climbed down from the rail and crossed to the bathroom and washed her face and changed for bed, and come out calmly, like a child, and crawled under the duvet and gone to sleep.

The next day was strained, and the one after that. He felt rotten and went to see a doctor, who told him he was in bad shape and his liver was, too, and that he needed to stop drinking altogether or at least half of what he took in now. He put him on something called Chophytol, which tasted bitter as hell but was supposed to clean him up, and something else called Drainochol, which was worse still. Somehow Fife had decided to believe him, at least on the surface. Whatever she was thinking, they lingered in Paris for twelve days in a deadly quiet truce, and then sailed for home on the Gripsholm through lurching weather. It was more than ironic that this was the very same ship they had booked for their Africa trip four years earlier. Nothing could have been more different now, particularly inside his head.

In their cabin, Fife took to bed with seasickness while up on deck he let the wind rail at him and the salt spray come like a slap with the wind, and wondered how he'd get out of this mess, or even through the night, since what he really needed but couldn't have was a god-damned drink or six.

That theory of God never giving you more than you could handle was about the wrongest thing he'd ever heard. If he were really smart, he'd just throw himself overboard and be done with it, because he wasn't only carrying more than he could properly manage, but also had gotten turned around and was headed backward through his own life. How else could you look at it when this had already happened years ago, except with Hadley?

Fife had to be feeling all that, too. She had to be, since she was the other woman then, and had set out to win him no matter what it took or whom she crossed. Whatever moral accounting she was doing now, he had to leave her to it. He had his own accounting to do, and very few answers. If this same awful story could happen to him twice, there might be something twisted up in him, possibly from the beginning. His mother and father had ruined him good, or he'd ruined himself. Either he couldn't be happy with just one woman or he hadn't found the right one yet.

Who could say, really? Who, when you got right down to it, knew a goddamned thing about love?

# 27

My speaking tour was supposed to be about the lessons of war. That's what I believed I had said yes to. But when I flung myself back to the States with force and launched state to state by train, zigzagging the country wildly and doing twenty-two lectures in one month, I realized that no one wanted to hear me praise the volunteers of the International Brigades for their dignity and nobility. They didn't want to hear me call Franco a butcher and a lunatic, or question America's position of neutrality. They didn't, in a word, want the truth.

Lecturing was the loneliest sort of business, I soon discovered. City after city, I talked out at rows and rows of people who never talked back. I had one hour and one hour only to distill everything I'd learned and say it fast, and passionately enough that it would wake them up to what was happening in the world. I couldn't stop feeling desperate and hysterical, but my audiences only nodded at everything, tucking my warnings into their handbags. When they shook my hand afterward, they told me I was inspiring, but I'd meant to terrify them. The situation in Spain was dire, and if things didn't turn somehow, and very soon, war would likely be coming for us all. And yet here they were chewing watercress sandwiches and then carefully reapplying their lipstick.

I wanted to scream, but who would hear me? With each engagement, the stakes seemed that much higher, and my energy that much more frenetic and despairing. I lost fourteen pounds because food had become sand. I couldn't sleep a wink and took to calling my mother late at night, threatening to quit the tour.

'Gellhorns don't back out of contracts, Martha,' she insisted. 'You'll find a way through.'

But I couldn't. In the end I forfeited my fees, most of which I'd meant to send to Spain, and made plans to go to Barcelona alone, borrowing money to do so. Each day's news from Spain was more sickening. Franco's army was bearing down on the Mediterranean, bent on severing Barcelona from Valencia and Madrid. Heinkels pounded the cities ceaselessly with bombs until the streets ran with blood. The Loyalist army was retreating on almost every front, with long convoys of refugees in its wake. Orphans filled the hospitals, long past tears, past wailing, their black eyes empty and haunted.

The next great war was racing toward us at terrifying speed, and Spain was on its knees. I felt so desperate and heartbroken, wrung out and diminished, that I found myself writing to Ernest. I sent a cable not to the Key West house but to Sloppy Joe's, his favorite Conch bar, sure it would find him, and it did.

'One last time,' I told him when he reached me by phone in St. Louis. 'It's all going to hell and we have to be there.' I heard my voice shaking and thought I would surely frighten him. I was frightening myself. I had sheaves of arguments at the ready, and wasn't at all above pleading.

But he only said, 'When you land in Barcelona, send word back and I'll find you.'

Instantly I felt steadier. My heart stopped thundering. I could breathe again. 'All right,' I told him. 'I will.'

'And Marty?'

'Yes?'

'When this is all over, come with me to Cuba. All the countries we really care about are going to come crashing down. Nothing will be the same soon.'

I'd worn myself so thin and ragged the tears came easily. 'We said we'd never have Cuba.'

'We were just trying to be brave, weren't we? I don't know that I can live without you is the thing.'

He'd knocked me sideways. Of course I felt the same, I had for a long time, but what did any of it mean, the wishing? The wanting? He wasn't offering a promise because he couldn't. 'It's hard to think ahead, now,' I told him. 'It's hard to believe that anything could be good again. When the war really does come for everyone, it's going to be the most awful and horrific thing imaginable. You've read what they're saying about Hitler these days. He's worse than Franco, even.'

'That's why we'd be wrong to do anything but bank on each other. You're the strongest woman I know. Who else would I want in the foxhole?'

I was too raw to answer him. We rang off soon after, and I lit a cigarette nervously, running my mind over the edges of what he'd said. *Cuba.* *Together.* What could be more impossible than that combination of words? *Happiness* and *peace*, maybe. The future and us in it, tucked safely inside.

# Part 4

# FOXHOLES

## FEBRUARY 1939-JANUARY 1940

# 28

The moment I stepped off the ferry in Havana, blinding outrageous sunlight flooded in from everywhere, splashing bright heat over my sandals and the tops of my shoulders, piercing through my white blouse as though it were nothing. Maybe it was nothing, here. Maybe the sun and the sea could melt through anything — my exhaustion and fear and heartbreak — leaving me clean and patched in the hurt places, able to go on.

I was counting on it. The past year had been hell. We'd gone back one last time, to Barcelona as it fell. Eighteen raids in forty-eight hours leveled the city, and still the bombers came, strafing anything in their path. The refugees were numberless, and they were starving. Most carried some small bundle with them, which amounted to all they owned now. And it was shocking to think that after such a prolonged and valiant struggle, they would end up so reduced and so hopeless. Countryless.

For six weeks, Ernest and Tom Delmer and I reported on the losses and the changing battle lines, traveling in caravans along roads full of retreating troops and families; farmers with oxen that looked beaten to the core. One night we heard and then saw thirty Italian bomber planes carving up the sky, louder than anything should be. We ran from the car and threw ourselves into the ditch. Crouching there, Ernest gripped my hand hard. We locked eyes for a moment, wondering if this might be the end, but they only screamed over us on the way to Tortosa. Looking up, I thought they were like brutal silver Valkyries bent on absolute destruction. This whole war had probably been futile from its beginning, but its ideals had been only beautiful. Whatever came next was going to be so awful I couldn't let myself imagine it.

When the Fascists finally reached the sea, we watched the wounded spill in an endless wave over the French border, and while I wanted to weep for every last one of them, Ernest got to work. He reached out to the American ambassador in France, asking for an evacuation plan for Americans. The British navy was drawn in to dispatch rescue ships to Spanish ports because we knew that as the Republican government crumbled Franco's troops would begin capturing, imprisoning, and even executing Americans caught behind enemy lines.

I had never seen Ernest act more tirelessly or selflessly. He helped raise money for those who'd been crippled and wounded, and when *Collier's* cabled that they were sending me on assignment, Ernest stayed behind, pitching in to help anyone in a tight spot. He hopped aboard a boat heading up the Ebro River, where groups of soldiers from the International Brigades had been stranded, sending word every few days from places that were like diminishing levels of Dante's inferno. I worried for him, but it helped that we were in constant contact now, not pretending we could bear anything else.

I spent almost a year crisscrossing through Europe on my own, writing steadily for *Collier's*, taking the pulse of nations on the brink of war. It was June of '38 when I left Paris for Prague. A little over two months before, Hitler had marched into Austria and claimed it for Germany. Now the same fate seemed more than likely for the Sudeten-German part of Czechoslovakia.

I went to all the frontiers, feeling worse and worse for Czechoslovakia's future. The small country was home to more than three million Sudeten Germans and surrounded on three sides by the German Reich. Hitler was putting pressure on the Czech president, Edvard Beneš, to concede. Meanwhile, Beneš was appealing to France and to England for aid in his struggle, while everywhere the mood seemed as dire as that of an operating theater with no ether being offered, not for any money.

The piece I wrote I titled 'Come Ahead Hitler!' meant to sound a loud warning to my American readers that war in Europe was on its way — not an *if*, but a *when*. Then I went to England, and on to France, hoping they would come to Czechoslovakia's aid while there was still time. But everywhere I went, there seemed to be a maddening level of denial and complacency. That actual war could come to them directly was inconceivable, I heard over and over, a song that was being sung even more loudly by British prime minister Neville Chamberlain.

While I was still in England, the Munich Pact was signed and Czechoslovakia was finished. I hurried back to Prague to find the border thick with Nazis. In another week, eleven thousand square miles of territory had been devoured, becoming the Sudetenland. Chamberlain and French prime minister Daladier had essentially hand delivered an entire country to the wolves. I could barely breathe to think of it.

I wrote another piece I called 'Obituary of a Democracy,' about what I'd seen, Jews fleeing for their lives from Germany to Austria, Austria to where now? The Czechs I'd seen beaten to their knees in Nazi-occupied Prague, the haunted-eyed children walking the streets alone, their parents already disappeared into labor camps. Nothing and no one could save any of them now. When I filed the piece, I was sure *Collier's* wouldn't use it, but they did. By the time it saw print, I was finished with Europe, swearing I would never go back. I wrote a long letter to my mother and also one to Eleanor Roosevelt, just trying to get some of it out of my head, the horrors of Kristallnacht, the cowardice I saw everywhere, the corruption, the helplessness, the anguish, the despair. I only felt very sick and weary now. I had no optimism left. I didn't know what to believe in anymore. 'I'll never regret Spain, though,' I told them both. 'It's the one thing I'm still grateful for.'

Then I fled.

# 29

Cuba had been Ernest's private hideaway for many years. When things in Key West grew too hot or his wife and family too demanding, he escaped on his beloved *Pilar* to the Ambos Mundos in Havana to write. Actually, he kept rooms at two different hotels, working at the Ambos and sleeping and collecting his mail at the Sevilla-Biltmore so that he wasn't entirely findable on any given day or night, not if he didn't want to be.

I wasn't at all comfortable with the symbolism of this arrangement. He had two lives and seemed to function well that way, or perhaps even preferred it. Which left me where, exactly?

Since Barcelona, when I'd given up trying to stay away or be sensible, and let myself dive into loving him, with all the prevailing risks and uncertainties, I had been trying to get a straight answer from him about Pauline. One day he'd tell me he meant to break from her soon, that he was committed to marrying me and bringing his boys to live with us. The next, he'd stall out, seeming confused and asking for more time. I had never seen him be passive about anything, and it terrified me.

'She knows I'm here, doesn't she?' I asked him just after I arrived in Cuba that February 1939. 'She has to.'

He shrugged, only half meeting my eyes. 'I

understand how awful this is for you, Rabbit, but it's going to sort itself out soon. I promise.'

'Rabbit' was a new nickname he was trying on me. We were trying it on each other, just as we were trying on this vague, unpredictable kind of love. All the right words were being said, except in limbo. Why did anything have to sort *itself* out, when he could turn at any moment to face the matter head-on? I didn't understand why he felt so stuck, so without options when the options seemed obvious.

'It *is* awful, actually. It feels like you don't want to make a choice between us.'

'That's not true. I'm only worried this is all going to be hell for the boys. Things have been one way for a long time. They like routine, even when no one's happy. At least they know what to expect then.'

'It's always hard to lose anything,' I said. Privately, I wondered if he wasn't talking about his own need for routine as much as theirs. Maybe this was a part of our being stuck in no-man's-land. He loved me, but he had also had Pauline and his sons and Whitehead Street in the picture for so long that perhaps he couldn't even imagine moving past them toward another life.

'If this divorce takes a long time and things go dark for a while, I hope you don't give up on me,' he said.

'Don't give up on me, either. I have just as much to lose.' *Even more*, I didn't say.

★　★　★

202

At least it was warm in purgatory. In the harbor, bright fishing boats danced and bobbed in deep-blue chop. There was a coarse beauty in the disintegrating seawall of the Malecón and the weathered strings of trawling nets, and in the crumbling old buildings along the bay in shades of melting ice cream.

Ernest was eager to show me everything, starting with the Floridita, his favorite bar in Havana, where we sat on corner stools at the bar and drank half-a-dozen daiquiris, cold and tart with a lot of good Cuban rum in them.

They seemed like a wonderful idea at the time, but the next day I woke late, my body overheated and snarled in the sheets. Ernest was gone — because it was morning, and unless the world had somehow tumbled from its axis, he worked every morning — and I was alone at the Sevilla.

I hadn't paid much if any attention to the room the night before, but now with the sun piercing through the wooden shutters, it was utterly unavoidable. Ernest was a pig. Everywhere I looked there was clutter, chaos, damp towels, debris. On top of the bureau, an open tackle box spilled lures over a pile of soiled shirts and socks. Every other available flat surface was covered with newspapers and darkened coffee cups, laundry, and tented books and scraps of food. Just as he had in Spain, he kept a larder in his room — tins of sardines and peaches, overripe bananas, hard cheese, half-empty bottles of red table wine. The habit had made sense in Madrid, where the siege had made even bread and beans hard to come by, but here it felt like laziness, plain and simple.

Sighing, I tried to get out of bed and nearly stumbled over a large cured ham that was only loosely covered in cheesecloth. Ham, on the floor. That was the last straw. It didn't matter how ill I felt, my head full of cotton and droning bees, I had to get out of there. Digging to find some aspirin tablets and space enough to bathe, I tidied myself up as well as I could, threw on a white skirt and espadrilles and sunglasses, and headed out to find some dense Cuban coffee, and some peace.

★　★　★

'You aren't really proposing we live in that hotel together,' I said to Ernest later, once he'd finished work for the day. We were in a café, and he was shoveling in smoked trout and onions and bread and wine and hard, sharp Spanish cheese. Still green to the gills, I could barely stomach a boiled egg and toast.

'Why not? It's not so different from Madrid and you didn't seem to mind then.'

'I did mind, though, and that was war.'

'We'll have the maid come more often.'

'She can take away the newspapers, but it will still reek of meat in there, and baitfish. And stale ashtrays. I want a real place.'

'This is fine for a while, isn't it? You don't have to have everything scrubbed with Dutch cleanser for you to be happy, do you? Nothing's clear about money right now, anyway. What if Fife fights me for everything I've got?'

I felt myself flinching at his nickname for Pauline, but knew better than to mention it. What could I possibly say? When you took away geography and hope, she was still very much his wife. 'I'm not unusually clean, you know,' I told him. 'I'm as tidy as any normal person.'

'I see. And I'm unusually, abnormally untidy. Is that where this is going?'

But I didn't want to quarrel or be baited. 'Listen. I've come halfway around the world to be here, and none of it's on my terms. I can't just sit waiting for you in the corner of a hotel room, don't you see?'

'You'll be writing.'

'I need a space of my own. I'm prepared to pay for more. I'll do all the looking, too. You don't have to think of it at all.'

★   ★   ★

I began my search the next day, and instantly felt better, just to be exercising any degree of control over my fate. I hired an agent, who showed me a string of small, acceptable houses in town, with neatly swept verandas and tiled breakfast rooms, and yards shaded with banyan trees. Some were even charming, but I felt nothing for any of them until we drove out of central Havana, past the dirty and smoke-encrusted parts of town that seemed to have been forgotten by everyone, and then up into the hills toward San Francisco de Paula, with its one dusty street of tiny shops and tumbledown fruit stands. Finally we stopped on a rounded sort of hill in front of a creaky, rusted gate with a chain. Beyond the chain, I saw only pure wildness. *Here?*

There were fifteen acres, the agent said, but it was hard to see much of anything with all the overgrowth. The house, when we reached it, was Spanish-style and looked abandoned. Thick vines strangled the peeling yellow shutters, parts of the roofline, and the terrace. A dilapidated tennis court sat behind, and there was a drained pool full of sand and empty gin bottles and tin cans. I should have run screaming, but the place had the feel of a fable. I couldn't say why exactly, but I had an instinct that something wonderful lay just under the surface, only lightly sleeping, like a kingdom cursed by a witch and waiting not for a prince but for me. For us.

La Finca Vigía, it was called — 'Watchtower Farm' — and no one had lived there for many years. Inside, the rooms smelled close and old and mildewy, and all the furniture needed to be burned. There were cockroaches in the kitchen, and years of dust built up, and so much to do everywhere. But if I squinted, I could picture myself writing in one of the bedrooms off the main sitting room, and Ernest hammering away at his typewriter in some other part of the house. We would be two writers under one roof, hiding away from everything but each other and our work.

'The view at least won't need repairs,' the agent said when we were behind the house on another wild terrace, gazing down the vine-matted slope toward Havana. The pink and yellow and white buildings along the waterfront were like something out of a painting, but it was the enormous ceiba tree rooted to the front steps of the house that really had my attention. It had grown up and through the foundation and now seemed firmly part of everything, body and soul. The tree had thick and fleshy leaves, so green they looked almost oily, and clusters of chestnut-colored pods. The trunk was like rhinoceros hide, thick and leathery and substantial — and everything about the tree added up to move me almost to tears, though I couldn't have explained why to anyone, not even myself.

'I'll take it,' I told the agent before reason could sink in. I meant the ceiba, but also every speck of dirt and cobweb and nest of dried leaves. Possessions had never appealed to me, and neither had permanence. But the war had forced me to rethink all sorts of things, and so had love. Time was different. Each day seemed charged and priceless now. Who knew how many years or even months anyone had left to live simply, just as they chose, with all this violence and struggle, whole countries crumbling under hate. So why not stake a claim while I still could? For myself, and also for Ernest, whether or not he understood its value yet.

★ ★ ★

The next afternoon when he was finished writing for the day I directed Ernest out of the city to take a look at the farm. I showed him the ceiba tree and all the other marvels — the slope behind the pool house that had eighteen

207

different kinds of mango trees, the sun-dazzled terrace and mimosas, and the trellis heavily bowed with fuchsia- and apricot-colored blooms — hoping he could see through the chaos to how happy we'd be here.

'There's a lot of land. But the rent's a hundred a month, you say?' He was paying just a few dollars a day in town.

'I'm writing the checks, you remember.'

'You mean *Collier's* is writing the checks.'

He was right. I'd been paid well for the pieces I'd filed from France and England and Czechoslovakia. 'You're being a mule,' I told him. 'Come look at my favorite tree in the world again.'

'What about the house?' He pointed to where the wan yellow paint was peeling in rubbery sheets to reveal the limestone beneath.

'Paint is nothing. We can choose any color we like.'

'And the pool? There must be two feet of garbage in there. It smells like hell. The tennis court looks like an earthquake socked it in the face. The well is dry. I don't know what you're thinking. We should be sprinting back to town.'

'That's just lack of care is all. No one's been here for ages. I plan to love it indecently.'

'Love has nothing to do with real estate.' He turned to walk back toward the car.

'Rabbit,' I said to his back. I was rooted to the path, my feet planted.

'Yes?' he asked without stopping.

'Let me try. I need this. I'm going to do it.'

208

# 30

In the middle of March, Ernest went back to the mainland on *Pilar* to see his family and most especially his eldest, Bumby, who was visiting over his school holiday. The moment he was out of sight, I hired workers from the village nearby, and we dug in. I decided it felt less terrifying, and less domestic, to begin outside, so the pool was unearthed first, like some ancient and derelict archaeological site. After the soil and debris were cleared away, the basin was a puzzle of jagged cracks, all needing to be patched. It seemed hopeless to me, but one day, when the structure was finally sound, and everything bleached white and painted and tiled, the workmen filled it with seawater, and I stood rooted, nearly mesmerized by the diamond glint of sunlight on the surface. It was blindingly beautiful and such an unlikely revival that it galvanized me for the work ahead.

And there was much of it. The tennis court needed reclaiming from the jungle, the vines beaten back, the bird and animal droppings shoveled away, and the entire surface and net replaced. The new surface was the shade of a well-fed flamingo, a color that made me so happy to look at I decided the house should go pink, too — a lovely soft ash pink that was like something belonging to Spain. Next, two gardeners came to liberate the terrace and tame the utter chaos of the yard little by little, bit by bit.

The place did feel truly magical. It shimmered with peace and serenity, even if I didn't yet. Once the interior of the house had been tackled, the plaster walls repaired and painted, the windows replaced, the curtains mended, I scrubbed floors with manic energy, fixing new paper to the kitchen shelves and drawers, attacking cobwebs with a stiff Cuban straw broom, while some part of me stood to one side, dizzy with fear and doubt and uncertainty — the vertigo of extreme transformation.

It wasn't at all typical, Ernest was right, for me to care about a place — an address, a plot of land. But everything had changed for me with the loss of Spain. The whole world was changing, and now the only thing that made any sense at all was to cling to anything that was good about life. A house on a hillside. A man who loved you, even if he couldn't tell you what tomorrow would bring.

More than a year had passed since Pauline had confronted Ernest in Paris about me. She had to know I was still in the picture, but she seemed determined to bury her head, to blind herself to every sign. They lived apart and called it a holiday for Ernest. A writing retreat. And he was just as culpable as she was in the lie.

All I could do was hope that at some point his central loyalty would shift to me. This house could help, I knew. If I threw everything into it, he would see how absolutely wonderful our life could be together. Two writers under one roof, hidden away from everything that no longer made sense. A home off the map, at the far side of the world. Our foxhole. The most beautiful foxhole that ever was.

★  ★  ★

I ordered a bed and table and other study furniture from a carpenter I found in the village. I brought in sheets and lamps and crockery, linen napkins and bath mats — and tried to stay focused on the tasks that needed to be accomplished, and not let myself think too much or smoke too much, or pace the terrace after dark. This had to work. It had to, so it would.

In three weeks, all the repairs were done and the workmen gone, and I was alone in the house. I poured a tall whiskey over ice and had a long bath and walked through the empty rooms in my pajamas, catching my reflection in the windows now and then and wondering, each time, for just a moment, *Who is that woman?*

This was all new, and I was shedding my skin, not quite the person I'd been before, and not yet who I wanted to be. I slept uneasily, unsure of where to rest in the large bed, and hearing the sharp almost metallic sounds of geckos chirruping in the eaves. I tossed and turned, and woke at dawn feeling thick and morose, a dark mood loitering like storm clouds. Without even making coffee, I went outside and sat on the front steps in my bare feet.

I was rarely up so early, and couldn't remember the sky ever being so pale and pearl colored and cottony. Spring heat pulsed from above and below. Great skeins of morning birds were speeding headlong over the treetops, backward and sideways, diving without fear toward their breakfast of gnats. Somehow the morning was louder than the night, here. The jungle around me seemed to exhale the sound of insects, billions and billions of them, holding up the trees invisibly with their music. The palms rattled. The round-faced spider monkeys crashed from bamboo to bamboo — and all of it was alive and insistent, hammering the same message over and over, about risk and hope, and where those two things met in me.

I was terrified of losing Ernest to Pauline — yes. I could go on gathering all the feathers for this nest only to find he didn't have it in him to leave her. I was just as terrified that even if he did finally choose me, our love wouldn't be the lasting kind. Yes, that could happen, too.

Just before me was the ceiba tree, gnarled and magnificent from every angle, old as an elephant graveyard. The tree was the keeper of the house, the witness for all that had come before. And it seemed to be saying, with its very rootedness and ancient patience, that my worries weren't extraordinary or unforgivable. This was an old story. The oldest on record. I had everything to lose, and also everything to gain — like any woman struggling with herself in love.

I went back inside, where all was clean and soothing and quiet — awash with morning sun. I brewed coffee in the new percolator, poured it into a new enamel cup, and went into the room I

212

would be using as my office. Not a single book stood on the shelf yet. I hadn't written a word in the house, not a telegram, not even a letter to my mother. In all this silence, it was up to me to sound the gong. No one else could do it for me. I pulled one of the new, stiff mahogany dining chairs over to a small table, and dug through boxes until I found paper and pencils and my typewriter. I snapped a blank page into the roller, sending a sharp report echoing through the house. The page was snowy white. It still held all of its secrets. There was nothing to do but begin.

# 31

From our back terrace at the Finca, we could look down onto Havana like minor gods from Olympus, the pale pink-yellow blur of it by day and the smear of twinkling lights after dark. No cars came by unless they were invited to come, and the quiet was like a dream, or like a spell.

I had chosen the house specifically for its distance from town. But though Ernest appreciated that, too, he insisted on keeping his writing room and mailing address at the Ambos Mundos.

'It doesn't mean anything terrible, Rabbit,' he said when I felt wounded. 'I have my habits, that's all. You've done a wonderful job with the place. I don't want to be anywhere else.'

'Good,' I told him, pushing away doubt as hard as I could. 'Neither do I.'

★ ★ ★

And so began the season of two writers writing under one roof. Ernest told Pauline he was staying in Cuba for the unforeseeable future and wasn't seeing any friends or guests. Then he put down roots made of words. He chose our bedroom for his writing space, beginning at first light each morning, at the standing desk he'd made out of a bookcase. Everything that he needed was there, well-sharpened pencils and

214

the wooden reading board he used to hold each blank page when he was writing longhand. The typewriter he turned to when things were going particularly fast and well, and the chart he always kept of each day's word count. It was a good place for him, just before the south-facing window. I would often wake and lie still for a long time with my eyes closed, listening to the rhythm of his pencil on the page, and the bees in the flowering jacaranda beyond him, dizzy with their own industry. When I rose, I didn't stop to speak to him and he didn't speak to me — something we agreed was important for mornings, and for writing.

I would pad downstairs to have coffee at my own desk, with bright sun flaring over the smooth tile floor and onto the golden wood of the new bookcase. We had hired two young boys from the village, Fico to cook, and Rene to manage the house. One or the other would leave a tray for me with a poached egg and toast, and small rounded pots of butter and fig jam. I would eat and feel warm as a cat, knowing that hours and hours stretched out in front of me.

I had returned to my notebooks and the instinct to write about Spain while it was all still fresh and sharp for me. If I could find the right characters, and a way to truly set down what I'd seen and felt in Madrid, I believed I could build on the success of my second book and maybe even make something extraordinary. Something that wouldn't dissolve with a whimper, or mock me for having literary dreams — but last, even

215

after my death, and speak the truth about this war.

I sat at my desk every day, courting inspiration, setting down hopeful sentences and bits of dialogue. 'Five-finger exercises,' Ernest called this phase of the writing process.

'Think of it that way, like piano scales,' he had explained early on, when he was still assuming the role of my teacher. 'You have to keep the muscles flexible and the mind, too, and then when something really comes, you'll be ready for it.'

I was still very much waiting for that something to take me over, and trying not to think about Ernest's marriage. Every few days, when he collected his mail, Ernest would get updates from Whitehead Street, notes from Pauline and the boys. I was dying to read hers, to know how things really stood for her, but even the idea of doing that was dangerous and self-destructive.

Meanwhile, he was on fire with a new novel. There were no five-finger exercises for him now, but rather a volcano thrusting up under the surface of everything and taking him over.

'At first I thought it was a story,' he told me late one night when we were wrapped around each other in our big good bed, my leg flung over his waist, his hands caught in my hair. 'But they're chapters. I think I've started the war novel I've meant to do. I know I have, actually. I've been worried to even say to myself what I'm up to. Something special is happening. The words keep coming, and I look up and I don't know where I am, or where I've been.'

'Really, Rabbit? That's wonderful.' It was
— for him. But terrible for me. Of course he
would be writing of Spain, too, I chided myself
in the dark. And do it better than I could ever
hope to. Jealousy came so sharply and
appallingly that I wanted to slink away under the
porch somewhere and begin to gnaw on my own
liver. I was still waiting and praying to hit on the
right story for my book, while he seemed to fall
there naturally, as if it were a God-given state of
being. *Where is my volcano?* I wanted to rail, but
couldn't. It was too small-minded, and he was
too happy. So I said, 'God, I'm thrilled for you.
Isn't that the best feeling?'

'There isn't anything better. I have the sense
there isn't a bottom to any of it. That I can just
throw my line down day after day, and the words
will be there.'

'How glorious for you.' I swallowed hard,
pinching the bitterness back, and fixed my eyes
on the shadowy ceiling. My book could still
catch fire. Any day now that could happen. 'Have
you told Max yet?'

'No, I won't for a while, either. It's all too
new.'

'I know what you mean. It's a little like
whispering in a house just after a baby is born.
You don't want to wake it up.'

'That's exactly it,' he said. 'I want the damned
thing to go on sleeping just this soundly until it's
walking.'

We weren't in competition, I tried to tell
myself. It only felt that way because we were

working in the same house, in plain sight of the other's fire pit. If it happened to be his turn to blaze now, my chance was surely coming. In the meantime, I would lean in close and warm my hands and smile for him. And love him.

# 32

June arrived with pulsing heat and the feel of storms that gathered and pressed at the edges of our view but rarely arrived. Ernest's book was coming like a freight train. He was writing as steadily and as well as he ever had, and he thought that if he could keep up this pace, he might have a finished manuscript by summer's end.

'It all happens in three days,' he said of the action. 'And yet it feels like all of history is in those days, and that Jordan is everyone who has ever lived. I made him up, but he feels more real to me than almost anyone right now.'

Robert Jordan was the novel's hero, an American munitions expert sent to blow a bridge and derail a Republican attack in the Guadarrama Mountains. I recognized immediately that he was based partly on Robert Merriman, and that the attack was a reimagining of a real battle, at La Granja, which had failed just after we'd left Spain the first time.

But that was just logistics. In the truest sense, the battle and this bridge were entirely Ernest's. The world of the book came barreling out of his imagination, so densely and fully realized that it was a bit of a shock to read his pages when he offered them, even a few at a time — like being slapped with absolute reality. I could smell the pine-needled floor of the forest, and hear the stream that ran along the side of the narrow road, and feel the sunlight as it pierced the canopy and fell on the steep mountainside. He'd put me there.

But when I went to my own desk, and tried to find my Spain, words mysteriously retreated. It should have been no strain to reach for that time. I thought of it every day, didn't I? But the sentences wouldn't come toward me when I called. I felt terrifyingly inadequate and tried not to panic.

'You know the girl Maria?' Ernest said one evening. We were on the terrace nursing a few scotches before dinner. The worst of the heat was gone, and the air was moist and heavy enough to lean on. Maybe it would rain later, or maybe it wouldn't. The result would be nearly the same.

'Yes, she's heartbreaking, isn't she? She's so wonderfully drawn, Rabbit. Really. It's magic what you can do with people.'

'She's not modeled after you exactly,' he went on. 'But she has your toughness mixed with softness. And all the stuff I write about loving someone. Well, that's you. I can only write it because I have you now.'

'Your book is going to be magnificent.'

'I have to be careful not to go too quickly, or I could lose it all.'

'You won't.' As I said it, I knew it was true. A gathering up was happening in him. Anyone could feel that, and know that something extraordinary was taking place. *He's writing the book of his life*, I thought with a start, and willed my jealousy away. 'You can't lose it. It's in you too deep for that.'

'Maybe so.' His voice softened, sounding bruised. 'I hope so.' Then he said, 'I've given Maria your hair.'

'I thought she was Spanish.'

'She is, and she has hair like a wheat field.' He sipped at his scotch, which was pale with melting ice, and said, 'She belongs to you, too. The book is ours. It's us.'

How I wanted to hold on to that, to believe it was true.

★  ★  ★

When I sat down at my desk the next morning, I realized that I had to let my own Spain idea go. If I didn't, I would always be measuring his work against mine, and coming up short. There was already enough anxiety and uncertainty in my life. I didn't need that, too. So I moved my characters to Prague instead of Madrid — and that seemed to solve something. My heroine was an American journalist very like myself, sent to write about the war only to fall hopelessly in love with a man she absolutely shouldn't want, but does. That was a story I knew, surely. And if I couldn't reach or even aspire to graze Ernest's talent with my fingertips, I could match him in terms of tenacity, and not give up on this book. Not if it took everything I had.

Real writing, I was beginning to realize, was more like laying bricks than waiting for lightning to strike. It was painstaking. It was manual labor.

221

And sometimes, sometimes if you kept putting the bricks down and let your hands just go on bleeding, and didn't look up and didn't stop for anything, the lightning came. Not when you prayed for it, but when you did your work.

# 33

All through that summer while the heat blazed and the thunderstorms crashed in and out again, and our mangoes ripened and disappeared in the night, carried off by who knows what sort of animal, we traded pages and nursed each other's ideas, and it was exactly as I'd hoped. His book was mine, and mine was his, and I felt more than I ever thought was possible — perhaps for the first time ever, truly — that I wasn't alone.

Each afternoon, when work was behind us, we played tennis on the newly resurfaced court, even in the full heat of the day, sweating out the toxins of too much thinking, and then swam until our shoulders were sore. At least one night a week, we blew off steam in Havana, settling along the bar of the Floridita, onto stools that seemed to always be waiting for us, reserved with our invisibly stenciled names. After a difficult day, it was wonderful to be in town, to see friends and be light. We loved all the little shops and cafés, the old aunties who sat on benches in their smocks and woven hats. We loved the boys with their white T-shirts and smooth dark hair, the loose way they walked, sometimes smoking, sometimes laughing, alive with youth and looking for trouble.

At dusk, *negritos* came from the cane fields in huge clouds, blurring the sky until they settled in the laurel trees on the Plaza de Armas. Their droppings painted everything that had collected beneath the trees during the day, cigarette butts and the flamed-out tips of matches, bits of paper and wrappers, and even the creamy tangle of someone's panties. Each morning, the old women would come with their straw brooms and stoop in their patient way, one square of earth at a time, and make it all new again.

★   ★   ★

We liked to walk along the Prado through Old Havana, past the strains of moody tango music from the dance clubs, the street hustlers, and the smell of rum, and the tight hollow leathery pops of the *batá* drums. We often strolled along the Malecón, too, and one evening came to a narrow and mostly bare park where a game was being played in the dimming light. A group of men faced a wall and swatted a small leather ball against it with surprising accuracy, stooping and pivoting, their feet fast and light. They seemed to be aware of one another's bodies naturally and blindly, like a kind of invisible choreography.

'It's pelota,' Ernest told me. 'A Basque game. I used to watch them play in San Sebastian. It's bloody wonderful, actually. I've heard it's the fastest game in the world.'

'Let's stay awhile. I think they're beautiful.'

They were. Running almost soundlessly along the clay, their arms swept out as if they could fly. Maybe they could.

We found a bench and watched the end of their game. There were teams, it appeared, and various ways of using the wall and bouncing the ball back to challenge the others — but all of it moved at such speed, I found myself focusing on the glowing white of their shirts, and the lightning-fast hazy shapes their arms made scooping the ball around and forward again, and on their legs, which never stopped moving, pantherlike, in the dark.

When darkness finally pushed in, and the game broke up, Ernest started a conversation with the players. There were six of them, of various heights and ages, though I guessed all were younger than Ernest, and they looked healthy and fit from the seriousness of their game. Before long we'd learned they were Basque, and that they'd come to Havana when Franco took Bilbao. They'd fought side by side in Loyalist brigades, and when Spain began to fail, to fall, they came here.

They were in exile, I understood sharply, and felt a kinship with them. Ernest and I were exiles, too, though we'd chosen it. They hadn't. 'You must miss your home very much,' I said.

'Franco took everything that was good from Spain,' said one of the players. 'How can you miss what no longer exists?' He was a little taller than the others, with a thick head of very black hair and a round face that looked ageless and untouched somehow. His name was Francisco Ibarlucia, he told us, but we should call him Paxtchi.

'What about your families?'

'We try not to speak of the past,' another man, Juan, said. 'Anyway, we are family.' He appeared

225

younger, perhaps twenty-five, with delicately drawn features and thick black eyelashes.

We told them a little of our time in Spain. They had known other journalists who had lived as we had, focused on the Republic and *la causa*, and so they seemed to understand us immediately, and we them. In the darkened street, Ernest motioned to a nearby hotel. 'Come and have a drink with us.'

'You shall drink with us,' Paxtchi said, 'it is Felix's birthday.' He gestured at a handsome young man with narrowly set black eyes and a wonderfully hooked nose. 'It's a sin not to celebrate.'

'I try to be more direct when I sin,' Ernest said cheerfully, and we followed the men to a small house off the Calle Campanario, where they all seemed to be living as one, with dozens of shoes piled by the door. It was all very snug and real — just the kind of place Ernest liked, where people lived simply. They had enough. They were together.

Off the back of the house, there was a small veranda with benches where we sat in the changing glow of candlelight while the men brought straw-bound casks of rich red wine. The casks had woven straw handles, and they had a way of hooking a finger and tipping the flask against the back of a bent arm, all in one motion, like a well-oiled dance. They managed to do it without spilling a drop.

Ernest already knew the method, had perfected it in another life, as I should have guessed. There was also *patxaran* to drink, a homemade liquor with a complex taste of blackberries and coffee and cinnamon, which we passed around, taking small thimblefuls in pinched cups. I liked it too much, and before I knew it we were all very drunk, the Basques singing mournful tunes, their voices rising and falling and running together, and then everyone growing silent while one picked up the notes and sent them out, ringing and clear.

Felix, whom everyone called Ermua, sang the truest, I thought. When I tried to tell him how wonderful he was, he shrugged and said, '*Normal, normal.*' But I thought I saw his shoulders lift perceptibly, and his eyes told me even more emphatically that he knew he had a gift, and that it was anything but ordinary.

Each of the songs sounded sad and complete and hopeful all at once, and several times I felt a ridge of gooseflesh run up my spine and the back of my neck. One must have been a favorite of everyone, because they sang it over and over. At some point, the words caught and sank in, and I began to repeat them, though the Basque syllables were as strange as the *patxaran* on my tongue.

*Baina honela*
*ez zen gehiago txoria izango*
*Baina honela*
*ez zen gehiago txoria izango*

*Eta nik,*
*txoria nuen maite*
*Eta nik eta nik,*
*txoria nuen maite*

'The word *maite*,' I guessed aloud to Ermua, when there was silence later, 'that's 'love,' isn't it?'

'It is, yes. It's a very old song, this one.' He sang a few more lines, like an angel. 'It's about a man who has lost a beautiful bird he loved and wonders if he should have cut her wings to keep her,' he continued, translating for me. 'But then he realizes she wouldn't have been the same bird if he had. In trying to keep her he would have changed her.'

'I think I've heard that story,' Ernest said wryly.

'We have all heard that story,' Paxtchi said and smiled at us like a wizard. He couldn't have been more than thirty-five, and yet it seemed as if there was already nothing he didn't know about love. Maybe it was true. Maybe, in the end, there was very little to know about anything. It seemed that way here on the veranda, where the candlelight quivered and dipped, and the wine was like cool velvet on my tongue.

I shut my eyes gently and listened as the men began singing again, letting the words fall without trying to catch them.

'You seem happy, Rabbit,' Ernest said in my ear.

'I am. I just remembered something.'

'Oh? What's that?'

'That life doesn't have to be complicated, not if we focus on what really matters. We have everything going for us.'

'Sure, we do.' He was smiling at me. 'But I think you're going to have a doozy of a headache tomorrow.'

'I don't care. I'm rooting for us, Rabbit. Do you know that?'

'Yes.' He leaned close, his breath sweet with the wine. 'I am, too.'

Then he kissed me, and the song began to rise again, and the night went on and on and on until it was morning.

# 34

We took to spending at least one evening every week with the pelota players, watching their practice games in the small park, or going to see them play seriously at the Frontón, buying a ticket like anyone else and sitting in the stands as each match unfolded. Now that I was learning the game, it was exciting to see the movement of the ball cracked against the wall and flung back, and then drinking as much as we could stand, sometimes weaving between bars in Havana, our arms linked to hold each other up. It was like finding a part of Spain again, an easy comradeship, and a wonderful way of being alive, though without the high explosives and the steady diet of fear.

If the Basques ever felt isolated from their own country and people, or ever considered leaving Cuba, they didn't speak of it. They seemed to live only for the here and now. A single pelota ball sailing back from the wall. A single walk at sunset with friends. One meal, which might be the last — who ever knew? — so it had better be the best anyone could find.

In July we invited them to go out onto the *Pilar* with us. It was just past noon when we left the harbor in Cojímar and shot east along the island, past a string of tiny nameless cays. Ernest was up on the flying bridge hatless with his glasses in one hand and the steering wheel light as breath in the other. The sky behind him was so blue and cloudless that he seemed cut out of cloth and set there precisely. He belonged on the boat, on *Pilar*. He was easier there than almost anywhere, his tan legs planted square, a glimmer of coconut oil on his nose as he squinted under the sun and against the wind, running out fast toward the Gulf Stream.

We had the feather jigs behind us and to each side. Ernest was always fishing, even in his dreams, I think. Most of the Basque men — I called them that, though many seemed like boys, and might always *be* boys in their hearts — were up on the long sloped stern with me, the sun beating down from its zenith, so that we sat on our shadows as well as the deck. It was a perfect day. The water beneath us went from gray-green to green-blue and finally to the deep navy we were always pointed at. Above us, half-a-dozen terns wheeled, screaming. Then we moved through a school of reef squid that boiled above the foaming whitecaps, their small bodies bouncing like sequins, just ahead of whatever hunted them.

It was clear the Basques were comfortable on water, and every part of the running out was easy. We'd brought a light lunch and ate with our hands — alligator pears sprinkled with lime juice, hard Spanish cheese, and olives and wedges of brown bread — saving our appetites for the real meal we would have later, a Basque feast we'd been promised.

Within a few hours we came to a small, protected island Ernest liked. I recognized its cupped shape. He'd brought me here before, to swim along the reef while he goggle fished with a spear and the heavy-soled shoes he used to protect his feet from the razorlike coral.

It was a beautiful place and utterly private, empty but for us — as if we had special-ordered paradise. Out from the windward side of the cay, the sea broke and collapsed like smoke over the knife's edge of the reef. Closer in, the water was clear as glass, translucent, with long white skeins of sandbars just beneath the surface. We made for the easternmost tip and then pulled around to the leeward side, where there was a small cove and white beach below broad, flapping palms.

Anchoring *Pilar* there, we went by skiff to the cove where the sand was very white and cool, now that the sun had passed to the other side of the island. The Basques had brought a bag of rice and another bag full of vegetables and a chicken and various mysterious items I knew would somehow become a wonderful dinner. Ernest built a cooking fire and then cleaned the few snooks and yellow jacks he'd caught from the trolling we'd done along the way, while Paxtchi began to cook over the open fire in a great steel concave pan he'd carried in his lap for most of the journey, obviously very proud of it. The rice and onions and peppers were mixed with stock and stirred with a great flat paddle, and then the chicken and the fish were added. It all cooked in layers and took a long while over the fire, so I went to swim down the beach a little, wading out to my chest and then pushing forward.

The water was wonderful. Ernest had given me a pair of motorcycle goggles that worked even better than a mask for swimming, and as I swam out to a spit of pale coral, a school of tiny, bullet-shaped fish moved beneath me, thousands upon thousands of them, their flesh so transparent I could see everything they were made of. Lower down, larger fish drifted slowly, bigger by far than me. It was a humbling feeling, but not a frightening one. I knew just how infinitesimal I was with the sea stretching out in every direction, on and on, and also below me, into cold black trenches where the strangest creatures lived, and where light didn't penetrate. I was small, and unimportant, and that was a relief in a way.

All the things I wanted to know about the future — whether Ernest would finally leave his wife, whether I could trust our love and the life we were building — those weren't just hidden from me, but from everyone. Mystery reached over everything. Loss happened the way the tide did, again and again, washing the white sand flat.

I flapped my fins slowly and filled my lungs with air to stay afloat along the surface, the tide rippling under my chest and thighs. Five or six feet below me along the bottom, nearly camouflaged, was a stingray, diamond shaped and very still, with pale sand billowed over the edges of his body. Just above him and close to the bottom, where they liked to feed, several dozen small pompano swam, their bodies silvery blue with yellow undersides and fins. They seemed oblivious to me and to the ray, too. I watched them for a while, and was just about to head back to the beach, when I saw a shadow gliding toward me from deeper water. I felt an icy finger of panic trail over me, but it was only a sea turtle. Her front flippers were arced up like wings, and spotted yellow-brown. She flew more than swam, eyeing me as I moved almost directly over her, my silhouette tracing her wide shell. I'm not sure I breathed at all, watching her, and then she was gone.

When I got back to the beach, the food was beginning to smell marvelous, and Ernest had a towel ready that he'd warmed in front of the fire.

'Did you see anything good?' he asked as he rubbed my shoulders under the towel and then handed me some wine. My hair was dripping.

'It was all good, but maybe the best thing was a hawksbill turtle. She had a lovely amber color to her, and let me get very close.'

'How did you know it was a female?'

'I know a broad when I see one,' I teased. 'We had an understanding, she and I. She was going to let me swim right up close if I didn't thrash around and overexcite myself about her wonderfulness.'

'Can you eat them?' Paxtchi asked. He was still stirring his masterpiece with the wooden paddle, sweeping it back and forth in rhythm.

'Yes, but if you touched this one, I'd have to shoot you in the foot. I told you, we have an understanding.'

'Hold the violence,' Ernest said, grinning. 'No one's going to lay a finger on your turtle.'

We all laughed, and then I left the men to their

234

cooking and talking and sat alone on the beach with a glass of tangy red wine. I pushed my feet deeply into the cool sand and watched the water moving over the breakers, each one like a seam of pearly blue that turned over and over before it spilled open.

The world was always changing, often violently. In Europe, the Nazis had recently signed the Pact of Steel with Italy, binding Berlin and Rome, Hitler and Mussolini, in an alliance that could only mean more senseless death. The threat was never very far away now, and it lent a particular intensity to moments like this one, the rolling surf and the laughter, the wine and the coming stars.

Paradise was always fragile. That was its very nature. But we were still here, inside it for the moment, weren't we? I turned to see Ernest. He stood before the fire with his back to me, and as he waved his arms wildly in some story, the flames rose and curled, licking past him. Climbing higher and higher.

# 35

Ernest's fortieth birthday came and, with it, a long letter from Pauline saying that there was no one like him in the world, and that she knew he would hit on what was best for them. It was signed with love and luck, and had us both pinned for a quarter of an hour in our long sitting room at the Finca as he read it aloud to me, and then over and over to himself silently. I didn't know why he was sharing it with me when he typically kept his family life very separate. I also had no idea what to say, or even to think, afterward. Either Pauline's resolve to save her marriage was more tightly woven and impenetrable than chain mail, or he had been secretly reassuring her. Both made me feel angry and sad and helpless, too.

We said we'd use the Finca to hide away from everything. Pauline never visited physically, for Ernest had staked his claim on the island long before as a private retreat. But she was always present in letters, cables, and phone calls about the boys; in bills passing from Key West to Havana, and bank checks passing back. Ernest rarely mentioned her name, but I always knew when she'd gotten a good jab in and hurt him. It was in his mood over drinks at the end of the day, or in the way he smashed the tennis ball in return over the crushed coral. Those smashes were never at me. This wasn't my war. But it was breaking my heart.

Why was he still holding fast to the marriage, I wondered, and the pretense that they were still a family? What did he want from Pauline that he couldn't get from our life together? What was still missing here, or inside me?

I wanted to phone my mother and ask her what I should do, but everything about this mess was so like what I'd already lived through with Bertrand that I couldn't bear to. So I waited, and fretted, and tried to hang on to everything that was good about our life at the Finca. The simple perfection of each day. The sun, the garden, our lovemaking, our work. It was all so unexpectedly rich that I sometimes woke at night and lay there with my eyes open in the dark, feeling like a dragon on a fat heap of gold. I had never been so happy, nor had I ever felt so fragile, so wary of what there was to lose.

Finally, I too was barreling down on the ending of my novel. A few more weeks would do it, I thought. I had recently found a title for it in one of Ernest's books about historic battles. Ernest liked to read the Bible when he looked for titles — that or crumbling tomes of old poetry — but I had a mystical approach to the naming of my books, believing that, if I just kept my eyes open, and paid close attention to everything I read, sometime something would leap off the page, highlighted by its own aptness. It was probably a silly theory, but it worked. I was peering over Ernest's shoulder one evening, only half paying attention to the book in his hands, when the phrase flared right up at me, as if shouting its own name. *A Stricken Field.*

'It's a little dark,' Ernest said.

'War is dark,' I argued. 'But it's a difficult thing to get right.'

'A title, you mean?'

'All of it. Everything. I want so much for this book to be good.'

'It already is, Rabbit. What you're doing is wonderful. You can trust that.'

'God, I hope you're right.'

★   ★   ★

Like every late August in recent years, Ernest would soon head to the L-Bar-T Ranch in northern Wyoming, one of his favorite hunting and fishing spots ever. Bumby had already gone west with Hadley and her second husband, Paul, and would be waiting for him at the ranch when he arrived. Gigi and Patrick would come out, too, after the end of their summer camp in Connecticut. Pauline had apparently left the country for her spontaneous trip to France, wanting to sail over before, as Ernest put it, 'all of Europe blew up.'

'I think I'll ask Toby Bruce to fetch them and bring them out by train,' he said, problem-solving. Toby had been a help to Ernest and his family for years, and was one of the few people he trusted absolutely to care for everything from his car to his guns to *Pilar* — and now the boys.

'I'm sure he'll do it,' I said, but I was distracted. Just because Pauline had gone to Europe didn't mean she wouldn't appear in

238

Wyoming eventually. She had plenty of time to get there, and a lot to lose if she didn't.

'Try not to worry, Rabbit,' he said, reading my face. 'I'm going to do my damnedest to get this all settled soon. You've been so patient.'

It was dim in the room, with the light from the lamps only stretching so far. The quiet was thick. We were both afraid to say more, but I was more afraid not to. 'It isn't really patience, darling. Is it?'

# 36

Leaving Havana was an elaborate migration when all was said and done. I traveled with Ernest as far as St. Louis, going first to Key West in *Pilar* to retrieve the car and give all the specifics to Toby Bruce about the boys. Then, loaded to the gills in Ernest's black Buick convertible, we launched ourselves at America, driving ten or twelve hours a day, the way he liked to travel, with very few breaks, and the windows rolled down, the radio blasting away.

He loved everything about this sort of cross-country trek — all the little motels in no-name towns, the filling stations and roadside stands, and eating bologna sandwiches for dinner, and pissing in ditches or open fields whenever he needed, just pulling the car over and not caring who might drive by.

I liked the open country and the warm air that pushed through the windows, but I was less charmed by primitivism and squalor. He had stopped shaving and drove barefoot, wearing the same canvas shorts with a piece of rope for a belt. It was all I could do to get him to wash his hands a few times a day.

'All women secretly pine for cavemen,' he said when I complained.

'It's an interesting theory.' I couldn't help laughing. 'But Mother won't let you in the house.'

'She's going to adore me — all mothers do.'

I very much hoped he was right. Aside from Ernest, my mother was the most important person in my life. It was too much to imagine that she'd approve of our relationship, since Ernest was still tied to another, but I felt confident that if she just spent a little time with us together, she'd see what was extraordinary about him, and why I was risking so much to be with him.

★　★　★

When we finally arrived, she had made a roast for us, and everything went better than I'd dared to expect. We sat up late, talking about the treaty Germany had just signed with the Soviet Union not to join with any other power or attack the other. During the war in Spain, Stalin had aided the Loyalists against Franco, but now it seemed more and more that the world's most powerful men were uniting. Soon they would be unstoppable.

Sighing, Mother changed the subject and asked Ernest to talk about his sons.

'Patrick is eleven. We call him the Mexican Mouse 'cause he gets so brown. He can read two or three books a day and says I should write a new one fatter than *Green Hills* so it will make me even more money.' He laughed. 'I don't have the heart to tell him that book was a bust.'

'Nonsense,' she said. 'He doesn't care about any of that. He's got to be proud of you. And your others?'

'Jack is fifteen and mostly away at boarding school. We've called him Bumby since he was a baby in Paris. Gregory's nearly eight. Gigi, and he's something, all right. Won ten dollars shooting craps at camp last week. He might support me one day, you know. He's like Midas with those dice.'

Mother looked alarmed for a moment. 'You don't really take him to the tables, do you?'

'Nah, at home he plays squatting in the alley like they do in Morocco. But I should take him to the tables. He could start sending me an annuity.'

She laughed then. 'Marty never cared about money, she only wanted to travel. One day she snuck out of the house and hid herself in the cart of the man who delivered our ice.'

His eyes lit up. 'Yes, I've heard that story. It's a good one.'

'What I didn't tell you is I couldn't sit down for a week afterward,' I said.

'Well, yes. But that was her only thrashing ever,' Mother was quick to add.

He winked at me. 'No doubt she deserved others.'

'No doubt at all,' I said, and we all laughed.

★   ★   ★

As the evening drew to a close, I felt a sense of accomplishment. It seemed as though Ernest was going to win over my mother without even trying. And she'd asked about the boys. That was a good sign, too. Someday, if all went as planned,

242

they'd be her grandchildren. *She* should *be interested*, I thought, letting myself be hopeful, just a little, that this would all work out in my favor, and soon.

The next morning, I helped Ernest load the car, which was already chock-full of rods and reels and all kinds of tackle, plus rifles, and sleeping rolls and canteens. Over his shoulder, the morning sun was fat and bright as a tangerine.

'Just get in,' he said. 'We'll figure things out when we get there.'

'Don't tempt me.'

He leaned against the side of the Buick and I pressed into him, draping my arms around his neck. The sun shone down on us, warming the tops of our heads. From the treetops, cicadas rattled their song, which was about the end of summer, and about us, too, it seemed. Maybe the neighbors were watching. Maybe my mother was standing at the window waiting for me. I only wanted to stand in this spot for as long as possible, to hold time still.

'If you get lonely, you know where to find me,' he said.

'I'm already lonely.'

'I don't want to be without you. We're going to have to do something about that.'

'We are. I love you something awful, you know?'

'Good.'

He kissed me for a long time, while I felt uncertainty pulse between us, and happiness, too, at having found each other. The two hovered

243

in a balance, difficult but true. Finally, there was nothing to do but let him go.

He climbed behind the wheel of the Buick, nudging over his tackle box and favorite rod. I kissed him one last time through the open window and watched him pull away, passing under all the bowed trees along the street, growing smaller and gauzier and fainter, until he wasn't there at all. Even then, I stood still a few moments longer, while my heart stretched after him, out across the spaces between us.

# 37

Days after Ernest and the boys were settled at the L-Bar-T, Hitler's troops marched into Poland. In no time at all, Britain, France, Australia, and New Zealand all declared war on Germany, and there was no place in the world far enough or deep enough to hide from the terrible facts any longer. The Second World War had begun.

In St. Louis, Mother and I huddled around the radio for hours and hours without moving or speaking, feeling drugged with sadness and worry, though we'd known this was all coming for a long while. The same broadcasts played endlessly with very little variation, but we kept listening. The living room went dark. Neither of us could even stand to turn on the lights.

When Ernest phoned, he told me it was the same for him and the boys. They had barely left their cabin. He was only sleeping a few hours a night, tuned constantly to the portable radio on his pillow. It was like no other time in Wyoming; that was certain.

'What do you think Roosevelt will do?' he asked through the phone line.

'I don't know. I'm not sure it matters. Wasn't everything lost with Spain and Czechoslovakia? We did nothing then, and now it's too late.'

Mother's phone was a heavy black monstrosity, with a receiver that must have weighed a pound. It was cool and dull feeling in my hand and against my cheek, and seemed to stand for something, though I couldn't have said what. I heard Ernest breathing, so near sounding, and yet impossibly far.

'The whole thing makes me sick,' he said.

'I know.'

We fell silent, and I could hear the sound the wires made, something between a hum and a heartbeat. 'Fife's back from Paris,' he finally said. 'She's flying out tomorrow.' His voice had dropped, and I knew he had been dreading telling me.

Jealousy rose up quick as anything. I didn't know why anyone ever said jealousy was green when clearly it was red. Rage red. 'I knew she hadn't given up.'

'I didn't. It's dawning on me I don't know very much about women. I'm sorry, Rabbit.'

I didn't know what to say. The phone felt hot, suddenly. I wanted to drop it, or throw it.

In the silence, he went on, 'I'm going to have to do something. I thought it might be easier for her to come to a decision on her own time.'

'Someone has to do something.' I'd snapped the words, making them a challenge, but he didn't bite. He was so deep inside his own worries it was very possible he couldn't even recognize mine.

'It's a hell of a trip already, I'll tell you that.'

★   ★   ★

I didn't hear from him for the next two weeks, while I camped out on the divan in the living

246

room, listening to the radio and feeling more and more vulnerable. The world was being turned inside out, and I was, too. I was plagued with terrible thoughts of Ernest changing his mind, of the tactics Pauline might use to hold him. But when he finally did phone, he told me it was over. He'd asked for a divorce — no more pretending, no more silent standoffs. Pauline had listened, seeming to hear, but he wasn't sure in the end, since she'd taken to her bed immediately afterward, locking the door, and hadn't come out for three days.

He was calling from a pay phone down the road from the ranch for privacy. I tried to picture him where he stood, mountains all around and pine dust, goshawks, a hard crisp edge to the air. He didn't sound angry or relieved, but like someone he knew well and had loved until he couldn't any longer had died.

'It's miserable business,' he said. 'She's strong as steel in some ways, but those are the ones who fall hardest when you get down to it.'

'She's still there, then?'

'Until the end of the week. Toby Bruce will get her and the boys back to New York. Bum will stay on a bit longer, and then go to Cody with Hadley and Paul.'

'The boys must be a wreck.'

'I think they're trying to be brave. Patrick hasn't really said anything. He just sits on the front porch and reads, quiet as a stone. He's there now. Gigi's trying to comfort his mother, but she won't let anyone near. He just waits at the door to her room and plays solitaire on the floor in the hall. It's like a goddamned funeral parlor.'

'How awful. I wish there was something I could do.'

He was quiet for a long minute and then said, 'What if you came west? I could almost stand this if you were here.'

'It wouldn't be fair to turn up the minute the door closes, would it?'

'What's been fair about any of it? I feel awful. I'm not sleeping. Come.'

The line crackled as we both fell quiet. For a long time, even after he was gone, I didn't hang up.

★　★　★

I began packing almost immediately, dragging the radio up to my room so as not to miss the latest apocryphal updates. The Nazis were defiling Poland as they marched. They'd reached the Vistula and were set to take Warsaw. Canada had thrown in with the Allies and declared war on Germany. In Washington, Roosevelt had called a special session of Congress to revisit our Neutrality Acts, but not much changed. His position was what it had been for years, that we wouldn't enter any foreign wars. We simply couldn't. He'd made that promise to all the mothers and fathers, and sons and wives, and he was going to keep it for as long as he was able.

'What's happening with Ernest?' my mother wanted to know. She'd come up to check on me and found me throwing things into an open suitcase. She looked worried, but only sat down to show me she was ready to listen if I was ready to talk.

'He's asked for a divorce.' The words were thick and strange in my mouth. I felt run through with guilt about Pauline, but also freer and more hopeful than I'd been in months. 'I'm going to join him out west. This has all been pretty ugly for him.'

'I'm sure it has.' There was something in her tone, chilliness or suspicion. 'But what about you?'

'What do you mean? I thought you liked Ernest.'

'I do like him. A more charming man never lived, but he seems to demand a great deal from the women in his life. What about your book? Won't that suffer if you drop everything to run to his side?'

'I'm not dropping everything.' I tried not to sound defensive, but I was. 'The bulk of it's finished. I'm onto the second draft now. And anyway, could you please try to be happy for us? It might not look like it should, but Ernest loves me.'

'Of course he loves you.' She settled next to me, picking up a pillow and gently smoothing the cotton with her fingertips. 'He'd be a fool not to. But he's been through two wives, now. He loved them, too, didn't he?'

'I assume so.' It was hard to hear her talk this way without rushing to his side. Or maybe it was my own side I was rushing to. They'd blurred together and now I couldn't tell the difference.

'He was so young the first time. People make mistakes.'

'Yes, and I'm trying to spare you one, sweetheart. Possibly the worst mistake of your life. Just be careful, will you, Marty?'

'I will,' I said, knowing full well that it was too late to promise any such thing.

# 38

Sun Valley sat in the Wood River Valley, surrounded by a symphony of mountain ranges, and the Sawtooth National Forest. There were flaring peaks, and golden jagged hills, and aspens rising tall and shapely against the sky.

After the Depression, Averell Harriman of the Union Pacific Railroad had had the bright idea that year-round play might save this part of Idaho from spiraling into worse straits. He'd sunk a lot of capital but hadn't been able to draw many visitors until he thought to seed the field with movie stars and other glittering sorts that would make Sun Valley look like the plum portion of heaven it actually was.

When he'd reached out to Ernest, offering a free vacation in exchange for a small amount of publicity, Ernest had actually turned him down at first. Then the war had come, and Pauline and all that misery, and suddenly a new place without any bad memories, or any memories at all, seemed like just the thing.

They gave us the corner suite on the second floor, the nicest the lodge had to offer, which had two large rooms, both with open fireplaces, a vast bed, and a living area wide enough for ninepins. It was almost too much, an embarrassment of riches with our current pangs of conscience and remorse — but I did feel something begin to loosen as we stood there and took in the view.

The window to the terrace was open, and the whole valley was laid out gold and green. Bald Mountain rose up out of the basin like a lord, the dry ski runs streaking down the sides as if something sticky had melted there. Soon enough there would be snow, and frost-tipped mornings and clear, crisp nights.

'We'll start writing again every day,' I said. 'That's what we both need. There's plenty of room for us to forget the other is even here. At lunch we'll ring a bell or yodel or something.'

'That sounds wonderful.' He looked at me, his eyes tired and unguarded from the night's long drive and also everything that had come before. All he was feeling and not saying. 'That might cure us. But we should have some sort of story to explain you.'

'Oh.' His words thudded. Pauline was gone, but of course nothing was truly settled. Not yet. 'You mean how I'm not Mrs. Hemingway.'

'Yes.'

'What would you like me to say?' I snapped.

'I don't have any answers, you know. I don't have the damnedest idea what's right. How do you think we should move ahead?' He sounded frustrated with my sharpness, but he'd never been anyone's mistress, never been where I was now.

'I guess that depends if you want to protect your reputation or mine?'

He looked stung. 'Yours, obviously. I'm not sure the shreds of my reputation would be worth the effort. We'll come up with something.'

'All right,' I said, unconvinced.

'For now, we both need sleep and a good meal and then some whiskey. If we just keep doing that over and over for a few weeks, we might be okay. We'll get to writing, like before. We'll fill ourselves up again and in the afternoons we'll fish or ride or shoot.'

'Shoot? What? I think you've got the wrong girl.'

'No.' He squeezed me against his chest and held me there while my questions and doubt went on ticking loudly inside me. 'For the first time in a long time, I've got the right girl.'

★ ★ ★

The plan was to stay for six weeks, and get straight again — straight with each other, and our work. To do this we had to forget about the world a little. The Soviets had invaded Poland and quickly turned Warsaw over to the Nazis, as if it were a toy to be bartered with, kicked back and forth. Reinhard Heydrich, who'd been second in command in Himmler's Security Service, was put in charge of the Sicherheitsdienst, overseeing intelligence for the SS, as well as the Gestapo and Hitler's Kriminalpolizei. It was too much if you let it all in, all the time, so we agreed to listen to the radio only twice a day, at lunchtime, after we'd written our quota of pages, and again in the evening when we had drinks before dinner.

Ernest was plunging forward on 'the Spain book,' as he was calling it, and I was elbow deep in my second draft of A Stricken Field, relieved

253

to feel fully inside the story now, completely absorbed. It felt real to me, this world I was making, almost as if it were a bridge I could stand on when so much else was erratic and unpredictable.

In the afternoons, we tried to be outside as much as possible, and to enjoy what was left of the nice weather. The country was so beautiful. Sometimes we went riding up into the hills on horseback. At first I wasn't sure I could sit a mount anymore, since I hadn't been on one since I was a girl and hadn't been very good at it then. But Ernest said it would be fine, and it was. He and Taylor Williams decided on a nice old gelding for me named Blue that was broad as a sofa across the backside and awfully patient with me when I hadn't sorted myself out yet.

Taylor was the lead guide at the lodge, a tall and narrow Kentuckian who shot and fished as well as Ernest. He was smart with the kind of biting sense of humor that caught you off guard sometimes, because it didn't seem to jibe with that lilting drawl of his — like spitting out honey-coated tacks. He could make us both laugh, and Ernest loved him instantly, calling him the Colonel.

You could ride east from the lodge, crossing the Big Wood River, and over a broad meadow flocked with rabbitbrush and sumac and sage, the grass nearly up to the horses' bellies. Trails went up into the hills, over stark-looking golden passes or through aspen forests, all of it so free looking and untouched by man it made you almost dizzy.

One day we went north instead, skirting the edge of Sun Valley Lake until it met Trail Creek, and then following that, lazily and happily, until we'd found a nice flat dry spot for the horses to graze. We tied them off and threw a blanket down under a tree on a soft berm and had our lunch before lying back, closing our eyes against the sun.

'We should stay until it snows, don't you think?' I said.

'Maybe we should,' he said. 'Or until Christmas even. I'll bet it's wonderful here, and quiet, too. No one's found out about this place. Part of me hopes they never do.'

'Don't tell Harriman that. He'll sock you in the nose.'

'Still. Things make sense here, and they haven't in a long while. There aren't any ghosts.'

'Oh, we've carried some with us,' I argued. 'You know we have.'

'Yes, but they're growing lighter.'

On a high branch above us, a blue jay craned his head one way and then the other, intent on all sorts of things we couldn't see. This was his kingdom. 'Where are you at now in the book?' I asked Ernest.

'Gaylord's. God, it's fun to be there again. To turn and know just where everything is, and how it looks in the dark, and what everyone's secrets are.'

'Gaylord's! Good Christ, I'm jealous. I want to go now, just for a drink, you know? To feel everything shaking apart, and then to come back here and feel very safe again.' I fell quiet for a moment, and then said, 'If you think about it, Spain is one of our ghosts, too. It broke my heart, but I wouldn't take any of it back. Places change us, don't they? Sometimes more than we can even guess.'

'Yes. Writing is one way to keep certain places alive. I've often thought that, and not just about Spain. If I know I'm going to write a story about Horton Bay, or Pamplona or Madrid, even, I feel better. As if I can't ever really lose that time, or who I was then.'

'How about Sun Valley? Will you write about this?'

'Maybe I will. When I know what the story is. Not every place has a story.'

I looked up at the jay again, the pine tree behind him, the sky hard and blue behind that, not wanting any of it to disappear. 'This one has to. Let's make sure it does.'

# 39

We took to having dinner or drinks with Lloyd Arnold, the lodge's PR photographer, and his wife, Tillie, a dark-haired, whip-smart woman with simplicity and honesty in spades. She wore her curls short, close to her head, and her brown eyes showed her thoughts and feelings as easily as if you were watching them played out through a pane of glass. Ernest liked her immediately, and I did, too, though she seemed to have very old-fashioned ideas about men and women. She didn't understand why I needed to work, for instance, or even why I would want to.

'Part of it's very practical,' I tried to explain. 'I've always paid my own way, and that's important to me. But I also have a passion for my writing. Sometimes, it seems like the only thing that makes sense to me at all.'

'I suppose it's what women are doing now. Modern, as they say.'

'I think it's wonderful. Why should we have to choose one thing or another?'

She smiled placidly, smoothing her skirt with her hands, but somehow she didn't look convinced. 'You really think you can have it all and not compromise anything?'

'Why not?' I heard her words as a challenge, and half wanted to say, *Watch me.* 'At the very least, I mean to try.'

A week later, in the middle of October, almost as if the gods had overheard me and thought to call my bluff, Charles Colebaugh at *Collier's* offered to send me to Finland. The Soviets were lately pressuring the Finns to cede land in exchange for some other territory elsewhere. The exchange was necessary for security reasons, they claimed, since Leningrad was only thirty-two kilometers from the Finnish border. But the Finns were refusing.

WE THINK YOU SHOULD BE THERE. THE SOONER THE BETTER, Colebaugh cabled, and I leaned in, realizing that although I still hadn't recovered emotionally from Spain, it felt important to go anyway, to be where essential things were happening, and to find the stories that needed to be told, no matter how hard they were to see.

'I'm a little worried about my book, though,' I told Ernest. 'And you, of course.'

It was midday, and we'd taken our lunch outside on a small patio off the main dining room. Around us, the Pioneer Mountains rose up sharp and clear, the edges of the peaks seeming hand etched against the high blue sky. Indian summer was upon us, and every moment outdoors seemed as precious as pure gold.

'You're so close now. Nothing's going to stall your novel, I'm sure of it. And this is a plum assignment. Most journalists would kill to have a shot at the circulation *Collier's* has, and obviously the magazine knows you can deliver

258

the material now. Think of the nest egg you can put aside, too.'

'Enough to keep me for four or five months, maybe. More if I economize. You'll really be all right, then?'

'Sure, I will. Maybe I can meet you there if I can break away. If not, we'll be back in Cuba together by the first of the year, happy as clams again.'

I phoned Colebaugh to tell him I was accepting the assignment, and then gave every drop of the time I had left to finishing *A Stricken Field*, and sending it to several editors in New York, hoping someone would love it as I did and see its value. Ernest kept insisting he understood both my total commitment to my novel, and this trip. That he supported me in every way. But when my travel orders arrived, he began to make pointed jokes at dinner with everyone in earshot.

'I'm being abandoned,' he said. 'And just when winter's coming on.'

'Poor you,' Tillie said, and turned to me. 'Can't you be a writer here? Why go halfway around the world? Isn't that dangerous?'

'To report on a war, you have to be where the war is,' I explained, keeping my eyes on Ernest, trying to gauge whether he was kidding or just now letting me in on his true feelings.

'You can look after me,' Ernest said to Tillie, lightly. His expression was smooth as a sphinx's, revealing nothing.

'Who'll look after Marty?' Lloyd asked.

'Marty can look after herself,' Ernest shot back coolly. He was smiling, but I didn't trust it.

259

'If you really don't want me to go, I wish you'd tell me outright,' I said to him later when we'd gone up to bed.

He was in the bathroom, running water into a glass that would go on the nightstand. 'Why? You're going to go anyway.'

'Yes, but we've talked about this. All the arrangements have been made.'

'Don't get so rattled, Rabbit.' He met my gaze in the bathroom mirror. 'I'm only teasing.'

'I wonder if you are.'

'Don't worry. I'll be fine. We're fine.'

'We are,' I told him. 'Because we have to be.' I kissed the back of his neck, working to push my fears away. 'I'll be back before you know it. Quick as a winklet.'

Then I kissed him again to seal the promise.

# 40

On November 10, two days after my thirty-first birthday, I boarded the *Westenland* in New York Harbor and we eased our way out of the wide mouth of the Hudson, past Brighton Beach and Rockaway, past Sandy Hook, its spit of land arched back toward the bay, while the pale strobe of the lighthouse pulsed eternally out to sea.

It was a strange thing to be on the way to war again. The conflict in Spain had made so much sense to me. I knew exactly what its aims were, and its ideals. This war was only about greed, it seemed to me, and insanity. Adolf Hitler was a madman — everyone knew that — but he was also a child, a red-faced, angry baby bent on total dominion. There had been a time, perhaps, when the world could have joined forces to stop him, but that had come and gone. Now, there was only a chance to temper the size of the catastrophe, to staunch the loss of lives, thrashing back against evil with torches or pitchforks. Or words, in my case, when the time came to write them.

The *Westenland* was a Dutch ship, bound for Belgium with just forty-five passengers, though there was space enough for five hundred. It was eerie walking past all those empty cabins, the silent darkened ballroom with no band, no dancing, no merriment. From stern to bow, hundreds of empty deck chairs smacked of all that was wrong with this picture. Most of the other passengers were Europeans trying to get home to family in time to keep them safe. You felt that persistently, knots of dread hovering over each bowed head at meals. The meals themselves were almost intolerable, chicken cutlets like wet paste, and wine that should have been poured straight overboard. But I looked forward to them anyway. In between, there was no way to properly fill the time. We drifted through the passageways like lost souls, nodding to one another with nothing to say, or standing on the bridge and smoking, collars up against the cold stiff wind.

I tried to avoid my cabin whenever possible. It had obviously been built with halflings in mind — halflings eager for pain, too, since the mattress seemed full of knobbly sticks and stones. When I tried to read, my stomach pitched and burned. When I bent over sheets of paper, wanting to write Ernest, I ended up staring at my hands, or at my single tipping porthole in a half trance. I missed him, and worried I may have made the wrong decision, but it was too early to concede that, wasn't it, when we weren't even halfway across the Atlantic?

For eight days, the torpor was barely broken, as we pushed toward England and the Channel. Then, on the ninth day, at breakfast, a story came over the wire that another Dutch boat, just one day ahead of us and headed for the West Indies, had hit a string of three mines and sunk in smoldering pieces. Six hundred passengers had been on board, and no one could do more than estimate for the moment how many lives had been lost.

When the broadcast was over, everyone fell silent as the coffee went cold. I felt a thickness in my throat, as if I'd tried to swallow more than what was on my plate — my heart, maybe.

I pushed my meal away and went out to smoke on the deck. One of the other passengers was there already, his wool coat sooty gray against the stark-white railing, his face pale as custard. He was a Frenchman named Laurence Gardet, and I'd spoken to him once or twice before, about his family in Provence, his unwell father with an aging vineyard he felt ambivalent about inheriting.

'But now there are the Nazis,' he'd added, explaining his situation. 'Maybe no one inherits anything anymore.'

I had agreed with him sadly, and we'd smoked a cigarette together. Now as I approached him on deck, he offered me another of his good Gauloises, and I took it, leaning into his flaring match, as if this were our routine and we were old friends.

War could do that to you. Helplessness could, too.

It was only a matter of stupid chance or accident, which vessels went down at sea. The Channel was strung through with mines, and even though our ship was posted fore and aft with signs that proclaimed our neutrality, what was the point of that? As if a floating mine could read, carefully consider politics and affiliation? It was ridiculous.

'The Germans have a new magnetic mine, I've heard,' Laurence said in his thickly accented English. 'They sit at the bottom, and if anything passes over . . . well. You understand.'

'How does it work exactly?'

'I'm no engineer. The ship disturbs something, I suppose. How does anything work?' He shrugged deeper into his collar and squinted against the wind. 'I'm more interested in what they might look like. It's a game I've played since I was a child. I used to draw things out from my imagination with pastels. Just bits of nonsense from my nightmares, or far-off things from the war in France I heard my parents talking about, sitting over the newspaper with coffee in the evenings. My mother kept all the drawings in a box, but secretly she probably thought I was mad.'

He was suddenly interesting to me and so human. I could picture his mother sifting through his drawings worriedly, smoking. 'What have you come up with about the mines?'

'Something like the *baleine*, or the *orque*. Killer whale, as you say, with hard black curves. Made of iron, obviously.' He gave me a funny look, as if he were trying to plumb whether I thought he was crazy, too.

'The captain says we'll anchor in the Channel overnight tonight, and try to shoot it by day tomorrow,' I said.

'They're beneath the surface in either case, aren't they?' He shrugged. 'And then there are

264

the torpedoes. They can travel up to six miles, you know.'

'I've read that, too.' I looked away from him and out at the morning sea, pale gray on darker gray, struck through with deep green and laced over with white foam. 'Shouldn't we be trying to talk of something else?' I asked, but he shrugged again, and closed his eyes, drawing in the smoke deeply.

I watched him, the skin of his closed eyelids pale blue and quivering almost imperceptibly, and remembered how it was in Spain when we'd heard an attack was coming, a bad one. At those times, it *had* helped to say the worst things out loud. Often we had talked all night, guessing, predicting the scale of the attack, how long it would last, how close the shells might fall. Somehow anything unknown was its own minefield. Waiting for shelling was worse than the shelling itself. Once the attack started, you knew exactly where you stood and could respond. But the waiting. Yes, the waiting was the worst part.

★   ★   ★

The next morning at first light we picked our way slowly forward toward the Strait of Dover. Many of us came up on deck to watch, because it was so much better than feeling trapped in the close tin boxes of our cabins, tethered to numbness. The wind whipped at us sideways, and that was real. Plymouth was real, off the port bow in the distance, and Weymouth farther on,

265

and the looming spit of land that meant Cherbourg.

Every now and then, we'd spot a contact mine or a string of them, bobbing like basketballs with rounded black spines, innocuous looking as teapots, far below the deck where we stood. Gazing at them should have set my hair on end, but it didn't. The real chill, the icy thing at the center of my fear, was reserved for something far below the rough green chop, something we would never see, not even if it sank us.

Late the next day, we'd reached the Downs, off Ramsgate, a safe zone protected by the English blockade. From there we heard more reports of vessels that had been sunk by mines, or by U-boats, and I found myself wishing the ship radio would stop working, at least for the night, so that I could get some sleep, though I knew that was foolish.

In the morning, we received clearance to move on toward Antwerp, but we were barely an hour past Ramsgate when the siren sounded ominously, and our captain's voice came through the loudspeakers saying another Dutch ship, one just ahead of us in the Channel, had hit three mines simultaneously. At least a hundred were dead in the explosion. There were several hours, then, made entirely of dread, my nerves frayed, and then we began to see the wreckage floating in the sea around us. As we drew nearer, shapeless objects became men and women. They all bobbed facedown, stiff limbed and gray, wearing the same yellow life vests strung along the railings of the *Westenland*, and

266

on her life rafts. I didn't want to think of that, or to really look at the bodies, but found I couldn't turn away. The long red hair on one woman streamed out like seaweed — though she wasn't a woman any longer, was she? No, only a casualty, someone who would never reach home. The ship had been neutral and full of passengers just like us, people who hadn't done anything more threatening or unforgivable than to be at sea.

Thankfully the fog came in an hour later, milky and dense, and we couldn't see anything else until night. A few hours more, and I heard the sounding of the whistle that meant landfall. When I made my way to the deck, we were moving past Ostend. It stood glittering at the edge of the North Sea like a fairy city. The clouds parted above, and moonlight spilled onto our ship, lingering on the curves of the bowsprit, and onto the Scheldt River as we entered it, nearing Antwerp. The whole world was quiet, and suddenly made of light, as beautiful as the hours before had been terrible. How could a single day — or a single mind — hold two such vastly different realities? It didn't even seem possible, but here was Belgium, cold and benign as a surgeon's table rising from the mist.

The Channel hadn't been a dream, and this wasn't a dream either. They were both true, somehow, and I had to stretch or bend or break in order to see that, and move on to the next place, the next thing.

★　★　★

I was standing on the gangplank an hour later, as everyone disembarked. When Laurence, my French smoking companion, passed by, I barely recognized him. He looked ten years older, as if he'd spent days and days swallowing broken glass.

'Good luck to you,' I said.

'To you as well.' He stopped for just a moment — his face wind chapped and haggard looking. He reached to take my hand, I thought, but it was a gift he was offering — a square blue tin with a familiar winged helmet. His Gauloises. His fingers grazed mine, and then he was drifting away from me, swallowed up by flocks of hurrying porters, while I clutched the tin and stuffed it deep in my pocket, close to tears.

It seemed unlikely that I would ever see him or any of the others from the ship again. Something had happened to us all, something that might never be fully comprehensible to anyone who had not come through it. That was the thing about experience. It took distant strangers and made them a family. A family of one moment. There was no other way to see it, even as we scattered to the wind.

# 41

That night, as soon as I closed my eyes, I saw the bodies floating in their useless life vests, rocking while the sea churned around them. With a flaring knot of panic, I groped for the lamp and turned it on. A cone of strange yellow light fell on the night table and water glass and the neat blank pad of notebook paper, and the blue cigarette tin, giving the objects a cold and detached feel, like things in a museum all made of ice.

*Don't think about home or any of the other places you want to be right now,* I told myself, training my eyes on the water glass, the still line of liquid like a simplified horizon in miniature. *Be a good girl and go to sleep, and tomorrow you will feel less breakable.* Then I pressed my eyelids tightly down against the yellow glare, doing my damnedest to shut everything out.

My hotel in Helsinki was sealed up with blackout paper on the windows. I didn't even know it was morning when the sirens began to wail. There was pounding at the door and the sound of boots running in the hall, and over all of it, the high steady scream of the air-raid sirens. I felt frozen and stupid, and sat on the edge of the bed trying to remember where my shoes were. The lamp on the night table was still lit, and as I watched, the water in the glass began to vibrate. Planes were coming, and they were coming now.

I found my shoes somehow and stumbled down the flights of stairs and outside onto the cold street where everyone was staring up into the heavy gray sky. The humming was like the noise of a wasp growing louder and louder until I could feel it under my feet. They must be close, I knew, but I couldn't see anything. The sky was still so dark with cloud cover, and it was a helpless feeling, waiting for something no one could see.

The crowd around me began to move — toward the air-raid shelter, I guessed. That's when the first huge silver trimotor roared in low, as if in slow motion, lumbering through the clouds, the sound it made now a roar. I began to run, still stiff and numb, half in a dream. And when the plane was directly overhead, its motor booming through me like thunder, it spilled its load.

I thought we'd all breathed our last; that everyone on the street would be dead the next instant, or horribly maimed. But as I turned to iron, waiting for the end, I understood that the flapping whiteness coming down all around wasn't death and wasn't snow, either. It was paper.

Propaganda leaflets fell in a crush, fluttering as they spun, depicting a mother grieving for her dead son, a Finnish soldier, with the eerie caption 'You're expected home.' And then it began to rain.

In the confusing silence that followed, people came out of the shelters and onto the street again, looking half asleep and disbelieving while the leaflets blew around and stuck fast to everything in the drizzle.

I went back to the hotel feeling angry and raw and humiliated. What kind of place was this, and why was I here? I ordered coffee and waited for true morning, but the sun simply didn't come. The sky had gone a paler, pearly gray, but the clouds never parted. By afternoon, many had returned to work and to school. The fog had dropped, thick and damp, and people felt safe, even cheerful.

'They can't come over in this,' the hotel manager said to a small group of journalists as we stood in the lobby. Two Italian reporters were there, too, and Geoffrey Cox, a New Zealander who wrote for the *Daily Express*. I'd met him once or twice in Madrid, and that was enough to make him a friend now.

'A Finn should know what his own weather can do, I guess,' Geoff said, but twenty minutes later, they did come.

Just past three that afternoon, the Russians attacked in perfect stealth. No sirens went off this time; there was just the deafening rumble of their bombers, zeroing in on a small section of the city. Nine planes in a narrow diamond formation came in at two hundred meters. In the hotel, we couldn't hear anything for the roaring. I lunged under a marble table in the restaurant, hugging my knees as the floor shook convulsively. Everything rocked and shuddered with the explosions. The windows concussed. I felt my teeth jarring and clacking as the bombs fell.

The attack lasted one minute, the longest single minute of my life. It was November 30, 1939. The Russo-Finnish War had just begun.

# 42

When I opened my eyes again, black smoke was everywhere.

'Gas. Gas!' I heard someone screaming, and I thought, *We're all lost now.* But they hadn't dropped poison. At least not yet. The smoke was just the calling card of high explosives. The sign of a city being blown apart.

In an odd, echoing stillness, I stood up and walked with a group of stunned others back out into the street. Everything was on fire. The avenue was an ocean of bright glass. Four large apartment buildings had collapsed as if made only of papier-mâché, or of air. A bus had been forced over onto its side like a downed bull elephant. The driver lay in the street. I guessed he was the driver, in any case, as he'd been spit through the wreckage and glass of the front windshield, his head wrenched with force from his body.

I looked at him and then away. He was no different from the hundreds of casualties I'd seen in Spain, except for his shoes. They weren't rope soled like the peasants wore in Madrid, but leather that had been very carefully patched who knew how many times, so that he might get more use from them. Somehow those shoes broke my heart like nothing else that day, and I wondered what I could say or write that would give his life and death the value they deserved. He had a wife, probably, a family, and where were they in this burning city? The dark was falling already, or not falling so much as pushing at you from the edges of the horizon as if it were always crouched or hovering there, like something calculating and predatory. Suddenly I wanted to be home in the sunshine so badly I almost couldn't bear it. To be sitting with Ernest side by side on our terrace — just that — the simplest possible thing, and the most unreachable.

Everything — the whole skyline — was veiled in flames, and a steady migration had begun. Straggling girls and boys, old men and mothers, moved away from their smoldering houses and shops and schools and out of the city. Of course they would leave, but what was peculiar was the silence. No one screamed or wept, not even the children as their mothers packed them into prams and carts and sledges. No one ran. There wasn't anything like panic, just a weary, frozen, resigned retreat. Heaps of blankets. Canned food in pulled wagons. A steady stream of faultless souls headed into the forests, hoping to be safe there.

On my way back to the hotel, I walked past young men trying to dig bodies out from under the rubble with snow shovels, and sometimes their hands. They would be at it all night, I realized, and the next day, too. In my room, I didn't take off my coat or even turn on the light, just lit a candle and sat on the side of my bed with a book for a desk and a pen and paper.

All this while, I hadn't been able to write Ernest somehow, but now the words poured out in a rush as my hands shook. *Dear Rabbit,* I wrote. *I love you. That's what absolutely matters now. I can try to tell you how it is here, but first you need to know this. I love you. I love you. We should never have left Cuba.*

# 43

Later, much later, this would be called the Winter War. From the last day of November until the iced-over middle of March, Russian planes came again and again while Finnish machine guns spit fire up at them into the dark sky.

The Soviets had three times as many soldiers as the Finns, thirty times the number of bomber planes, and one hundred times as many tanks, but the Finns had their resources. They knew how to use their weather to their great advantage, hiding in white coveralls on white skis, flicking through the forests invisibly to catch the Russians unaware. The landscape was on their side. Whole villages could be camouflaged beneath snowy bows of fir trees, further insulated by fog, invisible and quiet as the snow itself.

In Helsinki, the evacuation went on and on, with children being carted off in railcars and buggies and even hearses, anything with wheels. As the bombing continued, the Finns moved from their huddled forest camps toward nearby villages. From the villages they moved north and west, toward the Baltic Sea, in a rolling exodus that pushed out and out in waves. The people didn't seem frightened to me. They had a frozen resolve that seemed as much a part of Finland as the snow and the dark. Every afternoon the light rinsed away, as if a great blanketing shroud dropped from on high. I didn't know how they

276

got used to the eerily short days, but perhaps anyone could get used to anything.

One day a fireman took me into a bombed apartment building, through a knee-high river of water from fire hoses, and up several flights of concrete steps that seemed untouched, though the walls around them sagged in ruins. We went into one apartment where the door had been ripped from the hinges. Inside, the splintered wet black wreckage of someone's life, a bed and desk crushed under ceiling tiles, the curtains like cobwebs, a framed photograph of two small children on top of an icebox that had toppled to its side. The fireman explained that they had been digging here for bodies for three days, and that it might be another week or more before they found everyone.

Down the street was a technical school that had taken a bomb through the center of the roof, and now the entire building was a crater, all the floors and the cellar disintegrated so that you could see through to the sewers. A teacher had witnessed the collapse and seen most everyone in her classroom become pinned under the wreckage. Her husband, a plumber, was in one of the hospitals with a hole in his throat from a length of copper piping. She had a son, who was fifteen, but hadn't seen him since the last attack. When I spoke with her, I made sure to make a note of his name, his height, the color of his hair, the clothes he was wearing. 'In case I should see him,' I said, though I knew, with a lump in my throat, that I wouldn't. We were both playing at optimism, at resilience. At hope. But how else could anyone get through such a thing?

'Don't forget,' she said as I walked on to the next bombed place, the next battered person.

'No.' I lifted up my notebook like a promise. 'I won't.'

★   ★   ★

There was a routine to the bombing, which depended on the weather, and also on the light. Thick snow generally meant safety, and so did thick fog. Dark was the best of all, and we mostly felt safe until eight-thirty or nine in the morning, when the planes came roaring over from the east to drop their bombs or sometimes just propaganda leaflets. The most terrifying thing they could do was drop gas, of course, and we continually wondered if they would.

Rumors flew all the time that this would be the day, but I stayed in my hotel as long as I possibly could — stubbornly, I suppose. One night when I was sound asleep, Geoff Cox came pounding on my door to say that everyone had to leave the hotel immediately. Gas was going to be used in the morning. They were sure this time.

'It's time to beat it, Gellhorn,' he said when I opened the door.

I was still half asleep, my nightshirt probably on sideways and my hair bent in every direction. 'What the hell, Geoff? Have you been drinking?'

'Sure, but what does that have to do with anything? Everyone English speaking is pulling out.'

'They've done that twice already, and just end up coming back.' I rubbed my eyes. My head was throbbing. 'Please go away. I'll be fine.'

'Suit yourself,' he said, and went to the room next door, and began pounding there.

Thankfully, it was another false alarm, but we were all evacuated just the same. Sixteen Russian planes had been shot down, and a powerful retaliation was imminent. We went into the woods with everyone else. It was warmer there, and when it started to snow seriously, it was warmer still — a muffling, blanketing wet snow that flocked the fir trees and our canvas tents so that the sides bowed.

It felt like being in another, older world out there. We slept under stiff furs, like characters in a Tolstoy novel, while the thick-muscled horses all around steamed with the heat of their bodies, and stamped the snow. Their coats were shaggy, and they had matted chunks of ice in their long tails, so different from Blue, in faraway Sun Valley, that they might have been different animals altogether.

In the inner pocket of my jacket I carried two cables from Ernest that had reached me on December 4, and that I'd already reread so many times the paper had gone soft as cotton. He was proud of me, he wrote, and thought I was the bravest woman alive. *I can come over,* he insisted. *Say the word and I'll drop everything.*

I didn't feel brave, though. It wasn't bravery when you did what you had to do.

I was sick with missing him, yes. I felt so alone here, and more frightened than I'd been in a

279

long time. But none of that changed the truth. There were stories here that needed telling, and I couldn't leave until I'd done that.

Grabbing a steamer over to be near me would be terribly dangerous for Ernest, but also a waste of precious time. The book he was writing mattered more than it ever had, I realized. It would outlast all this chaos and senseless death. It would live long after all the stupid things humans did to one another had healed over. That's what great art was for, I thought.

# 44

At daybreak, several days in, I rubbed my
fingertips on the base of a lantern to get some
feeling back in them, and waited for the car that
was coming for me — a military chauffeur that
had been assigned to take me to general
headquarters for the Karelian front, four
hundred kilometers to the east.

'It must be nice to have Roosevelt in your
pocket,' Geoff Cox said. He was still irritated
that I'd ignored him in Helsinki, and he knew I
carried a letter that allowed me special access to
all sorts of places that were usually off limits to
journalists.

'Don't be stupid. This isn't about privilege, or
calling in favors. If I didn't have it, I'd never get
anywhere as a woman, and you know it.'

'You're right. I'm being an ass,' he said.

'It's all right. With this cold, we're all barely
human.' I took up the lantern I was using to
warm my hands and gave it to him. My driver
had arrived.

The car was long and white, aiming to
disappear in the landscape. I'd been granted a
young civilian chauffeur for the trip. He had a
schoolboy's face and a thin straight neck dotted
with pale freckles, and was also to act as a
translator between me and my military guide.
The guide's name was Viskey, a young lieutenant
so sharply and cleanly turned out he could have

been carved from a bar of soap. He wore high black boots trimmed in fur, and a charcoal wool greatcoat, with a black astrakhan collar. His hat was fur as well, and sort of magnificent, with high stiff sides and earflaps. I wondered briefly about the likelihood of pilfering one and smuggling it home for Ernest, but there was the actual business of the war to think of. For fifty kilometers or more we fell in behind a battalion of Finnish soldiers in heavy ammunition trucks. The line of trucks rumbled ahead in the dark, filled with supplies and sledges and bicycles and soldiers hunched on benches, their field rifles lying atop their knees.

It wouldn't be light for hours yet, and later still if there was fog, as there so often was. For the moment, the forest pressed black and dense from both sides of the road, and the driver was translating for the lieutenant about Karelia, which had apparently been fought over as a territory since the twelfth century or even before, with Sweden and the Novgorod Republic claiming and ceding it, again and again.

'Now others will have to die wastefully and stupidly,' Viskey said in Finnish, and the driver then relayed to me in French. I had managed to learn very little of their national language, which rose and dipped and curled, with complex elisions that had me wondering even where one word stopped and another began. 'Hopefully more Russians than Finns,' he went on. 'The Soviet infantry attacks in one solid line. Did you know that? We hide in the trees. We're everywhere out here.' He gestured toward the

282

dense inky forest. 'They make it too easy. One column, and we mow them down before they even spot us. It's sickening.'

'Sickening, yes.' It was. 'But perhaps you'll win this way.'

'No one will win,' he said simply. 'This is war, after all.' Then, 'Tell me, what do you think of Adolf Hitler in America?'

'In America? I hardly know. I haven't been home in a long time. I've lived in Cuba for quite a while now, and before that I was in Spain and other places in Europe.'

'Spain? On which side?'

'Madrid's, of course.' I felt myself prickling at the question. 'Do I look like a Fascist?'

'Who looks any way?' he asked, shrugging. 'Take off the uniform and remove the crowds and Hitler is a small, unremarkable man. Think of him at home in his bathrobe.'

I knew he was right, but I couldn't. It should have been impossible for him to do as he did and think as he did, and be at home anywhere, be loved or cared for by anyone.

★   ★   ★

An hour later the dawn came, wan and cold in a way that pressed through the car door, my wool trousers, and heavy jacket to get at my bones, so that I always seemed to be clenching. We drove without stopping, maneuvering over unmarked roads and tree-shrouded lanes, pushing forward where I didn't think there was a path at all. Often we drove in first gear, eking our way through wet snow, and I kept thinking the driver was awfully young to be so intrepid. At one point, he took us across a heavily mined bridge so slowly it seemed we were making our way inch by inch.

'It's only really dangerous if you skid,' he explained.

'Well,' I said, and then fell silent, my shoulders tense as trip wires. The bridge was only wide enough for the car, with less than a foot clear on either side. The road surface felt different here than before we'd met the bridge, glossy and flat as glass. *Slick enough to set us spinning like a coin*, I thought, but somehow we managed in a crawl and reached the other side. That's when we finally breathed.

'Last week one of our cars hit a mine on such a bridge,' Viskey said. 'Nothing was left of it afterward. The men were never found.'

I felt myself go clammy. 'What?'

'I don't mean to frighten you. I only thought you might be interested, for the story you're writing. Besides, Virtanen here is the very best.'

'I'm sure he is,' I said to be polite, but couldn't help looking again at the spattering of pinkish freckles on his neck. His hands were gloveless and pale, and his fingers were thin — even bony. Was he twenty? Twenty-two? How could he possibly have the experience and cool head required, I wondered, for this sort of driving? But then I felt my breath catch and every small question flew away from me. We'd come round a long slow curve and were pointed at yet another bridge.

★ ★ ★

All that day and through the night, we drove on and on while I slept as well as I could, sitting up and propped against the shuddering door, swaddled under blankets of scratchy gray military wool. Near dawn I had a snatch of a dream of being in St. Moritz, swimming through a forest of seaweed that seemed conscious of me, somehow, and even tender, accepting. When I woke, it was such a loss not to have St. Moritz, or even the warm glove of the dream, that I felt I might crack into pieces.

Viskey must have noticed my fragile state. He gave me a chocolate bar, which seemed a reasonable breakfast under the circumstances, and a small bit of aquavit, since there was no coffee to be had. The white countryside continued to flicker by. Sometimes we heard the rumbling of a battle, a blurred sound from miles and miles away. Every now and again, lightning flashed against the thick low sky, but it wasn't lightning. It was rifle fire.

Finally we came to Viipuri, a city on the Karelian front that had been heavily damaged by bombing. The houses that were still standing were gray, and the sky was a heavier gray, and I thought I was too cold to get out of the car when Viskey gave the sign that we'd arrived. At one edge of the city, a rail terminal had been turned into a barracks, with frosted windows and long lines of cots, and a coarse temporary commissary — everything bare and terribly sterile — but at least there was coffee.

285

My fingers aching, I shook hands with a young colonel. He had very thick, nearly white-blond hair and a cheerful manner as he unrolled a field map onto his breakfast table to show me where the infantry was, in what positions, with what reinforcements. Viskey had explained to him that I was going to write articles for an American audience, and also that I had published books. I assumed that was why he blasted off lists of specifics as if he were lecturing — how this number of guns was in each battery, and how that sort of shell was used. I took notes dutifully as he spoke, but this wasn't really the story I wanted.

More coffee came, and more maps were unfurled. The colonel was just getting started on a description of the Mannerheim Line, explaining how the southern front was perfectly situated in the geographical bottleneck of the Karelian Isthmus, when I stopped him and asked if I might see the prison. Viskey had told me they had Russian POWs, and I was eager to see them.

'Perhaps the airfield instead?' he suggested, looking at me with some pity, as if I wasn't sharp enough to know what was worth paying attention to. 'We have five new pursuit planes from Oslo.'

'I'm interested in people,' I said, insisting. 'All sorts of people.'

The colonel permitted the visit in the end, though he was shaking his head as we left, rolling up his maps and muttering, probably, about who would send a woman to a war front, when she took no notice of artillery?

＊　＊　＊

The Viipuri prison was a hulking stone building with cells deep in the earth. Viskey found the warden, who led us down into the icy honeycomb, adjusting and readjusting the silver pince-nez on his nose, and walking with a heavy determined clop, as if the soles of his shoes were made of iron instead of leather.

Finally we arrived at the cell of a Russian POW, a flier who'd been shot down and captured near Kouvola. He sat on a low cot, his back very straight against the concrete wall. He seemed to be sleeping with his eyes open until the guard clacked at the bars with the toe of his boots. Then he rose, looking startled.

He was tall and narrowly built, with a reddish growth of beard coming in, and sad pale eyes. He couldn't have been much older than I was, I thought, and he looked very cold. We had a brief conversation, a tangle of translation from Russian to Finnish to French and then to English. I wanted to know what he thought he was fighting for.

'To save Russia, of course,' he said quietly.

'From what?' I pressed.

'We hear this again and again,' the warden intervened. 'The government has told them Finland is the attacker. They fight because they think they must.'

'Is everything propaganda?' I shuddered and looked again at the pilot, who was here in this godforsakenly frigid place, and probably thought he was going to be shot at any moment. All

287

because his government had told a great lie. He was living that lie, and didn't even know.

'Ask him if he has a family,' I said to the guard. He did, but when the Russian pilot answered, the guard turned away because the man began to cry, holding his hand flat at the level of his waist to show the height of his daughter. His wife was pregnant with a second child, he pantomimed, while tears coursed down his cheeks into his beard.

The warden coughed, a half-strangled sound. Viskey looked at his shoes. I wanted to scream.

'Please, let's leave him alone now,' the guard begged, which I understood to mean he couldn't hear anymore, not if he was going to do his job and sleep that night.

We saw two more Russian POWs, who looked so lost behind their cell bars that I begged the guard to let me give them cigarettes. I was rattled at this point, distracted and emotional, and could barely look at them without wanting to weep. They had the thinnest sort of cotton pants, threadbare coats, and the wrong sort of shoes for this weather.

The men must have been almost mindless with cold, but they answered my questions solemnly and respectfully, and smoked my cigarettes as if they might never be offered such a pleasure again, drawing each breath in deeply before exhaling. Through the guard who stood there, they telegraphed the same general message the flier had, that they were fighting because they didn't know how else to save Russia. They'd only had ten hours of training before being shipped to

288

the front. They had families. They were afraid of dying.

'You have a soft heart,' Viskey said as we made our way out of the honeycomb later. I was breathing hard as we climbed, and not from exertion.

'Governments and world leaders should be punished,' I said. 'Not men.'

'I don't hate anyone,' he explained. 'But war insists we be practical, doesn't it?'

'It's just so sickening, that's all.'

He cleared his throat loudly. The sound bounced off the deep stone walls and echoed up and down the stairwell before landing back where we were. 'Yes.'

★   ★   ★

A short while later, we were at the airfield, though I hadn't asked to see it. The squadron commander was a version of the colonel I'd met that morning, and as he paraded me by the five planes, shiny with rivets behind camouflaging snowdrifts, I made sure to praise them and also scribbled notes to reassure him. When I was finally released to a nearby dugout, the men of the pursuit squadron stood around barrel fires, their faces glowing. One played a guitar with fingerless gloves, his touch light and effortless seeming. A folk song, a love song, an anthem — I wasn't sure of the sense of the words, but the music seemed to rise over the edges of the dugout as the snow came soundlessly down. I looked at Viskey, and his lower lip was trembling.

'I see you have a soft heart, too,' I said. Actually, I had begun to wonder.

'I know this song,' he said simply. 'It makes me forget how terrible things have been, a little.'

I felt it as well. How for a moment his voice seemed to lift us all beyond this war — beyond any war. Beyond what humans could ruin or distort. For as long as he sang, I could let go of where I was and what the world was up to. Almost.

★ ★ ★

For the next string of days, I dug in at the Karelian front, taking advantage of my special access from Roosevelt. I wasn't just the only woman there, but the only reporter who'd gotten through at all. As alone and as frightened as I felt, I knew that I'd been given a serious responsibility, and I meant to live up to that, or try with all I had.

It was almost surreal to watch the Finnish soldiers flicking through the snow-heavy, misty tree line on skis, aiming to surprise the Russians. To hear artillery fire half swallowed by a blizzard, and villages laid to waste almost silently. To see the whole white wet forest burning.

Back in Helsinki in a café, I tried to write what I'd seen and to keep out what I felt. *Collier's* wanted reporting, not histrionics or hand-wringing. Not tears. And yet how could I keep my feelings to myself? This was a war of gluttony. Because a very few people — Hitler, Franco, Mussolini, Stalin — wanted to control everything they could, ordinary people were dying in droves, and they didn't even know why. At least in Spain, there had been a cause, a reason for the fighting and the loss of life that gave a measure of dignity to both. But this, this was going to drive me mad if I thought about it too much.

It was three o'clock and also twilight in the far-north winter dark. I sat at the café table while my tea grew cold. It was raining and the fog was like damp and wretched bandaging coming apart. *Collier's* had sent word that I could leave as soon as I finished this piece, but apparently there were no planes going out now. Arranging transport during wartime could be difficult. You came and went in borrowed cars or convoys, cadging a seat on a plane when you could beg one, unless anyone more important needed it, which was nearly always. But here things had grown even more intense than I'd experienced before. The Russian fleet had moved from Kronshtadt, and the sea was unsafe, too. I wanted to send a cable to Ernest to let him know I might be stuck here indefinitely, but the wire communication had gone down completely.

I felt helpless and desperate. Now that I'd done my work, all I wanted was to be home again at my own desk while Ernest sat at his, with sun streaming in the windows from everywhere, and time to wallow and think and be quiet. I couldn't now remember any of the difficulties of the fall, or my worries about Pauline. There was only the love I had for Ernest and our life. I didn't want to be apart from him now, or ever again. If only I could get back to our precious foxhole again, I would tell him that, and then show him, over and over.

'Gee, Gellhorn, who died?'

I started, blinking, and saw it was Frank Haynes, an American military attaché I'd run into half a dozen times. We expats were a pretty small bunch.

'Hi, Frank. Sorry. I think I froze to death weeks ago, actually.'

'Looks that way. Maybe it's time you went home.'

'Don't tease me. I can't take it.'

'I wouldn't. I just got word there's a flight going out tomorrow. I can get you on it if you'd like.'

I nearly jumped out of my café chair and flung myself at him. 'Oh Christ, yes. Yes! Where to?'

'Sweden?'

'I can live with that. Oh, my God — Frank! Really? You've no idea how you just saved me. Do you think I might make it home by Christmas? Is that too much to hope for?'

'Maybe not. You can try.'

I did jump up then, and kissed him hard, full on the mouth, which had him laughing. But I would have kissed a lamppost. A leather shoe. A lump of coal. I would see my love, soon. I was going home.

# 45

From Sweden I headed for Lisbon to catch the Pan American Clipper bound for Cuba, but fate intervened in any number of ways. First I was waylaid in Paris, where I learned Gustav Regler, our colleague from long-ago Madrid, was languishing in prison as an enemy alien. They were questioning his Spanish citizenship and he had no one to help him untangle the snarl of red tape around the situation, so I wrote Eleanor Roosevelt to see if she could persuade the French government to see reason, and then visited his wife and gave her a little money so she could stay her course while she waited for good news.

I cabled Ernest saying it looked like I'd be home by the first of the year, now, but there were more delays in Paris. My exit visa needed sorting out, and there was a question about whether I could find a French plane to take me to Portugal, or anywhere at all, given the tense, tangled state of Europe. So I waited and bit my nails, and smoked more than was good for me, and longed for the Finca and my desk and Ernest's arms until they blended together into a steady, pounding ache.

The only thing that did anything for my nerves was Paris itself, which was quiet and cold and incredibly beautiful — more beautiful, actually, for the way the city didn't seem to know it

293

existed on borrowed time. War was coming here, too, of course. It was already an inevitability — but for the moment there was only a silvery snow falling on the empty Place de la Contrescarpe. Ernest had walked here as a young man, looking into all the café windows with a knot of hunger in his belly and a hole in his shoe. He had told me all the stories, and they seemed like gentle ghosts as I threaded my way through the Latin Quarter, past the good cafés burning *boulets* in their braziers, thinking of him.

★ ★ ★

Ernest looked scruffy and yet wonderful when he met me on the dock in a thick fisherman's sweater, his hair grown over his ears. The weather was unseasonably cold in Cuba, but I didn't care about that or anything else. When he held me, we were both shaking a little.

'Hello, Rabbit,' he said.

'Oh, Rabbit,' I said, pulling back to see his face. His face: my God, I had missed it. The feathered lines around his eyes. His strong straight nose. The dashes of gray coming through at his temples. 'Promise you'll tie me up next time I talk about going away, please?'

'Tie nothing. I was thinking chains. I haven't been able to eat or sleep for worrying about you.'

As we walked toward the car, I pulled my jacket more tightly around me, wondering if Finland's cold had permanently lodged in my bones. 'What's with this weather?'

'I don't know. The boys and I kept a fire going for days and slept in our clothes.'

'The usual lawlessness, you mean.'

'Without women, what do you expect?'

'Exactly that. Just kiss me, all right, and don't stop kissing me until I tell you to.'

He smiled. 'You have a lot of demands for someone who's been away for two months.'

'Two months and sixteen days, and I won't do it again. I promise.'

He stopped and reached for me, clasping his hands together around my rib cage until I felt the vise grip of his arms, strong and warm. 'I want it in writing.'

★   ★   ★

The next morning, I woke in my own bed and sank farther into the pillow, stretching long under the piled-up blankets. Ernest was working already. I could hear the keys of his Corona striking the paper against the roller, a steady pleasant clacking sound — the sound of things coming together as they should.

I lay there without moving and listened as the rhythm intensified, like a boulder rolling downhill and picking up speed. Then there was a silence as he read over what he'd written, and thought, and waited for what came next. His mind turning and turning, sifting through the things he knew, the true things he'd kept close to him for years and years, sometimes, waiting for the right moment.

Later, I would do the same. The places I'd just

been and the people who'd moved me were with me, ready to feed my work. And I saw now, in a way I hadn't before, how having the Finca and Ernest, too, made it possible for me to go away and return, changed and stronger, and better, and more myself somehow. It was a version of what I'd said to Tillie in Sun Valley, only truer. I didn't want to have this life with Ernest and my work to prove I could have everything. I needed them both in order to feel whole.

'Rabbit?' I called from the bed.

'Yes?'

'This is everything I love. It's all right here. We're our own country.'

★ ★ ★

My God, but I loved being back at my desk. The first thing I did was pore over the publishing contract that had arrived while I was away. I had sent *A Stricken Field* to a handful of editors in New York, initially planning to include Max Perkins at Scribner's. But Ernest had convinced me not to, saying that it might not be wise for two writers in the same family to also be competing for attention at the same house. I agreed, moving on to other possibilities, and had finally hit pay dirt with Duell, Sloan and Pearce. The book would be published the following March, and I was over the moon. I couldn't have loved it any more if it were my own child, and now it would have a place in the world, not just in my heart and imagination. I sat with the contract in my hands for a long time, absorbing the realness of it and the seriousness of the legal language that bound the book and me to a future.

It was Ernest's faith in me, and the rootedness we'd claimed together, that helped bring this book to life. I felt that profoundly, felt the value of what we'd made here. The future was as terrifying as ever, with Europe tumbling and shattering into awful shards. Ernest's divorce, too, was still only an idea. Hard words thrown down followed by awful waiting. But here was something solid. Ernest and I gave each other guts and roots, and a bright horizon. We filled our days with meaning and laughter and rich, real talk. I could never do any better, or have what amounted to more. I only had to say yes.

Reaching for clean paper, I snapped a sheet into the carriage and wrote,

*I, Mrs. Martha Rabbit Bongie Gellhorn Hemingway, do forthwith and otherwise swear never to undertake the leaving of my current love and future husband again, nor send him into wretchedness for two months and sixteen days, nor trouble his mind and heart, for he is everything that matters to me in this life.*

*Let it be known to these witnesses (imaginary as they might be) that I will endeavor to protect him from further loneliness and storminess of mind by staying put and loving him body and soul. And I promise this from the soundest and best of intentions, and with the squarest, most right*

mind I can muster for these proceedings, and with more love than I can properly state.

Martha Gellhorn Hemingway

# Part 5

# THE SUN AND THE MOON AND THE SUN

## JANUARY 1940-DECEMBER 1941

# 46

'She could put me out of business if she wanted to,' Ernest said of Pauline. We were still waiting for her to agree to the terms of their divorce and wondering if she could stall for months, or even years, to spite him. Us. In the meantime, she had sent the boys off to boarding school and shuttered the Key West house to be in New York with her sister. 'Jinny has too much influence over Pauline and always has. Things could get a lot worse now before they get any better.'

'Let's try to be optimistic,' I told him. 'Maybe she'll want to move on for her own reasons. She's still a young woman. There's plenty of life left.'

'Maybe,' he said, sounding unconvinced. 'In the meantime, I'm going to put everything I have into this book. I'm going to write so well that all the other books will seem small in comparison. That's the kind of optimism I can get behind.'

I understood the way he leaned on his work in the face of uncertainty. I was doing exactly that as I waited for A Stricken Field to finally land in the world, with its dedication to Ernest, and all my hopes and wishes for a lasting career as a novelist tucked inside its pages, written invisibly in all the spaces between the words.

But from the moment the first notices began to roll in, I crumbled. The story was too much like reporting, the critics said, too factual and journalistic, and not imaginative enough. Marianne Hauser at the *Saturday Review* went so far as to call my heroine, Mary Douglas, 'more noble than real.' She couldn't have hurt me more if she'd said the same about me, to my face.

'I wonder if they know how deeply we take this stuff in,' I said to Ernest, the latest notice in my hands. A hard, acrid lump resting just below my rib cage.

'There was Mrs. Roosevelt's piece. That was positive.'

It had been lovely, in fact. She'd praised the book in her 'My Day' column, calling it 'a masterpiece as a vivid picture,' but against the sea of mostly negative commentary, I couldn't trust her praise. 'She's just being loyal.'

'You should let me read them for you,' he finally suggested. 'You'll make yourself ill this way — or, worse, you'll start believing what they say.'

'That would be cowardly, wouldn't it? Not to even look?'

'Nonsense. It's self-preservation. What's the use of having two writers under one roof if we can't look out for each other?'

I gave in, and did actually stop reading them, until *Time* magazine arrived in a thick bundle from the mail boat, like a very quiet bomb made all of words. They'd given me a splashy feature — half a page — but it wasn't about the book at all. It was gossip, a biting piece about me and my 'great and good friend' Ernest Hemingway.

The photograph they'd used of me was far too large and vampish. I wore deep-red lipstick and sported a fashionable haircut, all of which worked to underline the journalist's remarks. My face was 'too beautiful' for a writer, he said. My long legs too 'distracting.' It was a goddamned exposé.

When I showed Ernest, he threw the magazine end over end to the other side of the dining room. 'These people are disgusting. They have no idea the trouble they're going to cause me, and the boys, too.'

Of course he was worried about what this meant for him. This was the first time anyone had dared to report that we were romantically involved. It was also the first mention anywhere of Ernest and Pauline's impending divorce. But as much as I understood his anxiety, I was still fuming, still raw. With no effort at all, the magazine had stolen my credibility as a writer, and reduced me to Ernest's concubine.

'Listen to this,' I said, as I retrieved the magazine from the corner against my better judgment. ' "Gellhorn is headed to San Francisco de Paula, Cuba, where Ernest Hemingway is wintering.' How do they even have that on record? Have reporters been following us?'

'Probably.' His tone was defeated, flat as slate. 'It doesn't really matter now. Fife's going to come with her guns blazing. You can bet on it.'

And she did. The next day, a telegram arrived. She'd changed her mind about the boys coming to Havana that spring for Easter vacation. *The environment won't be healthy for them*, she'd written.

' "Environment," ' he repeated sourly. 'You'd

303

think I was running a whorehouse here. She can't keep my kids from me.'

My head felt so heavy I had to rest it in my hands. 'Can't she, though?'

'Maybe. Oh, hell,' he said. 'Maybe she can.'

He wrote her a long letter immediately trying to plead his case. We waited for her reply, both of us ill at ease and able to think of little else. I wrote several damning letters to *Time*, threatening to take legal action, and sat at my desk for long hours, trying to read and feeling lower than low. It was one thing to receive bad notices, and another thing entirely to have one's work be made cheap and meaningless when it was not that. I'd worked hard — incredibly hard — for a year, and now all the public would remember was my sordid association with the most famous writer in America.

That famous writer wasn't writing, either. The real world had grown too loud, and was drowning out Robert Jordan and everyone else in the book, there in the middle of chapter 28. Ernest began to panic. He told me he wanted to go away for a little while, just until the dust cleared, to see if he could get back in. I agreed to stay behind to field the mail and keep an eye out for snooping reporters, but then immediately regretted it. I needed peace just as much as he did, and to believe in the value of my work again. I wanted to run far away until the dark voices in my head quieted. But his needs upstaged mine.

He left for Camagiiey, an inland city on the plains of Cuba, hundreds of miles from us. It was far away from everything, and just what he'd been looking for. He wrote me every day, telling me that his head was clearing a little at a time, and that the book was coming back.

I was relieved for him, but I was also in mourning for my own book, and feeling very alone with it. From the beginning we had made a promise that our books would be our children. That we'd tend them together, him mine, and mine his. I still needed to know that we were in this together, even when things grew difficult, like now. I understood that he was overwhelmed, but I was, too.

I wrote him a letter telling him just how much I missed him and was looking forward to having him home again, as it should be. Then I closed the door on my office and my work. My articles for *Collier's* had been posted, and I had no idea what came next. Someday I would be ready to think about that. For the moment, I only wanted peace and forgetting.

# 47

Ernest came home in the later part of March, just in time for Patrick and Gigi's arrival from the mainland. Pauline had finally relented, though not happily. On the day they were set to come, I went around and around the house nervously wiping away nonexistent dust and rearranging piles of books, trying to distract myself. I still hadn't begun to get over my book and what its failure meant. Overseas, the Soviets had begun bombing Viipuri until finally Finland submitted to their terms of surrender. I thought of the Finnish people, all their quiet determination and their dignity, and now their country would fall anyway. I felt awful, and didn't know what to do with myself, so I washed and rewashed every glass in the sink, and then scoured myself in the hottest shower I could stand.

'They won't care what anything looks like,' Ernest said. 'They're kids.'

'I want them to be comfortable here,' I said.

'And they will. You'll see. Just give it time. They're going to love you, you know.'

'God, I hope so.'

★ ★ ★

The moment he saw his sons on the gangplank of the ferry, Ernest rushed at them, somehow managing to scoop both of them off the ground at once. The look on their faces was beautiful. The pure, unadulterated joy of belonging to someone. Of coming home to love.

'How d'you do?' Patrick said with a warm and delicate smile when Ernest brought them my way. He had a straight fine nose, brown hair brushed down from the crown of his head, and beautifully shaped feathery eyebrows. Immediately I recognized his gentleness, the quiet that he kept at the center of himself. It was right there, as plain to see as his blue-checked cotton shirt.

'H'lo,' Gigi chirped. He put his warm slim hand in mine, his eyes black as glass buttons. When they darted up at me in the middle of the handshake, I could see the comic in him instantly. This was a funny story already in the making, just below the surface, where he was trying to be good, and I was trying to be good.

'You can call me Marty if you like.'

'That's your name?'

'Yes, part of my name. It's Martha, actually, but that's too serious sounding for me, most of the time anyway.'

'I think my name's too serious,' Patrick chimed in, 'but no one around here uses it. I guess that's lucky enough.'

'You're the Mexican Mouse, aren't you, because you were brown and small like a mouse when you were a baby?'

'I'm brown as a mouse in the summertime, too — browner than either of my brothers.'

'Say, I can get brown enough, too,' Gigi said.

'Sure, you can,' Ernest broke in, 'and you'll both get plenty of sun this week and we can have a contest and Marty can judge.'

We sorted the boys' luggage in the car and settled them in the back before starting home the usual way, passing through the heart of the city and then winding up the hill out of town. It was the usual way, but already anything but ordinary. It was livelier, moving through the countryside with the boys talking and noticing things. The windows were down and Patrick had his hand out lightly, riding the air pressure.

'Can we go goggle fishing later?' Gigi asked.

'Sure, if the water's not too cloudy,' Ernest said. 'We'll go plenty of times, so don't worry if today's not right.'

'Do you like goggle fishing, Marty?' Patrick asked.

'Why sure.' I turned around to face him, resting my arm over the top of the bench seat. 'Not the fishing part so much as the swimming and looking at everything.'

'Whoever heard of not liking to fish?' Gigi's question was good-natured and honest, coming as quick as thought, the way only children seemed to allow — not yet burdened by trying to rearrange themselves for others.

'It doesn't matter,' Patrick said. 'She can do as she pleases, can't she? There are plenty of things to be good at.' He gave me a diplomat's smile. He was clearly a natural mediator, as middle children often were, less on the side of any particular person than on evenhandedness in general.

'Maybe I can learn to like it,' I offered.

'You're a writer, aren't you?' Gigi said. 'Like Papa.'

'Yes.' Unexpectedly, my throat tightened. None of the tidying or preparing for the boys had touched that sore place in me. 'No one's quite like your father,' I said. 'But yes, I am a writer.'

★　★　★

Time began to swing like a hammock as the boys settled into their vacation. They had no set bedtime and sometimes fell asleep at the dinner table, or on the floor in the middle of a game. The refrigerator was always open, no matter how close to either side of any meal we might be.

'Boys need food,' Ernest said simply.

Obviously that was true, but I had no idea of the scale. Entire hunks of cheese vanished. If I bought a dozen eggs, three dozen were needed. And the milk they could put away — it was shocking. But there was also something wonderful about coming into the kitchen and seeing one of the boys emptying a foamy white glass into his mouth without even breathing, and then gasping afterward for the coldness, and wiping his lips with the back of his sleeve.

They slept on cots on the long sun porch, strewing their bedclothes and dungarees and T-shirts and pajamas on the floor. Their socks, I found everywhere, which was funny, because they rarely seemed to wear them. Ernest laughed at this and everything. He seemed to have only two house rules, no properly filthy swearing before 4:00 P.M., and no sand inside. If we came back from the beach or an outing on *Pilar*, he made them rinse their feet and legs with buckets of rainwater on the terrace. All sorts of other things got tracked in, of course — rocks, bark, shiny leaves, and, once, a yellow-flecked, opaque-eyed lizard, but these were somehow permitted. And if it was after four, when the boys let everything rip, well, watch out.

'They're actually making a great effort to behave for you,' Ernest said, as we were getting ready for bed one night. 'I know it doesn't seem that way, but just wait. Your newness will wear off and everything will go to hell. Maybe you won't be as fond of them then.'

'I guess I can stand it,' I said, slipping into white cotton pajamas. 'They're children, after all.'

I could see I'd surprised him. 'Miss Dutch Cleanser,' as he liked to call me. He gave me a funny look and then sank into bed and stretched out long. 'I wish I could get some sort of special dispensation as their father.'

I flicked off the light and lay beside him, kicking the sheets clear. 'I'm afraid it doesn't work that way.'

'I'll tell you one thing. I sleep better when they're around. It's the sound of their breathing. Even when I can't hear it, I know it's warm and even and untroubled. They get to sleep that way. They haven't ruined anything for anyone yet.'

'I'm hoping they're going to be around a lot. They bring life with them, you know?'

We lay still for a long time — so long that I was sure Ernest had fallen asleep. Then, in a voice so low it was almost a whisper, he said, 'I'd like to have a daughter.'

He'd caught me off guard. I felt my pulse speed up instantly. 'Would you?'

'Yes. With you, I'm saying. I'd like us to have a child.'

I felt a flashing up of excitement and terror and everything in between. I was glad we were in the dark, and that he couldn't read my eyes. 'Do you really think we're ready for that? We're not even married yet.'

'The wedding is a formality at this point, isn't it? We're already together in every way that matters. And anyway, no one's ever ready for a child. I learned that with Bumby in Paris. You could have knocked me over with a feather at first. I just kept thinking of all I was losing, not having any idea how he would be a whole real person with his own wonderful mind. Not knowing how much he would bring.'

'Do you feel something's missing, not having a daughter? Is that what this is about?'

'That's part of it.' He rolled onto his side, releasing a complicated sigh. 'But it's also something I want us to have together. And I don't know, there's just a feeling I have thinking of her. Sometimes she seems so clear and real to me I can almost believe she's here already.' He swallowed hard, his voice thick with emotion. 'She has your hair and your eyes, and everything fine about her is what's fine about you.'

'And what will you give her?'

'Not much until she's older. Then she'll learn to fish and swim and sail like her brothers. She'll swim early, like a small otter, and freckle in the sun.'

Hearing him talk was stirring all sorts of things in me I wasn't quite prepared for.

The more he went on, the more I could begin to see her, too, this small shining essence of a daughter, a bit of gold leaf quivering in a shaft of sunlight. 'An otter with two rabbit parents?'

'That's right,' he said. 'And she'll read three books before breakfast, just like the Mouse, and be funny like Gigi, and decent and kind like Bum. She'll have all of us in her.'

'Well, she couldn't sound more lovely. Who wouldn't want that person around?' I paused, steadying myself. We'd plunged so far forward in one conversation I needed to catch up. 'Maybe after we've married will be a good time.'

'Sure, if you need to do things the conventional way.'

'We couldn't bear any more scandal right now, and you need to finish your book. When the time is right, we'll know it.'

'We're going to be so happy,' he said, curling toward me. 'No one saw that coming in Spain, did they? Not even us.'

'No,' I said quietly. 'Especially not us.'

# 48

It was a bright clear day — a day of frigate birds and flat white quilted-looking clouds and languorous bottomless sunshine. *Pilar* was tethered off one of the small numberless cays we frequented, rocking in a light wind. Ernest and I were on deck, and the boys had taken the dinghy out to the reef to goggle fish with Bumby, who'd just arrived the day before from the mainland. He'd spent part of his holiday with Hadley and Paul in Miami, and he was already brown from the sun — with tousled, sandy-blond hair and finely sculpted shoulders and a face that was so lovely it made you think of Achilles or Apollo, the absolute cream of Mount Olympus.

He was sixteen and utterly devoted to his brothers. Just now they swam along the lee side of the reef, with their rubber-framed masks squeezed tightly to their heads, their light wood-shaft spears floating atop the waves, which only had the slightest chop, the weather being so fine, while they kicked their long legs and bare feet.

All three boys seemed incredibly comfortable in the water, but there was so much of it all around, the vastness of the ocean and everything it contained just beyond the shallow stretch of the reef.

I shaded my sunglasses with my hand so I could see them all more clearly. 'Do you think they're all right?'

313

'Sure they are,' Ernest replied. 'They're with Bum, and they know to stick together.'

'They don't seem afraid.'

'Not Mouse — he was made for the water — but Gigi knows about the things that can swim over the reef and worries about them. Not that he'd want his brothers to know that. It's so important with brothers to appear braver than you are.'

Ernest went below and came back with two very tall glasses of rum and coconut water, with chipped ice and wedges of lime. The drink was cooling and delicious, the lime fizzing over my tongue, but I couldn't quite relax with the boys out there. 'Do you think something really could come over the reef at them?'

'I suppose that's always possible. The tide is up.'

'At least the water's clear.' I stood and continued to watch them, my drink in my hand, the boat swaying beneath me. I could see the shape of the reef, the way the tide boiled around the dark prongs of coral. Patrick had gotten a nice-sized grunt, bright yellow, and Bumby had stopped to help him take the fish off the point of his spear. They were both laughing as they threw it into the dinghy, but there would be blood in the water now. I turned to Ernest. 'Maybe we should be closer.'

He looked at me curiously. 'It's nice that you worry about them, I guess.'

'Is it nice? It's hard to care about people. You end up fretting all the time and feeling helpless, hoping they'll live forever. Only no one does.'

'Yes, that's love for you.' He squinted into the sun, and then pulled the anchor, using the winch. Climbing up to the helm on the flying bridge, he started up the smaller Lycoming engine and used the controls to nose over until we were almost touching the dinghy, with *Pilar*'s portside to the reef, but not too close. All the while, I kept my eyes on the boys, thinking that Ernest must be right. Love came with risk by nature. But that didn't mean any of it was easy.

'How's that for you?' he asked when he was back down beside me again and the anchor was set.

'We can see everything now. Thank you.'

He came over and put his arms around me, resting his chin on my shoulder. 'Yes, little mother. We can see everything now.'

★   ★   ★

The boys swam safely all day, seeming tireless, and caught lots of fish, which we cooked up that night when we were back at the Finca. Yellowtails and grunts and red snapper they cleaned for themselves — even Gigi could gut and scale anything with the precision of a surgeon — and we ate them with bacon and onions, and knobs of the Spanish cheese that Ernest liked to always have on hand in the icebox. Rene made a beautiful tomato salad to go along, and an apple cake dusted with confectioners' sugar, with soft spoonfuls of homemade ice cream. It was a feast fit for the day we'd had, and we sat at the table for a long time afterward, with only the candles

315

lit, as if it were Christmas, while the boys told me their favorite stories.

Patrick and Gigi wanted mostly to talk of summers in Wyoming and the L-Bar-T, about how once they saw a black bear that got all the horses good and spooked. Ernest had the touchiest horse, and had been thrown wide into rail fencing that split his forehead something wicked. They had lots of stories, most of them involving scars and tumbles and tough scrapes they'd come through together or separately. Gigi talked loudest, offering loads of details like a natural tale-teller, but I could also sense that it was important to him to assert himself about the summers he shared with his family, since many more of them had been spent with his nurse in Key West on their own in the Whitehead Street house, or with her family in Syracuse, New York, until he was old enough to make the trip.

Everyone seemed happy to concede to Gigi's place as the entertainer of the family. He went on and on, his eyes bright, until Ernest took over, telling stories of Paris when Bum was a baby. About the apartment over the sawmill, and the constant high-whining sound of the mill running, and of the sharp smell of the wood dust in the air; of Bumby in his pram in the Luxembourg Garden on chilly fall days, warming his hands on pigeons Ernest had downed with his slingshot; of sitting in cafés like Lipp's and the Closerie des Lilas and getting small sips of café au lait while Ernest talked to interesting friends.

'You were a good Parisian baby, Schatz,'

316

Ernest said. 'Everyone loved you desperately. You were so beautiful and solid and well behaved.'

'Tell Marty about F. Puss,' Gigi urged, and Bum obliged him, describing the large plush Persian that had possessively guarded his bassinet when he was an infant, not letting anyone come near.

'He was a wonderful nurse,' Ernest said. 'Better than our *femme de ménage*.'

'Not really,' I said. 'You didn't leave the child alone with the cat.'

'Like hell we didn't. He would curl up at Schatz's feet and keep him warm from drafts when he had a cough. That cat would have lit into anything or anyone, make no mistake. He knew why he was there.'

'Now I've heard everything.'

'He was the best friend I ever had,' Bum said. 'We should get a cat here, shouldn't we? Or maybe bring one over from Key West. You always have cats around, Papa. It feels strange not to have at least a few.'

'I'm swearing off cats.' Ernest's eyes were bright, his voice full of good humor. 'They eat too much.'

'I don't believe you,' Gigi said. 'You let them eat from your hands at home, right at the table.' He turned to me, his face alive in the candlelight. 'Papa calls them love sponges. You like cats, don't you?' he asked me, and I recognized a pleading in his voice. I'd already said I didn't like fishing. Perhaps he thought this was my last chance to fit in with the gang, to be one of them.

'I do. Very much.'

'That's settled then,' he said, clearly greatly relieved, and everyone laughed.

⋆ ⋆ ⋆

Ernest wrote smoothly and well with the boys at home. The typescript was already over four hundred pages long and was an impressive thing on his desk while he worked, a neat white tower next to his sharpened pencils and his notebooks.

I couldn't think about writing yet, and didn't know when I'd be able to have that much hope again. So I dug into each day, instead, surprised at how gracious the boys were with me, sharing themselves as easily as they did their books and their games — inviting me to plunk pennies with them into a line of muddy cans, or join them in a mock-fencing battle with broomsticks and tennis rackets, or watch them climb into the alligator-pear tree and then rocket to the ground again and again. I was even more surprised at how easily I took up the role of stepmother and friend. I loved my long talks with Bumby, or Bumble, as I'd taken to calling him, as we walked the perimeter of our property, or sat on the terrace in full sun, both of us keen to soak up the warmth like happy golden lizards. He was good company for me when Ernest was busy, and I liked to hear him musing about his future, wondering about college boards and where he should think of flinging himself. Or maybe he wouldn't go to university at all?

'Sure, you'll go. You're so bright. What else would you do?'

'Fish? It's what I'm best at.'

'Fish for a living?'

'If there was such a job, I'd gun for it, that's for sure. I think about it all the time, and dream about it, too, all the browns and blues and rainbows. Montana or Wyoming, or up in Michigan.'

'You sound like your father,' I told him.

He smiled sideways, looking pleased. 'I guess I do.'

'It's nice of you to be my friend,' I teased, 'when I haven't ever caught anything. Those flies in the box all look the same to me. That's unforgivable, isn't it?'

'You can still learn. Anyone can. And it's not like I'm going to test you on the names or anything. Hell, we don't even have to use flies, we can use grasshoppers.'

'You're a good one,' I told him, which was exactly what I felt, as well as the truth. He glowed with goodness, with fineness of character. What a remarkable boy Hadley and Ernest had made together. Then I said, 'I'm awfully glad we're getting to know each other.'

'Me too. I haven't ever seen a woman stand up to Papa like you do and just be herself.'

'Do I stand up to him?' I had felt myself shrinking inside since the release of *A Stricken Field*, and it troubled me. I would have to find a way forward soon, somehow.

'Seems like you do. Anyway, I think he likes you better for it.' He cut his eyes at me, suddenly

319

shy. 'I hope that's okay to say.'

'Sure,' I told him, inwardly pleased by what he'd noticed. 'You can say anything to me.'

'That's another thing I like. I was just telling Papa I've never met a woman who was so pretty and also swore.'

'Ha!' I felt the laugh burst from me, delighted and also slightly horrified. 'Please don't tell your mother.'

'It's all right.' He was blushing now, the way boys did, bright pink striping his cheeks vertically. 'My mother swears, too, every now and then. And anyway, I think she'd like you.'

Hadley had been the angel of Ernest's youth, the best thing about his Paris years, and the loss he most regretted. She still shone brightly for him, the way only the past could. And though I didn't know if I was a large-enough person to shake her hand without feeling threatened, I loved Bum's wanting to knit us together, even with words. 'What a nice thing to say,' I told him. 'The very nicest.'

# 49

After the boys left, I decided to behave more bravely than I actually felt and locked myself in my office, determined to begin something new. In one of my notebooks, I found some sentences I liked about Finland and began to work them into a story about an American reporter in the midst of the Winter War. It felt good to be back in that country as it was before it fell. Almost as if this were my way of honoring the place and reviving it, even a little, for one small moment.

'It might be called 'Portrait of a Lady,'' I told Ernest of the new story one afternoon after I'd worked well.

'I'm happy you're back at it, Rabbit. But I do worry a little. Your subjects are so dark. Wasn't that a lot of the guff you got about *A Stricken Field*?'

'The world isn't exactly a cheerful place these days,' I snapped. 'Or hadn't you noticed? Only grim things have gone on for years. Am I supposed to pull a happy story from my hat?'

'Now, now. I'm on your side, remember? I just don't want you being boxed in as just one kind of writer.'

'I know,' I told him, but there was something in his tone that rattled me. He knew more about writing, certainly. Maybe he even knew what my career should look like better than I did. But in order to hold myself up and keep moving forward on my own steam, I had to do what felt right to me. I needed his love. I needed his support and then some, but the most dangerous thing I could possibly do was shift myself to get his stamp of approval. He never waited for mine, did he?

These days, Ernest was on a strict regimen of work and little else. He'd cut back on drinking and was watching his diet, weighing himself each morning, and then recording the number on the wall above the scale in pencil. All of this so that he could go more deeply inside his book. Sometimes it felt like he wanted to close himself up in the pages like another skin. He'd stopped telling me about the scenes he was working on, his characters, or moments of dialogue. I understood why he couldn't, how it was only when you gave a book everything that it gave everything back to you, and then some. But the house was a lonelier place, just the same.

In the meantime, the monsoon season had begun and every day brought in torrents. As if on cue, the roof grew spongy and began to sag precariously. The plaster in the living room loosened with the damp, falling with a smack on the tiles. There were buckets and tarps everywhere, wadded soggy newspapers and useless mops.

In early June, I met my mother in New York at the Carlyle, telling Ernest I just needed a week of sunshine and her company, but actually the weather was only a symbol of what prickled at me. Europe had been at war for nine months, and though England and France had both declared war on Germany after Hitler's capturing of Poland, only now were things escalating for the bulk of the nations involved. A full attack had recently been launched by Germany on France and the Low Countries. Holland, Denmark, and the Netherlands were swept under so quickly you'd think they'd been made not of flesh and blood but paper.

As bad as things were, I felt comforted to be near Mother. She'd always been my North Star, but nothing helped for long. Each day's headline was more terrifying than the last. The Nazis had crossed the Meuse River, punctured the Maginot Line, and were swinging their way south through the Ardennes with great force. France was poised to fall.

I chewed my fingernails raw, and didn't want to leave our hotel room, but Mother insisted on dragging me out for a walk. We headed up Madison Avenue for twenty blocks, slowly, arm in arm. Crossing Central Park near the North Meadow, we wound our way down again, as if by tracing the city with our feet, we could ward off some evil.

But it came anyway. We were having tea in the Algonquin when we heard the news, and we sat there, numb, while the service staff disappeared and our tea went cold, and the cress sandwiches wilted. The Germans had done it. Tanks were rolling into Paris.

★　★　★

The world was in the hands of madmen, and Roosevelt still wouldn't act. He froze all

323

American assets of the Axis powers. He made speeches to condemn fascism and aggression, arguing loudly and with vehemence, but he held the same line as ever. America would not enter this war unless attacked.

When I raced back to Cuba, taking Mother with me, I expected to find Ernest tuned in to the wireless, but we no longer owned one. He'd done away with it.

'You can't be serious.' I whirled on him. 'Nazis are marching down the Champs-Élysées.'

'Who wants tragedy and disaster screamed at them from their own parlor?'

'Tragedy and disaster are happening. It's irresponsible to be so insulated. The mail takes four days.'

'I wish it took a week. It's so distracting.'

I could hardly believe him. 'That's like saying a fire alarm is distracting when flames are licking up the wall!'

'Listen, if someone's army comes battering down the door, by God I'll fight to save what's mine. I'm not ignoring anything. I'm making a stand.'

I could see that Mother was uncomfortable with our arguing, but I was just about to lunge with another point anyway when she broke in. 'How about lunch? I'm famished.'

'Your daughter seems to want my liver,' Ernest snapped.

'Yes, but I was thinking oysters,' Mother shot back, and we laughed nervously.

★　★　★

In the end, I had to admit that Ernest's utter commitment to this book about war while the world raged on and on *was* his stand. I found it hard to agree with him, and might not ever, but I had to respect the work itself. He'd begun sharing pages with me again, and they were magnificent, as good as anything he'd ever done or might do. Max Perkins had set October as the date to publish, and so Scribner's needed the pages now, if not yesterday.

In the meantime, the boys had come to visit and left again, and the summer heat closed tightly around our days. I worked on my stories in the morning, took swims with Mother in the saltwater pool, and then we would go to town. We had to, now, to get any news.

One afternoon we'd just taken several papers to the Floridita when a man walked through the door of the café. He looked like any other gringo you might see in Havana except for one small thing. He was wearing a Nazi uniform, crisply turned out, with leather strappings and epaulets, bright-striped insignias and a stiff high-rising hat, and jet-black boots. But your eye only wanted to go one place — there on the left arm, where a swastika blazed vividly, almost luridly red.

I reached for Mother's hand under the table because she'd gone absolutely stiff. 'It's all right,' I said very quietly. 'Ernest and I have seen him before. There are quite a few Germans in Havana.'

She looked at me sharply and I knew exactly what she was thinking. *He's not just any German.*

He stood at the bar now, half turned away with one boot on the rail, making some remark to the waiter. Meanwhile, our lunch had arrived, but Mother could only pick at hers. I couldn't remember seeing such an intense reaction in her before. After he left, finally, she leaned toward me and whispered, as if he had informants in the room or might yet come back, 'I can't believe anyone would go about like that.'

'Well, they mean to instill fear. It's very effective.'

'I hate it,' she said simply. 'I hate everything about this war.'

'Sometimes I pray that a nice bolt of lightning would strike Hitler. It would simplify so much.'

She looked nervous that I'd said such a thing out loud, but what else could you think, really? Lightning or tornado, or great sweeping typhoon, some very specific and acute natural disaster delivered right to his doorstep. It wouldn't solve everything, but it would be a start.

When we got home, I told Ernest what had happened, trying to explain how upset Mother had been. 'It was as if she'd seen a wolf on two legs. Maybe we've gotten used to having them around here, but that's a mistake. When you stop noticing ugliness. Maybe I should write something about them.'

'Instead of your stories? You're liking them, I thought.'

'I am. But I don't want to pull a blanket over my eyes, especially not here where we live.' I was thinking of being in France and England when

326

Czecho was falling, and how a Nazi in your newspaper wasn't at all the same thing as one in your café. 'Being with Mother today reminded me of how when you really see something for yourself it can change the way you feel. Change you.'

'Yes. But don't change too much, Rabbit.'

'What do you mean?'

'I just wondered if you were thinking it wasn't enough to be here anymore. That you might want to be part of the action.'

He was right. I had begun thinking in a fragile, shadowy way about what it would mean to go to France, just for a short while, to be involved with things, and face them head-on, and maybe write an article or two that could make a difference to someone. But admitting as much would only hurt him, and now was not the time anyway. 'No,' I told him, and then reached for what was true. 'I love our life.'

# 50

Though I'd often wondered if Ernest might be writing this book forever, the ending finally came. The bridge was blown, and he had finished off Robert Jordan, and now was as wrung out and empty as if he'd killed off a part of himself to do it. He had, really, since Jordan was in him deeper than most real people in his life would ever get.

He went up to New York to be on hand as his proofs came in. He stayed at the Barclay, sweating through the heat wave that was punishing most of the country just then. He wrote me saying that I should think of him in pajamas, in a puddle of sweat and effort, the fan going around the clock. Every time he finished proofing and correcting a section of the book, it was rushed to Scribner's by a runner who was always ready nearby, and then on to the printer — forty-three chapters all told, each as dear to him as a child. Each day he raced to keep just ahead of the typesetters. But I could also tell he was buoyed up by all the urgency and expectation, the thrill of the deadline.

When he was finished, bleary eyed and spent, he took the train to Miami and then boarded the Pan Am Clipper to Havana. Mother and I met his plane, and though anyone could see how exhausted he was, there was also a clear sense of triumph. He had the Scribner's contract in his shirt pocket, and it was a doozy — promising 20 percent on copies once he reached twenty-five thousand copies sold — an almost unheard-of royalty. The Book of the Month Club was also sniffing at the book for their October selection, and if that came through, they would print one hundred thousand copies immediately, and the number would just go up from there. Scribner's was going to devote all its window space on Fifth Avenue to display copies, and there was even talk already of the movie rights being snapped up in Hollywood, with Gary Cooper playing the lead.

I was thrilled for Ernest, I really was. But it stung to see the red carpet rolled out for a book that wasn't even published yet. I had been just as devoted to *A Stricken Field*, and it had vanished into the ether almost immediately. I had poured my best self into those pages, but instead of triumph, or some sense of personal accomplishment, I'd been sucker punched. It still hurt that work I loved and had suffered for could be so easily dismissed. It enraged me as much as ever that even the few good reviews I'd received had been hijacked by the larger story of my being Ernest's new girl. But I didn't know how to say any of this to Ernest, particularly now when his book was poised to be the biggest novel of the year, and perhaps the most important thing he'd ever done.

And it was beginning to dawn on me fully just what all this meant. The book already glowed with a rare incandescence most writers would have killed for — to stand in that light for even a moment. It was a dark and shimmering star, creating its own atmosphere and gravity. It was the biggest thing in our lives.

\* \* \*

Now that Ernest had finished writing, he could turn his energy to other things, like harassing Pauline about the final details of the divorce, and talking about our own wedding, which was on his mind more and more. I had always known it would happen eventually, and had aimed a lot of my own energy at wanting the worries with Pauline to finally be settled so we could be together completely, without any barriers or strife. But it was strange and surprising, now that our marriage finally felt imminent, how I began to feel anxiety and rising dread. I didn't understand it, exactly, which troubled me even more.

Ernest seemed not to notice — he was too immersed in his own whirlwind — but Mother did. When I drove her into Havana for her ferry to Fort Lauderdale, I knew right away she was intent on speaking her mind.

'If you're having second thoughts, you should honor them. Your intuition is there for a reason.'

'I don't want to lose him.'

'I'm not suggesting you leave him altogether. Enjoy the interlude. This is paradise . . . I see that. But paradise never lasts.'

'Please don't say that. Not now. I'm feeling too fragile as it is.'

'Well, tell me what you're worried about. What do you want?'

'I want him, but he's such a force of nature. He pulls everything into his orbit and seals off the corners and any route of escape. He does it all without trying, and with very little self-awareness. And this book. He might be finished with the writing, but it's not going away, not in the least. Some sort of wave is beginning. I can feel it.'

'What does your heart tell you?'

'That's just the thing. I seem to have two hearts where Ernest's concerned, and at least two minds.'

'He's a big person, that's certain. But so are you, my darling. Don't sell yourself short. You're as strong as anyone I know inside. And whatever happens, you can take it on.'

'I love you, you know that?' I said, and kissed her. 'Are you sure you can't stay?'

★   ★   ★

All the rest of that day, I chewed on my thoughts. Ernest had already been through two wives, both of them strong women if I could believe his stories. And yet they hadn't been strong enough, or their love hadn't been. Either way, the end had come sadly and irrevocably. Could I bear it, if that's what fate had in store for us as well? Could I bear walking away in fear, not having tried at all?

'I've been thinking I need more time,' I finally told Ernest, having spun on questions over and over, reaching no answer. I meant to be gentle, but Ernest flinched just the same.

331

'You sure know how to hurt a guy.'

'That's what I'm trying *not* to do,' I protested. 'I love you, I just want to be sure this is the right and wisest thing.'

'Wise? Since when has love been anything of the sort?' There was a scoffing tone to his words, and his mouth had hardened and seemed almost cruel in this light. 'Marriage isn't science class, you know. It can't be reasoned out. And anyway, you sound awfully cold to me. Actually, you sound calculating.'

'Oh, Rabbit, no. Not that. I only want to be sensible and listen to myself.'

'Enjoy yourself, then,' he said flatly. 'I've heard enough.' He went off to bed, slamming the door as he entered our room.

I was afraid to push things any further, and so stayed up later and later, the words of my book swimming in dim light. I nursed a small scotch, then another larger one, and finally fell into bed past two, muffle headed and morose.

In the morning, I didn't hear him get up, though I guessed it was before dawn. When I woke myself, there was a fat letter on the nightstand, saying how gutted his heart was, and that I'd felled him just when he needed me most. It was hard to read the rest, particularly when the letter began to list all the ways I should be grateful that he'd helped my career. Even in Spain he'd been helping me, he wrote, believing in my work long before I believed in it myself. He'd read every word of *A Stricken Field* ten times over, and urged me to work on stories. Then he said that if I was sure I didn't want to go through with the wedding, I should come clean now. He was going to have to take *Pilar* to the mainland in September, and that would give him ninety miles and plenty of hard, empty time to think about how goddamned busted open he was. That was if he made it to the mainland. Maybe he wouldn't this time.

I held the letter, which seemed to quiver and smoke in my hands. It was every one of his moods, all his sides on full display — bitter, wheedling, threatening, guilt mongering. But all of that only very thinly covered a profound loneliness and fear. I saw that and understood that any awful thing he said only pointed squarely at the fact that he didn't want to lose me. Didn't want to lose us. In the end, I didn't want that either. I wasn't trying to walk away, only to keep myself from being so sucked in by him — his wants and needs, his friends, his appetites. His books. *His* books, which glowed and soared and roared into the world while mine faltered, even with his encouragement.

I bathed and dressed slowly — still nauseated from the scotch and my ever-more-jumbled thoughts, and from what I knew I was about to do.

I found him at the dining table reading through piles of mail, and though I waited for him to look up, he went on gutting the letters with a vengeance, slicing through seals with the opener in small decisive bursts of violence.

I forced myself to come nearer anyway, the ceramic tiles cool under my bare feet, my eyes swimming with unshed tears. 'I can't lose you,

333

Rabbit. I won't. That would be pure idiocy and I'm no idiot. I want us to be married.'

He finally turned his gaze on me, his eyes glassy and unyielding. 'I don't believe you.'

'Please don't punish me. I've been punishing myself enough as it is.'

He stilled his hands, then, softening infinitesimally, but softening. I knew he would listen now, and forgive me for hurting him, but part of me was angry with myself for seeking that forgiveness — for capitulating — when I'd only been trying to honor my own very real doubt. And that doubt was still there, the same as ever.

'We're each so independent,' I said as gently as I could, 'so bent on having our own way. How is that going to sort itself out?'

'I never feel you get in the way of anything,' he said, missing the thrust of my point. 'You just make it all better.'

'I don't know any happy marriages. Even between lovers who know how to compromise.'

'We'll make our own rules, then, and damn everyone else. We're the best thing going, and we're going to be so stinking happy no one will be able to stand us. We'll barely be able to stand ourselves. You'll see.'

*How, how, how can it work?* I should have cried out. *You're the sun and I'm the moon. You're iron and I'm steel. We can't bend and we can't change.* But what I did was go to him. I put my head on his broad, impossible shoulder, and I nodded and I kissed him, swallowing back all my doubt and fear. My wisdom. 'I love you so much,' I said.

# 51

*For Whom the Bell Tolls* launched to reviews that weren't raves so much as paroxysms. Even the staunchest critics couldn't deny the power of what Ernest had done, and the effectiveness of the book. *The Atlantic* called it 'rare and beautiful,' full of 'strength and brutality.' *The New York Times* said it was 'the fullest, truest and deepest' thing Ernest had written. *The Saturday Review* thought it 'one of the finest and richest novels of the last decade.' But the notice that seemed to make Ernest happiest, and the one that rang out all through that fall, was from Edmund Wilson. For years and through several books, he'd been loudly disappointed with Ernest's writing and Ernest himself, it seemed, but now he was equally emphatic in sounding the prodigal trumpet, saying, 'Hemingway the artist is with us again; and it is like having an old friend back.'

Because I had the closest vantage point, it was impossible to miss how the success of this novel worked to cure every other publishing disappointment. Hurt fell away like iron scales — and not because everyone loved the book, though that was wonderful, but because he had doctored his own ills. For nearly a decade, he'd been accused of macho posturing, of writing prose that was akin to wearing false hair on the chest — as Max Eastman had so meanly scolded in print for all of America to read. But Ernest knew there was more inside him, and he'd gone to Spain to find it, to access the raw and elemental sort of experience that he knew would bring him to life again as a writer. And it had worked brilliantly. He'd written the precise book that would rocket him past any further doubt from the critics as to his ability, and to quiet the demons in his own mind.

It also didn't hurt that the book was flying off the shelves.

'Like frozen daiquiris in hell,' Ernest said of the sales figures Max Perkins sent on.

'Just as it should be when the gods are actually on our side. Now you can rest.'

'Rest nothing. It's time to enjoy myself.'

★  ★  ★

It was high season in Sun Valley when we arrived. The publicity campaign seemed to have worked, because the lodge was swimming with socialites and celebrities. It looked like a film set and might well have been. No one talked about Hitler or the latest cataclysm coming over the wire — or about anything, really, but the movies they had just seen or had just made, or wanted to make. I thought it was all incredibly shallow and shortsighted, but since Hollywood had grown keen on adapting Ernest's book for the screen, it was the only thing he could think about, so I knew to keep my opinions to myself.

Dorothy Parker was hoping to write the script.

336

'Over my dead body,' he said when she was out of earshot.

'Her writing's very clever,' I allowed.

'Which is the opposite of what anyone should value.'

'Yes,' I agreed, privately thinking that Sun Valley was a strange place to even mention values.

One day Gary Cooper arrived with his very beautiful and very groomed wife, Rocky. Everyone thought he was a shoo-in for Robert Jordan, but the part of Maria was up for grabs.

'What about Ingrid Bergman?' Cooper suggested over drinks. When he leaned toward his overfull martini, his suit jacket followed his every movement, and my eyes trailed along appreciatively. Ernest wore the same shirt for days on end. I'd almost forgotten how good a man could look in the right clothes. Cooper would have looked even better if he knew how to be quiet, but he and Ernest had just gotten started.

'How about Marty for the part?' Ernest said. 'She's the real Maria.'

'What do I know about acting?'

'You'd be grand. You'd play her straight and simple and true.'

Rocky's eyes grazed over me. She wore a net hat and gleaming sable jacket, a deep-red stain on her lips. 'Hmm. Who else? Garbo would be marvelous.'

'With those false eyelashes? I can't see that.' Ernest motioned to the waiter with two quick tugs of his hand through the air. Our drinks were still half full, but that was how things went now

337

that Ernest wasn't writing. The clock went unwatched. Hangovers didn't factor in if you could sleep the day away.

'Without the eyelashes, then,' Cooper said smoothly. Everything about him was smooth, I had to admit, but the talk went on this way for hours, dull and empty and artificial. I had to stop listening.

'Does the movie really matter so much?' I said to Ernest later. 'The book is wonderful all by itself.'

'The money won't hurt,' he said. 'You know Pauline's going to keep exacting alimony until I'm dead. And my taxes are suddenly so outrageous I might need a tourniquet.'

'Well, all right. I just think writers who cater to Hollywood end up soft and spineless. Too well fed. Please tell me you won't get sucked into all that. I couldn't bear it.'

'I don't think I could after what happened to Scott out there.' He meant Fitzgerald. Everyone knew that as soon as he'd indentured himself to MGM, he'd written almost nothing and turned into a sad and spongy impostor of himself, drinking and drinking and trying too hard to please everyone, forgetting altogether what had driven his work, and what really mattered. I couldn't think of anything more tragic.

But even if Ernest did privately hold up Scott for himself as a cautionary tale, the moment we were among others, he raced to be the first with a drink in his hand, talking louder and more forcibly than anyone else, never dimming even in the wee hours when I could barely hold my head

338

up. The endless gossip and the highballs and the elaborate menus felt frantic to me, like angels dancing wildly on the head of a pin while the larger world was in chaos.

★   ★   ★

Once Hitler had conquered France, he'd turned his gaze across the Channel and sent his bombers streaming over London in an attack we would later know as the Blitzkrieg. All through September and October, the attacks went on, night after night, week after week, decimating the city, while we played doubles tennis and fished and complained about the coming rain. It was almost too much to believe.

I tried to work on the stories I'd brought with me but had a hard time focusing. I couldn't concentrate with so much going on, and felt myself growing dangerously edgy. But Ernest didn't want to listen to my fears or anxieties. He'd earned his break, he insisted. Could we just get through this holiday?

Finally, the boys arrived to save the day. When the rain cleared, we organized a long pack trip along the Salmon River, taking our horses over twenty-three miles of trail, as the fall colors burst and then bled, and the air went crisp as an apple. I'd never loved camping, but the boys made anything better, even sleeping on the ground. Gigi taught us an elaborate card game to play around the fire in the evenings, and Patrick read out portions of The Call of the Wild with such feeling and sensitivity I got a lump in my throat.

Bumby was quieter than usual, even pensive. He was about to turn seventeen and had just started his senior year of high school, but he still didn't know what to point himself at, or what he should care about beyond fishing and the occasional role in a school play.

'Don't be so sure you need college,' Ernest told him. 'At least not right away. You can work awhile, can't you? Catch up to yourself?'

'Sure,' Bum agreed. 'That would leave a lot more time for getting after steelhead.'

'You bet. There's only one life, as far as I've been told. Why not get as many as you can?'

'The war could land here and turn everyone's plans over,' I cautioned. Just that week, Japan had joined the Axis powers, signing a treaty that said an enemy to any one of their countries was an enemy to all. It was a prophetic moment. America had avoided conflict so far, but now it seemed obvious that we could be forced into the theater at any moment. Japan was awfully, eerily close to the South Pacific, where we had a strong military presence.

'It's not here yet,' Ernest said.

'I think I'd make an all-right soldier,' Bum said, and I felt a chill pass over me, head to toe.

'Don't grow up before you have to,' I told him. 'Not a minute before.'

★ ★ ★

The more time I spent with the boys, the luckier I felt to have fallen in with them. Like their father, they surrendered to the natural world,

340

becoming absolutely alive in whatever they were doing — flicking for trout, wading through yellow eelgrass, catching mallards on the wing. Ernest had taught them what to do, as his father had taught him — where to stand, how to hold a knife, how to walk through grass without a sound — but he also made plenty of room for them to make their own discoveries and mistakes. He left them the plum shot, even if they might miss. He moved down-stream so one of them could have the prime location for fly-fishing. He also listened to them intensely — all their stories, their funny schemes and long-winded jokes. And when I saw him this way, with them and at his best, I felt guilty and disloyal for doubting him. This life I was building with Ernest and his boys was a good one. And I was about to be married, wasn't I? To make all the promises that would mean I wasn't only myself anymore, but part of a family, *this* family, the one that wanted to make me feel whole and loved and just where I belonged. If only I would give in and believe it.

★ ★ ★

On November 21, 1940, in the gently moth-eaten dining room of the Union Pacific Railroad in Cheyenne, Wyoming, I became the third Mrs. Hemingway. We had roast moose for supper and passable champagne, the very best that could be found in Cheyenne or for a hundred miles, probably, and we were giddy, both of us — giddy and rash and determinedly hopeful.

Ernest had been divorced for only two weeks, but I did my best not to think about that. I tried not to remember my mother saying how Ernest didn't seem to know how *not* to be married, either, or how these last months had been so difficult, with him and Pauline fighting and clawing over money, because that was the only thing left to fight about.

For almost four years, Ernest and I had been together — immorally, in one way, if you thought like that, but also cleanly and honorably, because we wanted to be. Now there would be insurance policies and codicils and all the sticky bindings of matrimony. But it was done. I could only face the future, drink my champagne like a good girl, and be fiercely, dizzily merry.

Afterward, we headed east in Ernest's brand-new Buick, which wasn't black, for once, but a glittering color called paradise green. Ernest looked happy and relieved — weightless — as he slid behind the wheel, as if the physical fact of his shiny new wedding ring held him in place and made him feel sure of life again. My own ring was the loveliest thing I'd ever seen — a platinum band studded with small diamonds and sapphires, part of the spoils of this new book and what it could buy. It was so beautiful, I was almost afraid of it. I found myself looking at it again and again, as if I might catch it in the act of becoming something else.

# 52

It took us most of a week to travel from Cheyenne to New York, where Ernest had promised me a honeymoon at the Barclay. Along the way we talked of the book he might do next. He'd had an idea to write about the Gulf Stream, deeply and factually, obsessively, as he had bullfighting in *Death in the Afternoon*.

'I'd love it if I could do something for the boys, too,' he said. 'I don't know what exactly yet, maybe an adventure story. Something they'd like to read.'

'That would mean so much to them. Now, obviously, but also for someday. A real legacy.'

'How's your work coming?'

For a moment, I thought of how to answer him. He'd been so preoccupied, I couldn't remember the last time we discussed my work, or he'd asked to read pages. 'I'm pretty far along on a collection of stories. They might be too gloomy for your taste, but I like them.'

'I don't mean to tell you what to write. I'm just trying to look out for you.'

'I know.' I gazed out at Nebraska, the shorn cornfields, silver with hoarfrost. The land went on and on, empty and unspoiled. 'But it's almost as though I have to relearn everything with this book. The last one broke my heart. I've forgotten how to trust my own instincts.'

'I know, Rabbit. They don't all bust you to

pieces, though. I promise.'

It was easy for him to say. He was riding the most glorious wave of his life. I swallowed hard and said, 'I just have to toughen up and write the damned book and take my chances like anyone else.'

'I think you should let Scribner's do it when you're ready. Max would put it out beautifully and respect your thoughts, too. I'm not saying you should decide anything now. Just mull it over.'

He meant to support me, to protect me, if he could, from another potential failure. Still, I felt a shadow of unease. 'What happened to your idea that the same operation shouldn't publish two writers in the same family?'

'I'm not sure I trust anyone else. This is my wife we're talking about.'

★ ★ ★

The Barclay was Ernest's favorite hotel in New York, and he treated our suite as he might his own living room, often keeping the door open to the hall, and inviting all sorts of old friends by, literary folks and sports personalities, and reporters seeking interviews. We could barely keep our bar stocked. The telephone rang off the hook.

Certainly I understood why Ernest was relishing the chance to receive everyone just now — life was on his side, and he was the talk of the town. But I felt even more frayed and exasperated than I had in Sun Valley. My

344

husband belonged to everyone and seemed to like it that way. Where had the quiet gone, and the privacy?

'Do we have to be on display all the time?' I complained.

'I guess not, but I can't really see wishing this all away so soon. Seems like bad luck to even think it. Can't you hang on a bit longer?'

'I'll try,' I promised. But it all wore on me. There seemed to be no moment that someone might not burst in the door wanting something — a chat, a drink, an interview, a photograph. We were never alone, and sometimes I could scarcely recognize the couple we'd become — and in such a short time.

The only company I actually relished was when Bumby came down from school on two of the weekends we were there to stay with us. Ernest thought it would be fun to give him a few boxing lessons at George Brown's Gym on West Fifty-seventh Street, a place he'd loved for years. They went suited up in thick gray jersey with towels around their necks and spent hours training with the bag and working on footwork. Ernest believed that boxing was one of the best ways to stay trim and also sweat out the liquor he was taking in. Bum didn't even try to sneak shots from his father's flask, as far as I knew, and was already a perfect physical specimen, but I could tell that heading into that masculine sanctuary with his father by his side felt like a particular rite of passage. He'd crossed an essential threshold and had a right to be there now.

But where was my place? That wasn't at all

clear. Almost immediately, I grew tired of being trotted out as the new wife. It was almost impossible to work in our suite with so many comings and goings, and so one day, desperate to be free of the vortex, I made a lunch date with Charles Colebaugh at *Collier's*.

'Is there any possibility of an assignment?' I asked him over shrimp cocktail at the Russian Tea Room.

'Well, there's the Burma Road to cover, and the war in China. But I wouldn't think of you for that.'

'China?' I felt jolted. It was difficult to stay in my chair. 'Why not?'

'You just got married, Marty, or hadn't you heard?'

'Married isn't dead, Charles. My work still matters the same as ever.'

'All right, all right. Don't get your nose out of joint. I was just thinking you wouldn't be as free to travel now. It's a reasonable assumption.'

It was a reasonable assumption, and yet I felt an urgency to run at this chance now, while I still could, to claim something for myself before I became completely swallowed up by Ernest's career, his fame. 'I'll make myself free.'

★   ★   ★

Though China and Japan had been battling for resources for decades, in 1937 an all-out war had begun, and now the Japanese occupied almost two-thirds of the Republic of China, including the coastline. The only way to get supplies into

346

the country was the Burma Road, seven hundred seventeen miles stretching through ruggedly mountainous terrain and linking Kunming with Lashio, Burma, and, farther along, Rangoon. Britain had been aiding the Chinese since the conflict had begun, and protecting their crown colony along the way, but recently Roosevelt had become involved as well. Defending China was a way to secure it as an important ally now that Japan had joined the Axis powers. No one liked to think that Japan might openly attack us, but it was naïve to ignore the possibility. The Burma Road was a big story — an important story — and I wanted to be the one to tell it.

When I got back to the suite, Ernest was looking through a large stack of magazines for new notices while Bumby gobbled lunch enough for six from room service. The timing wasn't perfect, but I thought Bum's being there might dilute some of the tension if the conversation went south. And it did.

'China?' Ernest barked. 'Are deprivation and difficulty some kind of flypaper for you?'

'Oh, stop. It's a plum assignment. There's so much happening in the Far East now, and I've always, always, dreamed of going there. Ever since I was a child, really. All of those place-names . . . Hong Kong, Singapore, Guam. The *Orient*. Doesn't that sweep you away?'

'Someone's read too much Somerset Maugham.' He narrowed his gaze. 'What kind of honeymoon would China be anyway?'

*Honeymoon?* 'You'd go along, then?' He'd surprised me.

'I think it sounds swell, Mart,' Bumby said from his chair.

'Can you really free yourself up now? I'll be fine on my own. I still remember how.'

'I have a signed contract saying you'll never leave me again, if you haven't forgotten. And there's another contract, if you remember. Some words spoken in Cheyenne. This might be the only way I can see my wife.'

'Of course I haven't forgotten.' I went over and draped my arms around his neck, touched that he'd concede rather than fight me on this. That he would follow me where I was going when it was almost always the other way around. 'Thank you, Rabbit. It will be wonderful to have you there.'

★   ★   ★

That week, before the ink had dried on my paperwork from *Collier's*, Ernest contacted an editor he knew at *PM* and had a contract of his own to write a series of articles on the 'real China.'

I knew everything would go more smoothly if he had work of his own to do, but I'd just begun to like the scenario I'd painted in my mind, that for once he would be subject to the demands of my schedule, traveling as my husband, my entourage, my cheering squad. I should have known better. To get my own glimpse of 'the real China,' I would now have to compete with him, elbow to elbow, and pen to pen. I would also get no break at all from the chaos his fame created.

Even on the far side of the world, he would be the great Ernest Hemingway, of course. And I would be his wife first, and myself only if I fought constantly to make it so.

# 53

The first order of business was submitting to an awful series of typhoid injections. Then, achy and bruised, we went to Washington to arrange the necessary visas and be briefed on China. From there, we made the long flight to Los Angeles, spending two days in Hollywood, where we had lunch with Gary and Rocky Cooper, before heading to San Francisco to meet Ingrid Bergman. When David O. Selznick had told her she had only a narrow window to catch us before we headed to the Far East, she'd driven through most of the night to make it happen. What a baffling thing life could be, for there was Bergman, tall and slender without a stitch of makeup, as natural as a length of birch bark, sitting across from us in a restaurant on Sacramento Street. She wore a camel-colored wool coat over a turtleneck and dark pants — simple traveling clothes she looked anything but simple in.

Ernest and I were both a little in awe of her, not because she was a star, but because she seemed to glow. It was an ordinary light she had — she just had more of it than anyone else.

'Your book is so romantic,' she told Ernest. 'I can't tell you how much it moves me.'

'You'd have to agree to have your hair shorn. It would be sort of a shame to ruin what you have.'

'Not at all. It's such a part of Maria's story. Who'd flinch from that for vanity's sake?'

'I'm glad you see it that way. I don't suppose you'd show us your ears.'

'Ernest!' I said, feeling horrified he'd be so fresh, but she only smiled and obliged him, lifting her brown hair and turning side to side. Of course they were perfect.

'I think it's wonderful that you haven't let Hollywood change your looks,' I told her.

'Oh, they were after me. You have no idea. My hair was too long, my name was too German, and I was far too tall. Oh, and my eyebrows were all wrong. I can't think of the meetings they had over my eyebrows.' She smiled as if none of it touched her now. But I'd felt the power of that sort of scrutiny when *Time's* journalist had weighed in on the shape of my face, the length of my legs, when the way I looked had nothing at all to do with being a writer. We shared something, a particular kind of sisterhood forged by outside pressure that perhaps only women understood.

'I wish I'd never touched mine,' I said. 'They never grow back, not really.'

'Nothing does, not the way it was before.'

A short while later we said goodbye on the street while Ernest hailed a taxi.

'What do you hope to find in China?' she asked.

'I don't exactly know, but it feels important to go there. It feels important to go everywhere one can and see all there is to see and try to understand it. Everything's changing so fast. I

351

want to believe in something while there's still time. I want to tell the truth, even when it's difficult. And I want to find the story I'm meant to write.'

She was looking at me with those soft, large, intelligent eyes, and I felt a sudden wave of insecurity that I had babbled on too long or been insensible. But she only said, 'You seem to know a lot about what you want, actually.'

'I hope so,' I said, and looked back at Ernest waiting by the cab, his body squared against the open door while traffic streamed past. 'I'm going to need it where I'm going.'

★   ★   ★

Ernest and I had been thinking the sail over to Honolulu would be full of banquets and buffets; that we'd sit in deck chairs and be waited on hand and foot while paradise rolled nearer. Instead, the journey was like a small death. We were plunged first one way and then the other until we were green as frogs. Bad weather trailed us, and the high seas never stopped pitching with dark chop. I wanted off almost immediately, but there were days and days of unbroken misery. Finally we went belowdecks and tried to stay drunk. Ernest had a theory that with enough liquor you could fool your stomach or sense of balance or whatever it was that made you wish you'd never seen food and never would again. But even whole jugs of whiskey only helped marginally.

'Who knew the Pacific was such trouble,' I

told him. 'Isn't an ocean an ocean?'

'Obviously not.'

When we reached Pearl Harbor we were anxious as could be to stagger off the boat and find solid ground, but the moment the gangplank was lowered, scores of well-wishers scrambled aboard to greet us, flinging leis around our necks and making speeches and saying 'Aloha.' Photographers snapped publicity photos. Strangers pumped our hands and thrust more garlands on us until we could barely see over them.

'You'd better get me out of here.' Ernest had his jaw clenched, his smile like a barracuda's. 'The next person who touches me will get a sock in the nose.'

'Careful, darling.' It took effort not to break my own stricken smile. 'They're all here for you, you know.' In truth, I wanted to punch someone, too, or scream my head off, just to clear the air. Instead, I said, 'Thank you, thank you so much,' over and over, a hundred times or more. I was green to the gills, delirious with fatigue, but smiling, smiling, doing my very best impression of Mrs. Hemingway.

# 54

We traveled to our hotel by rickshaw through the choking heart of Hong Kong, the cramped streets seeming to close in on us as our driver navigated through bicycles and tumbledown food stalls, bodies and more bodies. There were scraps of red and white paper wherever you looked, litter from the firecrackers that seemed to go off every few seconds. There were chickens in the street, and also babies. Who knew how the traffic moved at all?

Our hotel in the swarming downtown was ancient looking with touches of gentility. Broad paddle fans swept back and forth across the ceiling of our room, and heavy brass spigots trimmed the heavy soaking tub in the bathroom. I said a prayer for small mercies, climbed in up to my chin, and didn't come out for two hours while Ernest went to get the lay of the land.

'I found someone to shoot pheasant with,' he said when he came back. He'd found a Chinese newspaper, two huge bottles of warm beer, and a colorful array of fireworks he wanted to try setting off right there in the room.

I grabbed them out of his hands, thinking of a hiding place. 'Pheasant hunting? Where? You know there's a war on, right?'

'It's here somewhere, I suppose, though not obviously.'

And that was true. The Japanese army

354

surrounded Hong Kong on three sides, but the most serious problem seemed to be overcrowding. Apparently the colonial government was attempting to evacuate its citizens, but hadn't made a dent in the number of bodies. For common people, food was scarce, and clean water was a myth. There was staggering poverty everywhere you looked, but Hong Kong was also like nothing else we'd ever experienced. The air was full of smells we'd never smelled before. Smoke hung on the air and filled the alleyways, where mysterious offerings swung from hooks, and children squatted in the sewers. This was life, as teeming and raw and strange as it came. I wanted to understand it all the only way I knew how, which was to go out and fling myself in up to my neck, talking to everyone I could, taking every little alleyway by foot, getting good and lost until I found a picture, a story, a moment. Something that called to me alone.

Ernest, in the meantime, held court in the hotel lobby, letting his story find him, with absolute confidence that it would. His celebrity drew all sorts of people to him — Cantonese bankers and expat rugby players, cabdrivers and card sharks and even an intelligence officer for an expat warlord general. He took over the choicest corner of the room, spreading out his books and magazines and highball glasses, receiving his subjects from a tufted cordovan leather chair, and listening to tale after tale. He was in his element.

★  ★  ★

Four days after we arrived, I boarded a primitive, metal-clad DC-2 bound for Lashio on the border of Burma. It was before dawn in early February, the air frigidly cold and black as anything. There were only seven other passengers, all Chinese, in the dark cave of the cabin. The seats were rickety-looking metal with the barest canvas coverings. The lavatory sat behind a green canvas curtain and was, essentially, a lightly covered hole that everything dropped straight through to whatever or whomever lay below. I couldn't even look at it without shuddering.

Our pilot was an unflappable American named Roy Leonard. He was tall and blond and corn-fed looking in his tan flight suit, as comfortable behind the controls here in war-torn China, it seemed to me, as he might be driving a tractor in the middle of Indiana. The plane was owned by both the Chinese government and Pan Am. He flew this route regularly, he said, mostly in the dark and at an elevation that put him out of range of Japanese antiaircraft guns.

I tried to scribble these and other observations in my notebook in the dim cabin, but it wasn't long before we were locked in the middle of a hailstorm. The plane bounced and rocked. Ice pelted the windows, sounding like penny nails in a jar. When the airspeed dial froze, I watched Roy open his window to see if he could gauge it for himself by eyeing the ground. I felt sick and terrified, my clammy palms gripping my seat — and this is how it went all the way to Chungking, over seven hundred miles away.

Five hours later, we dropped out of thick, wet cloud cover to land on a crude airstrip on the middle of an island in the Yangtze River. The river itself seemed carved by hand, with high yellow cliffs rising to each side, flocked with vegetation like a mossy crown.

While the plane was refueled, we ate a breakfast of sticky rice and fried egg, with bowls of foul-smelling tea.

'How'd you come to have this job?' I asked Roy, who was nose deep in his tea bowl.

He shrugged. 'I'm never bored.'

I had to smile at that. 'No, I don't imagine you are. Do you think there's more dangerous flying anywhere in the world?'

He grinned back. 'I'd probably have found it if there were.'

Before long we were back on board with a new handful of passengers, climbing out of the rough-hewn dramatic valley and into a sky now starkly, deliriously blue.

'Isn't it safer to be socked in clouds as before?' I shouted up to Roy.

'I'm watching for them,' he shouted, meaning the Japanese antiaircraft encampments and enemy planes, I guessed.

*Good grief*, I thought, and tried to focus on the scenery instead, far-off rice paddies, shining in the sun like silver foil, steeply terraced mountainsides and river valleys and rich wet farmland. We flew all day, landing at Kunming just as dusk fell, staining everything purple. More fuel, more rice and tea, and then onto the final leg, over high mountain passes I had to imagine, since we tunneled over them in inky darkness again, the plane vibrating with effort.

Lashio was essentially nowhere, and yet all of China depended upon its existence if it was going to keep on fending off Japan. The snaking, vertiginous Burma Road began and ended here, a modern *ouroboros* spiraling into the Himalayas and back while the Japanese dropped their bombs in regular raids. As soon as the skies cleared, the Chinese road builders flew into action, making the repairs that would be destroyed again with the next attack. And so it went, on and on. Japan had might, and that was undeniable. But China had determination and an ancient bottomless patience. My money was on them.

I spent most of that night scrawling notes for the story I would post, and then finally crawled onto the cold wooden platform that was my bed, shutting my eyes and thinking of Ernest. Perhaps he was sleeping in our posh hotel with the fans sweeping overhead. More likely he was still in his tufted leather chair in the lobby swilling whiskey and trading true-life stories, utterly dug in. That was who he was and how he was happiest. Tomorrow he would do more of the same, while I saw what there was to see in Lashio, and then boarded a late flight back to Kunming, reversing my journey through the treacherous combination of high altitude, weather, and war hazard. I was exhausted and frightened, but also felt stronger and more capable than I'd been in a year. Without Ernest nearby, it was easier to trust myself, and I liked that.

As demanding as these days had been, they were also exhilarating, flaring with life. Ernest was holding court, and I was on the move. We were both exactly where we needed to be.

# 55

I found a guide willing to take me anywhere in Hong Kong, into the steaming, dripping squalor of cement bunkers where whole families slept in cell-like conditions on the bare ground, into cold and badly lit factories and mah-jongg houses and brothels where many of the prostitutes didn't look much older than fourteen. I went into several opium dens, too, where you could buy two loaded pipes for what amounted to pennies, and disappear that way into platform bunks arranged in stacks, with filthy woolen blankets and not much more. Still, I thought, who wouldn't prefer an opium dream to the actual conditions in these areas? On one of the platforms, two ravaged-looking men slept. But no, I had to remind myself. It wasn't really sleep, they were stunned and vacant, propped against each other, their mouths open. On another bare slab, an old woman in rags leaned against the wall, which was rotting away from moisture and general decay.

No one seemed to be in charge, unless it was the girl who was tamping black tarry-looking wads of opium into pipes with her fingers. She may have been fourteen or a hundred to look at her face. Her shoulders were stick thin, jutting from a dirty shift, but she was also almost painfully efficient in her movements, heating lamps, tidying the heaps of filth. Everywhere,

360

thick smoke hung with the smell of sweet decay.

'How much is she paid for this work?' I asked my guide.

'Maybe twenty cents a day, maybe less?'

'Less? How can she feed herself on that?'

He shrugged and mentioned she might have a family.

*Might*, I repeated mentally while my fingertips grew clammy around my pencil. I was tempted to give her everything I had, starting with the clothes on my back. But she was only one girl. There were thousands like her all over the city, and many hundreds of cities in China, I guessed, where this particular scenario repeated over and over, and might never stop.

Before we left, the girl motioned us over to a narrow slit in the wall where she wanted to show us something in a white bucket. Bending closer, I saw it was a small leathery box turtle she was keeping as a pet. She lifted the bucket and it scrambled against the side, its claws sounding desperate to me, and trapped. But she looked pleased somehow, and watched my face, obviously wanting me to be pleased as well.

'It's wonderful,' I said through the translator, my heart crumbling to pieces — not for the first time that day, or the last.

'I don't think you should let me leave the hotel again,' I said to Ernest when I returned.

He was reading on top of the made bed, and took off his wire-rimmed glasses and looked at me for a moment. 'You want to save everyone.'

I poured two fingers of scotch. 'That or scream myself hoarse.'

361

'That's the problem with going into the world, isn't it? You actually have to face things you find you don't want to know.'

'I do want to know. Only it makes me feel terribly helpless. You should have seen this young girl in an opium den. I nearly died to see how she lived.'

'At least consider that she might not be as miserable as you imagine. It's what she knows. It's her life, not yours.'

'Maybe so. But if I wrote her story, something might change.'

'You're awfully naïve if you think so. And she might not even accept change if it came. People like what they know. It's human nature.'

'I can't agree.' The scotch hit the back of my throat with a burning sensation that felt right. 'At the very least, I'm going to try.'

'Suit yourself,' he said as I huffed off to have a bath, letting the door close after me a little too hard.

★ ★ ★

As it turned out, we'd only begun to disagree about China. Ernest surrendered to every local delicacy and custom, drinking spring wine seasoned with pickled snakes, not caring about the heat or the lice, the rats or the bedbugs or the ghastly smells in the street. I took to bathing three times a day and was rewarded with dysentery and a dire case of China rot, my hands peeling and yellow with a maddening leprous fungus.

'I'm going to lose my mind,' I told him, trying not to scratch or retch or sob.

'Who wanted to come to China?' he asked cheerfully, and then sauntered off to buy more fireworks.

He was rubbing my nose in something, but what exactly? That here was one trip that wasn't his idea? That he was thriving while I struggled?

Even though I didn't understand his position or like it, 'Who wanted to come to China?' became Ernest's favorite refrain as we headed into the interior, first by air, then on bedraggled ponies that weighed not much more than I did, through torrential, unceasing monsoon rains. At one point we traveled by sampan along the North River, past villages flying the black flags that meant cholera epidemic, then by transport truck. Eleven days of slogging in all to reach the Canton front in Free China. The road was more rubber cement than mud, and then there was no road at all.

The actual front looked to me like a mountain. Like two mountains, rather, with the Japanese holding one and the Chinese holding the other and all quiet between. We saw one Japanese bomber soaring over and likely meaning to attack Shaokwan, a hundred miles or more to the north of us, but mostly what we encountered during our time inland was propaganda. In every village we came to, posters in English proclaimed WELCOME TO REPRESEN-TATIVES OF RIGHTEOUSNESS AND PEACE. When we met General Wong, who'd been holding this particular line for years now, he welcomed us with rancid-tasting rice wine and a single message. If America would only send planes, weapons, and money, China could finish off Japan very quickly.

'And if we don't?' I ventured.

'You see how it is,' he said, gesturing out and out, meaning, I supposed, that everything that had already happened would go on happening, possibly forever. The Japanese had all the planes, and the Chinese had all the bodies, and an endless capacity to bear hardships. What the Japanese destroyed, the Chinese would rebuild, with their lives, if need be. What was four years in such an ancient and long-suffering country?

★   ★   ★

'This is the damnedest war I've ever seen,' I told Ernest when we reached Chungking.

He had arranged a meeting with Generalissimo Chiang Kaishek, the democratic leader in China, through his numerous contacts in Hong Kong, and was champing at the bit. This was just the kind of thing he'd hoped for in coming to China. A story no one else had, and a chance to report back something of consequence to Washington when we returned home. I was less excited. In fact, I'd decided I already despised General Chiang and his wife before I met them. It seemed poignantly clear to me they cared nothing for their people. Millions were starving. The orphaned and the dying begged in the street, while they themselves and all those graced with wealth and power lived like kings on the

364

backs of those beneath them.

Madame Chiang was a famous beauty and femme fatale who spoke of working slavishly as the savior of her people. She spent most of her time trying to charm Ernest and effectively ignored me. When I asked why her country didn't care for its lepers, she smiled witheringly and told me, 'China had a great culture when your ancestors were living in the trees.'

I glared at her, taken aback, while Ernest suppressed a laugh. The next instant, she shape-shifted, rearranging her smile and offering me a jade brooch set in silver. I didn't know what else to do but accept it and thank her. Meanwhile, the lunch went on — the main dish being propaganda. General Chiang presented himself as the democratic hero of the people, a tireless leader in the struggle with Japan, when his real enemy was in fact the Chinese Communists who might lead the people to revolt, breaking their chains of misery and servitude. Chiang's only goal was to stay in power. He was an overlord, and Madame Chiang was a jewel-encrusted viper, and I couldn't write any of this for *Collier's*. China was our ally.

'What happened to objectivity?' I wailed to Ernest, wanting to throw the jade brooch against the wall.

'It went out with the dodo. Is that even a real question?'

'I thought it was. Oh, hell.'

★   ★   ★

Later I would be ashamed of the pieces I turned into *Collier's*. Nowhere were my actual opinions and fears voiced. I called Madame Chiang 'entrancing,' as glamorously put together as 'the newest and brightest movie star,' because that's what everyone needed to hear. We had to keep China on our side and occupying Japan's resources in the Far East lest they come breathing down our necks instead.

Everywhere I looked there was ugliness and hypocrisy, and I had let myself become part of it. But I couldn't fall into cynicism about reporting, believing that journalism had no power to right wrongs, or even elucidate them, as Ernest insisted. That would mean I had no power either, and I couldn't even bear the thought. I would simply have to do better, fight harder, and stand my ground.

# 56

With royalties from *For Whom the Bell Tolls* continuing to roll in wavelike, Ernest decided to use some of them to buy the Finca outright. We'd been renting since I found the place, and making repairs out of our own pockets, but by the time we returned from China, it was ours, every last stitch of it, right down to the cluster of mauve orchids on the ceiba tree and the locusts rattling in the palms. We celebrated with a raucous party, inviting our Basques and everyone else we knew from town, and somehow the mood of celebration just kept rolling forward for the rest of the summer. The house was never empty, and the liquor never stopped flowing.

I was missing the boys, but Ernest and Pauline were in a custodial tug-of-war at the moment, and it looked like we wouldn't see them until the fall. So we continued to drift through our days. We woke when we wanted to, took our meals whenever it struck us, had our first drink before noon, most days, and then slept in the sun. Ernest had stopped watching what he ate and also stopped recording his weight, or caring, it seemed. And though there were tennis games and shooting matches to help sweat out the rich food and toxins, I found myself feeling blue at odd moments.

I had sent Max Perkins my finished stories,

367

and he'd accepted them as a collection I was titling *The Heart of Another*, after something I'd read in a Willa Cather story. The proofs would be arriving any day now, and I felt a harrowing mixture of excitement and dread. The disappointing reception of my last book was still with me, and knowing that, though I hadn't asked, Ernest was doing everything possible to make sure this one was done right. He had suggestions for the promotional copy and wanted to help choose the dust jacket. My last author photo hadn't shown me in my best light. He offered to take one himself, so I'd appear as natural as possible.

'Does all of this really make a difference?' I asked him.

'It can't hurt,' he offered. Then, 'You should think of using your married name. That's something you haven't tried.'

'You mean capitalize on your reputation?' I was instantly on guard. 'That's what everyone's expecting, isn't it? You read those reviews.'

'It is your name. Why shouldn't you use it if you want?'

I felt heat climb my neck like a ladder. ' 'Gellhorn' is my professional name. It's the only thing I've ever published under.'

'Would you rather have your pride or good sales?'

'You don't think I can get there on my own.' I heard the stridency coming through in my voice and forced myself to breathe. 'That's what you're saying, isn't it? That I ride your coattails or perish?'

368

'You're being overdramatic. I only mean to help.'

'Maybe so, but it's my work. I have to give it my name.'

As he studied me, it was clear he thought I was making a mistake, but he only said, 'Do what you like, of course,' and then walked off to read his mail while I fumed alone.

It wasn't a matter of doing what I liked. He was missing my point completely. There was nothing slight or prideful in this choice. I was Gellhorn and a writer before I knew him. I had to be that now before I was his wife, or anything else for that matter.

★ ★ ★

More and more I was beginning to understand just what a creature of habit Ernest was. He shifted with the calendar, following a migratory path like some order of butterfly, returning to the same places at the same time, year to year. It didn't matter that we'd only recently returned home from months away in the Orient. Fall meant Sun Valley, and that was where he meant us to go.

'What about Arizona or Mexico instead,' I suggested one evening, trying to see if I could stretch him a little, and do something that would interest me more. 'The boys would love the desert.'

'But everything's all arranged. It's been arranged for months. What's this about?'

'Sun Valley is beautiful, but haven't we already

seen everything it has to offer and then some?'

There was a furrow between Ernest's brows. I watched it deepen, realizing I'd hurt as well as surprised him. Just as essential as his migratory pattern was his needing to believe I felt the same about everything; that we would forever point in the same direction. 'Are you suggesting I go alone?' he asked warily.

'No, no. But maybe I could trail you there, if there really is no way to change our plans. I could stop in St. Louis to see Mother and then come out to meet you when the boys turn up.'

'In October, then? The middle of October?' He was looking at me with an intensity I recognized. He hated to be alone. He couldn't keep his head right without me nearby — that's what he always said — and I understood that about him. It was his nature. But I was also realizing that my adapting to his needs came with a challenge to keep watch on my own head, too. My own nature.

'October sounds just right,' I said as cheerfully as I could muster. 'All the colors will be out then, too.'

'Yes. All right.' His stiff tone meant woundedness. 'If that's the way it has to be.'

\* \* \*

In early September, Ernest left for the mainland on *Pilar*, loaded down with the usual gear. There was a tightness around his mouth as he said goodbye, and I knew he didn't understand my point of view at all. He'd been sulking for weeks, feeling betrayed, I knew, and it was work, real work, not to give in as he wanted me to and let him have his way.

I would miss him, of course. I always did. But as soon as he was off, I felt lighter. When I got back to the house, it was like a different place without him — not just quieter, but more expansive. The air itself felt changed. I walked from room to room, marveling at the stillness. I stood motionless in a patch of sunlight, my feet bare on the warm floor, and realized that for days on end I didn't have to think of anyone else's needs or entertain or compromise or stretch to accommodate. I sent away the cook and the housekeeper and got into fresh cotton pajamas, vowing not to get out of them until I absolutely had to. And it was wonderful. I lay in one place and read, soaking up the peace and stillness, and feeling only a little guilty for being so happy alone.

★   ★   ★

I was in St. Louis when Max reached me with the very first copy of my new book. I had seen all the plans for the dust jacket and knew what to expect, but the actual book was so lovely and perfectly made I found myself rooted to the spot. The cover was blue and green with the title in artful type, and my name across the top. And everything was beautifully done, from the type to the heft of the spine, to the endpapers.

'It looks awfully grown up, doesn't it?' I said, showing my mother.

'It's just wonderful,' she said. 'A work of art.'

'I've been sick and scared inside,' I admitted, 'but seeing it makes me want to be stronger. I like these stories. I'm glad I've written them.'

'You should be proud,' she said, handing the book back. 'They did a beautiful job.'

'Maybe the only time to truly love a book is before you let it go. Before the critics have their say, or the sales figures come in to surprise or disappoint you.'

'I can only imagine how difficult it is to have something you love be pored over and picked at. But even the worst reviews can't take your book from you, can they?'

'It's worse, actually. You start off by being so hopeful and so full of faith, but the clips come in and they whittle away at you. At first you disagree with them or you feel angry, but little by little you begin to believe every terrible thing you read and forget what you ever liked about it. And then your faith is gone. No one has to take your book. You give it away.'

'Oh, sweetheart.' Her look was soft. 'Ernest has had some terrible reviews, too. Years' worth of them, and yet he goes on. Have you asked his advice?'

'I'm not sure he remembers anymore what it feels like to be at the bottom this way. There isn't a more successful writer in the world right now. And it doesn't matter that he hasn't written a word since. He could rest on this one for years and years.'

'That would give anyone amnesia, I suppose. But I know he wants you to succeed.'

'He does. It used to be simpler, though. We used to feel like a team. I think that's what I'm missing most. I don't know how to get back to that place. It might already be too late.'

Concern moved over her face like a raft of clouds crossing a blue, blue sky. 'Is there anything I can do?'

'Tell me it will all be fine.'

'It will all be fine,' she said. 'Oh, Marty. I hope it will.'

# 57

Everyone thought they knew what would fix him. Max wanted another big novel, immediately if possible. Esquire wanted a long article about the West and the American male of the species. They were willing to pay prettily for it, too. Every time he turned around now someone was throwing money at him in great stinking handfuls, when all he really wanted to do was fish Silver Creek all day and have his wife nearby to talk to in the mornings and at night. His wife, by his side. Was that really so much to ask?

He had seen her independence from the first. In fact, he had liked how strong she was and how brave in Spain. But that was war. Once they'd settled in and built a life together, she seemed to love it as much as he did. Hell, she'd found the house, he hadn't. She had pushed for all the work and repairs. She'd made a home out of nearly nothing, and made him as happy as he'd ever been, so that he had trusted and believed in what they were doing. Two writers writing under one roof. She had wanted it, too, and reached for it, so why now did she only seem to feel strangled and ready to bolt like a racehorse? This St. Louis trip, to see her mother, made no sense at all when Sun Valley had been planned months and months before. It was their place, together, and he was here alone.

At least the weather was fine and the fishing

would be good. He knew this river well now, and it was always better when you did. If you had a map for this fork or that bend or shallow pool in your mind and then returned, the memory of the place and the actual moment merged to form a sharper etching, a deeper map, and also worked to cement you more into your own life. Marty had said they'd seen it all, this place, but that wasn't true. You could never see everything of any place nor anyone, but the trying of it made all the difference and made you who you were, maybe.

He put his rod case on the bank, settled his fly book in his pocket, and waded into the stream. The water was a notch above fifty degrees, he guessed, and was a good kind of cold against his legs as he felt his way forward with the current, the creek rising around him. Just upstream a big trout broke the surface, feeding, and came down splashing a bright prism of water droplets. He didn't need to go after that one. The creek was full of them, bigger ones, too, and the day was fine and he was happy in every way, nearly.

He released his line and felt it run out cleanly in an arc, making the corrections in the air so that it dropped just where he thought it should. He had always enjoyed knowing how to do a thing well. The cold pressed and eddied against his legs, and the smooth river stones shifted under his planted feet, and downstream, just under his line, a big fish was rising to the surface like a secret, every possible color along its rippling flesh.

If he let the rest go, this moment felt as good

375

as anything he knew. But could he? Could he manage the thing inside him? That was the real question. He kept wanting to bring Marty closer, feeling worried that he could lose her. But the problem wasn't that she didn't love him enough. No, the problem was he loved her too much.

The American male of the species indeed, he thought. That was rich.

But this creek was perfectly itself. Each fork and tributary had a name, and the ones he hadn't learned yet, he meant to. He meant to learn the Silver again and again, one cutthroat at a time, making notes in his fishing log to build his map. If everything else went south, he would have that tucked safely away. He would know where he'd been, and where he was going, because they were the same thing.

# 58

In November, *The Heart of Another* launched into the world, and with it came the early notices, sent on to Idaho by Max.

'I don't think I even want to read them,' I told Ernest. 'It's the business of the writer to write, not to care what people think.'

'You know you care.'

'But I wish I didn't.'

'They're going to be wonderful, because the book is wonderful.' He slit open the packet and began scanning the clips while I lit a cigarette shakily.

'Well?'

'This one from *The New Yorker* calls your stories 'affecting and intelligent.''

I exhaled a cloud of smoke, feeling a little lighter. 'That's all right, isn't it?'

'It's wonderful. And *The New Republic* says you have heart and substance.' I saw his eyes moving farther down the notice, but he didn't read out anything else, only folded the clips back into the envelope.

'Is that all?'

'Pretty much.'

'Ernest.' I reached for the packet.

'I thought you didn't want to read them.'

'I don't, but you're shielding me.' I held out my hand more forcefully, and though I could see it pained him, he finally relented.

'Please don't take it too much to heart, Marty. What do those assholes know anyway?'

'Nothing. They know nothing, and they have all the power.'

I took the packet and made myself read every word of the four clips inside. To be fair, there were nice comments in each of them. *Kirkus* might have been the best of them, calling my stories 'more sparse and emotional' than my earlier work, and 'more tuned to the agonies of unexpressed emotion.' But in each of the others my style was compared to Ernest's. *The Yale Review* critic said she wished I'd lose my 'pronounced but not incurable Hemingway accent.' The *New Yorker* critic wrote, 'She's read too carefully the works of Mr. Hemingway . . . an amiable trait in a wife but dangerous for a writer of fiction.' She'd gone so far as to call Ernest my 'Svengali.'

'This is ridiculous,' I told him, a cold flicker of rage wavering inside me. 'I'm the same writer I was before. No one compared me to you before we were married . . . they're *looking* to say this sort of thing just for the copy.'

'Exactly. Just ignore them, Rabbit.'

'I can, but what about everyone else? People read these damned things, you know. They'll pick up my book looking to see if it's true. Or they won't pick it up at all, thinking they've already read you and that I'm nothing but your shabby mirror.'

'Marty . . . ' I watched his face twist. He didn't know what to say to me, or how to help me through these waters.

'Oh, the hell with it,' I snapped, suddenly exasperated. 'I'm proud of this book and I won't have anyone ruining that for me.'

'That's my girl.' He reached and pulled me close in against his chest, where I could feel my heart fluttering, a small loved bird caught and held. I was his girl. There was no changing that. Try as I might, there was no stepping out of his shadow.

*　　*　　*

When new reviews came, I fed them into a yellow envelope with a sigh. I was trying to write again, sitting at the desk in our hotel room for a few hours each day, but each time a sentence came to me, I would find myself reading it over again as soon as it was on paper, while an insidious voice slipped into my head to ask if the words were really mine, or counterfeit. I grew weary and snappish and even more critical of the company at the lodge, even of the Coopers, whom I mostly liked.

'I can't sit through one more dinner,' I told Ernest. 'These people are embalmed.'

'Be fair.'

'I'm being more than fair. You know Hollywood is killing Scott.' Everyone had heard the gossip and understood he couldn't go on this way, pawning his talent for studio executives. He was no kind of writer anymore. He was unrecognizable.

Now Ernest's face grew still. He couldn't argue with me. 'It's just a few more weeks.'

379

'I won't make it.'

'You don't think you're exaggerating just a little?'

'Is that what you think? I wouldn't be here at all if not for you, you know.' I was shouting at that point and doing a pretty good impression of a grade A bitch. But I didn't care. 'Do you really just assume everyone wants exactly what you want, at the moment you want it?' I didn't wait for a reply, just stormed out of the room, slamming the door loudly behind me. He didn't follow, and that was fine with me. All I wanted — all I wanted in the world at that moment — was to be alone.

★ ★ ★

The next morning I woke to an absolute horror of a hangover, the old-fashioned kind, with roiling waves of nausea, a crucifying ache between my temples, and a shuddering feeling everywhere else. I wanted to bury my head under the pillow and sleep forever, but Ernest had been waiting for me to rouse. He sat on the side of the bed wanting to talk, so I rolled over, wincing, and propped myself up on the pillow to listen.

'I'm an ass. We can go whenever you want. I should have thought of you.'

'You are an ass, but you're my ass.' I tried to smile, still green and queasy. 'I do need to be out of here, and someplace where there are no parties, and no one's fashionable, or showing off or trying to be clever.'

'The moon, then. Or Arizona.'

'Oh, I'd love that. It won't be as much fun now that the boys are away, but let's do it. We can drive all the way down through Nevada and into the Mohave, and bake ourselves silly in the sun and get really and truly lost.'

'All right.' He was nodding, but there was some sort of sadness lurking in his gaze, a shadow of a mood I didn't fully understand. Maybe he didn't either. We were both straining to bend and compromise for the other. But that was what marriage was about, wasn't it?

We shoved things into suitcases and put Sun Valley behind us, heading south and ever more south, through tiny nowhere frontier towns, past gas stations and diners the size of telephone booths, and great spans of lion-colored desert that stretched and stretched, swallowing everything. Finally I began to feel I could breathe again.

We had the radio on and the windows down, stopping to see pockets of Indian country and little bars with no one in them, and talking to almost no one but each other. I had a no-frills Brownie camera and snapped funny-looking signs and billboards and other things no one cared about but us. Nothing was slick or sanitized, and nothing wanted too much of our attention until we'd cleared Arizona and half of New Mexico and were crossing the border into Texas at El Paso. We'd stopped at a cantina on the side of the road — a weathered and browbeaten thing with a tin roof and an erratically blinking COLD BEER sign. Ernest had just started instructing the bartender on how to make a very cold daiquiri with no sugar and plenty of lime when the door to the saloon fell open with a loud crack and a small Indian boy came in. He had bare feet and a red-twisted bandanna around his neck, like a Spaniard. His arms were full of newspapers.

'Con la guerra,' he announced with a hoarse little voice that made me think he'd been shouting for some time. 'Con la guerra, la guerra,' he said over and over, going table to table as everyone turned to watch him, recognition growing.

While we'd been driving and thinking of nothing, free as dust in the wind, the Japanese had bombed Pearl Harbor. America was finally at war.

# Part 6

# A SEASON OF RUIN

## DECEMBER 1941-JUNE 1944

# 59

The attack hadn't come from nowhere. Nothing ever does. Through the summer and fall, tensions had mounted dangerously. Roosevelt had sent warnings that the United States would be forced to 'take steps' if Japan attacked neighboring countries. Japan had sent warnings back, saying it would be forced to take steps of its own if the United States wouldn't let up on the economic blockade. We'd all been preparing for the worst for some time, which was why Roosevelt had moved the Pacific Fleet and all those bomber planes to Pearl Harbor in the first place. Ernest and I had seen them for ourselves when we passed through Hawaii on our way to the Orient. Eight battleships, three cruisers, three destroyers, and nearly two hundred planes had all been lined up and waiting like sitting ducks. Our richest military arsenal, and the clearest target imaginable.

Simultaneous attacks were launched on US-held areas of the Philippines, Guam, Malaya, Singapore, Hong Kong, and Wake Island. It was absolutely sickening to think of the lives lost, and even more sickening to think ahead. Roosevelt had finally made the call to arms. Tens of thousands of young men were being recruited as soon as they turned twenty. Bumby wasn't old enough yet, but would be soon, and it was something we could barely stand to think about as we made our way back to the Finca for Christmas with the boys.

'I'm not afraid,' Bumby said.

'I'm afraid enough for all of us,' I told him. 'And your poor mother.' I shook my head and lit a cigarette. Nothing could happen to this glorious boy. It just couldn't.

'Maybe it'll be over before we know it.' But I could see he didn't believe it for a moment. No one did.

'Just go back to school and stay in school, all right?' I said, as Ernest came into the room.

'What's going on here?'

'The Mart is worried about me.' There wasn't the smallest bit of irritation in Bum's voice. 'It's all right. I don't mind. She's my other mother.'

Without any warning, tears sprung to my eyes. I turned so Ernest couldn't see them, surprised that I could feel so much. But the truth was I couldn't feel any more for each of these three boys than I did. They were rooted in my heart now, and that was that.

★   ★   ★

Later that evening, after the boys had gone to bed and the house was relatively quiet, Ernest came to me where I was reading. I could tell from the look on his face that he was wrestling with something. 'Maybe now's the time to start a family. We're always saying we will.'

'With the nation at war? It couldn't be a worse time.'

He sat down hard in the chair next to me. 'When then?'

'I don't know, Rabbit. We shouldn't be talking of it. You'll only feel worse.'

'That's right, I will. And why shouldn't I?' His voice had an edge I knew well by now. He was angling for a fight, just to release the pressure. I did it myself all the time, but I wasn't going to bite, not with him tensed up this way. I'd never win.

'It will happen, I promise,' I said as gently as possible. 'I know how much you want a daughter.'

'I want one. That's right . . . and that's the problem, isn't it? If you wanted a child, we'd already have one. You've only been pretending.'

'Oh, Ernest, that's not true,' but he was already striding out of the room and I was alone with his words as they bounced against the closed door and echoed back, challenging me.

Did I want a child? *Did* I? I had to admit that the dream was a perfect one when it remained a dream, shimmering out ahead of us like the lilting mirage of an oasis. Our daughter, with my hair and sense of adventure, and Ernest's wits and his brown eyes, goggle fishing beside him in the reef, or scrambling up the path behind the pool house barefoot, an orchid tucked into her braid. Oh, it was lovely, that fantasy, but the moment I let myself think of how life would really be with a child, I hit against the truth like a submerged bit of sharp reef. Ernest loved his children, but he had the freedom of hunting or fishing with them on holidays, enjoying their company, while Pauline and Hadley did all the daily caring for them, particularly when they were young, making sure they were fed and well, their tears soothed, their skinned knees bandaged, their cares and worries listened to, their teeth brushed, their schoolwork done.

The list went on and on, and all of that would fall to me, I knew, as the mother. It was hard enough already to fight for my work now. With a baby, it would become a secondary consideration, while Ernest's would go unchanged. My ability to travel independently would dissolve, but whenever Ernest needed to go anywhere, he would. Of course he would, because I'd be behind at home making that possible, tending our child and keeping everything going for him. It might be selfish to sit on this decision a bit longer, but I had to think about how much of myself I was willing to give up.

★ ★ ★

Christmas that year was somber and thin feeling, all around, and when it was over, there was only relief. Ernest still wasn't writing, and though I had told my mother he didn't really need to write anything new now, since *For Whom the Bell Tolls* was still selling incredibly well, and had been one of the most successful books anyone could remember, Ernest was a writer before he was anything else. He needed to work to feel solid and like himself, but when I asked, he insisted he was fine. 'I just haven't hit on the right thing.'

'You're not afraid, then?' For that was my new suspicion. 'You're sure something will come when you're ready?'

'Whose side are you on, anyway?' he asked, narrowing his gaze.

'Yours, of course. Always.'

'I'm not worried. A book always leaves me feeling swept out for a while. And this one took so much. That's all.'

I wanted to believe him, but couldn't quite. He had gained ten or fifteen pounds in the last six months, and his skin looked sallow beneath his suntan. He'd also just mixed his third martini, and it was barely past noon. 'Just try working tomorrow,' I said, though part of me knew it wasn't wise to push him. 'You have to begin somewhere.'

'Now *you're* instructing me? That's rich.' There was acid in his voice. I felt a warning sensation, a prickling at the back of my neck, and swallowed the words I should have said. I felt them for a long time after, like small burning stones.

# 60

One day Ernest came home from an all-day trip to Havana with two wriggling long-bodied cats in his shirt.

'This is Good Will,' he said of the one that was a rich-brown-and-gray tabby with a plush feather duster of a tail. 'We can use some of that around here, don't you think?'

'We definitely can.' Though inwardly I wondered if he meant our disagreement about having a child, I was smarter than to bring that up again. 'Who's his friend?'

Both cats had jumped from Ernest's arms and were exploring tentatively, noses glued to the floor. The second had a shorter face and was solid gray, gray as a storm cloud. 'This one?' He touched the lanky side of the cat's body with the toe of his sneaker. It arced away from him like the curve of a bow, and then back again elastically. 'This lovely girl has no friend.'

'Friendless.'

'Precisely.' He grinned.

'Poor lovely starving things. Wherever did you find them?'

'Fighting over a rusted can of beans in the alley behind the Floridita.'

I dropped to my knees and waited for one of them to venture my way. 'We can do better than that, can't we?'

'Hell yes, we can.' He called Rene, and told

390

him to take one of the filet mignon steaks he had set aside for dinner and chop it very fine and leave it for the cats on two plates in different corners so they wouldn't fight.

'He thinks you've gone mad, you know,' I said when Rene had gone.

'You have to feed them meat if you want them to be good mousers. Everyone knows that. How else will they grow to like the taste of blood?'

'Because they're animals?' But he only swatted me on the rear. He was deadly serious about these creatures already. Already they were his children.

When Rene came back with the meat, Ernest pinched some of the pieces even finer with his bare hands, saying that next time he should use the grinder so the cats wouldn't choke.

'You want for them to have this meat every day?' Rene's thick brows were knitted, his brown hands cocked at his waist. You could see that, in his world, felines didn't eat better than their human counterparts. It was simply absurd.

But Ernest didn't care. 'Why not? They'll think it's the Ritz and never leave.' Then he settled on his haunches and watched with great pleasure as the cats fell on their plates like wolves.

★   ★   ★

Even though Ernest still wasn't writing, I decided I would try my hand at another novel or die trying. I hit on a story that I liked — at least in my head. It was about a Caribbean girl named

391

Liana and her marriage to a much older man, a white man she doesn't love. It was far more romantic than anything I'd ever tried, and had nothing to do with war. I wasn't sure where the plot would take me, or what would happen to Liana in the end. But that was part of the intrigue.

In the meantime, our animal inventory was expanding at a terrifying pace. Ernest had found and adopted three more cats — Princessa, Boise, and Fatso — as well as a dear little bitch dog he'd plucked, half wasted with hunger, out of the gutter at the Frontón. She was inky black with a delicate muzzle and a tail that curled up decorously at the end. Negrita was her name, and he made it his project to feed her as lavishly as he did the cats, our 'cotsies,' as he liked to say. Salmon, tuna, chicken breast, and freshly peeled shrimp: nothing was too good for them, or too much trouble.

I was half worried that nothing was going to grab Ernest's attention again beyond our animals and a very cold martini, but then he began talking of trying to develop a private intelligence network in Cuba. He'd gotten the idea by talking with our good friend Bob Joyce at the American embassy in Havana and didn't want to let it go. At first I thought it was madness — what did he know of espionage? But it *was* like Ernest to want to be on the inside of things, and to seek out opportunities for daring. What could be more daring and more covert than messing about with spies?

He and Bob decided to seek support from higher-ups at the embassy, and that's when

Spruille Braden became involved. Braden was newly posted as US ambassador to Cuba, a squat, jowly man with flesh that pressed at the buttons of his shirt and vest. He seemed ill suited for Cuba to me, but Ernest liked him and respected him, probably because he took Ernest seriously. Cuba did need a counterintelligence group now, he agreed. In April, the embassy had sought out and immediately arrested more than fifty men — German, Japanese, and Italian — for 'illicit activities on behalf of the Axis powers.' No one was saying more than that, but they didn't really need to. Several freighters had been sunk off the coast of Cuba in the past few weeks, and enemy subs were suspected.

More and more, it seemed the sea was where the war was actually taking place. When we went to town now, rumors flew about predatory German U-boats lurking in Caribbean waters and off the coast of Florida, sinking scores of freighters and oil tankers, anything large and useful. Dozens were torpedoed every month, and sometimes more, it was speculated, but speculation was all we had. Strict censorship kept real news from reaching us either in print or over the wire, and this only increased the feeling of unease. The Nazis were out there, who knew how many, and how close, or how lethally armed. But they were there.

Ernest was going to get his shot at them, too.

★ ★ ★

Naval Intelligence for Central America would give Ernest a five-hundred-dollar monthly

393

stipend to patrol the waters off the coast of Cuba, with more allotted to outfit *Pilar* as a Q-boat and assemble a crew. Ernest would call on the people closest to him: the Basque pelota players; his favorite waiters at the Floridita; his frequent first mate on *Pilar*, Gregorio Fuentes; and Winston Guest, an aristocrat he'd met years before on safari in Africa, who'd recently been visiting us at the Finca. The mission was dubbed 'Operation Friendless,' after our favorite of the cats, though Ernest immediately began calling it the Crime Shop, or even the Crook Factory. Stacks of egg crates full of hand grenades and small-fuse bombs were loaded on board, along with machine guns, a supersensitive shortwave radio, and a life raft. Their first mission was in June, and they went off full of fire and conviction and derring-do. If they ran into a German sub, they would pretend to be a group of scientists gathering specimens for the Smithsonian. When the Nazis sent a boarding party, Ernest would gun the engines, close the distance to the sub, and signal his men to start shooting, throwing grenades or bombs down her conning tower if he got close enough for that, and then disappearing into the night, safe as butter in a jar.

'Don't worry about me one bit,' he insisted as he outlined his plan for me. 'There are things I know about these waters that no one else does, not anyone. There are numberless places to hide. I can find every one of them.'

I nodded and kissed him, wishing him luck — all the while biting my tongue. I knew better than to say what I thought, that this mission smacked of fantasy, and avoidance. He would be hunting subs instead of facing his fears head-on, sweeping out that empty place inside him, and beginning something new. Or perhaps this was his way of coming to terms with all that plagued him from the inside, only instead of wearing their own faces, his demons would look like German U-boats. If everything went well, he would blow them to smithereens, perhaps without ever having to see them fully. And all without writing a word.

★ ★ ★

If Ernest really wanted to do something for the war effort, I wished he would go over to one of the fronts in Europe as a journalist and add his voice to the resistance, as he'd done so brilliantly in Spain.

I was dying to go myself, but now that this was our war, too, the American military had decided that female journalists shouldn't be anywhere near the front lines. It wasn't like Spain, or like anything that had come before. Magazines were still hiring women, just not where it counted. Any battle zone would be off limits for me.

I pleaded with Charles Colebaugh at *Collier's* to see what he could do to stretch the rules for me, but it was nothing doing. The closest I might get to action, he wagered, was a stint in the Caribbean, trying to see what the effect was there of all this submarine warfare. How did that sound?

The assignment wasn't at all what I'd hoped for. I wanted to be at the center of the fray, where things of real consequence were happening. That's where I felt alive, and useful and involved. Still, sweeping through the Caribbean was better than staying home, hounding the servants to polish the silver, and feeling soft and domesticated and safe, safe, safe. So I took it.

The plan was to go island to island looking for anything interesting — informants for the Nazis, stashes of supplies for the subs, lifeboat survivors. The Germans were most definitely in the Caribbean. Allied ships were being blown out of the water almost daily, but what I saw wasn't a battle zone but a postcard, the glinting blue surface of the Windward Passage shifting and concealing everything but itself.

I was sunburned, ant bitten, seasick, catatonically bored, disgusted by cockroaches and fish smells and the ceaseless porpoiselike rolling of the boat. And though I never saw what I'd come for, the secret thrust of a periscope on a still black silent night, I wrote anyway, sending *Collier's* eleven thousand words that didn't amount to much more than a travelogue of the horror journey of all horror journeys.

I came home with dengue fever I'd contracted in Surinam and the feeling that my bones were slowly breaking. I also missed my husband terribly. When Ernest finally returned from his latest Operation Friendless patrol, he was sunburned, with a thick, scraggly beard. He smelled of fish and men and close quarters. As far as I could see, he hadn't changed his clothes or bathed the whole while. He'd also lost his shoes somewhere.

'We're a pair, aren't we, Rabbit?' I asked after he'd held me for a long time and then poured us both a scotch. 'Did you find your sub?'

'No. Did you?'

'Not even close.'

He collapsed on the other end of the sofa, the cue for Princessa, who'd been drowsing nearby in a patch of sun, to perch on his chest and purr like a sputtering Model T. 'There must be a lesson in here somewhere.'

'I can think of one,' I said, beginning to ease off his clothes. I led him to the shower, where we stood for a long time under the warm spraying water, then I began to rub him with soap and a soft cloth, kissing each part of him after it was clean, reclaiming him bit by bit.

'Go easy,' I said when he started to wash my hair. 'I'm still a little tender everywhere from the fever.' But his hands were wonderfully gentle, easing away the exhaustion, and all the efforts of travel, and the strain of our months apart. And there, in the total surrender, I felt us come back to each other. Here was the man I had fallen for, not being able to help myself. He hadn't disappeared entirely.

Later, when we were curled in bed together, half knotted in the damp towels that had trailed us from the shower, it was lovely and peaceful in the old way — before Pearl Harbor, before the rising wave of his great book and the sinking troughs of my disappointment, and the doubt that had crept in that we weren't on the same side anymore.

'We can't lose sight of what really matters,' I told him, easing against his neck and shoulder and kissing him there.

'Hmm?' he asked sleepily. 'We won't.'

'I mean it, Rabbit. Even when other things come in loud, we have to keep choosing each other. That's marriage. You can't only say the words once and think they'll stick. You have to say them over and over, and then live them out with all you've got.'

He made another soft noise and I realized he was already tumbling toward sleep. He couldn't hear me.

'This is what I want,' I said softly, anyway. 'I choose you.'

# 61

All through the fall, Ernest came and went often, not saying much about his Crook Factory business. I didn't ask many questions, either. I didn't really understand what he was doing or why it mattered to him, or how he could justify his being away from home for such long stretches, when he always hated my being gone. But if I was going to be here, I decided I might as well be writing.

I dug through my desk to find the pages of the long story I'd begun the year before, about the Caribbean girl, Liana. There were good things in the pages, things worth salvaging and polishing. I wasn't sure if the material was rich enough to sustain a novel, but there was only one way to find out. I would start at the beginning again, I decided, setting the book in the Caribbean, since my mind was so full of the place now. It would be my private joke, taking my horror journey and making it Liana's home in paradise.

I knew something about paradise, didn't I? Only it seemed to me more and more that you couldn't turn your back on heaven any more than you could turn your back on love. They both wanted to go wild on you — and would quicker than you thought if you didn't tend them properly.

All I had to do was go room to room for evidence of this. The rains had come again, leaving trails of mildew. In the back bedroom, chunks of the tile floor were being forced up by a thick system of roots as if the outdoors was trying to tunnel its way inside to wreak havoc like everything else. The kitchen paint was peeling from damp. The silverfish were at our books.

I tackled what I could and hired out the rest while the cats chased one another from room to room. The population had doubled in the last several months, and though I loved all of them as much as Ernest did — the fat white Persian named Uncle Wolfer, the two black-and-white toms, Dillinger and Thunder, and the gray tabby who looked so much like Friendless we called him Friendless's Brother — I realized that if we didn't do something about neutering the toms, there'd be no way to stop the rising tide.

I found a veterinarian in town, congratulating myself on being so practical. But when Ernest returned to refuel and collect his mail at the end of October, he was absolutely furious over what I'd done.

'You may as well cut *my* balls off,' he spat out. 'Or shoot the cats outright. That would be kinder.'

'Don't be dramatic. The doctor said it's very humane. They don't feel much. Not like us.'

'Like hell they don't. And now they're women, the poor bastards.' He shot me a sharp look. 'You want to kick me some other way while I'm here, or have you had enough?'

'Oh, Ernest,' I said, feeling exasperated, but he was already striding away.

400

Later, when I went to seek him out and talk it through, Boise was perched on the table by Ernest's plate while he fed the cat soft ripe slices of alligator pear with his fingers. As soon as he saw me, Ernest began to mutter to Boise about how terrible it was that a woman had taken the only thing that was truly his, his power.

'We don't like wimmins now.' He was only looking at the cat. 'I'd keep your distance.'

I could hardly believe he wouldn't let the matter go. 'You're acting like a child.'

But he only went on feeding Boise and stroking his head, the two of them conspirators in some war I didn't even understand. And yet apparently it had become my war, too, without my consent.

'I'm going to bed,' I finally said. 'Are you coming?' He'd been out for weeks; surely he was going to drop all this.

'We don't like wimmins,' he said again, not taking his eyes off the cat.

I strode off to our room, letting doors rattle behind me on the way, and lay awake for some time, boiling over with exasperation. My thoughts spun on themselves, and I knew it was no use. I would never find sleep this way. Reaching over to Ernest's side of the bed, where he kept a bottle of small red sleeping pills, I took one and waited for the slow film of it to lower over my brain and my muscles like a heavy and good annihilating fog.

I woke with no hangover — thankfully — except the emotional one. Here was my husband, sleeping beside me. Here, but far, far

401

away. It was a silly argument and I missed him. Even when he was wrong, I missed him.

★ ★ ★

Day after day, while the cats ran and tumbled and moused and waited for their feast of ground-up filet mignon, and mourned their lost sexuality — if indeed they'd ever prized it — I shut myself in my office and sailed away on my pages as they took shape. Liana was an unschooled young woman, and a great beauty. Her cold, white plantation-owner husband, Marc, had married her to spite the woman he truly loved, and kept her as a kind of trophy. He had no true feelings for her, and she didn't know what love even was until a handsome young French teacher, Pierre, entered her life and began to teach her the ways of the world.

In one way, it almost embarrassed me that I was so taken in by this small and personal story that was not about war or social justice or any larger thing, but only people. I was taken in, though, and ecstatic to be working so well. The days felt very full, suddenly, and alive and also hopeful. Hitler's army was still raging overseas and out in the Gulf Stream, menacingly invisible. Things with Ernest weren't entirely calm or simple, but I was happy and occupied and feeling strong.

Soon, I had almost twenty thousand words, and they kept coming, flowing from some point beyond rational thought where imagination lived like a rare white dragon. I didn't know anyone like Liana, but she felt utterly real to me, and also terribly tragic. I loved her and was moved by her life, and finally grew brave enough to share what I'd written with Ernest.

'This is *wonderful*, Rabbit,' he said when he'd read the pages.

'Really? You like her, then?' I was so relieved, I could have cried.

'I do. You've drawn her so well. And the whole world has texture and it sings.'

'Oh, God, I'm glad you think so. I've been so happy doing it, but that never means anything. We never really know what we're doing.'

'That's the truth, but keep going. Don't stop for anything,' he insisted. 'I'll be waiting to read the next installment when I come in again just before Christmas. You're the writer in the family now, Marty. I'll be your editor, and if you don't want that, I'll be the person who cheers you on no matter what.'

His tone had been light, but I still felt alarmed that he'd say such a thing. 'You'll start up again soon,' I told him. 'There are two writers in this family, and always will be.'

'Sure,' he said weakly while a shadow flickered through his eyes.

'Don't go out again,' I said suddenly, feeling that everything had become so fragile between us, inside and out. 'I've been craving you awfully, you know.'

'You miss me, do you?' He came over to where I sat, and as he pulled me to my feet, we tucked into each other like a lock and key, my head under his chin, his hands clasped at the base of

403

my spine. I wanted to stay like that, exactly like that, for years and years.

'I miss *us*. Let's hide away from everything. Remember when this was our foxhole and we were alone for months at a time?'

'I'll be back before you know it.' He nodded into my hair and then squeezed me tightly, and let me go.

# 62

When they came through the channel and saw the little island with its bone-white sand and its clusters of date palms in a cove where they could beach the dinghy, he knew it would be as good a place as any to hide from himself.

Not that the boys knew anything about it. He'd tried very hard to conceal his worry and the strain he'd been feeling, like a lead weight in his chest, and thought he'd done all right by them. Now he banked to starboard and then cut the engine, letting Pilar swing toward the sandbar, which was rippled and white and looked like flesh beneath the clear waves. Like a woman's thigh swung out casually as she slept.

He told the boys to get the dinghy and take a look at the beach. 'If you find any Krauts, you know what to do,' he called out to Gigi, who loved this game. Then he went below to make himself a drink and came up again, looking out and out, trying to spot the shadows of mako sharks.

Everything had a shadow, he knew. Clouds shading the surface of the water darkly. Long thin gars that streamed in silvery lines against the current, and tuna that hovered under his boat like monsters. Words had shadows you could feel long before they reached you, and love had a shadow, and so did he.

Ever since he was a boy, he'd had moods that

405

could steal in and leave him almost breathless. Sometimes they came so quickly and seemingly from nowhere that he took to fearing what could happen inside him, the terrible transformation from one feeling that could be handled to another, more horrible one that couldn't.

More and more lately he had felt the dark space thickening in him, threatening to crush his breath. But he hadn't given himself over, not yet, and wouldn't if he could help it. Once, in May of '36, he had been alone on Pilar hours out of Havana and heading toward Key West when a wind had come tearing up without warning, waves running up and over the bow, the foam bright and shockingly cold when it struck him over and over.

That was a night that had pulled anchor and stretched free of time. His compass had shuddered and swum. He couldn't leave the stern to check the fuel stores or to see how much water he was taking in below. He didn't even know his position until dawn came like a gray paw and he felt worse somehow, for now he could see exactly what was against him and his small boat.

The dawn had muddied into morning and the wind roared on, and waves were concrete walls to crash against. Finally, sometime after noon, he reached the edge of the storm and pulled free. He was closer to home than he'd thought too, and was soon pointing at the harbor in Key West. He was wrung out and spent, but another part of him swelled to know that he'd done something difficult and brought the boat in safely, and brought himself in with it. That he'd come through.

Sometimes shadows bore blacker shadows when they found you. Yes. Some storms had darker, more terrible storms inside them. But even then you could come out of them and see a known shoreline. You could look up to see that somehow, some way or other, you'd found your way back.

# 63

December came and with it the first anniversary of Pearl Harbor. Bombs only bred more bombs, it seemed. The United States had just attacked Naples. The RAF was bombarding the Netherlands. Japanese destroyers had taken the US cruiser *Northampton* at Guadalcanal. And on and on it went, terribly.

The boys were all home for Christmas. Gigi from Key West, Patrick from his new boarding school in Connecticut, and Bum from Dartmouth, where he'd transferred after swearing off the University of Montana. He'd thought it was the place, not his course work, that had put him off college, but now it seemed Dartmouth wasn't sticking for him, either.

'Do you think Papa would mind if I dug in here for a while?' he asked me. 'Just until the dust settles and I can think of what comes next?'

'You can stay forever, darling, no matter what Papa says. But please tell me you'll go back to school. You'll be enlisted if you don't.'

'I told you I'm not afraid of going over there.' He lifted his chin, his eyes clear, and I could see he meant it. 'Maybe it would even be a good thing. I could use some growing up.'

'Nonsense. You're perfect now.' *And you're alive*, I didn't say.

'I've got some friends who've enlisted and they

say it's a relief, actually. Rather than waiting for some ax to fall.'

'Can we not talk about it anymore?' I tried to keep the anxiety out of my voice, but it was nothing doing. 'Why don't you move your things into the Little House? We've made it over, and it's awfully nice when we can keep the cats out.'

'I think Princessa's hurt,' Gigi said, carrying the big blue-gray Persian into the room, half draped over his shoulder. 'She's bleeding.'

'That's the fruit rats, I'm afraid.' I rubbed at the patch of red he pointed to just under her chin. 'She's the most brutal mouser we have. Usually she bathes better, though.'

Gigi's look of concern had changed into a kind of thrilling regard, and I recognized it as the way he sometimes looked at his father. His swashbuckling, daredevil heroic father who was now out fighting Krauts in the Gulf, taking them on like a cat might fruit rats, which is to say fearlessly and with some gusto.

That was the fantasy, anyway. That was the story. But more and more I began to wonder if Operation Friendless wasn't something infinitely more complex. Either Ernest was using these missions as a way to hide from trouble and all he didn't want to confront, or he was secretly hoping to get a book out of his adventures, much the way he'd found Robert Jordan by going to Spain. But Spain had been terribly real, full of challenges and daily tests of courage, and legitimate heroes. While in the year he'd been patrolling, untold hours spent sweeping the Gulf, he'd spotted a sub only once — a distant black shining thing off Mégano de Casigua — and that had led to nothing.

It made me feel worried for him, and sad. He didn't look well to me, and was drinking too much. He'd always been a drinker, but there had been a rhythm to it, a rise and fall. Two drinks at lunch after a full morning's work, then two or three with dinner. Now there wasn't even the ghost of an anchor, and no reason at all not to be drunk all day.

The boys noticed it, too, I realized, and I wanted to reassure them that Papa was just going through a dark time and would be back good as new. But did I believe it myself? Could I?

On Christmas Eve, we went into town for dinner at the Floridita. Ernest had been drinking on and off since noon, and now there was a string of double frozen daiquiris ferried to our table by Constantino. I tried to meet his eyes surreptitiously, a hidden plea for him to slow down, but he seemed not to notice. He was Ernest's ally, not mine, in any case.

Our meals finally arrived and we'd just begun eating when a man approached our table, a tourist from some southern state, a drawl on his lips and his hat in his hand as he asked Ernest to sign a copy of For Whom the Bell Tolls.

Ernest's glazed eyes flicked over him. 'She'll sign it,' he said, meaning me.

'He's kidding,' Gigi jumped in quickly. 'He'd be happy to do it.'

The man laughed nervously and produced a pen. He darted off as soon as the deed was done, and I didn't blame him. A murky energy hung

410

over our table, and it was Christmas. Surely we could do better, for the boys if not for ourselves. They were bent over their plates, pretending we were a family in the middle of a nice meal, while Ernest bent over a fresh cocktail, his eyes glassy. I felt sorry for all of us.

'Don't you think you've had enough to drink?' I said.

'I feel fine. How do you feel?'

'Awful. Embarrassed.'

'Then maybe you should drink more. I might like you better if you did.'

Patrick's eyes flashed up to meet mine. I thought he might say something in my defense, so I shook my head pointedly and motioned for the bill, only wanting the night to be over.

When the waiter came, I told Ernest and the boys that I would take care of it and meet them outside in a few minutes. They left to get the car while I found the cash in my wallet and then lit a cigarette, hoping to clear my head and get a moment to myself. I breathed, shakily at first, and then a little easier. We would go home to bed and both sleep off this terrible mood, and tomorrow would be another day. A better one.

When I walked out on the street not even five minutes later, though, Ernest and the boys were gone. I thought I'd miscommunicated the plan somehow or they had, and went looking for them. I walked around the block, looking into every bar and café, wondering where they might have tucked in. I took the next block a bit faster, and then raced back to the Floridita, wondering if they might be waiting for me there. But they were gone. The truth dawned on me with a chilling shock. I would have to find my own way home. I was being punished. Ernest had left me.

\* \* \*

The boys were horrified when I saw them the next morning, but no more than I was. Ernest had gone to the US embassy to give his monthly report, and was nowhere to be found.

'Is everything all right, Mart?' Patrick asked me, looking pained.

'I can hold my own with Papa, Mousie,' I said, but he didn't seem to believe that any more than I did for the moment.

'It's not fair,' he said quietly.

'No.' I put one hand on each of his shoulders, and felt tears rise. 'It's not. People are awfully complicated. I don't know how else to say it. And sometimes they lose themselves a little. Papa will come back to us.'

'He doesn't always, though.'

I felt something knock hollowly in my chest. It hadn't been that long since he'd watched his parents battle out their differences, plenty and publicly. He must have been sick thinking that the whole awful story might repeat itself now, just when he'd started to believe the dust had settled, and that life — our life — was something he could trust.

'It's all right, Mouse. Please don't worry. Everything's going to be fine. You'll see.'

He was fourteen going on a hundred just then, and though he let me pull him toward me and

412

tell him again that all would be well, I could feel doubt as a stiffness in his body. I had my own version. I wanted to believe that Ernest could wrestle his darker nature and come running to my side, but I wasn't sure that things could ever be truly simple again. The world was a more complicated place than it had been before. Time was different, and more costly. A page had turned, and we had, too.

# 64

Over the next few days, Ernest and I tiptoed around each other, keeping our interactions brief and light and cool and civilized for the boys. It was Christmas, after all, but I couldn't help but feel saddened and defeated by the effort. It shouldn't be so hard to be kind, I thought, particularly to the person you're supposed to care about more than anything.

People, as I'd told Patrick, were complicated, and so was love itself. In fact, it was more and more complicated all the time. I decided to go to St. Louis to visit my mother and get a small respite.

'I'm just so tired,' I told her when I arrived. 'I want to pull the blankets up over my eyes and not think for a bit.'

'Of course, darling. Take all the time you need. I should tell you, though, that Ernest has rung twice. He doesn't sound very well.'

'No, he's not well. I don't understand. Oh, Mother. Honestly. Where did we go?'

★   ★   ★

The next day I phoned the Finca and got Ernest on the first ring. We didn't speak long. International calls were incredibly dear, then — and there was little to say. He was sorry and I was sorry, and we would try to be better for each

414

other when I returned home in January. In the meantime, he would enjoy the boys and I would rest and work on my novel, which I'd brought with me.

'This is a beautiful book you're writing, and you're beautiful. You're the most beautiful woman I've ever known and I'm going to learn how to do right by you. I haven't loved you well or strong enough. I see that.'

'And I haven't loved you well enough either, Rabbit. We can both do better. We have to.'

★   ★   ★

All this time at sea had been hard on his mistress, *Pilar*. She needed a new engine and other points of care. While she was laid up in dry dock, I had him back in my arms, but unfortunately that came with a price. His crew came along in the bargain, and all sorts of friends from town who had missed his company all these many months. The house was full to brimming and loud at every hour.

One night, an acquaintance drove his car into a corner of the house and fell on the horn. I ran out in my robe thinking he was dead, but he was only drunk. No one was around, either. They'd all gone to town for a nightcap.

'I can't work this way,' I told Ernest.

'Maybe you should go to town? To the Ambos. I can make sure they reserve you the best room.'

'I don't want to live in a hotel. This is my home. But why can't it be the way it used to be — with peace and quiet? Just us two? What happened to those days?'

'Looking back will only sink you,' he said, hearing my cry for the past as a complaint. 'This is our life now. Are you with me, or not?' His voice was challenging and his look was, too. He was wondering if I'd run off again — but I wouldn't. I was too close to finishing *Liana*, and I wasn't going to lose traction on the book for anything or anyone. Not if I could help it.

⋆ ⋆ ⋆

I locked myself in my office, rolled up my sleeves, and plunged in for one last push to finish the novel. No travel, no articles, no lunches in town, no distractions of any variety. There was only Liana and her world, which felt dizzying and wonderful and terrifying and maddening, just like love. Three weeks later, on June 27, I wrote the words *The End*, and then sat looking at them, shivering and full of joy and disbelief and astonishment and gratitude. The book was really and truly done. I'd poured everything inside. Whatever happened next, I hadn't spared anything or hedged my bets or been cowardly about a single word.

'Do you think it's actually good?' I asked Friendless. She was sitting atop one of the books that were spread everywhere and looking at me with those eerie green eyes that were like nothing of this world.

Cats' eyes sometimes seemed to bounce your own questions back at you, and Friendless's eyes did that now, blinking and steadying. *Do you think it's actually good?*

'Oh, God, I hope so. I do hope so, more than anything.'

I piled up the pages and rested my head on them for a moment, saying whatever prayer it is that writers have for the gifts that come from somewhere both inside and outside. And then I walked through the dark house to the pool and shed my clothes at the edge and slipped through the cool skin of the surface, plunging down and kicking hard, my mouth trailing bubbles. This too was a prayer.

# 65

I had long feared that Bumby would be drafted, but that wasn't what happened. He enlisted, breaking my heart and his mother's, no doubt. Ernest swore he had no fear for Bum, and that he was proud of him, but I couldn't see how when he could be taken just like that, and his courage with him, and his fine heart.

'Try not to worry so much,' Ernest told me. 'Nothing will happen to him at Fort Riley, and maybe by the time he goes over, the worst will have come and gone already.'

'I hope to God you're right,' I said, and wrote to Bum in his officer's training facility in Kansas telling him that I was sending two angels to watch over him, one for each of his beautiful shoulders. He might not feel them at all, for they were very light-footed angels, but they would be with him always and bring him home. And when he did come back, we would walk under the fruit trees at the Finca and talk about everything, just like we always had, because there was nothing better than talking with a good friend.

I posted the letter and then, to keep from fretting, tried to get the house ready for Ernest's forty-fourth birthday, and myself as well. I had let my hair go something awful and my body, too. I began to watch my weight again, bronzing myself from head to toe and slathering myself with lotions and creams and unguents.

It was right in the midst of all this preening and priming that I heard from Charles Colebaugh at *Collier's*. The Allies had begun bombing Rome and were hoping for a surrender from Italy. There was also a whisper that we would invade France soon.

I was intrigued, and full of questions. 'I thought there was a sanction against women at the front,' I told Colebaugh.

'That's still true. You wouldn't have formal military accreditation. But if you launched at England first, then made your way to Italy and France, we know you'd find good stories. You always do. We can stake you three months of expenses.'

After we rang off, I stood there a long time, looking at the phone and feeling powerfully moved by Colebaugh's faith in me. This war was the most terrifying thing the world had ever seen. Who knew how any of us would survive it? Who knew what to do at all except cling tightly to those we loved, and hope? But there was something else, too. I could write about it. *Collier's* had an audience of ten million readers now, and they could all see what I saw if I gathered the nerve to plunge over. This was a rare chance. How could I not take it?

★   ★   ★

When Ernest finally arrived home, he had a coal-black beard, and a singed nose that was peeling. I folded him up in my arms and kissed

419

him a dozen times, and then took him to bed. For two solid days, we only left the bedroom to go to the pool, and only left the pool to crawl to our deck chairs. We sat in our robes, squeaky clean and bleached by the sun, and sober. The cats sprawled beside us, lanky and at ease. Boise with his purr that was entirely silent. Friendless on her back, flicking her tail.

'I wish it was always this easy,' I said.

'It's easy enough right now, isn't it?'

The light was behind the trees, making them look cut out — carved painstakingly and leaned very gently against the sky. I looked and looked at them, thinking. Would I be as thrilled by the idea of going off to war if I didn't have Ernest and the Finca waiting for me? And would I be truly content here if I couldn't also go away sometimes and do my work? The questions hung there for only a moment, their answers obvious. I didn't want to lose anything I had. I also didn't know how to move forward without risking everything.

'I never want us to be so married that we can't be ourselves anymore,' I said.

'All right.' I heard a thread of caution in his voice. He likely smelled my dilemma, even if it wasn't my intention to share it. 'What would you have instead?'

'Instead of being polite and awfully safe, you mean?'

'Yes.'

'Just for there to be room to be as wild and free as we actually are, and to be able to really talk to each other. That's what I miss when

420

you're away. You've always been my favorite person to talk to.'

'That's nice.'

'It is. It *is* nice, Rabbit, but I have these other sides of me, too, and I'm not always sure how they fit together or even if they can. I want to be passionate about things and feed my mind and travel the world. I'd rather be darkly and dangerously happy, like living on a knife's edge, than lose my way and forget my nature.'

He'd been watching me seriously as I talked. Now he said, 'This is why you've never agreed to have a child.' It wasn't a question but a statement, and it was laced all over with sadness rather than bite or malice.

'I do love children. I love yours terribly. I don't know. Maybe we should have done it ages ago, as soon as we were married or even before. It just seems like the window has passed.'

'I know. I feel it, too. Only it seems awfully unfair when I think of it. Men can long for a child but not do anything about it. The woman always has the final say. And if that's no, then no is what you have to live with.'

There was a stillness and a matter-of-factness to his words that gave me a sick feeling. 'I'm sorry,' I said, because I didn't know what else to say. And then I said the truest thing I knew. 'I love you.'

★   ★   ★

We'd bought a hog from a neighboring farmer for Ernest's birthday and set out to roast it,

421

hosting a feast for all our friends with enough liquor on hand for several times their number. The house and grounds were as beautiful as they'd ever been, and everything went smoothly, and the food was sublime. Ernest gave several speeches, and Gregorio, Ernest's first mate, recited part of a poem and caught everyone off guard, and the pelota players sang and played beautifully, and everyone got slightly drunk and then very drunk, and then roaring drunk.

It wasn't the drinking that troubled me and made me feel a little apart from the events of the evening. It wasn't that the Basques had started to throw silverware and then hard rolls at one another at the table. It wasn't even that I couldn't hear myself think for all the noise and chaos. It was a song that undid me. A favorite of mine that I'd heard countless times by now, 'Txoria Txori,' about a man who loves a bird that has flown away.

'If I had clipped its wings, it would have been mine,' the lyrics went, 'it would have never flown away.' The song had always struck me as wistful and a little romantic, about the difficult lessons of love. But as Felix sang it tonight, his voice high and clear and plaintive, I heard something new in the song. It was just as much about the bird, I realized, as the man. When she flies, it's not because she's cruel or cannot love the man, or because she loves another, or for any other reason, really, except that she's a bird. She is what she does.

I tried to meet Ernest's eyes when the song was over. I wanted to tell him about Europe now

422

— *now* — before I'd lost my nerve, and while I still felt the song as a beautifully clear blazing of wisdom. *Listen,* I wanted to say, *when you fell in love with me you must also have been in love with my wings. Love them now. Love me. Love me, and let me go.*

# 66

I hadn't seen London in five years and couldn't help staring in disbelief by how changed it was. Over a million houses had been damaged or destroyed in the Blitz, and many of the most familiar landmarks had been bombed to unrecognizability, so that the entire skyline seemed altered. Perhaps it always would be. Every other person on the street was in uniform. Nurses walked in pairs with the crimson lining of their wool capes flaring and billowing around them. The berets of the boys from the parachute regiment were redder still. Clean shaven and beautiful, they stood out in a sea of American GIs who were everywhere, everywhere, awaiting orders for the invasion of France, which was still months away, though no one knew how far. It was a whispered plan, a wish, a dream — the thing that would turn the tide in this war. If only it would finally come.

I took a room at the Dorchester, which reminded me so much of my room in Spain I felt instantly at home there — with the same slightly faded cretonne curtains and fabric on the chairs; the same pinging radiator and tiny bathroom sink. Ginny Cowles had a room at the Dorchester, too, as did many of the correspondents I'd known in Madrid and later in Czechoslovakia and Finland. I felt heartened by that and comforted — as if we were all still a kind of fraternity or even a family. I'd missed that dearly.

★ ★ ★

*I know you don't understand why I have to be here, I wrote Ernest, but please don't give up on me. You belong to me and I belong to you. Don't ever doubt that, or that I love you.*

★ ★ ★

*Loving me from London isn't exactly the most satisfying option I can think of, he wrote back. Come home quickly, Rabbit. I know I haven't shown you much lately, but I admire your courage and your mind and your heart more than anything I ever saw, and please be careful when you're over there because I couldn't rightly stand it nor find a way to go on without you. Without you, please understand, is no longer any kind of life for me. Already it feels like sadness and loneliness have their grip on me and I wonder how these weeks and weeks will go. The cotsies have called a powwow and are watching me, worried. They send you love and say, as I do, come home.*

★ ★ ★

I read his letter over and over until I'd memorized it. The tenderness in his words made my heart hurt, and so did thinking of him there alone with the cats, feeling lost. He was trying

425

his best to let me do what I needed to do. I saw the effort and wanted to reach across the ocean between us to hold him, and to tell him that without him was also no way of life. No way at all.

Maybe distance was sharpening something for us both. I hoped so, as I waited for my official correspondent tags and my first assignment. When they came, I headed to an airfield in the country, at Woodhall Spa, in Lincolnshire. The British Lancasters, which were among the heaviest bombers in the war, flew in and out of the airfield a dozen at a time, the air so full of vibration when they did you'd think you were going to shake apart or go a little mad. I watched them buzz away in their lethal black formation, and then watched them come back again after dropping their cargo and in the meantime took loads of notes about the base. There was one small country hotel where the pilots who waited for their next mission drank vats of milky tea and read borrowed dime-store novels in long wooly cardigans and slippers by the smoking wood-stove. I saw a story in that, the way they seemed like anyone anywhere, staying warm, biding their time before the signal came. Then they suited up, climbing into those great hulking terrible birds to bring death on the wing.

I started writing about 'the bomber boys,' as I'd begun to call them in my head, on my way back to London, but along the way caught an awful cold that stuck and stuck, becoming the flu, and then gastritis, all of that at once. I couldn't keep my fever down, nor eat a bite, and

426

felt like some sort of dying animal. Even worse, Ernest's letters had stopped coming.

I knew he wasn't at sea, with his crew, since his mission had been held up indefinitely. His silence was all the more troubling, too, because he'd reached out so lovingly just a week ago. Had he fallen lower at home, and turned to drinking himself sick at the Floridita and the Frontón? Had he slid further away from me, to where I couldn't reach him? It was maddening, and made me feel helpless. I knew my being gone for so long must be chinking away at him, but I couldn't see his eyes and talk to him about it. I couldn't pull him back toward me and tell him I was his own, and always would be, no matter where I'd gone in my travels. I couldn't really do anything but worry, sick and thick-headed, and wait for some news. And hope it was the good kind, and that we would be okay.

# 67

The trick when things got bad, he knew, was to be very still, first in his body and then in his mind. If he lay still enough, long enough, he could drop down and down until he found that pocket of quiet inside himself. It was always there, the quiet place, but you couldn't always reach it.

The flooring they'd put in the house was woven matting good for this climate, and also good, it turned out, for the cats and for him, too. There was furniture everywhere in the room, comfortable furniture you could sink into, but nothing felt right until he lay on the floor, and put his legs against the armchair, and pulled the lamp over until the light formed a soft circle just off his shoulder. The matting was stiff, but that was all right. He put a blanket down on top of it as if he were camping, and then pulled a pillow off the sofa and he had a fine place.

In a few moments, Friendless swayed, walking over to him, then settled against his right side, at his waist, just under his arm where he held his newspaper up to the circle of light. Boise wouldn't have anything but the best spot, in the center of his chest, and he curled there with his warm weight and a stillness that always felt like love to Ernest. In the same way that fish had quickness, cats had a way of being still. That was their gift, and you could learn a lot by watching them get there. If you lay close with them, and matched your breathing with theirs, you sometimes thought you had a great and very rare secret.

He hadn't always understood the thing about cats. He hadn't always understood himself, either. When he was young, it had often seemed as if nearly anything could finish him off. He felt too much. That was the truth of it. He noticed too many things in people's eyes, so that even a meal with his family could make him feel split open and exposed. His parents soon guessed how it was for him because he'd not learned to hide it yet, but they couldn't help him. No one could help him until he began to learn how to seal over the wounded, flinching place inside and feel an almost surgical relief. It had taken time to learn, and a lot of concentration.

The first time he had known he could do it and count on the method to carry him through was after Agnes's letter had come, the one saying it was all over and that she'd been wrong to lead him on. They were supposed to be married and he'd believed her. He'd told his friends and his mother and he didn't think he could bear trying to explain that it was all a mistake, or worse. He hadn't thought he could live through losing her, but he had. Later, he would know how much more there was to lose, and just how deep love could go, and how it could shred you and everything you thought you understood about life. When you loved two people and were terrified, knowing you could lose them both at any moment and have nothing. Or when you loved one person too much and couldn't be sure who you were anymore without her. That's when you would need every trick you'd learned, and more.

Now the wind was picking up outside. He didn't have to go to the window to see how it would be coming from the west, blowing the trees and rocking their branches. In the lane that led up to the house, and out behind the pool where the jungle grew up thick and tall, everything would be shifting now, back and forth like dark water. But Boise had his own rhythm and wasn't troubled. If the cat felt the wind, he didn't show it. He only grew heavier and more himself, as if he was falling more deeply into his bones. Surrendering to the way things actually were. Ernest registered all of this against his chest and began to make the necessary adjustments, slowing his breath, feeling the rise and fall of his chest and belly beneath the cat until he felt heavier, too, against the blanket and the matting, everything below him and all around.

He reached for his glass, and held the whiskey in his mouth for a long time, letting it burn him in a good way. And then, when he knew he had gotten to a place that was very quiet indeed, and very still, he made the final adjustment. The warmth and gravity of the cat's body sank into him and through him. And that's when he knew he was strong enough, and quiet enough, to let himself feel that Marty was really gone. He wouldn't get her back because he'd pushed her away. Something had broken between them, or was it him who'd done the breaking?

In his head and way down at the center of him he blotted her out, now, to see if he could bear it. She wasn't away, he told himself. She wasn't working, nor following her assignment until she could come home to him. She wasn't traveling by convoy or talking to people trying to hear their stories. She wasn't in her hotel, sleeping curled on her side like a child, but utterly gone and finished. She wasn't his wife, because he had no wife.

At this last thought he'd stopped and just listened to himself breathing beneath the cat's weight. His heart was still going. The floor was still there beneath him, and the blanket against his back. Boise opened his golden eyes and then opened them again, the second set of lids flashing like something metallic and strange, blessing him.

'If only you liked whiskey,' he said to the cat, 'then everything really would be all right.'

The cat didn't stir even a little. It sat on his chest, still as a sphinx and quiet as anything. This would be a very long night, he knew. He closed his eyes and felt the house all around him and him inside it. The weather made a halo around the house, and the sky made a halo around the weather, and the ocean pushed out all around everything and touched its way east until it found England, and that's where she was, though she was also nowhere. He could feel her absence even in the place he'd tried to kill. He could feel it moving through him like his own blood. Yes, goddammit, it would be a long night.

# 68

In many ways being a woman meant I was relegated to the outskirts of the war in Europe, but there were interesting people at those outskirts, and I talked to as many as I could. In train stations and barracks, in storefronts and pubs and mess halls, I looked into their eyes as I asked questions, and wrote down what they said, and what I felt listening. At night I sat up late by the single bulb at my bedside, or sometimes walked through London's blacked-out streets and thought about what I had seen and heard, turning everything over for myself until I felt that I was slowly and little by little coming to understand what this war was. I'd always been someone who needed to take things in on my feet and with my own eyes. I was doing that now and trying to stay focused on each day, each encounter, and not fall too low about my marriage.

The pieces came fast, tumbling out of me — most of them concerning ordinary people, which had always been what I most cared about and felt pulled toward. I stood beside them, watching until I thought I could glean what was particular about their story, what was true and worth knowing.

Maybe the most difficult of all the stories I heard came from a Polish refugee who'd only barely fled his village with his life. The Germans

# The Curve

William Street,
Slough, SL1 1XY
Renew books by phone  0303 1230035

Borrowed Items 21/08/2019 16:21
XXXXXXXXXX9206

| Item Title | Due Date |
| --- | --- |
| 30130503648036 | 11/09/2019 |
| 30130505630720 | 11/09/2019 |
| 30130503665625 | 11/09/2019 |
| 38067412576502 | 11/09/2019 |
| 30130503690067 | 11/09/2019 |
| 30130503665691 | 11/09/2019 |
| 30130502309985 | 11/09/2019 |

Space Chase free children's Summer
Reading Challenge
Read 6 library books. Collect rewards. Get
a medal and certificate when you finish.
Ask staff for details.
Thank you for using Slough's Self Service
Unit

www.slough.gov.uk/libraries
Did you know? There are no overdue fines
for children aged 13 and under!

had taken most of the men for forced labor, and whichever of the wives and daughters they found desirable for brothels on the eastern front. The other women were made to work, or sometimes ordered to claw a shallow grave where they stood before they were shot without ceremony. Some Poles became servants or serfs on their own stolen farms. Most Jews were killed immediately, wherever they were found.

I watched the man carefully as he told me all this. He was rail thin and jaundiced, with wide yellow circles beneath his eyes. He couldn't have been more than forty, I guessed, and had seen things no one should, not at that or any other age.

'They're killing millions of Jews,' he said.

I heard him. His words rang in my skull like something hammered out on an anvil, but I also couldn't fully take them in. The number was too vast, too hideous. The suffering almost unimaginable. 'How many have found a way to escape, like you did?'

He shrugged. 'Maybe one day we'll know, but not enough. In my village, anyone who even gave a Jew a piece of bread was shot on sight.' His face changed as he told me that his parents had been sent to a labor camp. 'I can't believe they're alive. I don't know where my daughter was taken. She's fourteen.'

I found I couldn't say anything. I wanted to touch his hand, send up a prayer, weep for all that had been stolen from him, but nothing would have been right or enough. Finally I thanked him for his honesty and told him how important it felt to me that we'd met, that now readers in the States would know exactly how sickening and abominable things were in his country and elsewhere. Then I watched him walk away, feeling like I could barely stand up.

I met another Pole who told me about the Warsaw Ghetto, where there was a wall ten feet high and sealed all around with guards. Inside the walls, four or five hundred thousand people had been driven, and there they starved and fought off typhus and watched Nazis hunt through the streets randomly, murdering anyone they liked, just as it struck them. He'd escaped by jumping from a train that was taking him to a labor camp in Prussia. When he got back to Warsaw, he'd altered his appearance, changed his name, and paid to have new papers forged. The man he'd been before was dead. He didn't know how to reach his living family members with the truth until the war was over.

I wanted to tell him the war had to be over soon, but I didn't believe it, and anyway, even if it ended right then, at that precise moment, it would already have been far too late for the Jews. Learning the truth and taking it in felt like swallowing poison. The pieces I would write would take that poison and give it to each of my readers like a terrible dark kiss — that's why I was here and not at home, and why Ernest truly needed to be here as well. But he couldn't be, I realized with a very particular sadness. He'd lost something, something utterly essential to him, and had grown afraid. Maybe writing the book of his life had given him too much, after all, and he couldn't take risks now. Maybe it was the middle of his life breathing down his neck, or Bum being sent over to France soon, which he still wouldn't acknowledge. Whatever it was, I saw that now the war terrified him and so did his own death. And me, too, and himself. Everything.

I wrote him again, from the absolute bottom of my heart, saying how much I needed him to be here — for me — and for all the readers who needed to hear the truth as only he could write it.

His reply couldn't have been clearer. He said I might be exactly where I wanted, as I usually was, but that he could not possibly come. His war work in Cuba was too essential to walk away from. He was going to stick it out there, because that's what he was meant to do. Meanwhile, he was lonely — terribly, awfully, disgustingly lonely, *like someone with my heart cut out*. He ended not with the word *love*, but with *so long*, saying that maybe he would see me soon, and maybe he wouldn't.

I'd been away for over four months, longer than I ever had. Too long, I realized. His loneliness had hardened and turned. He was only bitter now and he wouldn't budge in my direction, or couldn't. We seemed to be at a terrible impasse, and he was cutting my heart out, too, and I didn't know what to think, or what to do. So I read it all again, holding the letter away from my body, like something that meant to do me harm, and already had.

# 69

By the end of January 1944, I'd finished and sent off six of the seven articles I'd promised to *Collier's*. They were pleased with my work and told me so. They even printed a photo of me next to a short column saying that, 'among gal correspondents,' I stood out, coming 'pretty close to living up to Hollywood's idea of what a big-league woman reporter should be.' I didn't know about or care about Hollywood, but I loved knowing I had a real following now, readers who looked for my take on things, and recognized my voice when they came across it, what a far cry that was from how I'd started.

I decided to set out for Italy, where the Allies had been stalled by a brutal German defense for months and months, just below Cassino. Ginny Cowles had already headed there and written back to say she'd run into Herb Matthews and that they were waiting for me with a giant flask of whiskey.

My heart swelled to think of seeing Matthews and working beside him, as in the old days. As I readied myself to leave London and head after him, I received a packet of notices for *Liana*, which had just been released in the States. Only one of them was dismissive, referring to me merely as Hemingway's wife, and saying nothing substantial about the book. The others used my own name and applauded what I'd done. I'd come of age artistically, one said. Another mentioned that I seemed to be able to handle characters — particularly female ones — with more delicacy and restraint than my far-more-famous husband. The dizzying charge of that statement was followed by a letter from Max saying how pleased Scribner's was by the early sales figures. The book had already sold out its first printing of twenty-seven thousand copies and had hit all the major bestseller lists.

I was ecstatic — I truly was — but the good news also seemed to belong to another Martha Gellhorn. This one was packing a satchel and hurrying to Algiers and then to Naples, where I threw in with a long convoy of trucks and Jeeps and tanks and ambulances stringing their way to the front through a deep constant paste of mud. It rained for weeks until everything was slick and wet and brown, the small villages we passed at a crawl, reduced to rubble from heavy shelling, the blown bridges and ransacked farms and displaced families that were working their way south while we headed steadily north, toward the Germans.

Ahead were the mountains the French were holding with their lives, and ones they were trying to take back, inch by inch. Ahead, I kept telling myself, were Matthews and Ginny Cowles keeping a place for me in some mud-spattered tent along the side of the road, warming whiskey with their hands and saving a laugh for me and all their best stories.

The convoy kept moving through the damp, past minefields and encampments, while the sounds of gunfire and shelling grew louder. My shoulders ached with knots. I was terrified, but also filled with admiration for the French soldiers who were dug in here and fighting with everything they had as a way to get home — right through the German army and back to France, by way of Italy.

When we came to Sant'Elia, seven kilometers from the front at Cassino, an ambulance had just been shelled where it stood, parked to one side of the Rapido, just below the village. The murdered driver had been brought to the hospital field tent on a cot, and there were flowers in her hands that one of her friends had placed there — her friends being the other French girl ambulance drivers who had come to see her where she lay, and now were headed back to their vehicles, to the treacherous road and the mud and the whistling shells with her face in their thoughts. She had the most beautiful features, and hair the color of summer corn, and she was absolutely gone and not asleep.

I watched the doctors and the stretcher-bearers doing their work in the unremitting cold, with improvised equipment, while a transistor radio in the corner played swing music on a station from over the Swiss border. When the number of wounded had ebbed to a trickle, the surgeon invited me to his living quarters down in the cellar of a nearby building. It had a dirt floor that had been covered over with peeling wooden doors taken from the rubble that was every-where. The doors were damp and cold, but the floor was far worse, so we perched there on mattresses by a stingy coal-burning stove, and listened to the mice in the walls.

The surgeon offered me some Italian cognac he'd been saving, which smelled of singed peaches and lilacs and tasted like quivering fire on my tongue. I drank it gratefully, and sent up a silent toast to Matthews, wherever he was, and to Ernest, too — wishing with every last cell in my body that the three of us could be together right now, here with the damp doors and the endless mud and the mortar fire and Tommy Dorsey, and death. If we could lean on each other, we could bear anything, anything at all. Nothing had ever felt as right as that, and Ernest would remember it, and take it in, and maybe be saved a little by it. He would, if only I could get him here.

★　★　★

Before I left Italy, a letter from Bumby found me. He was stationed in Algeria, serving as a military police officer in charge of a special unit. He was fine, he promised, but had seen no action and was growing restless.

THANK GOD FOR THAT, I shot back by cable. YOU RESTLESS IS THE LUCKIEST THING I'VE HEARD IN AGES.

He told me he was going to be on leave soon, in Algiers, so I made arrangements to meet him there, en route back to London. Even for a single night, I thought it would be worth any amount of trouble. And it was.

As soon as I arrived in Algiers, I managed to

439

get us both invited to a dinner being thrown by Victor Rothschild. He'd just won the George Medal for valor for his service in dismantling undetonated bombs in the London Blitz. In years to come, there would be a great deal of talk about whether or not he was a Soviet spy trading British secrets, but for the moment he was only our incredibly dashing host, recounting high-risk tales over pressed duck and plum pudding while Bumby gobbled up all of it, leaning on Victor's every word.

'Don't get any ideas,' I told him. 'Papa and I need you in one piece.'

'I'm only listening,' he said with a wink. 'You can't arrest me for that.'

He seemed to have aged two years since I'd last seen him at Christmas. It was the trim cut of his uniform and his sharp haircut, but also a look in his eye. He was finished with being safe and sheltered, only he knew better than to tell me that.

After dinner, I followed him over to where Victor was perched with a Pimm's Cup and a massive cigar, talking of parachute jumps with Randolph Churchill, son of the British prime minister. Randolph had just narrowly escaped capture, and probably death, after dropping into Yugoslavia. To hear him tell it, there were only thrilling, fearless moments. He was eager to go back immediately, right into the thick of things.

Randolph was at least as dashing to look at as Victor, if not more so. They both could have been film stars, even without the help of their very famous families. And now I knew there was no chance in persuading Bum that a sleepy post was lucky. As the evening flew by, he pressed both men with questions, nodding the way I'd seen him do when Ernest instructed him on some point of shooting on the wing or fly-fishing. He wasn't dreaming; he was taking essential mental notes.

'I should steal you away to London and keep you as my special pet,' I told him when we had to part.

'What about the firing squad I'd get for desertion?' he asked, smiling and patient with me as ever.

'Oh, that. Well, the threat of a firing squad might be useful in drawing Papa over.'

'You're worried about him.'

'Nearly always. Isn't that stupid? I swear I'd worry less if he wanted to parachute into Yugoslavia with you. At least then he'd be behaving like himself.' I felt my emotions rising dangerously and shook my head quickly. 'I'm sorry. I shouldn't be talking like this.'

'It's all right. I know things haven't been easy lately.'

'What would you do? Tell me.'

'Drag him here in a large wool sack?' He shrugged a little, trying to make light. 'If only he were the dragging type.'

'I might try anyway,' I said, and then I pulled him close and hugged him hard and for a long time, not wanting to ever let him go.

# 70

Although Bumby was more than right about Ernest's temperament, by March I'd decided that I was far too concerned about my husband not to head home, at least for a short while. I'd been away for five months — twice as long as we'd ever been apart — and I almost didn't recognize the Finca when I arrived. Empty liquor bottles were strewn everywhere and the cats had taken over the Little House, spraying wherever they liked. Six or ten of them were new. So was the man that looked at me with Ernest's face, but with a mood that was so very dark and sour I was almost afraid to go near him.

'Did you forget something?' he asked coldly, before I even settled my luggage properly.

'Please don't punish me, Rabbit. I've missed you like no one's business.'

He only shrugged and told me that Operation Friendless was no more. All counterintelligence activity in South America had recently been handed off to the FBI, which had examined his activities and pronounced them 'amateurish.' He grimaced at the word, repeating it.

'I'm so sorry,' I told him.

'Like hell you are. Two years of steady patrolling and we don't even rate a *thank you very much*. How's that for duty?' Bitterness and pure rancor shone in his eyes and the turned-down corners of his mouth.

442

He seemed so much older to me suddenly. His eyes were lined and flat and without fire. His cheeks seemed to sag, and there was salt in his beard, I noticed in the light. When I tried to talk about Europe, the coming invasion of France, any portion of the future ahead of us, he flinched and twisted on himself, and then struck out at me.

He was intent on rubbing my nose in everything that was wrong with me, everything I'd ever done to cross him. He spat entire lists of things he'd had to suffer through because I'd needed to have my way, China and Arizona, Finland and the Caribbean, all the weeks and months he'd had to be on his own when he'd told me how rotten that was for him. The way I'd ruined the tomcats, and now was trying to sink him like every other woman. He snarled about my spoiledness, my terrible spending habits, my ambition. My *ambition* — that seemed the dirtiest word of all.

At first I refused to be baited, insisting that I loved him and wanted what was best for both of us. But finally I couldn't take the bullying a moment longer.

'What's my crime, exactly?' I lashed back. 'To be working and at war when you weren't? Why is it that a man can do his work and just get on with it, but a woman has to drop everything for her place at home or else she's selfish?'

'You are that.' He ignored my question, simply batted it away. 'Selfish beyond belief. You have to have excitement at every moment, or you'll make it yourself, like a kind of sickness for adventure

443

and for trouble. I should have seen it in you right away, but I guess I was looking at your legs. That was quite a trap you set, by the way.'

'I *trapped* you?'

'Some would see it that way, sure.'

It wasn't enough that he had to rewrite everything that was happening between us. He wanted to rewrite the past, too. It made me sick and sad. And it didn't end there.

'I used to have a wife,' he ranted. 'I married one woman and now seem stuck with another.'

'Stuck? Then why don't you blow it all apart? You've done it before. Hell, you're doing it now. Tell me you aren't.'

'I'm only trying to save myself,' he said. And the battle raged on.

We fought about his drinking — which had become bottomless, unstoppable — his boasting, his need to control everyone and everything around him. We fought about the house, about money, about work — everything that might be dragged out to spit and snarl over, chewing it to pieces. Once it might have felt cathartic for us to row like this, but now I only felt shredded and fearful and terribly unprepared. We had been drifting apart for a long time, but so slowly I could push the thought away. Now it was as if the glacier of unease we'd been standing on for years suddenly exploded. Ice had become fire.

And when I thought about the boys — Mouse and Gigi, and Bum — and how I might lose them now, I almost couldn't bear it.

'I wish I could break into pieces,' I told him one night, just a week after I'd come back. 'That

444

would feel better somehow. Isn't the worst when you can keep on walking and breathing and writing letters and going to the market and all the things you do when you're alive, but really you're blown apart?'

'That's called self-preservation, darling.'

'I don't want to be a preservationist, then. I don't want any part of that. I want to be honest.'

'Have another whiskey.'

'I've already had too much. I can't feel my fingers.'

'Then it's doing its job.'

★ ★ ★

I didn't know what to think or what to do except go back overseas. I called Charles Colebaugh and told him I was ready to finish the work I'd begun, but instead of the usual enthusiasm I'd come to expect from him, there was a strange tension on the line.

'Ernest is going to write for us. He rang the other day. I thought you knew.'

'What?' I was so surprised I couldn't even speak for a moment. There was a lump in my throat the size of a starling. Finally I said, 'He didn't mention it.'

'We can only have one accredited journalist over there. I'm awfully sorry.'

'Twenty-six pieces, Charles. You've published twenty-six of my pieces since I first went to Spain, and you're throwing me over for my own husband?'

'I think you know what a difficult spot I'm in.

445

I have to think of circulation. And don't forget he came to me. Please forgive me for saying it, Marty, but maybe you're arguing with the wrong fellow.'

When the line went dead I held the phone in my hand for a long time, trying to quiet the roaring in my ears. If anyone had asked me years or even months ago if I thought Ernest was capable of such a thing I would have laughed. He loved and admired me too much to sink me. But this was pure retaliation. In his mind, I was the one doing the betraying. I had abandoned him for my work and my own ends, and now I would be made to suffer as he had suffered.

I couldn't stand to think of what all this meant, or what it would possibly take for us to become allies again. I barely recognized him now. His demons had set up house, taking him over, and it seemed he didn't recognize me, either. I saw no love anywhere in him for me, and this made me feel desperate.

His timing couldn't have been worse, either. The invasion of Normandy was coming at any moment. I had been preparing for it since October, learning what I needed to learn and thinking of just how to cover it so that when the time came, my voice could chime in with the others to chronicle one of the most crucial moments in the history of war. But now I no longer had any official capacity, and no guarantee that anything I wrote would find a home. It was as if I'd been plunged back to the beginning, when I was wet behind the ears and headed to Spain.

For the first time in years, the memory brought me no comfort at all.

★　★　★

When I confronted Ernest, he only scowled, his jaw set against me, his eyes stony. 'You pushed me to go all this while. You haven't stopped pushing for a year. You only have yourself to blame if I finally took the hint.'

'You could have gone to any magazine in the world, absolutely any of them, and you took mine. I didn't know you had such a cruel streak in you.' My face was hot.

'Well, with any luck I'll get blown to smithereens. You'd like that, wouldn't you?'

'Don't you have any feeling for me at all?' I asked, but his face remained closed.

When I walked down the hallway to bed I was light-headed. I reached out to touch the walls with my fingertips, feeling I'd gotten hopelessly lost in the dark. So lost I knew it would be an utter miracle if I somehow found my way again.

# 71

Ernest left for New York almost immediately. He was catching a seaplane for Shannon and then London. At first I thought he might have a few drops of civility left in him and try to find me a seat on the plane, too. I had no expense account now, and no one paying my way, and had already run through my Scribner's advance for *Liana*. But he said it wasn't possible. It was an RAF plane, and women were expressly forbidden.

I appealed to everyone I knew for a way over, and it was then I learned that Bumby had applied for a transfer to the Office of Strategic Services and got it. Almost the moment his security clearance came through and his training was complete, he volunteered to parachute behind enemy lines in a German-held part of France. He'd never launched himself out of a plane before, but he'd heard about it, I thought, feeling awful and terrified for him, and awash with guilt for exposing him to Rothschild and Churchill that night in Algiers.

I pressed my contacts for more information, but they could only tell me that he'd tucked a fly rod into his jump pack before he launched himself out over France, swearing to his commanding officer that it was a radio antenna. I hoped to God that he would stay safe, somehow, and wished more than anything that I could be near Ernest again, as he used to be. We needed to bind together now, to lean on each other. How else would we get through?

When my chance at transport finally came, I almost couldn't believe it. The Norwegian freighter was outfitted to carry the two-and-a-half-ton amphibious assault Ducks, to be used in the D-day landings — that and loads and loads of dynamite. I was the sole passenger. There were no lifeboats anywhere, no place I might get a drink, since the ship was dry, and I wasn't allowed to smoke on deck. The journey would take twenty days, a good long time to think about where I had just been and where I was going.

All I knew was that a hollow, haunted feeling followed me wherever I went. I thought of Ernest nearly nonstop and wondered if my heart had been somehow carved out of my body. I lay in my cramped bunk, staring at nothing. I paced between the hulking Ducks until my legs turned to jelly. When night finally came, I slept like the dead.

For days upon days, we had terrible fog. I stood at the railing of the ship desperate for a cigarette and anything that felt like peace while, all around us, the air remained thick and white as concrete. Over and over again, the freighter sounded its horn through the murk, announcing its presence. Every time, I jumped, feeling the sound reverberate through my body, vibrating the rungs of my rib cage, the ladder of my spine. The future was like this pressing fog, or like an endless wall of shadows. I was a shadow, too, and I found it was impossible to think of what might

449

lie ahead for us — if there was any way to recover who we used to be together. The task seemed immense, and hope was nowhere — a thing that belonged to other people who were sturdy enough to carry it.

★  ★  ★

Day followed night, or so it must have. The sun rose and set behind thick curtains. But finally, as we drew nearer to England, the fog began to lift. I woke one morning, and knew it was morning. A cold clear wind blew on deck. It pierced my wool peacoat and clawed at my face, and I needed it. I stood and watched the sea until I was so chilled I thought I might never be warm again, because there, in the bone-cracking clarity of that feeling, I could actually breathe. Off in the distance, there were icebergs. At first they were formless, only great smears of white here and there, like sunspots. But as we grew nearer, they shifted and winnowed and stood out more and more clearly, like pieces of architecture, or art, crystalline and bright and wild and alone. One was like a genie's lamp, curving and spiraling up and up, made entirely of diamonds. Another floated like a mountain, while another sprouted the wings of a sheer-white pigeon or a dove, cracked through with light that radiated and flared and made my breath catch. There was no reason at all to feel any hope. There wasn't, but in that cold exquisite moment, I couldn't help myself.

# 72

When my Norwegian freighter finally docked at Liverpool, I gathered my things and went ashore. Almost immediately I ran into two correspondents who were talking about Ernest. Two days before, he'd been in a car accident after a party at Belgrave Square. The driver had been drunk and plunged them both into a steel water tank. Ernest had been thrown against the windshield, cracked his scalp, and banged up both his knees. He was now in a London hospital with a serious concussion.

I flew to the recovery ward without waiting to hear more. Even with things as terrible as they were, I had to go to him. What if I had lost him now, after everything? We'd been so stupid to push each other away, when love was the only thing that made sense anymore, given the way the world was going.

I found his room, ready to say anything, do anything, but I could barely push my way inside. There was a cocktail party going on. Extra chairs had been pulled in, and pals of his sprawled in them, joking and telling stories. A dozen or more empty whiskey bottles spilled from beneath Ernest's bed, where he sat up cheerfully, not seeming at all surprised to see me. Other than an enormous snowy bandage wrapped around his head like the turban of some self-imposed pasha, he seemed perfectly fine to me.

In an instant, my mood turned. 'I was told you were hurt.'

'Hello to you, too, Wife. I have fifty-seven stitches, for your information. Not that you actually care.' He said this right out loud, as if everyone there already knew the score about us. Of course they did. They'd heard every sordid detail straight from him.

'How can you be drinking with a concussion? Does your doctor know?'

'Who do you think brought the bottles in?'

As angry as I was, I pushed closer. 'Have you heard Bum's in France?'

'I got a letter yesterday. Apparently he's getting nice fish.'

I could only stare at him, disbelievingly. His cocky expression, the hangers-on, this pretending that we hadn't said the worst sorts of things to each other. It was all too much. 'What are we doing? Please send everyone away, will you? Talk to me.'

But he ignored me, plunging ahead with a string of accusations. 'I could have died in that car, and where is the tenderness, the sympathy? You can only think of yourself as usual.'

'I'm here,' I said, but I realized he couldn't see it. Couldn't see me at all. There was only disappointment standing in my place, the way we'd hurt each other, the arguments we'd been bludgeoning each other with for months. There was so much wreckage all around us, and if there was a way to break through, I couldn't see it. I found I had nothing to say, either in anger or in love.

Shutting my eyes tightly, I turned quickly on my heel without saying goodbye, and hurried out into the hall. The dim corridor was full of nurses and men in uniform. The rooms were full of wounded men and the smell of ether, and camphor, and death. I steadied myself and slowed and tried to catch my breath, but nothing felt real. Not my body in the hallway. Not the scene behind me. Not what lay ahead.

I'm not sure how I reached the Dorchester. I don't remember anything of the journey, only that I wanted to sleep forever when I arrived.

'Ah, Mrs. Hemingway,' the clerk said, looking at my passport. 'Welcome back. Your husband's room is on the second floor. Shall I give you the adjacent room?'

I was worn so thin at that point I felt my legs buckle. This was what we'd come to, then. As far away from our beginnings at the Hotel Florida as hope was away from despair. As love was from hate. I gripped the desk in front of me, focusing on my hands to stay upright. 'Please no,' I said, not caring that tears were coming, or that my face laid everything bare. 'Put me on the highest floor, will you? Far, far away.'

# 73

Ernest always said there was a season for everything. A season to love and be loved. To work and rest your bones and your spirit. To dream and to doubt, to fear and to fly. What season was this, then, if not one of ruin? Of utter defeat? For seven years Ernest had been not so much in my heart and mind as in my very blood cells. And now I would have to learn to live without him. How? Where could one learn to do that kind of amputation, and walk away alive, and still be the same person?

★ ★ ★

For years now the Allies had been preparing for the invasion of France. Operation Overlord. D-day. More than two and a half million men were awaiting deployment in Britain for the surprise attack across the English Channel. Hundreds and hundreds of journalists and photographers were poised, too, everyone jockeying for a place at the vanguard. Ernest would be going on the *Dorothea L. Dix*, I heard, but there were only so many spaces aboard the ships and assault crafts, and certainly no room for a second-string reporter like myself with no official credentials. So I stayed behind in London with all the other unlucky correspondents, waiting for news that the invasion had begun.

This moment had been so long in coming, I think we were all afraid to exhale or move, or hope. We had all been briefed, so we knew when it was set to happen, down to the last second. And we stood there, watching the clock all together and knowing that nothing would ever be the same after the attack was launched, and that reporters and novelists and historians would be telling the story for a hundred or two hundred years. And it was happening now.

You expected some sort of explosion, the great seam of the world ripping open and spilling a cry. But there was only a strange silence. I didn't know what to do with myself, and so walked around London in the cold morning air. It was a wet bleak day, with a steady mist that got in your lungs and in every joint. Over my head, the hulking black British Lancasters, my bomber boys, roared toward Normandy. I felt tense and more than a little helpless, pinned here while the world was changing utterly. And I knew I had to at least try to be there for it. If I found a way to the battle, I could gather the material I needed to write the piece I'd planned for months. If it was good enough, *Collier's* would have to publish it, I told myself. And even if they didn't, I could do better than to give up. Besides, what else did I have now?

I headed to the train station, and got myself as far as Dover, hoping I could find something, anything, to get me over. The docks were dark, and I felt like a prowler. I suppose I was. Just as I was eyeing possible ships, a military policeman approached me and asked for my credentials. I flashed him my *Collier's* badge too quickly for him to see it had expired, and pointed to the nearest vessel, which was a hospital ship, the most obvious thing around with its bright white hull and huge blood-red crosses.

'I'm going to interview nurses for my magazine,' I told him, the lie flying to my lips the moment I opened my mouth.

'Right, then,' he said, not even blinking, and waved me through.

I could hardly believe it could be so easy. I almost laughed, but thought better of that and hurried on board. It was nearly ten o'clock by this point, and everything was quiet. Still, I knew if I was caught, I could be thrown off or even arrested, so I found a toilet with a locking door, stowing myself away. I'd never done anything so bold. I didn't think about what would happen next, or what I'd do if I got caught, just squeezed myself into a corner, sitting cross-legged on the floor, and reached for the whiskey flask in my satchel. Thank God I had it. After a while, I heard the groan of machinery and movement as the ship weighed anchor, and felt very scared, suddenly, about everything. In the loud silence and the dark, I drank as much as I could stand, wondering about the future. Would I be caught and turned back? Would the ship be targeted and all of us blown to bits? Would I see Ernest again, or ever return to the Finca, my home? Would I be able to write the boys and explain or even see them, or was I expected to launch forward entirely on

456

my own and without looking back, as if those years and all that love had never happened?

★   ★   ★

I slept on the floor that night, using my arm as a pillow. It was luck alone that no one discovered me there. At dawn, though I felt green as could be, I got brave enough to let myself out of my small prison. On deck, no one questioned me. Too much else was happening. We'd come all the way through the mine-filled Channel and now were sitting below the high yellow-green cliffs of Normandy surrounded by more ships than I had ever seen in my life or even knew existed. Thousands upon thousands of them made up the armada, massive destroyers and transport vessels and battleships. Small snub-nosed boats and cement barges and Ducks carried troops to the beaches, which were alive with pure chaos. Once they made the beach, there were two hundred yards or more of open ground to survive and then the cliffs. Overhead, the sky was a thick and billowing gray veil strung through with thousands of planes.

There had never been anything like it, nor would there ever be.

It turned out that the vessel I'd stowed away on was the first hospital ship to make it over. The wounded began to arrive almost immediately, and I found that it didn't really matter how I'd come to that place; now my hands were needed. Every hand was. I became a stretcher-bearer and bandage-bearer. I lit cigarettes, made beds,

457

poured coffee, took messages from one man to another. They were each of them incredible to me. But I couldn't stop long enough to admire them; there was too much to do.

Late that night, when I already had thick blisters on my hands and feet, I loaded into a cement ambulance barge with a handful of doctors and medics, crashing through the surf around floating mines lit up by a flashing strobe. Soon I would know we'd landed on the American sector of Omaha Beach, but for the moment there was only horror and chaos. We bumped through severed limbs and the bloated forms of the drowned. Artillery fire shattered the air in every direction. Planes roared over us, so close my skull vibrated, but there wasn't even time to wonder whose side they were on.

Near the beach, we flung ourselves out into the icy water and waded to shore. The surf came to my waist and tugged at my clothes. I stumbled, feeling chilled to my core, but I couldn't be dragged down. I had to hold up my end of the stretcher and stay between the white-taped lines that marked the places that had been cleared of mines.

Seeing those lines, and knowing what they meant, was terrifying. But everything was. The gunfire was deafening. Flares whistled and exploded blindingly, rinsing the scene with red light, and showing me things I would never forget. Terrified waves of men running headlong into death. Bodies wrenched apart. Eyes filled with an almost animal agony. Hands clutching my pant leg, desperate to be saved.

458

High above on the cliffs, shells slammed into German positions. There were POW cages for the captured, and haunted faces there, too. We picked up everyone, anyone, even Germans, and assembled them all on the beach for triage. They were young and scared and cold and hurt, and it didn't really matter how they'd been wounded, or who they were before this precise moment of need. Every last one of them made me feel gutted, and there were hours of this. Blood-soaked bandages, flares sailing like red silk over the beach with a pop, tanks, and bodies. Men and more men. Men with boys' faces. Boys spilling their lives into the tide, and the tide taking each drop and churning, changing, crashing out and back again.

The more exhausted and helpless and raw I grew, the more the faces blurred and transformed. I might have been delirious, but there on the wet strand, just past the smoke and the screaming, I recognized the blown-apart Frenchman who'd shown me his branch of mimosa long ago in Madrid. And there, just beyond him, falling to his knees, was Laurence Gardet with his blue tin of Gauloises. The soldier from Belchite, who'd dreamed of St. Louis with me, was in a transport boat, his neck wrapped in red gauze, while the Russian pilot in the Viipuri prison who'd wept and trembled for his wife and child gripped his hand tightly. They were all here, and I didn't question it — nor how, as I bent to lift bodies, one young man after another became the boy from the square at Santo Domingo, his face, every face. And each time, I wanted to scream and weep, to tell him I loved him, that I needed his forgiveness. That he'd been with me for years. That he always would be.

★ ★ ★

It was the strangest and longest night of my life. Later I would learn that there were a hundred thousand men on that beach and only one woman, me. I was also the first journalist, male or female, to make it there and report back. Ernest had been stranded offshore along with so many others — but that sort of accounting felt petty now, and inconsequential, particularly since I'd lost so very much to get there. My life was a ruin just then — there was no other way to see it — and much more suffering lay ahead, whether or not I thought I could survive it.

And yet no one could take away anything I'd seen, or the blisters on my hands, or what it meant to be here, feeling myself cracking further and further open as the tide churned and the sky rattled.

I looked into the eyes of the man on the stretcher before me. We were loading him into the water ambulance.

'You're awfully pretty to be a nurse,' he said. 'Maybe you're an angel.'

'Actually I'm a writer if you can believe it.'

'Really?'

'Yes, that's right.'

'Are you going to write about me, then?'

I nodded and felt stronger suddenly. His story would be mine, and mine would be his. We would remember through each other, for each other. We weren't strangers, and we weren't lost. We weren't alone. 'Yes,' I told him. 'That's something I'm going to do.'

And then we laid him down and I held his hand tightly as we plunged back, wave after wave, toward the white boat.

# Epilogue

The morning after Omaha Beach, I was discovered and arrested for crossing into a war zone without any authority or permission. The military police took away my travel papers and packed me back to London. On the way, I started writing the pieces I'd send on to *Collier's*, but also couldn't stop fuming. I'd been a war correspondent for seven years, in Spain and China, Finland and Italy and Czechoslovakia. I was as qualified as nearly anyone, and now couldn't do my work or even stay in Europe unless I went AWOL. But I would stay, somehow. I had to. What other choice was there?

Aiming to get back to France, I charmed a ride with a Canadian regiment, which didn't seem to mind having a woman around as long as I flirted with the right officers and could tolerate camping in fields or throwing myself into the occasional ditch when German planes dove from above. Later I would find that lies and tears worked, too, an invented fiancé at this or that front I had to see one last time or die trying. It made me livid that I had to cajole and sweet-talk my way forward, when no man with my experience would ever have to lower himself to do anything of the kind. But when the latest issue of *Collier's* found me, finally, it was something to see my name and Ernest's on the masthead as 'invasion correspondents,' side by

462

side. They'd published my D-day story and would go on printing what I sent, I knew, if I could find a way through.

★   ★   ★

D-day had been the beginning of the end, and now we'd come to the middle, and there was still so much tragedy to see. In Florence, the Ponte Vecchio sagged in ruins while German and British soldiers battled it out, one burning street at a time. The Pitti Palace was overrun with refugees, and the dead filled the parks, unburied, since all the cemeteries still belonged to the Germans.

By mid-August, I'd fallen in with a Canadian regiment that was sweeping north along the Adriatic coast. I wrote as I went, posting stories back, and asking everyone I met about their lives and how they thought the future looked now, when the war was finally going our way. Sometimes I got blank stares back or flat incredulity, but more often I saw worry about those still fighting, because what would be worse than dying now, when the end was so near and home was a palpable thing?

I didn't ever think of going home myself, because I was all but certain I no longer had one. I hadn't heard anything from Ernest since London, months before, not a letter, not even an angry cable challenging me. My marriage was surely over, but neither of us had spoken the words. When I finally reached Paris, I heard almost immediately that he was dug in fast at the

Ritz, claiming he'd liberated it. He wasn't alone, either, apparently. Just next door was an exceptionally pretty journalist named Mary Welsh, who'd had by-lines in *Time* and *Life*. I didn't know her, and didn't want to think that Ernest could become involved with someone so quickly, and exactly the way we'd been at the Florida, when we first fell in love. It was too much, and threatened to topple me, so I found a room as far away as possible in another hotel, and tried to stay busy, and breathing, and upright.

Some parts of Paris were so unchanged you wouldn't know anything had happened. You could walk along the Seine, where the booksellers had never shuttered their little kiosks, and count every lovely intact bridge, feeling the sun on your face, and telling yourself the occupation had only been a terrible dream. Or you could turn and look for the hungry, who were never very far away, or the lost, who were everywhere. Women wandered through the cemeteries, searching for the names of their vanished husbands on tombstones. Tens of thousands had disappeared during the occupation, likely tortured or shot or abandoned at the edges of the city. In one barely standing shack in Montmartre I crouched to see the words REVENGE ME scratched into the wooden slats of the door, and walked away, my eyes swimming with tears, hoping there was a way to do just that.

Fall was coming, and there was no coal anywhere, and very little food. Good coffee could still be found at press headquarters in the Hotel Scribe near the Paris Opera. Any stories I posted had to be brought there for censoring, and though at first I feared I'd be turned away or worse with no proper credentials, everyone had so much more to worry about. I slunk in and out, and sometimes caught an earful about Ernest. Apparently he'd recently left the city with the Twenty-second Regiment in a convoy headed to Belgium, through minefields, past roadblocks and entrenched Germans. Some said he was not only carrying weapons but using them, too. Others suggested he might be court-martialed and stripped of his credentials if found out.

It was hard not to worry about him, even though his behavior seemed foolhardy. If he was bent on getting into Germany, even being a civilian would be dangerous, but it seemed he didn't care about that at all but only wanted to play soldier and run patrols, and risk his neck. It was surprising to see him so driven to boldness when all he'd done for years was insist on staying in Cuba and minding his own damned business. Something was pushing him now, and I couldn't stop thinking of that, and wondering how his head was, and if he was sleeping. He was still rooted in me, I realized. My mind knew it was all finished, but the heart never knows, or if it does, it does only at the very last possible moment.

A few months later, a dashed-off note from Ernest appeared at my hotel, inviting me to dinner. I was hesitant about going, but thought it was more than time we finally talked, and I'd never fully stopped thinking and fretting about him. I accepted reluctantly and worked to bolster myself by walking to the restaurant near his hotel with my coat open to the wind, hoping to feel stronger by the time I arrived. But I needn't have bothered. When I saw him, all the same impossible feelings flooded back, starting in my knees and climbing me rung by rung until I heard a buzzing in my ears. *I shouldn't be here*, I thought immediately. I wasn't tougher yet at all, if I ever would be.

He was sitting in a snug rounded banquette with a group of people I didn't know, and didn't stand when I approached. I wanted to run and keep running and not face any of it, but a waiter came around, urging me to squeeze in, and then handed me a glass of champagne. I tried to compose myself and behave normally, but could barely focus on the conversation. Ernest was regaling the men around him with his scrape in the Hürtgen Forest, a bloody battle that had left more than seventy men in his battalion dead. As he talked, at first I saw only bluster and bravado, but there was something else just beneath, too. A small flash of the old light in his eyes. Aliveness was waking up in him. He'd gotten something back with all that risk, something pure and cleansing that reminded me of how he'd been in Spain. And it made me feel relieved for him, no matter what else had happened.

'Any news of Bumby?' I asked later, once the hangers-on had finally left us alone. He'd been missing in action for months, and I'd never stopped thinking of him or praying he'd come through.

'Yes, I just heard. He's safe, or at least alive. He took a hit or two, and grenade fire. He's in Nuremberg, at a POW camp.'

'Oh, God. Will he be released soon?'

'I think so. Try not to worry.'

'Easier said than done,' I told him. My eyes found his and landed there, and I felt rocked. Every emotion woke at once, love and hate, hope and despair, sorrow and more sorrow. 'I hear you have a new girl,' I said. 'I hope she'll be good to you. I wish you so much luck, Rabbit.'

His face softened at our nickname for just a moment, but then he was far away again, his gaze flinching and racing away, his heart closing with a click. 'Yes. I'm going to marry her.'

'Oh,' I said. I'd gone utterly numb. 'I suppose you should divorce me, then.'

'You left me, you know. Over and over. I guess you thought I'd wait around like a sap.'

'We left each other, didn't we? It was either that or burn to bits.'

'Maybe that would have been better.'

'Maybe. I don't know. We'll never know now.'

There was a long moment when I couldn't feel my body enough to make it move. But finally I was able to put my glass down with stiff fingers and stood, somehow, and straightened my face, and walked away very carefully, trying not to fall to pieces or scream or rage or cry. I felt as alone as I had ever been. Scorched, and almost weightless, and so terribly free I wondered how I could even stay in my body.

For seven years I'd known exactly who I was and what mattered. Now I had nothing. No

467

husband and no home, and no idea what to cling to, and no future at all but this one, broken as it was. Ernest would return to Cuba soon; of course, he would. And he would take Mary Welsh with him. I imagined her sweeping through my house as if she were turning over a nest, one I'd made with great care, with my own hands and heart, for Ernest and me. She would empty my office, rename the cats, pluck the blossoms from my ceiba tree, and put them in a brand-new vase. She would go room to room erasing me, and she wouldn't stop until there wasn't a trace or a wisp anywhere, anywhere.

★   ★   ★

Ill and strange and hollow, I stayed in Europe, going to Belgium and Norway, and then to London, and finally to Germany, where the Allied troops had just discovered Bergen-Belsen. All through the summer and fall, I'd been hearing whispers about the concentration camps, but couldn't believe any such thing might actually exist. Then I met a Frenchman, a refugee, who'd managed to escape from Treblinka and had witnessed thousands being gassed. He told me everything, how he'd smelled bodies burning in incinerators, and had seen the dignified and incredibly brave faces of those marching into death chambers. As he spoke, I shook with rage and disgust, and I knew I would never again feel the same about the world.

For twelve years, hundreds and hundreds of thousands had suffered unspeakably, had been degraded and tortured and murdered, and worse, while the Allies had waited, hiding their eyes and deluding themselves that it would all be over soon. There could be no words for this sort of evil and horror, but I would have to find them. That would be a kind of revenge, however inadequate.

I left Dachau for Belsen, and then returned to a Paris I barely recognized. It was VE Day and every church was tolling its bells. The streets swam with people cheering, kissing, weeping, pouring wine down their shirtfronts. I pushed my way through the bodies until I reached the Hotel Scribe and found the first correspondent I knew and cried in his arms until I was spent. We stayed up late talking of what we'd seen, and then he went off to sleep and I took out my notebook and pencils and began to work.

It was harder than I imagined to read my notes, and harder still to look back at the last months of my life and feel what had happened and know it fully. When Ernest crossed my mind, I tried to dive back into the sentences in front of me. And when I thought of all the other things I'd lost — the boys, my desk in the sunlight, the Finca, happiness, and the dream of happiness — I knew I had to find some way to sever myself from all of it, everything, even if I had to break my own heart to do it.

*At least I'll get my name back*, I thought, grasping at straws, and found I felt a little stronger. Outside, the cheering went on, and the dancing, and the terrible bells. I felt separate from all of it, and past all hope, but this was something solid, and mine. A very small place to begin, and all I knew to do.

*Gellhorn.* It was what I had now. I would take it.

# Author's Note

Martha Gellhorn went on to become one of the twentieth century's most significant and celebrated war correspondents, reporting on virtually every major conflict for sixty years — from the Spanish Civil War to the Bay of Pigs, from Vietnam to El Salvador to Panama, where she covered the invasion at the age of eighty-one. She also published a total of five novels, fourteen novellas, two collections of stories, and three volumes of essays along the way, and never stopped traveling avidly and passionately, exploring more than fifty countries, and setting up house in half-a-dozen exotic locales, including Africa, Wales, and Cuernavaca, Mexico.

By all accounts, Hemingway never forgave her for leaving him — the only one of his wives to ever do so. Famously, she spent the rest of her days avoiding not just the man himself but even the mention of his name. Though she was a fiercely private person, and determined not to be waylaid by gossip, most of all she refused to be seen as 'a footnote' in his life — or anyone else's — and hated the way her writing style was continually compared to his.

And yet if there is tragedy in the devolving of their love story — once so ardent and intense — into professional rivalry, acrimony, and betrayal, it's more tragic to me that neither knew happiness with another for long. Hemingway remained married to Mary Welsh until his suicide in 1961, though most of his biographers characterize the marriage as less than nurturing for both, and Gellhorn (quipping in a letter that the role of 'Countess Tolstoy' wasn't 'a becoming one') found her mercenary and a fool. In 1954, Gellhorn married *Time* magazine editor Tom Matthews, but the union ended badly after nine years. Publicly she claimed to find marriage 'boring,' but in letters to her closest confidants, she confessed to feeling enraged when she discovered Tom had been having a longtime affair. When she left him, she swore she would 'never try it again,' meaning marriage. But I don't think she knew how to be fully herself when she was with a man or could feel anything but baffled by the competing demands of career and domesticity. Her struggles are poignant and real to me, and all too familiar.

In 1949, Gellhorn adopted an Italian orphan, Alessandro (Sandy), but this relationship, too, was often an anguished one. As her son struggled with his weight, with drugs, with a direction for his life, she struggled with impatience and a critical nature. They reconciled eventually, but the bond lacked the closeness she'd had with Hemingway's sons, whom she was essentially exiled from until after Hemingway's death, in 1961, and also her stepson, Sandy Matthews, with whom she kept a tender correspondence for over twenty years, and whom she later left in control of her papers and estate.

Gellhorn would hate that there's lingering gossip about her — that she was a dilettante, a clotheshorse, a pursuer of other women's husbands (while reportedly hating sex). But she had no patience for small-mindedness in any form. She hated liars and cowards, and also nostalgia. Looking back saddened her, so she plunged forward instead, setting off for far-flung destinations where she could swim alone in strange seas. She loved her friends, and good whiskey neat, solitude and dizzying vistas, and words stripped to the bone, so they could tell the truest version of the truth.

Her most enduring passion (apart from her mother, Edna, her True North) was her work. In 1998, at the age of eighty-nine, she was nearly blind, and also struggling with cancer, and couldn't read the page in her battered typewriter any longer. Getting her affairs into meticulous order, she burned piles of old papers to ash (including letters from Hemingway) and, using a special pill she'd held on to for such a moment, took her own life, as Hemingway had done nearly forty years before.

I wish I'd known her — that '1,500-watt bulb,' as one friend described her, beaming 'vitality, certainty, total courage.' I admire her voice and vision, the way she railed against injustice, telling the stories of ordinary people, and doing it impeccably, with absolute conviction. She was outspoken and tenacious, a straight shooter and a world-beater. She lived all the way out to the edges of herself, no matter the risks or what she lost along the way. We can't have enough heroes like her, if there ever was another like her at all. And if I've lifted my pen to find her, I lift a glass of whiskey now — neat, of course — to her matchless life.

— *Paula McLain*
*Clevelands Ohio*

# Acknowledgments

When I had the idea for *The Paris Wife* ten years ago, my career changed completely. I went from having three part-time teaching jobs and stealing time away from my family at a nearby coffee shop to being a full-time writer with a home office, readers who were as passionate about my characters and stories as I was, and an entire team of people doing their damnedest to make each book a success. All of this is to say how grateful and *lucky* I am to have the encouragement, support, and faith of many, many talented and remarkable people.

My agent, Julie Barer, has been with me from the beginning of this wonderful ride, and even before. Her instincts, guidance, and friendship mean everything. This book is dedicated to her for a thousand reasons, including the day she put on a killer red suit and went to bat for me when the stakes were high. Julie, you are irreplaceable. Thank you.

A shout-out goes to the entire team at The Book Group, which is an extraordinary operation and family: Nicole Cunningham, Brettne Bloom, Elisabeth Weed, and Faye Bender. Rock stars, every one, as is the marvelous Jenny Meyer.

Susanna Porter has been my editor for many years, but never stops impressing me with her insight and level of investment. She's in this book elbow deep, on every page. She's made me a better writer, too. Thank you doesn't really suffice, but I'll begin there.

So many folks at Ballantine Books and Penguin Random House need to be thanked (and thanked and thanked) for their enthusiasm, support, and excellent work. Kara Welsh, Kim Hovey, Susan Corcoran, Jennifer Garza, Allyson Lord, Quinne Rogers, Benjamin Dreyer, Steve Messina, Anastasia Whalen, Caitlin McCaskey, and Emily Hartley. Sue Betz did a wonderful and thorough job of copyediting the manuscript, and Dana Blanchette has come through again with an absolutely stunning design. Thanks to Paolo Pepe, Robbin Schiff, and the top-notch art department for their ongoing excellent work and to Anna Bauer Carr and Debra Lill for this magnificent cover, Gina Centrello for her ongoing investment in my work, and the entire sales force for getting my books into the hands of booksellers and readers, and out into the world.

I owe much to Ursula Doyle at Fleet, my brilliant editor in the UK; Susan de Soissons and David Bamford at Virago/Little, Brown UK; Caspian Dennis of Abner Stein; Michelle Weiner at Creative Artists Agency, and my wonderful team at Penguin Random House Canada and Doubleday Canada, especially Lynn Henry, Kristin Cochrane and Sharon Klein.

While working on this book, I made an essential trip to Cuba for research, master-minded by my longtime friend and sometime travel assistant, Brian Groh. Luly Duke of Fundación Amistad was instrumental in putting us in touch with all the right people, including Esperanza García Fernández, curator of the Hemingway Room at the Ambos Mundos in Havana; America Fuentes, granddaughter of Gregorio Fuentes, captain of the *Pilar*; and Gladys Rodriquez Ferrero, Hemingway scholar and former director of the Museo Hemingway Finca Vigía. Ada Rosa Alfonso Rosales, current director of the Museo Hemingway, was incredibly generous with me during my visit, as was her patient, helpful staff. My translator and guide, Aixa Roche Pozas, was a complete *gem* and made every day a pleasure. Further excellent translation of interviews and help in perusing archival documents came from Alejandro Jose Acosta.

Many friends have supported me in crucial ways over the years, and honestly I can't thank them enough: Lori Keene, David French, Greg D'Alessio, Sharon Day, Pam and Doug O'Hara, Brad Bedortha, Steve Reed, Beth Hellerstein, Michelle Lipp, Patti Henry, Laura McNeal, Eleanor Brown, Sarah McCoy, Becky Gaylord, Denise Machado and John Sargent, Terry Sullivan, Heather Greene, Jim Harms, Chris Pavone, Scott and Cherie Parsons, Karen Rosenberg, and Nan Cohen. The East Side Writers — Terry Dubow, Sarah Willis, Toni Thayer, Charlie Oberndorf, Karen Sandstrom, Neal Chandler, Lynda Montgomery, and Justin Glanville — have always been on my side. I miss you guys!

Charlotte Fowler and Allie Lustig kept things running smoothly on the home front. Bless you both! My son Connor stepped in as nanny, cook, dog walker, and all-around superstar at a tough time, and made life actually doable. Every day he would come into the kitchen where I was working, and where the same William Fitzsimmons record was on over and over. 'You should thank him in your book,' Connor said one day, so here you go: Thanks to William Fitzsimmons for being the soundtrack to literally thousands of hours of writing time.

Love and thanks go to my mother, Rita Hinken, and also to the dazzling Tom Persinger, for the fireflies, the music, the moon on a string, and for generally arranging to be found. What have we done? My children, Beckett, Fiona, and Connor, are the most extraordinary people, and I feel lucky to know them. They and my sisters have been, and will always be, home.

# A Note on Sources

My work is always a blending of fact and fiction. For the past ten years, as I've been completely absorbed in writing about incredible women from history, I have trusted my gut response to lead me to a particular life that inspires me, or, rather, completely obsesses me. Then I begin the difficult but also joy-filled task of sifting through the historical facts on record to find the story within the larger story that I want — and need — to tell. That part is pure intuition, too. I follow my heart, and then trust my imagination to jump on board. And away we go.

But I know I couldn't get to the dreaming, feeling part of my process without the concrete, absolutely essential source material that grounds my research. For that I am indebted to many fine writers and biographers. I want to especially acknowledge Caroline Moorehead for her remarkable biography *Gellhorn: A Twentieth-Century Life*, and for curating and assembling Gellhorn's correspondence in *Selected Letters of Martha Gellhorn*, both of which were crucial in bringing MG's voice and story to life for me. Bernice Kert's *The Hemingway Women* was also instrumental, as was *Hemingway and Gellhorn* by Jerome Tuccille.

Reading Gellhorn's own work was a pleasure and a revelation, particularly *The Trouble I've Seen, A Stricken Field, Liana, The Honeyed*

Peace, *The Heart of Another*, *The Face of War*, *The View from the Ground*, and *Travels with Myself and Another*. I also discovered a wonderful play, *Love Goes to Press*, which Gellhorn co-wrote with Virginia Cowles, and which really helped illuminate the life of female war correspondents. It's also hilarious, and the dialogue is tops!

There were many texts that helped me understand the very complex political terrain of the Spanish Civil War, and also what it meant to be *there*, fully part of that crusade, including *The Education of a Correspondent* by Herbert L. Matthews, *The Starched Blue Sky of Spain* by Josephine Herbst, *Spain in Our Hearts* by Adam Hochschild, *Hotel Florida* by Amanda Vaill, *This Time a Better Earth* by Ted Allan, and *Looking for Trouble* by Virginia Cowles.

For important insight into the arc of Hemingway's life and the man himself, as much as can be understood, I need to acknowledge *Ernest Hemingway: A Life Story* by Carlos Baker, *Hemingway: The 1930s* and *Hemingway: The Final Years* by Michael Reynolds, *The True Gen* by Denis Brian, and the gorgeous and utterly affecting *Hemingway's Boat* by Paul Hendrickson.

I'm always reading and rereading Hemingway, and learning more all the time. For this particular novel, I'm indebted to *For Whom the Bell Tolls*, *Islands in the Stream*, *The Fifth Column*, and *To Have and Have Not*.

Finally, I think it's important to say that my Gellhorn isn't *the* Gellhorn, for how could she be? That woman is a mystery, the way we're all mysteries, to our friends and family and loved ones, and even to ourselves. And yet the woman I discovered, in trying deeply to understand her, I couldn't admire more. Whatever her flaws, she was incandescent, a true original, and I won't ever forget her.

In the course of my research, there were many moments when biographers contradicted each other, and places where Gellhorn herself made errors of memory. Some were quite small. For instance, she went over to Finland on a boat called the *Westernland*, as we know from passenger manifests, but she wrote *Westenland* in letters. It would be easy to correct her on this count and others, and no doubt many writers would choose to do just that. I've decided that it's more important, and means more symboli- cally for me, to tell an embodied and emotional truth about her life rather than to be 'correct.' Whatever my own errors and failings and idiosyncrasies, I hope my fondness, admiration, and empathy for her — and for Hemingway, too — ring through.

We do hope that you have enjoyed reading this large print book.

Did you know that all of our titles are available for purchase?

We publish a wide range of high quality large print books including:

**Romances, Mysteries, Classics**
**General Fiction**
**Non Fiction and Westerns**

Special interest titles available in large print are:

**The Little Oxford Dictionary**
**Music Book**
**Song Book**
**Hymn Book**
**Service Book**

Also available from us courtesy of Oxford University Press:

**Young Readers' Dictionary**
**(large print edition)**
**Young Readers' Thesaurus**
**(large print edition)**

For further information or a free brochure, please contact us at:

**Ulverscroft Large Print Books Ltd.,**
**The Green, Bradgate Road, Anstey,**
**Leicester, LE7 7FU, England.**
**Tel:** (00 44) 0116 236 4325
**Fax:** (00 44) 0116 234 0205